T0380096

EVERYTHING ABOUT YOU

Everything About You

ROBBY WEBER

STORYTIDE
An Imprint of HarperCollinsPublishers

HarperCollins Children's Books, a division of HarperCollins Publishers,
195 Broadway, New York, NY 10007

HarperCollins Publishers, Macken House, 39/40 Mayor Street Upper,
Dublin 1, D01 C9W8, Ireland

Storytide is an imprint of HarperCollins Publishers.

harpercollins.com

Library of Congress Control Number: 2025939019
ISBN 978-1-335-00897-8

Typography by David DeWitt
25 26 27 28 29 LBC 5 4 3 2 1
First Edition

This one is for the readers,

merci, je vous aime.

Chapitre Un

À bon chat, bon rat.

That's a French idiom I learned recently, and while the translation is literally "to a good cat, a good rat," it basically means someone has met their match.

The cat is a skilled chaser, but the rat just as cleverly evades.

I'm not exactly a cat person, and I'm definitely not going to call myself a rat, but luckily I don't have to be either for a while. Up until now, my entire life has been all about competition and adversaries, so I'm relieved to finally be done for a whole summer.

I'll still have to work hard, but I've *already* beat the competition. I've already won, and that's why I'm here, in Paris, where perfection just might actually exist: There is a feeling everywhere like you'll just never find anything better. The grass is greener, the treats are sweeter, and the art is bolder.

Plus, the drinking age is eighteen, which means I can enjoy a bottle of Sancerre with my best friend without a sketchy fake ID claiming I'm a twenty-seven-year-old from Michigan.

We're sitting at a tiny bistro table outside a cafe near the base of a bridge, crammed in with other people who also have their backs to the windows, and across the Seine, against the bright blue sky, is the Musée du Louvre.

This was the cafe we stumbled upon after a day at the Musée d'Orsay, which Celeste had somehow thought was the name of a macaron flavor when I'd sent her a list of activities this morning. I posted my first Parisian TikTok with the iconic gilded clock, wearing some white European tennis shoes I found at Nordstrom, thrifted jeans, and an oversized Ralph Lauren oxford from the nineties.

Il est arrivé.

"*Mon dieu*, Milo," Celeste says. "I still cannot believe this summer is real." She has her eye on a pink YSL crossbody passing us on the sidewalk. Wearing a lacy top and high-waisted jeans, with her blond shoulder-length hair perfectly crowned by a black beret, she sips her wine and quirks a brow. "Well, I sort of can believe it, actually. If anyone could make this happen, it's you."

I reach for a square of the buttery croque monsieur we're sharing straight from a cast-iron skillet. "And everything turned out so perfectly. For all the stress and moving parts—the sleepless nights and phone calls and emails and the panic over passports and student visas and arrangements and *outfits*."

"I always knew it'd be fine," Celeste says coolly. "This is destined, honestly. We've been manifesting a summer abroad for years, it's only fitting."

We wasted no time after graduation, which was two days ago, before zipping our already-packed suitcases and offering *au revoir* and *bisous bisous* preemptively to anyone we encountered before our flight. Immersion is important, after all.

"You'll stage a coop at Maison Dauphine, and I'll find *amour*."

I laugh, ignoring that last part. "It's a coup, *ma cheri*. And I will not. It'll be a friendly takeover."

"Of course, of course." She snaps her fingers, pointing across the street. "Nineties Chanel tweed."

"Nobody in Citrus Harbor is that chic," I say.

She shakes her head. "Except maybe your mother. We've made it to paradise. Or—how would you say it in French?"

"*Paradis*," I say, nodding in agreement. "We have made it. We're here. In Paris. For the whole summer."

"We're here!" She grabs my wrist and squeals. "Our European summer!"

Celeste's bubbly *joie de vivre* might lead some to the conclusion that this was effortless. That we woke up in luxurious baroque chambers wearing satin pajamas as breakfast was served on silver platters and Edith Piaf drifted in through the *portes-fenêtres*.

In fact, the road to Paris from Citrus Harbor was anything but simple.

It was March, and it was three o'clock in the morning in Florida.

Maison Dauphine, one of the biggest fashion designers in France—in the world—posted about a new apprenticeship. Open to students internationally, it was a true talent-scouting situation. One student would get an internship on crack, training and learning for a full-time role at the end of the summer.

I saw it around 6:30, when I was trying to find the motivation to get up for school.

One student? In the whole world? Out of billions of people?

Milo, *c'est impossible.* Right? Why even bother?

By lunchtime I'd plotted no less than three flawlessly designed ideas for my entry. By the final bell of the day, I had three more.

Ideas have never been my problem. For this, especially, they came effortlessly—referencing my own knowledge of Maison Dauphine's iconic collections and history, speculating about the future of the design house.

I'm great with ideas, but I tend to struggle with deciding. Executing.

Because everything has to be perfect.

I'm not someone who can just pick something and hope for the best. I have to forecast and optimize and plan contingencies. That's one of the reasons I love tennis so much. I can control and calculate and command the court exactly how I want to.

By dinner, the numbers on the apprenticeship posts were daunting at best. Comments, likes, shares—they all added up to one lump sum of competition. I figured I'd have to do something drastic, but *what*?

I only had one idea, and it definitely felt like it would make a statement.

My older brother was the first person I consulted. He thought the idea was absolutely nuts and would get me blacklisted from the brand. I decided not to even ask my mother, who owns a high-end boutique and would probably have seized my phone before letting me post.

Celeste, however, totally believed in me.

"Fuck them if they don't get it," she had said while we ate tacos by the pier. With queso all over her lips—one of the only foods she'd ruin her Hailey Bieber lip gloss for—she'd rolled her eyes.

"You're amazing and so talented and smart. You deserve that apprenticeship."

My best friends from tennis were also very pro-Totally Wild Idea. Chip, in particular, was adamant that the only way to win was to make sure I got their attention.

So, I got their attention.

I decided it must be true that all press is good press and leaned in to that. The concept was one thing, but the execution was key.

Considering that Maison Dauphine had recently been lambasted for launching a bag that was so exclusive the Kardashians couldn't even get one, and considering this criticism was likely why they were trying to rebrand with this generous offer for young talent, I figured it was a chance to look directly into the belly of the beast.

So, I submitted a Photoshopped luxurious lifestyle vignette with Maison Dauphine products. It was all gold, diamonds, pearls, champagne, and excess, but the focus was the Waitlist, lined with the most rich and famous fashion icons, dead and alive.

It was a risk, but it was calculated.

Le reste appartient à l'histoire.

"I wonder if you'll find love too," Celeste muses. She stares off, wistful, and exhales as if expressing her hopes and wishes to the universe through the simple act of wanting.

"I'm not here for love." I sigh. This is so Celeste.

Don't get me wrong, we both have had our share of boy-crazy moments, but Paris is different. Paris has to be different. The guys I dated back home were distracting dead ends, so if that's what I have to look forward to in Paris, I'd rather focus on the apprenticeship.

"Isn't it the city of love?"

"No," I say. "Not for me. I'm here on business, remember?"

"Of course." She catches my expression immediately. "Okay, but it is still our last summer before college. Before *I* go to college." She corrects. "It is sort of absurd I'll be in college, and you'll be starting your *career* with Maison Dauphine."

"As long as I crush the apprenticeship," I say. "It's contingent on everything going well. HR was almost too clear about the fact that they could revoke my spot for any reason."

"Sure, sure. Still, this summer can be business and some pleasure." She wiggles her brow as a group of shirtless cyclists speed by. "We deserve to have fun too!"

"There are plenty of fun things that don't rob you of your time or, like, your soul," I say, swirling the Sancerre in my glass in an effort to distract her.

Celeste groans, then flicks her hair over her shoulder, pouting and glancing up the Quai Voltaire. "Currently I think the most fun thing would be a tall, tan *garçon* in a Saint Laurent suit."

"Non." I roll my eyes. *"Absolument pas."*

Undeterred, she shrugs. "You never know what's going to happen, Milo. No matter how hard you try to control things, this is our summer in Paris, and it might just be unpredictable. There might just be boys."

I'm fairly convinced there is not a guy out there for me. There are just too many boxes to check, and the odds seem slim, if even at all probable.

That's a rabbit hole for another day, though.

"I doubt I need to remind you, but—"

"Our summer in Paris is only the start." Celeste parrots back my mantra. "Well, hopefully. It might be good to relieve some of the pressure and start with fun—"

I shake my head. "What are the odds of a random Citrus Harbor High School student winning a social media contest and getting an apprenticeship with one of the biggest fashion houses in the entire world? This is, quite literally, the chance of a lifetime. I can have fun after I get a real job with the company and am more secure in Paris. Right now, everything is riding on this summer going perfectly and me giving a hundred and ten percent."

"One of my favorite things about you is that you're never intense at all."

Chapitre Deux

I wake up from a dream where I am tasked with scaling the Eiffel Tower to retrieve an evening gown. A nightmare, more accurately, and one I don't need a psychologist to deconstruct.

Still, I muster up a glare of confidence in the mirror of the bright, marble-laden guest bathroom, surrounded by all the bougie skincare products and framed black-and-white photos of models in editorial shoots around Paris. The diffuser on the stool by the toilet smells of citrus, and I pump onto my palm some body lotion that is absolutely women's—an almost sickeningly sweet mix of vanilla and some sort of fruit—but I'm honestly too riddled with nerves to care. My hair is also decidedly more fragrant than I'd choose for myself.

Fuck your nerves, Milo. Get it together.

I am here, in Paris, and I am going to do this. I'm going to make this happen for myself. I got this far, anyway. I can do this.

It's my first day at Maison Dauphine, and I don't have a clue what to wear. I considered a suit with sneakers, but that could come across as trying way too hard, so I've settled for trousers with a short-sleeve pique tee that hugs my biceps in a way that helps me feel more confident when I've never been more self-conscious. I don't know what they expect from a male apprentice at a fashion house that only designs women's wear, but I'm hoping I can scout some other guys working there today and adjust accordingly.

I pull on some of my white Nike crew socks, a bit worn after years of playing tennis in them, because they remind me of home and pair nicely with a pair of limited-edition Nikes my mom got me for this specific occasion. I haven't worn them yet, in hopes that there will be some sort of good luck attached when I walk through the doors of the office.

My backpack isn't giving fashion apprenticeship, but if it's egregious or gets terrible looks, I'll try to find one here in Paris. I don't think it's particularly offensive—a Nixon from Sun and Surf, since I'm still just a boy from Citrus Harbor, after all—but it has a padded laptop sleeve and a mesh pouch on the side for the Nalgene bottle they gave us at the state championships.

The bottle is definitely not giving fashionable . . . and do people in Paris use Nalgene bottles?

Is Nalgene French, maybe? Nal-jean?

Probably not, Milo, you idiot.

Fuck, I look like such an American.

"You look so cute, oh my god."

Celeste is leaning over the counter eating yogurt and scrolling on her phone when I emerge from my room. She's wearing a big T-shirt and satin pajama shorts, her hair up in a ponytail.

Her aunt's apartment, nestled above a quiet and cobbled street in the 7th Arrondissement, is something out of a magazine. This makes sense, of course, since Celeste's aunt is an incredibly successful interior designer. She splits her time between Paris and New York, and though she'd normally be in Paris now, Celeste is her favorite niece and barely had to try to talk her into letting us use the apartment.

"Do I look like I'm trying too hard? Or not hard enough?"

Celeste shakes her head. "No, I think this is great. Effortlessly cool."

Effortless. Right.

Except for the fact that, at this very moment, the sight of Celeste's yogurt is enough to make me dry heave. My anxiety is swirling around in my stomach—no, actually, it's not swirling, because *swirling* is too whimsical. My anxiety is crushing and squeezing and wringing out my insides. It's like this thick, heavy tar.

It's motivating, usually, but now I am so aware of what's happening. I'm so aware of every fault and deficiency—I haven't even found a place to take French lessons, for instance, and I know my two years of French at Citrus Harbor High School are hardly enough for what I'm about to get myself into. One of my worst fears is offending someone with my lack of fluency.

"I can do this," I say, breathing through tight lips. I open the refrigerator and grab a glass, pouring some grapefruit juice from a carafe. "I can figure anything out. . . ."

Celeste nods. "Milo, you are going to be amazing."

"What are you going to do today?"

"I'm doing a 'romanticize my life' TikTok, because . . ." She gestures around. "Obviously. So, I'm thinking a walk through some gardens, a bit of shopping, maybe wander through a museum. I'm going all in on being an American tourist in Paris. And if I bump into a gorgeous Parisian man who wants to take me to a candlelit dinner and teach me about French wine . . ."

I study her, holding the glass just below my lips. "Make sure you let these Parisian men chase you. Not the other way around."

"Right," she says, standing up straight. "Totally. I mean, to be fair, today I actually am more interested in cheese and vintage stores, but I'm keeping my options open for the right European romance."

Then she raises a finger. "And you need to make sure you don't go in totally guns blazing."

"I won't." I nod. "I'm going to take a more passive role today. Listening, learning, figuring out my place. I'm assuming they'll have me doing grunt work until they realize how much I have to offer."

"Patience," Celeste says.

Patience is more foreign to me than the French language will ever be, but this isn't the time to reinforce that thought.

"Right. Patience," I nod, taking a sip of juice. "I can be patient. I will be patient. Because I'm here, and as long as I do a great job, it'll all work out the way it's meant to."

"Exactly, you don't have to control everything. . . ."

This is one of our things. We give each other these pep talks, where we know the other one is probably thinking, *Right, but . . .*

Still, it's one of our love languages, and I'm sure it helps us to stay at least five percent more grounded.

"You might even make some cool French friends who can show us around."

I shrug. "Maybe. There aren't any other apprentices, and the summer interns won't start for a while, so I'm not sure."

"That sucks."

"It does not," I say. "No competition. I can stand out."

"Okay, well, when they do get there, maybe you don't have to view them all as competition."

I down the rest of the juice and set it in the sink. "Right, of course not. I should just be best friends with all of them. In fact, maybe I should just ask if any of them would rather do my tasks so they can score points with Pascal."

Pascal Dumas is Maison Dauphine's current creative director. It might be slightly delusional to imagine myself getting any face time with him, but I'm going to do everything in my power to make it happen. I'd love to learn how he manages to be so innovative and accomplished and confident.

"Well, they're interns," Celeste offers. "And you're the apprentice. Right? So you're the only one who is guaranteed a job."

"*Tentatively* guaranteed a job," I say. "But yes. The interns only get credit for a course."

"Exactly. I'm only saying you might like some of them!"

The idea of making friends at Maison Dauphine is nice, but it's also terrifying. The moment you trust an opponent, you are weak. I know this from years of studying the best tennis players at rival schools. The ones who make me nervous aren't the players who simply manage a high ace count or have a menacing backhand—no, the ones to watch are the kids who smile in your face and try to befriend you so you're off your game and don't see them for exactly what they are: the only thing standing in the way of a win.

"Wish me luck." I exhale.

Celeste grins. "You're going to be the best they've ever seen, *mon amour*!"

I give myself a final once-over and try to nod as confidently as I possibly can when I pass the floor-to-ceiling mirrors in the foyer. AirPods in, and sunglasses on, I hear Celeste repeat herself, this time higher pitched—"*The best they've ever seen*!" Excited, and willing me to believe her.

As soon as I find myself on the street, I'm invigorated and scared shitless.

I was going to take an Uber, but it's a nice morning, and I'm running obscenely ahead of schedule on account of nerves and having been up pretty much all night just waiting for my alarm to go off. So, instead, I decide to walk. I've already clocked that the walk from the apartment to headquarters is seventeen minutes, but my legs typically operate at lightning speed even when I'm not nervous, so I don't expect it to be anywhere near that estimation.

Once I'm heading up the Avenue Rapp, I'm a bit surprised. I expected it to be like rush hour in New York City, but it's not. It's busier than I've seen it when just traipsing around with Celeste midday, but there seems to be a more relaxed slowness to the culture overall, especially when most of the tourists are all still sleeping.

I'm not sure if I've romanticized this so much that it's becoming a self-fulfilling prophecy, but it really does feel magical. The classic architecture is something you'd never see in Florida—the old light-gray stone that's warmed by the rising sun, with wrought-iron balconies and gates adorned with gilded details. I love the sloped roofing and the bright flowers perched on the ornate window guards, and even appreciate the newer, more modern buildings closer to the Seine.

The trees are bright green, the air smells of fresh baked goods—there's a sweetness to this morning as I reach the bustling Quay d'Orsay, and across the arched bridge is a picturesque vision of Paris so stunning I stop, betraying any attempt at looking cool and nonchalant, to take a photo.

It's wild to me that I'm here, doing this apprenticeship on my own. It almost feels like I'm cosplaying as an adult or something, being so far away from home—my siblings and parents are still asleep, and here I am, on my way to live a literal dream come true.

The magic of it all is helping to ease the nerves. The fact that this is real, and this is my life, and that I've somehow pulled it off.

The Seine is sparkling, albeit a tiny bit smelly, and as I walk across, I note I am making great time and haven't broken a sweat.

Celeste is so right. I *am* going to be the best they've ever seen. And though I know she has slightly idealized, if not utterly unrealistic, opinions about making friends there, this is really going to be even easier to win than a tennis match because I am only competing against myself.

I remind myself of this several times as I keep walking. I repeat positive affirmations as I make my way past the gorgeous Théâtre des Champs-Elysées and the iconic Hôtel Plaza Athénée, until I can see the Maison Dauphine headquarters on Avenue Montaigne, standing tall like a prestigious Parisian palace.

I take the deepest breath anyone has ever taken, and I know I need to savor this moment as much as I savor any sugary sweet dessert or French wine—this is a momentous occasion, after all.

My whole life begins when I walk through these doors.

I hear the most gorgeous French music playing in my mind.

The city is veiled with a rosy hue. This is going to be the most amazing summer of my entire life.

When I snap to, having floated on a romantic cloud—painted like one of the impressionist masterpieces—I'm outside Maison Dauphine's flagship store and headquarters. The inside is dimly lit, since the boutique is closed, and I wait for someone to see me through the large glass doors so they can come unlock them.

I finally catch the eye of a woman who is scurrying around in a black dress and heels, though she seems to be preoccupied with something else behind me.

Turning on my heel, I realize that outside of my little daydream, there's an entire ordeal happening around me. The flashbulb of a camera causes me to blink a few times, and then another.

Paparazzi are shouting and snapping photos, and they seem to be growing in number.

"Over here!"

I follow their shared line of sight until I realize why they're here.

Holy shit.

Chapitre Trois

"Rhodes, over here!"

Rhodes Hamilton is walking toward me on the sidewalk.

The Rhodes Hamilton.

Golden sunlight filters through the verdant trees, floods the sidewalk, and shines on the blue awnings of Harry Winston. It highlights his bright blond hair, illuminates his piercing blue eyes, and dances over his long eyelashes. He's ethereal, with glowing skin and deep pink lips.

It's like he is straight out of a fairy tale.

If princes had reputations for excessive partying, polluting the planet with private jets, and breaking hearts while wearing watches that cost more than a car.

Come on, Milo. He's hot, but he's Rhodes Hamilton.

London's resident fuckboy, if I recall the wording correctly.

His outfit is cool, which is to be expected: nineties-cut denim, mid-height Adidas, a patchwork plaid shirt over a white tee, and a green Nike belt bag across his chest. Plus, a gold chain around his neck that's probably worth more than I can even imagine.

These types of guys are always in effortlessly cool outfits. This is textbook *I don't even have to try, and you can't even help but look at me.*

I want to roll my eyes.

What are all these paparazzi doing here anyway? Rhodes shouldn't even be famous. He's famous by association—his *family* is famous. Rhodes is a walking tabloid headline.

When he's closer and our eyes lock, it's like an involuntary surge of electricity starting at the base of my feet and shooting through my entire body, all the way up to the top of my skull. I don't know what the feeling even is. He's objectively very attractive, but all I can think is how I know guys like him.

Just this past spring break, I had my own run-in with one of Citrus Harbor's resident fuckboys. Guys like that have this way of making you feel like you're different—you're the exception. They make you feel special before they disappear. It's all about the chase and getting what they want.

My stomach sinks just remembering how shitty it felt to stare at my phone waiting for a text that was never going to come. Celeste and I listened to podcasts about how some guys are lessons and sometimes you have to give yourself your own closure.

If that podcast was right, the saddest part is that he wasn't the only guy who seemed to embody this particular lesson, and I somehow still hadn't learned it by the time he came around. Practically every guy I dated was some version of the same truth—snakes with different stripes, but all venomous.

Another paparazzi shouts something and Rhodes Hamilton glances over, offering a slick grin and a slight wave.

Guys like this only care about one thing: themselves.

Rhodes stops in front of me, and now I am the victim of that captivating smile.

"Sorry about all this." He holds out his hand, and after I don't take it for a moment, it falls back to his side and he laughs it off, eyeing the photographers before turning his attention back to me. "You're Milo, right?"

I blink.

In what world does Rhodes Hamilton know who I am? What the fuck is happening?

"I am." I clear my throat and stand up straight. "How did you . . . how do you know my name?"

I wonder if Celeste and I have ingested some of her aunt's mushrooms or something. I'm sure she has them in her apartment, honestly, given some of her more abstract tendencies.

Holy shit, Celeste is not going to believe this.

Chip and the rest of the guys are all going to absolutely lose their minds.

And just wait until I tell my brother—

"Milo . . ." Rhodes furrows his brow, now a bit more serious. "Milo Hawthorne, the tennis star? You're playing at Roland-Garros, right? In the French Open?"

"What?" My jaw falls open. "I am definitely not playing at Roland-Garros, nor do I see that happening in the near future. Or, like, ever. I'm—"

Rhodes laughs now, patting me on the shoulder. "I'm only joking, mate. I looked you up. Saw your submission, of course. Cheeky."

My face burns. So, what was that? Some condescending excuse of a fucking joke?

This is exactly what I'd expect from some douchebag who comes from a family of world-famous athletes. Just because I'm not playing in the French Open, my entire award-winning career as a tennis player can be reduced to some punchline.

"Funny." I almost want to wipe my shoulder free of any trace of his touch.

He narrows his eyes. "Sorry?"

Shaking my head: "Why did you look me up?"

He points over my shoulder. "I'm an apprentice too."

Then he breezes past me.

"All right, boys, that's enough for today. If you're good, we can arrange something another time, yeah?"

I turn to watch him put his hands in his pockets and smile as they get their final shots.

The doors to Maison Dauphine swing open, and the woman I saw before is giving Rhodes Hamilton the biggest, warmest greeting I've ever seen, complete with a hug and a squeeze of the shoulders.

But. Wait . . . *what*?

I'm stuck in a vacuum where Rhodes's words play on repeat.

There was only supposed to be one apprentice.

"So happy you are here," the woman says. Her French accent is beautiful, but when she turns to me next, her top lip curls up like she's smelled something bad and her brows turn down like she's been given a surprise she'd have been fine without. While I wouldn't say she's quite *disgusted*, I certainly don't imagine she's happy I'm here. She's my height in heels, with perfectly coiffed shoulder-length brown hair and a pearl-and-gold necklace that is attention stealing but not gauche. "And you must be Milo."

Rhodes gives me an odd look, one brow lifted, and mouth half turned up. I have no idea what it means or what he's thinking, but he must catch himself, because he switches back to his more charming grin and then turns back to the woman.

"Yvette. *Quel plaisir de vous revoir!*" Rhodes says.

Yvette, whose name I recognize from some emails, is very pleased to hear this. She giggles, in fact, ushering us into the boutique. "Oh, your French is getting better! *Bien joué!*"

While trying not to obsess over what it *means* that Rhodes is also an apprentice, I am still in awe of the size and luxury of the store. It's all a bright ivory, the main floor broken up into three large rooms: apparel, accessories, and beauty. Throughout the store, however, there are tall, slender mannequins in various poses that are effortlessly chic, like a group of Audrey Hepburn-esque models.

Each mannequin wears a piece from the current season—pieces that are not to be seen anywhere else. A silk midi dress, a feathered gown, a fitted tweed suit, the feminine blushes and creams sparkling and just asking you to touch them to see if they're possibly as soft as they look.

Farther back and to the left, where even more expansive shopping continues, some of the best-known garments are displayed as an exhibit for visitors who will recognize and appreciate the history of the house.

It's strange to be here like this—with only a few lights on, no music, no bustling customers or elegant salespeople in their tailored black suits. The normal ambiance is removed, and yet there is another that seems to exist entirely within the clothes on the mannequins and hanging from the racks—not in large quantities, but by threes, like art displayed purposely for sophisticated patrons.

"We'll head back this way," Yvette says, walking by a round mahogany table of carefully folded silk scarves. "I trust you both had no trouble finding us this morning."

"Of course. Everyone knows the Maison Dauphine flagship," I offer.

Yvette doesn't say anything, and I notice Rhodes looking at me from the corner of his eye.

Okay, don't try so hard. Noted.

It smells of vanilla and something else sweet, but a bit more earthy—overall, a gourmand scent, which Maison Dauphine is famous for.

Rhodes scans the room while we walk.

"Yvette, the dress you chose for my mother to wear to the Grand Prix was absolutely stunning. I meant to tell you sooner, but that one over there reminded me."

"Oh, you're sweet. It was such an elegant look on her. She is the perfect Lady Dauphine."

So sweet. My chest is on fire. He's deploying his charm on Yvette, and she's eating it right up.

We go through a heavy wooden door and are let into a stairwell that is certainly not as aesthetic or glamorous as the boutique, all while Yvette and Rhodes giggle about how gorgeous his mother looked in one of the spring dresses.

As we climb the stairs, I get a wave of nostalgia. Or rather something a bit worse.

I'm reminded of a summer tennis camp where I was constantly snubbed because the coach preferred his best friend's son over me. It was entirely personal and not at all merit based.

But this isn't some tennis camp at the country club. Even if Yvette clearly likes Rhodes more than me, it doesn't matter. It's not like she's going to be my boss.

"As I am the director of public relations for Maison Dauphine, I oversee the PR assistants, interns, and now apprentices."

Okay. Shit.

Well, not everything is a competition, Milo. It's fine. He's not here to steal your thunder.

But he is. Completely and without even trying to at all.

It seems his reputation is no problem here. All that matters, apparently, is that he's famous and wealthy and incredibly attractive. Of course anyone is going to dote over him, and the staff at Maison Dauphine is only human. His mother does wear the clothes all the time. I'm sure his motive isn't to upstage me.

He just does it naturally.

I take a sharp breath.

The problem isn't that I want attention for the sake of having attention. I just envisioned this going so differently. I imagined I'd show up and there would be a team of people who were just so thrilled to see me. They'd be *so* excited to meet the young, creative, innovative mind behind the Waitlist campaign. They'd want to pick my brain or tell me they thought I'd done such a brilliant job—after all, they must think that, since I was chosen out of all the other entries.

But this is the opposite of pomp and circumstance.

And even as I recall my expectations, I realize it was a bit pie-in-the-sky to imagine a bunch of chic and prestigious Parisians fawning over an American eighteen-year-old guy who can't even speak their language.

We are let out of the stairwell onto the third floor. I've seen these bustling and glamorous offices in a couple of documentaries now, so walking by the bright white reception desk, in front of the wall with the black serif Maison Dauphine Paris logo, feels like walking through a movie set. It's unreal.

"Bonjour." The receptionist greets Rhodes specifically, but her eyes do dart to meet mine for a split second.

"Bonjour," Rhodes and I say at the same time. His is more elegant than mine, and his voice goes up at the end more casually than mine, so while I'm embarrassed, I'm slightly grateful that it masked my own weak French.

Fuck, Milo. You can't even say bonjour *right.*

We take a left down a long hallway of offices behind floor-to-ceiling glass panels. Runway photos are printed and pinned to boards. In some offices, fabrics are stacked on lacquer desks, and in others, various products like perfume bottles and compacts are lined on cabinets and shelves.

All the employees, mostly in all black or dark gray, have their eyes on Rhodes as we make our way down the corridor.

The glamour of this place distracts me from the fact that nobody cares I'm here.

I'm walking the same hallway as the founder, Renard Florin.

Or the famous Three Ps—the last three creative directors of Maison Dauphine, Philippa, Pierre, and Pascal. Pascal currently acts as the genius behind the brand. Honestly, I can't even begin to imagine the absolute legendary greatness that has graced this hallway.

We push through a pair of double doors at the end of the corridor, and when Yvette pulls them open, we're welcomed into a square room fully lined with built-in closets. Fabrics of all sorts are tucked in so tightly, it's almost a surprise there aren't cracks in the foundation. Taffeta, silk, satin, tweed, sequins, sparkles, tulle—it's like an explosion of seasons and seasons of Maison Dauphine. Thanks to my hours of research, a quick scan tells me these garments are all sorted in order, by show and by look.

Above the garments, there are bags and sunglasses and random stacks of jewelry, while shoes are displayed below the garments. It's a mix of perfect organization and some clear improvisation: Some of the shoes are paired neatly together, some are in plastic, some are in dust bags. It's not quite clear how this chaos is controlled, but it seems carefully maintained.

In the middle of the room, there are two wooden Parsons tables, connected to form one long desk, with Macs and expensive-looking cups full of expensive-looking pens. There are, of course, less expensive-looking highlighters and pencils and measuring tools scattered about on the ends of the desks, atop printouts and magazines.

"This is our main PR closet," Yvette says. "These are the sample garments. Mostly used for magazines or editorial shoots—sometimes for display at events or even to be loaned out for our

VIPs for red carpets, things of that nature. These garments must be kept in pristine condition."

I want to say something, to try and earn a smile or even a tiny, minimal nod of approval, but I don't. I stay quiet, studying the room.

Yvette opens a closet door on the far-left side of the room. "Here are supplies. We use only Maison Dauphine garment bags or our premium shopping totes to send accessories. Magazines and agencies should know to never send back samples in their own bags, but if they do, let us know quickly. We like to keep a standard.

"Most of the time they will send a representative to pick up garments," she adds. "We do not like them to use messenger services. Regardless of season or demand, no Maison Dauphine is any less exclusive in the eyes of the house. All pieces should be treated as if they are"—she eyes me—"the *Mona Lisa*."

I straighten up. I think that was a slight dig at me because I'm an American and she thinks that's the only way I could understand.

I nod.

Yvette shuts the closet door and takes a step toward the desk. "And this is where you'll be working. Milo, your computer is on the right, and Rhodes, yours is on the left."

We nod.

"I hire good people, so I let them do their jobs. Meaning I'd rather not micromanage. I will let you determine how you divide tasks, unless it becomes an issue, which I trust it will not."

Rhodes smiles. "Of course not."

I agree. "No issues."

"Any other questions?" Yvette sighs, passing us and heading back toward the double doors.

I rack my brain. "Well, I was just wondering . . . do you think we will have any opportunities to network or share ideas or . . . ?"

Yvette raises a brow. "To *network*? Or share ideas? Milo, it's day one. Let's just make sure our external requests are all handled, first and foremost. Once you two are proficient, we could perhaps begin to assess opportunities for growth. I will be as forward as possible about this, however . . . Maison Dauphine has the highest of standards, and we expect all representatives of the house to maintain and progress those standards. Simply doing your job will be the bare minimum expectation."

Rhodes doesn't look intimidated by this at all, but the severity in her tone kind of makes me want to hurl my grapefruit juice all over the closet.

I told Celeste I wouldn't go in guns blazing, and I already have annoyed Yvette.

"We are in the final stages of preparation for our resort show, which I'm sure you know takes place in three weeks. It's a bit later than in previous years, but this has only seemed to drum up excitement."

The resort show is one of the things I'm looking forward to the most. In addition to the spring/summer and fall/winter shows every year, many big designers show a cruise or resort line. Resort wear is a huge trend in the market for competitors like Dior, Chanel, and Saint Laurent, and Maison Dauphine always makes a splash.

"So, until then," Yvette says, "there will be absolutely no time for 'networking' or 'sharing ideas.' I must insist that you do not attempt to distract any employees in the meantime. Is this understood?"

I nod. "Of course. I would never want to distract anyone. I know how important the resort collection is."

Our computers make a dinging noise, and Yvette gestures toward them. "That'll be your email. Seems the day has begun, boys."

Chapitre Quatre

"Are you all right?" Rhodes asks. His eyes are glued to me.

We're sitting at our desks, and I'm trying to sign in to my email account with no luck. There's a sticky note on my desk with the username and password, but for some reason it doesn't work.

I nod. "I'm fine."

This fucking stupid computer.

"Are you fine?"

Finally the password works—turns out the caps lock was on—and with the sense of relief that I don't have to call tech support and sound like a total moron, I turn to Rhodes and let my gaze meet his.

"Yes." I lift my brows. "Everything is great."

"I'm not sure," he says. "You seem . . ."

"What?"

"Well, you seem annoyed or something."

I roll my eyes. "Why would I be annoyed?"

"Dunno."

Cheeks warming, I mean to look away . . . but there's something magnetic about his eyes.

"I'm not annoyed."

"All right." He straightens up in his seat and points to the computer. "Seems we've got loads of emails already. How are we even meant to—"

The doors burst open behind us, and we both spin so quickly in our chairs I think we might resemble blurry cartoon characters to the two girls standing before us.

"Thank goodness you're here."

One of the girls has slick blond hair that stops just above her shoulders. The edges are as severe as the jut of her cheekbones and the sharpness of her chin. She's wearing an oversized gray sweater and a black midi skirt, and she pushes up the sleeves as she takes a step toward us.

"I'm Haydée," she says, arching a brow and studying me before looking to Rhodes. "Public relations senior manager."

"I'm Zoe," the other girl says in what I believe is a posh British accent. She's a bit mousier—quieter, shrinking into the blue shift dress she's wearing and standing a few feet behind Haydée. "Public relations senior manager, as well. Only . . . well, I've been learning under Haydée, so sometimes I feel like I shouldn't even be a senior manager. I mean, I'm qualified, but—"

She forces a chuckle and Haydée furrows her brow, shaking her head slightly and keeping her attention on us.

Not awkward at all.

"We've got a project we need you to complete quickly."

"*Très rapidement*," Zoe says.

Haydée lifts her chin. "*Ah, oui. Je voulais vous demander si vous parlez tous les deux français? Couramment?*"

Wait, what?

Rhodes looks to me and then shakes his head. *"Non, je suis désolé. Nous ne parlons pas français couramment. Nous pouvons en comprendre un peu."*

Huh?

"Vraiment?" Haydée purses her lips. *"Il semble que vous avez compris. Vous avez répondu rapidement et votre français semble bon."*

"Notre français est très limité," Rhodes says.

They're speaking too fast. What is happening?

Haydée then turns to me, no longer speaking to Rhodes, and narrows her eyes. *"Ah. Est-ce vrai? Votre français est-il à tous les deux très limité? Ou seulement le vôtre?"*

I have no idea what is happening. It sounds like maybe they're talking about breakfast food or something. With a drop of sweat forming above my brow, I force a smile.

"Sorry, I'm still learning."

"I thought so," Haydée says. "It might benefit you to pay attention as Rhodes speaks French. We'd prefer if you both were able to converse with our French-speaking clients and colleagues."

Rhodes's face goes red, and I'm sure mine is quick to match.

"We need you to do an inventory of the current season," Haydée says, pointing toward one of the closets behind us.

She runs us through the process, and it's fairly simple. There's software that acts as a database across all of Maison Dauphine, which categorizes every single sample from accessories to clothing and indicates the status and whereabouts of everything. We'll just scan the items with the iPad cameras and use the app to mark that, as of today, the sample is here in the Paris office.

"We need these all done before you leave for lunch today."

Haydée doesn't leave any time for questions, comments, or

concerns. She and Zoe are gone, with the doors shut behind them, and we are left with iPads in hand and an absurd number of items to scan.

"What about all those emails?" Rhodes asks, starting to unzip a garment bag on a rolling rack. "We're already behind, I think."

"How can we be behind if we just started?" I groan.

Rhodes nods toward the computers. "There are a bunch of emails we haven't even started on."

I squint. "I know. It was a rhetorical question."

He laughs now. "I see. Dunno, seems like this is going to be the kind of job where we're always behind."

"We'll be fine. All we need to do is scan all of this and then we can breeze through the emails, and we'll be caught up."

We begin working in silence, and I keep catching Rhodes glancing over at me.

Finally he sighs.

"All right, I think I know what this is."

"What do you mean?"

"Look, Milo. I know it's probably kind of weird . . . the paparazzi and stuff. But I'm honestly just a person—"

A laugh escapes my lips with such fervor I clap my hand over my mouth, nearly dropping the tweed hat I mean to inventory.

"I'm serious!" he says.

I swallow another laugh, eyes bugging. "I know you are. Celebrities—*they're just like us.*"

Judging by the way his face falls, he realizes almost instantly that his theory is incorrect. "Not the right thing to say, I guess. I don't know. Sometimes people treat me really weird before they get to know me. I just thought . . ."

"You just thought I was starstruck?" I scrunch up my nose and shake my head. "I'm sorry to disappoint, but that is not what's happening here . . . I mean, you're . . . yes, I know of you. My brother is, like, obsessed with your brother."

Rhodes's eyes go wide, and his lips remain in a wide smile. "Yeah?"

"Not obsessed." I groan. *Idiot.* "That's—no, he just loves soccer. *Football*, I mean."

"Does he?"

"Yeah, it's, like, his whole life." I scan a barcode sticker that's been placed on the size label of a sequined dress. "He's been following Ollie's career through the academy and all that. He follows him on Instagram and TikTok, and he doesn't normally follow a ton of players."

Bit of a lie, because he follows most of the Clyde Circus club. I think if it weren't for Ollie being more of a personality and having such an iconic player for a father, he wouldn't follow him at all.

Because while Rhodes's twin brother, Ollie, has just signed and will soon debut with Armoury United, my brother is a huge Clyde Circus supporter. Armoury and Circus have one of the most famous Premier League rivalries.

I smile as it hits me that this might finally get Rhodes to leave me alone: "He loves Clyde Circus."

Rhodes scoffs. "You're kidding."

"I'm not."

Rhodes brings his hand to his mouth. "What an absolute tragedy. Your brother's taste is . . ."

It's harmless teasing, but it might cause steam to burst from my ears.

"He has great taste, actually."

Rhodes lifts his palms. "I'm only calling it as I see it."

"You don't know him."

Maybe sensing the sterner tone, he studies me for a beat. "Fine. I know he's supporting a losing club, but . . . fine." Then he gives me an up and down. "Don't tell me *you* have a Eun Seung-hyun poster above your bed."

Scanning a bag of jewelry, I shake my head. "Definitely not. I do have a Clyde Circus keychain that he gave me. And I have a scarf from when he dragged me to go see them play in an International Champions Cup match back home."

"Dragged you? Not a football fan yourself, then?"

"No. I like tennis, as you already know."

"But you went with your brother, that's nice."

I nod. "Of course. He's my brother."

Rhodes's eyes seem to soften at this.

"That's nice," he repeats, scanning some shoes. "You guys are close, then?"

"We are. I don't know what I'd do without him."

"That's brilliant. Is he here with you? In Paris? Did you come with your family?"

"Nope, he's back in Florida. They all are."

Rhodes considers this, biting the inside of his cheek and tapping his fingers on his desk. "Right. Are you here with, like . . . your boyfriend?"

I shift in my seat. "Uh. No."

Was he just asking me *that*? Like, was that a loaded question? Surely it was not a loaded question.

"Why'd you say it like that?" He chuckles.

"Like what?"

"Sort of like it was an absurd suggestion."

I inhale. "I just don't have a boyfriend."

"You're anti-boyfriend?"

"What? No, I'm not anti-boyfriend." *Where did this leap come from?* "I mean, I guess kind of. But not fully, just . . . I have goals and I'm busy and, in my experience, dating isn't worth the complications."

Rhodes pokes his tongue against his top lip, then nods. "Sounds like you've definitely dated the wrong guys."

"Oh, right."

"I'm serious."

I cock my head. "And what does that mean, Rhodes?"

"Nothing bad. Really!" He shrugs. "Not everyone will appreciate a catch."

With a lump and any possible chance of a coherent thought stuck in my throat, I poke my thumb into my palm.

My chest warms, and I don't mean to so openly blush, but he's actually impossibly charming. And despite my best efforts to not be the most basic American in Europe, I might also find myself swooning just a little bit because of his British accent.

Wait. This is it. This is the kind of thing London's resident fuckboy says. Right?

Rhodes, a fuckboy *and* a mind reader, wiggles his brow. "I'm not trying to butter you up or something. I'm just explaining what I meant."

Sure, sure.

Then: "So, you're in Paris all alone?"

"With my best friend. We're staying at her aunt's flat."

"Oh, nice, where?"

"The 7th."

He smiles. "I actually am staying in the 7th as well. My parents have a flat there." He pulls a face. "Does that sound so cringey? 'My parents have a flat?' I do make my own way, as well."

"I'm sure you do."

Woof. That came out way snarkier than it probably should have.

Rhodes takes it in stride, though. "You're interesting, Milo."

"*Interesting*," I echo with a scoff. "I'm sure you meant that as a compliment."

He lifts one shoulder. "I did."

Our eyes meet.

I always sort of wondered if celebrities look as good in real life. There can't be any way there is just this class of humans who are somehow gifted with having perfect skin and hair and smiles and posture and style. Right?

But in real life, Rhodes looks better than any photos I've ever seen of him. His rosy cheeks and sapphire eyes—a handsome portrait, painted with only the best colors and the finest strokes.

This Rhodes seems different from the one I've expected, really.

"For what it's worth, Armoury isn't exactly my thing," he says, waving it off. "I support them, of course, and I'll certainly give a Circus fan a fair amount of well-deserved shit, but I don't care nearly as much as my brother or dad."

Different from what I expected indeed.

"So, is that what it was, then?" He hums. "You don't like me because your brother goes for Clyde Circus?"

I shake my head. "I don't *not like you*."

"But you don't like me."

"You'd think it's the first time this has happened to you."

The corner of his mouth lifts again. "You really are interesting."

We work through the clothes, only running into a couple of smudged barcodes or missing pieces that we are, thankfully, able to locate in other drawers or hanging on other racks. I'm not sure who's been managing the closet until now, but it's almost meticulously organized. I imagine sometimes it's easy to, especially in a rush, place a dress on the wrong rack or a pair of shoes in the wrong bag, but it seems like the PR team at Maison Dauphine is as scrupulous as Yvette has indicated.

I catch myself admiring Rhodes several times, which is incredibly irritating. He is endlessly charming and he's open enough that he's easy to talk to. Anyone else would think they'd hit the jackpot—he's not only ridiculously handsome, but he's also funny and has great banter. It's just like having the perfect volley partner in tennis.

Once we're wrapping up, he places his iPad on his desk and stretches his arms over his head. The flash of his stomach causes a lump to form in my throat and I quickly look away.

"I'm—um. I'm only missing one belt," I say. I look around the closet. "I've looked everywhere."

Rhodes walks over to me. "What does the belt look like?"

"It's a little black one with the gold monogram. And there are pearls on the clasp."

Rhodes snaps his fingers together. "Ah, no, it's not missing. Looks fifty-seven and twenty-eight both share the same belt. So it's accounted for."

I stare at him. I am disproportionately impressed that he

remembered this. I'm also fighting a feeling I know all too well—competition.

How did he figure that out before me? How did I not put two and two together? It's so simple, and this is only day one.

"You already remember the look numbers?"

Rhodes nods. "I guess so. I sort of picked them up as we went."

Here I was being a total idiot, caught up in Rhodes's eyes and smile and effortless wit, while he was retaining details that are going to be valuable to our apprenticeship.

Remember, Milo? Guys like Rhodes. They're always charming. Always handsome, and just sweet enough to confuse you in the beginning.

I'm going to have to be better about resisting that charm if I'm going to stay on top of my game. I have to do my best work this summer.

"Anyway, that means we're done, then." He takes my iPad and locks it. Smiling down at me. "We make a pretty good team."

He's less than a foot away from me, and as he adjusts to hold the iPad behind his back with both hands, I can practically feel the space between our bodies warming up.

"Crushed it, I'd say." He smiles, eyes still locked on mine.

And then his gaze lowers to my mouth, his own cherry-red lips turned up ever so slightly.

I've become good at reading people. Opponents, mostly, but I know what it's like when a guy wants to kiss me. I've noticed the way even eye contact becomes tonal. Noticed the subtle ways people inch closer.

This can't be that, though. Right?

We just met. And it's Rhodes Hamilton.

Surely he's not about to kiss me, even if he's unashamedly

staring at my mouth. Even if, when he makes eye contact again, he licks his lips and takes a sharp breath.

My own breathing halts.

"Look, Milo . . ." Rhodes's voice is a bit lower now. A bit gruffer. "To tell you the truth, I might have been trying to butter you up just a bit earlier."

"What?"

"Only a little," he offers. "I'd like to try and get on your good side, I think."

I swallow. "Why do you want to get on my good side?"

With a quiet, breathy laugh: "Well, you seem . . . cool. I guess."

"I seem *cool*?" I furrow my brow.

Another laugh. "You're funny. You're obviously driven and seem clever. Plus, you've got this whole loyalty thing—like you going to bat for your brother when you don't even like footie. And if you really want me to say it, you're fit. I don't know, it's just—I think it could be fun to go for dinner after this. Or something casual, if that's more your thing. In case you're worried you might get sick of me rather quickly and not want to be sat at a dinner table for the entire duration of a—"

I cackle—he can't be serious.

Except he tilts his head. He *is* serious.

He looks at me like a wounded puppy. "Silly of me, apparently."

"Sorry, I'm just trying to get this right. Were you just asking me out?"

"I think I was attempting to. And failing."

"We're coworkers."

He looks at me expectantly, like he's waiting for me to offer up another, more useful point.

"We should keep this professional."

Rhodes chews on his lip. "Right."

"Don't give me sad puppy eyes." I furrow my brow. "You're Rhodes Hamilton."

"What's *that* supposed to mean?"

I exhale. "You know what it means. I am sure you will have no trouble throwing a stone and finding someone else who is driven and fit in Paris."

"Maybe not. So, there's no part of you that would want to go to dinner?"

Guys like Rhodes . . . Guys like Rhodes . . .

"No. I know how this whole thing goes."

"Oh, do you?"

With a quick nod, I glance away. "Let me guess? You're interested, but you just want something casual? And you're mostly interested in something fun and carefree for the summer?"

"Who said—"

"Casual may work for guys like you, but in my experience, I don't love it. And it doesn't end well, and we can't afford something like that, because we need to focus on Maison Dauphine."

"For guys like me—" He sighs and opens his mouth to say more before closing it again. Then, after a beat: "Right, I see. All right, then, Milo. Okay. Loud and clear. I'm sorry if I made things weird at all. Hopefully we can just pretend this never happened. And let's agree to stay a good team. Yeah?"

"It's fine. And yes, of course. We'll be a good team."

He sighs. "Okay, good. I just know how these things can get. I think you and I will do well together, so I don't want the competition to change things."

I'm almost distracted by the absurdity of him asking me out. *Almost*. "Competition? I mean, Rhodes. We don't have to compete."

"For the job?" he asks.

And now it's like time has stopped.

When I don't say anything, Rhodes takes a step back, cocking his head. "You didn't know?"

"I'm confused. What do you mean *the* job?"

"They're only going to give one of us a job at the end of all this," Rhodes says.

"What? That makes no sense. Why would they only give one of us a job? We're both apprentices. And the whole point of the apprenticeship is that there's a job at the end of this."

Rhodes shrugs. "I don't know all the details, but I guess HR only approved one role. It's a bit experimental, isn't it?" He frowns. "Shit. I thought you knew."

"No, I thought . . ." I exhale. "So, we're competing."

"Yeah, that's why only one of us gets to work the resort show. Since by then they'll have a good idea—"

"Only one of us is working the show?" I balk.

With a heavy sigh, Rhodes grabs the back of his neck. "But we're starting to get on, you and me. I don't want this to change anything."

Of course he doesn't. Everyone absolutely adores him here. Yvette seems to know him personally. Haydée loves that he can speak French. He's already memorizing the looks. He's ahead of me in every way, and it seems he doesn't even need to try.

Now it's my turn to take a step back.

"Milo?"

"I just can't believe this," I say.

I don't stand a chance against you.

If there's one thing I have learned in tennis, though, it's that showing weakness is not an option. You've always got to be on your game.

And then there's this terrible sinking feeling as I replay the flirting and cute smiles.

I bet that was all on purpose. He was already playing the game.

I was right about him, even if I didn't know exactly how.

"I don't want the competition aspect to change anything," Rhodes repeats. "That's all I was trying to say."

I frown. *The competition aspect.* As if there's really anything else now. "But this changes everything."

"It doesn't have to," he offers.

"Have you ever competed for something?" I laugh. "I don't know if this nice act is some kind of tactic—"

"A tactic?" Rhodes scoffs. *"Nice act?"*

"Look, I don't intend to lose, Rhodes."

"Well, neither do I, but—"

I hold up my hands. "Then there's our answer."

"I assure you, I can separate friendship from the competition."

"Maybe you can, but I can't. I don't have a backup plan. I'm four thousand miles from home and I'm here to get a job with Maison Dauphine at the end of my apprenticeship."

"That's it, then? We're competitors, and nothing else?"

Those pleading cerulean eyes are so tempting. It's almost illogically devastating to turn them down—after all, they're brand-new to me and shouldn't have such a profound effect.

Which is exactly what he wants.

"That's all we can be, Rhodes."

CLOTHES MINDED: RHODES HAMILTON TAKES ON MAISON DAUPHINE PARIS

Bienvenue à Paris, monsieur! Rhodes Hamilton, nineteen, is following in his mother's footsteps as he begins a summer-long apprenticeship with international fashion house Maison Dauphine. Former supermodel Rosie Hamilton has had a long-standing affiliation with the designer, so it comes as no surprise that one of her sons should venture into the fashion industry.

This news is not without controversy, however, as Rhodes's father, Armoury United legend Liam Hamilton, also has a relationship with a French fashion house. Rhodes is said to have "changed his mind" about a brand partnership with Louis Vuitton. Some outlets have called this "disrespectful," and many on social media have shared thoughts, such as a Tweet claiming, "Rhodes clings to his mummy's legacy since he can't follow in his dad's footsteps."

Many in the fashion industry are watching closely to see if Rhodes has what it takes. An anonymous staff member at an Italian fashion house expressed the buzz around their office as employees placed bets on the numerous outcomes.

"There's a very good chance he somehow makes it work, but there's a better chance . . . well . . ."

The apprenticeship was originally announced as a scouting opportunity for young, fresh talent, open internationally;

a submission from a Florida student caught the eye of the house.

Another anonymous insider at a casting agency questions if the apprenticeship—and specifically Rhodes's somewhat controversial appointment—is part of the fashion house's attempts to distract from the recent criticisms surrounding gatekeeping practices in the luxury world and Maison Dauphine's role as a central player.

No stranger to controversy, Rhodes has become a paparazzi favorite as he's frequented clubs and high-profile parties with countless different girls. Following the divisive ending of his relationship with former *Love on a Boat* contestant Imogen Evans last year, some have labeled him a "selfish cad." Friends of Hamilton have defended his right to "be young and have fun."

Rhodes's twin brother, Ollie, will soon be making his debut for Armoury United and has received acclaim and enthusiasm from fans around the world.

We're eagerly watching to see whether Rhodes joins his brother as a prodigal titan in his own regard or if he opts for a French exit.

Deuce Bags

Chip: Did you see this?!

Miguel: a florida student

Isaac: Milo with the Florida Man vibes in Paris

Me: The vibes are definitely not Florida Man

Chip: I can't believe they didn't include your name

Isaac: Pretty fucked up

Isaac: Citrus Harbor Boys Tennis Legend, Milo Hawthorne

Me: It's not a big deal

Me: That piece is about him, not me

Miguel: overall pretty sick you're working with Rhodes Hamilton tho

Isaac: I might get Ollie for my PL Fantasy

Isaac: Maybe you'll get some insider knowledge

Chip: Which he wouldn't be able to share with you

Chip: Legally

Isaac: Right, legally

Miguel: we missed you at McGuire's tonight, Milo

Isaac: We really did, they had a pop culture category for trivia

Isaac: You would have killed it

Me: Damn, so you guys didn't win a month of milkshakes?

Miguel: sadly not

Isaac: I gotta run but keep killing it, Milo

Chip: Yeah, Milo, make it so they can't possibly leave out your name next time

Chapitre Cinq

"And you know, Chip and Isaac are right. My name should be included! But article aside, I just don't understand why Maison Dauphine would do this. Why would they pit us against each other? What is this—the Hunger Games?"

Celeste has picked me up from Maison Dauphine like a Citrus Harbor Day School mom picking up a whining toddler.

She's wearing a baby tee and denim skirt with white sneakers, paired with pink-lensed sunglasses that are definitely only for appearances since they're nearly translucent.

"Who is the rat here anyway?"

Celeste gawks. "Huh?"

"*À bon chat, bon rat!*" I exclaim. "There is no way I'm the rat. Right?"

"So this means you're *not* going to dinner?"

"No, we are definitely not going to dinner. I have made it very clear to him that we are the furthest thing from going to dinner."

Celeste frowns. "This is devastating, Milo."

"I know. And of all people to compete against."

"Not that," Celeste says. "You were going to go on a date with Rhodes Hamilton! Not only a date, you were going to go on a dinner date in Paris. This is literally, like, a Hallmark movie." She winces. "Or it *was*."

"It's not a Hallmark movie, Celeste. I shouldn't have to remind you that this charming thing he does is . . . it's performance. At the very least, he can't stand that I'm not googly-eyed over him, and he probably wanted to prove he could make me fall for him just like all his other poor victims."

Celeste's eyes are trained on the ends of her hair as she pulls at a split end. "Then it's even more of a Hallmark movie. Those types of guys are always—"

"Those movies are propaganda," I say. "Because in real life, *those types of guys* are not going to change or surprise you or save the inn or end up being Santa Claus."

"Do you *want* Rhodes to end up being Santa Claus?" Celeste asks very seriously.

"I am going to have to figure out how to take him down."

"Milo, Milo, Milo. Do you hear yourself?"

Taking a deep breath as we stroll up the avenue, I nod. "I do. I hear myself, Celeste, and you know I would never play dirty. There must be some fair, just way to squash him. You should see the way everyone fawns over him—"

Celeste stops walking, throwing her hand across my chest. "You are not *squashing* Rhodes Hamilton."

"Like a bug," I assure her.

Sure, this is a daunting task. And, to Celeste's original point, it is a disappointment. A massive, earth-shattering disappointment. This was supposed to be my perfect summer.

"Maybe instead of taking him down, you could just show them that you're better suited for the job."

Celeste is such an idealist sometimes.

"You're right. In fact, I think that's Sun Tzu verbatim. Right? Who needs war?" I roll my eyes.

"Okay, look, I get that you aren't going to dinner. But I don't know, it might be good to keep him as a friend. I'm sure Sun Tzu has something about allies, right? Would it be such a terrible idea to have a friend in Paris?"

I shake my head. "Unfortunately, I just don't know how to be his friend if we're going to spend all day every day consciously trying to outdo each other. I don't know how that could be possible, and I just don't think he can be trusted. Anyway, I already have a friend in Paris, remember?"

We continue to walk for a bit, toward Avenue des Champs-Élysées. I'm not sure what food is around, but when we get to the giant five-way intersection—which I am completely uncertain how these cars even navigate—I pull out my phone and start to look for nearby restaurants.

"What are we in the mood for?"

Celeste hums. "What?"

"For dinner?"

"Oh, right. I'm not sure. I don't have much of an appetite."

"Did you already eat?" I glance up from my phone, studying her. "What did you end up doing today? I'm sorry, I was just droning on and on about Rhodes and I didn't even ask you a single question about your day. Tell me everything."

She laughs, and I think I might recognize a bit of her nervous giggle.

Oh, god. What did you do, Celeste?

"I had a bit of a late lunch. I walked around the Jardin du Luxembourg, which was beautiful. I planned on making a TikTok, but . . . Well, anyway, I wandered the city a bit after that. I went to this super-famous bookstore, Shakespeare and Company. It was so cute. And then I saw Notre-Dame from the outside; I somehow ended up browsing around a tiny little outdoor produce market. . . ."

She's saying all of this in a long, drawn-out, sort of whimsical way, and I know she is avoiding telling me part of it. But what? And why?

"I did meet a guy." Celeste pauses as we cross the street, concentrating on the crosswalk as if she's considering how much to divulge. "Nothing really came of it, but he was handsome and had the most amazing French accent. It was just a quintessential romantic moment—a cute guy stopping next to me at the market to introduce himself. . . . Which, by the way, how ironic is it that you were the one who was like 'No romance in Paris!' just yesterday, but then you got a guy's number and were asked on a dinner date first thing in the morning—hours before I was?" She pulls a face. "Sorry to bring that up again. Just thought it was ironic."

"So ironic," I echo. "Okay, what is it? You're doing that thing where you dance around something you don't want to say."

Celeste takes a deep breath once we're on the other side of the road. "Right. I know. I have to tell you something."

Of course I don't know what to expect, but this has at least temporarily killed my appetite and added a giant pit in my stomach.

What the hell could Celeste have to tell me that has her acting so bizarre?

The anxiety from today, which I've barely processed, mixed with this sudden flood of nervous energy and jitters, makes me want to hurl into the nearest trash can.

"Celeste!"

She nods and nods, looking around as if to find the words. "I don't want to—are you sure you don't want to talk about Rhodes for a bit first?"

"What is going on? You're scaring me. Is it something bad?"

Again, she nods. "Yeah. I mean . . . it's not good."

"Celeste, for the love of god. Have you never had someone deliver bad news to you? This is the worst, most drawn-out way—please just tell me what the hell is going on."

Poking her tongue in her cheek, she shuts her eyes. "I have to go home."

"What?" I give her a once-over. "Are you okay? Do you not feel well? I can get us a car, I bet it's, like, a five-minute drive from here. Can't be more than ten."

"No, I don't mean home, like my aunt's apartment. I mean home. *Home*, home. Citrus Harbor." When she opens her eyes, they're filled with tears and her brow scrunches up tight, lip quivering. "I was so excited for our summer in Paris, you know that. I don't want to leave you, and I thought you'd have the best day of your entire life today and it'd be easier to tell you, but then . . . I know this is all a lot harder than you expected, and I'm so sorry."

I stare at Celeste, drawing in a breath through my mouth, but my chest is so tight, my lungs barely expand at all. My jaw and chin feel numb, like there isn't enough skin to stretch across the bone. My throat is closing, and everything is going hazy. Paris softens, like it's trapped behind a blurry lens. Now, involuntarily, I think my eyes might be filling with tears too.

How did today go from the most exciting to the absolute worst? How did everything go to shit so incredibly quickly?

"I don't . . . I don't understand. Everything was fine this morning?"

She bobs her head up and down quickly, wiping away tears from her cheeks. "It was. Everything was great. But Gran isn't doing well. Like, she's *really* not doing well. And I can't . . ." She stifles a sob, holding her hand over her mouth.

"Oh my god, Celeste, I'm sorry." I pull her in for a hug, and she pats my back. "I am so sorry. Okay. Of course. Right. We'll go back and—"

Celeste pulls away from our hug and leans back, hands on my arms. "Milo, no. *We're* not going back. You have to stay in Paris and do what you came to do."

I shake my head. "I can't just let you go back alone."

She waves that off, sniffling. "Yes, you can. And you will. I'll be okay. I just have to go be with my family. And when you get back . . . I mean, even when you get a big job with Maison Dauphine, you'll come back home before you move here, right?"

This tidal wave of emotions has thrown me, and I suddenly have no recollection of my goals or plans or hopes for the future. I nod, though, because I figure I'll go back, at least to pack my things.

"Celeste, I really don't think you should go back alone. I want to be there for you. This is a big deal."

Lips turned down into a deep frown, she lifts her shoulders. "It is what it is, Milo. And I love you so much for wanting to be there for me, but what would really make me the happiest is to Face-Time you and see your spectacular view and some really pretty clothes and still feel like I get to go on this big, once-in-a-lifetime adventure with you."

I really don't even know how to process this. I'm certainly crying now. For Gran, and for Celeste and her family, and for this special summer that we were going to share. All the memories we were going to make together.

"I don't know if I can even do it alone," I admit.

Celeste shakes her head. "You can. Milo, please. You can literally do anything. And you know that. You're Milo the Great. When you set your mind to something, you make it happen. You inspire me all the time, and I know you're going to inspire me this summer."

My nose is running now, and I am turning into somewhat of a hysterical mess on the sidewalk. Celeste is also crying, and between the two of us, we must look absolutely batshit.

"Only we would have a dramatic sob fest on the Champs-Élysées," I say.

She laughs, wiping her face again. "I know. This is so us."

"When do you leave?"

"Tomorrow," she says. "First thing in the morning. My mom is already driving to Orlando now, so she'll be ready to pick me up from the airport."

I exhale. "Oh god. Tomorrow."

Celeste squeezes my arm. "Aunt Angela obviously says nothing changes with the apartment. It's all yours."

Swallowing, I try to continue with some deep breaths to stop crying like a toddler. "All right. I'm going to have to think about this. I don't know. Look, I hear what you're saying, but I don't know if I can stay here by myself. I don't know if I even should, honestly."

"What do you mean, if you *should*? Of course you should."

I shrug. "I won't have you—I won't have anybody here. It just sounds a bit . . . well, there's also the fact that I might be spinning my wheels with Maison Dauphine. You're right, anyway, I'm not going to squash Rhodes Hamilton. He's unsquashable. They all love him, and he's going to work the resort show, and that job is probably already his. He's *Rhodes Hamilton*. There is no competing with him. This is a losing battle."

"I don't even know what to say," Celeste says, her expression hardening a bit. "I honestly don't. You never give up, Milo."

"Maybe sometimes that isn't a good thing."

"Do you remember when you tried to do the leg-press machine at the gym and you hurt your glute because you jumped ahead and did, like, an absurd number of weights? And Coach Marshall told you to sit out the tennis match, even though it was a huge deal? Remember, you were playing that guy from Miami? With the youth records?"

I groan. "This isn't like that—"

"You beat that other kid to a pulp on that court, and you didn't even look like you were in any pain at all."

"But I was. And I had to rest for a week and a half after that."

"You won, though! And you recovered, and then you kept winning."

"Stubbornly competing through injury is not quite the metaphor I—"

She folds her arms. "I think it is. It seems like right now, your ego is injured because you believe you're somehow less than Rhodes Hamilton. And while I very much would like to see you have a friend and an ally in Paris—and while I would like it to be Rhodes Hamilton because I can only imagine the kind of invites he'd give us—I know you could squash him if you had to. Even if the odds were stacked against you."

Celeste might be right.

But she might be wrong.

"I'm going to see how things go, and if this is just going to be some massive disappointment, I'm going to nip it in the bud and concede."

Chapitre Six

At five thirty in the morning, I squeeze Celeste in a tight hug once she has wheeled her luggage up to the front door.

She never even unpacked, and we aren't sure if that is more convenient or a melancholy reminder of the lost summer.

She didn't even get a chance to hang up the baby doll dress she bought to wear to the Louvre. Never got to wear the vintage Chanel bag my mom let her borrow. Didn't get the chance to fill the extra space she left in those bags for souvenirs or new clothes.

Of course, I completely understand why she's leaving and that it's more important than outfits or plans that will wait for another time. Part of me feels like, despite her vocally expressed wishes, I'm a bad friend for not jumping on that plane with her and being there for her and her family during this.

After so many dinners and pool days and shopping trips with Gran, it feels like I'm letting everyone down. Gran would be there for me—always has been—and I'm not going back.

When Celeste leaves, I slip back under the covers, clutching them over my chest.

I'm fully alone now, with everyone and everything I know halfway across the world. I hate feeling so soft, but my temples are stained with streaks of slow-sliding tears.

Though I long for the echo of city sounds to remind me I'm not fully alone, it's dead quiet as I lie in the dark.

Two days ago, I was sitting outside a cafe on a gorgeous day with Celeste, imagining how perfect this Parisian summer would be, and it's all dashed, a sunny day waterlogged.

My alarm finally goes off, but I can barely find the motivation to get out of bed now. My body feels like it's sunken into the mattress, become hollow as a symptom of the quiet, still and silent like moss overgrown on a forest floor.

I have to get ready.

I have to turn on upbeat music, take a hot shower, drink some grapefruit juice, eat one of the yogurts in the fridge, and try to muster up something that resembles confidence.

I also have to avoid any unproductive thoughts about Rhodes. It's now my job to stay rational: to forget the way my heartbeat quickened as I briefly questioned my own judgment because of his bright blue eyes, and to make sure I never imagine Rhodes in some romantic golden hue.

Eyes on the prize.

I connect to the sound system—a perk of this bougie apartment—and shuffle my Spotify. Of course, there must be some kind of hilarious irony in the fact that the opening instrumentals of "Love Story (Taylor's Version)" start to blast through the speakers.

While the shower heats up, I do everything in my power to lift myself out of this hole. I remind myself, through brute force, that I got myself here. That, in and of itself, is something to be proud of, and something to provide a source of motivation. Past Milo would tell Current Milo to get a grip.

Being alone in Paris isn't the end of the world, surely. I can do all the things I planned to do with Celeste on my own. I can explore by myself.

And I *will* get a job at the end of this apprenticeship.

When I get to Maison Dauphine, there is a much different energy than yesterday. Voices drift down the hall and fill the lobby. Not just the overlap of voices, either—high-pitched *giggles*. People are laughing!

It seems the entire staff is stuffed into the first conference room, gathered around the large oval wooden table in the center of the room, which has been converted to some sort of patisserie. Overflowing from colorful Pierre Hermé boxes and scalloped brass-tiered trays are macarons and cakes and flaky golden pastries. Vibrant and decadent tarts sit among pralines and other little rectangular treats adorned with powdered sugar or chocolate.

Haydée and Zoe are whispering in a corner, and once we've made awkward eye contact, they stiffen before shuffling over to me.

"All right, now all eyes are on you to see what *you'll* bring to the office," Haydée says.

Zoe giggles.

I just furrow my brow. "What do you mean?"

"Well, Rhodes brought in this gorgeous spread from Pierre Hermé—it's Yvette's favorite."

Which means he will be too.

"Right," I say.

Damn. I really wanted one of these delicious-smelling pastries, but knowing they're just here as Rhodes's way of bribing his way into everyone's favor makes them significantly less appealing.

Still, I can't turn down sweets, so I grab a small vanilla tart, tucking into it before making sure there are no crumbs on my person. There can be no evidence that I enjoyed this little stunt of Rhodes's.

I walk back to the fashion closet, and Rhodes is sitting there with a hot takeout coffee beside his mouse. He's wearing a black cap and a white hoodie with no logos or indication of brand, but something about the material and the thick strings just tells me it's ridiculously expensive. He's paired this with camo pants and Nike sneakers, and he doesn't look like he'd work at Maison Dauphine at all, but I'm sure Yvette and the rest of the team all told him how *trés cool* he looks.

I didn't wear my backpack, bringing only my wallet and phone, which both fit in my pant pockets. I snap my AirPods shut and place them on the desk beside him.

This causes Rhodes to look up at me, smiling. "Did you grab a pastry?"

"I prefer Ladurée." I narrow my eyes. "What kind of tactic is that, anyway?"

"Tactic?" Rhodes asks. "What are you talking about?"

"Bringing in Yvette's favorite? In fact, don't you think it's a bit transparent?"

Rhodes's face pales. "Do you think it's—is it too much?"

Groaning, I sit in my chair and log in. "You don't have to pretend this wasn't some calculated move to make yourself look better than me."

"It wasn't." He swallows, color returning to his face in the form of burgundy across his cheeks. "I just wanted to do something nice for everyone. I don't know. It's the kind of thing Mum and Dad do—for everyone at Armoury, they always bring in breakfasts. I didn't realize it'd look that way."

A sense of agitation bubbles inside me.

"Okay, Rhodes. Sure."

Rhodes nods. "Actually. And I am honestly sorry if you felt slighted by it. I wasn't trying to make myself look better than you at all. I just thought it'd be a nice gesture." He winces. "You do think it's too much, though, don't you? Reckon everyone thinks that's why I did it too?"

I deadpan. "Who knows? In general, I'd say money can't buy friends, but bringing Pierre Hermé to Maison Dauphine might be the exception."

"God, I can be so thick." He forces a laugh, turning back to his computer and dragging and dropping images from his desktop onto an email. Based on our training yesterday, it seems he's already getting ahead on a magazine request.

Of course he is getting ahead. More fucking tactics and mind games.

"How is the inbox?"

"There are actually several emails from New York," Rhodes

offers. "I figure maybe you'll lead point on those. The American offices are probably . . . familiar, right? Also, that PR assistant, Sophie, uses a lot of exclamation points and smiley faces. Very American."

Very American. Where does he get off saying these things?

Of course, clicking into our emails, I can see he's right. Sophie is certainly expressive. And she signs her emails "xx Sophie," which seems odd, except for the fact that further in this email thread, I can see that a fashion assistant at *Glamour* also signs with two little Xs. It does seem like something only Americans are doing, but I'm *not* going to start signing "xx Milo."

Haydée has also posted into a big PR department group Teams chat.

> Si vous n'avez pas visité la salle de conférence, assurez-vous de ne pas manquer les délicieuses pâtisseries. Merci, Rhodes. C'est une merveilleuse façon de commencer notre journée!

I don't know what it all says, and I don't want to risk Rhodes catching me as I paste it into a translator, but her thanking Rhodes tells me everything I need to know. That and all the subsequent "*Merci*, Rhodes!" that follow.

It is hard to imagine I will survive this for the entire summer.

I click my tongue against the back of my teeth. "What if there was a way we didn't have to compete?"

Rhodes stops typing, and when he turns to me, his expression is different. It's softer. It almost makes that tightness in my chest completely transform to a glowing warmth.

"Really?"

I shrug. "It's not like I signed up for a competition."

He smiles. "That's really big of you, Milo."

"What do you—"

"Look, I really appreciate this. You know, if you want tickets to a Clyde Circus match or something, I'm happy to make some calls. Get your brother over here, you two can take the train into London and make a weekend of it."

I shake my head. "I'm not conceding. But I'm saying maybe we can convince Yvette to let us both work the resort show, and there must be some kind of compromise. Maybe there are different roles we could each get after the apprenticeship."

"Yvette has made it clear," he says, sighing. "It's only going to be one of us. And I'm sorry, Milo, but there is no way it isn't going to be me." He looks a bit pained when he says this, gaze falling from my eyes to my mouth, his own nearing a frown, before he turns back to his computer. "It isn't personal."

And just like that, the tension is back. I don't know how Rhodes manages to keep me on this emotional seesaw, but I'm instantly defensive.

"Well . . . that's not . . . what makes you think I can't do it? I need this, Rhodes. I came here all the way from Florida. This is a huge opportunity for me, do you have any idea? I mean, I don't have a famous family or connections that can get me any job I want."

His cheeks go red instantly and he places his palms on the desk, swiveling in his desk chair to face me. "You don't know what you're talking about. And for the record, you're not the only one with things on the line here. I need this too."

"How? How could you possibly need this?"

"Well, first, there's the fact that I turned down a huge campaign with Louis Vuitton to be here."

I raise my shoulders, looking around. "Do you hear the words that come out of your mouth, or do you just sort of—"

"There were literal articles written about it. *WWD* called it disrespectful, considering my father's past campaigns with them. Now, once news breaks of my apprenticeship here, I've publicly committed to Maison Dauphine. I can't just back out, Milo. How does that make me look?"

"God forbid you have to negotiate another deal to be the face of a different luxury fashion house. How incredibly difficult for you."

Rhodes's face is only growing redder. "That's only the tip of the iceberg. I've got more on the line than you could understand. I'm sorry you flew here from Florida, and this isn't your magical Milo in Paris summer."

"I'm not trying to be *Emily in Paris*, you—"

"You . . . ?"

"I don't know, okay, I'm not going to call you a name. I just . . ." I take a deep breath. "Look, you're right, I don't know your life or your problems, but there must be some way we can make this work. This is important to both of us."

Rhodes presses his lips together. "I wish things were different, but this is where we're at. As a courtesy, I'm going to tell you now that I'm not a fan of losing. And if it's only going to be one of us, I'm not gonna just roll over on this opportunity."

"But I don't understand why it has to be *this* opportunity. Why does it have to be my—*this* apprenticeship, this summer?"

"Do you hear the words that come out of *your* mouth?"

"I just don't get why you gave up a perfectly respectable campaign for a PR apprenticeship. Like, why did you choose something internal? Something corporate? Something that was supposed to go to *one* international student? I'm sure Maison Dauphine would have loved if you just did a campaign like you would've done for Louis Vuitton."

He sits up a bit straighter, blinking quickly.

"Oh my god. You could have, couldn't you? You could have done something else."

Rhodes swallows, crossing his arms, and the corner of his mouth twitches. "Milo, I'm getting the impression you fancy yourself as the center of the universe. And that isn't entirely shocking for people in our age range, and it's clearly gotten you pretty far, but I have to be honest. It's incredibly presumptuous for you to question my—"

"Why didn't you do a campaign? Or a collaboration? Or any other number of things influencers normally do with—"

"I am not an influencer." Rhodes holds up a finger. "And while I don't owe you an explanation, I wanted to do something different from the typical *celebrity* partnership."

I blink. "Then do you mean to tell me you're only doing this apprenticeship to prove a point? That you're not like other nepo babies?"

"Wow," Rhodes scoffs. *"Nepo baby."*

"Feel free to disagree."

Now I've *really* struck a chord. Rhodes practically has steam coming out of his ears, and his eyes are darker now, the crystal aquamarine pools turned stormy.

"You've got some nerve, Milo."

"Don't tell me. Your father made a call and got you this apprenticeship."

"He didn't, actually." Rhodes scowls. He opens his mouth to continue, but the doors fly open and Yvette appears, eyes trained on an iPad, strutting through the threshold in a slinky gray dress and black heels.

"Bonjour," she says, but without waiting for us to respond, she drags her finger across the tablet screen and sighs. "Let's go over the upcoming itinerary. You both will be staff for the majority of the summer PR events. This is a very important time for Maison Dauphine, especially as we are looking to build up the mystery around the resort theme. There will be hints at each event, little clues, if you will."

"Just like Renard Florin used to do," I say.

Yvette glances up, and for the first time, she smiles. It could be an involuntary twitch, except for the fact that she nods slightly as well, and even adds, "That's right, Milo. *Très bien.* Yes, this year's resort theme is L'or des Fous, an homage to Renard Florin's signature gold campaign."

Rhodes shoots me a look.

Oh my god, did I just get on Yvette's good side?

"This is all extremely confidential. This information cannot leave this room. Do not tell your closest confidants. I mean this very sincerely. Now, on to the schedule."

Our computers both ding as an email pops into our inboxes.

"There we are. Okay, the three I want you to focus on: We will hold a pop-up at the Versailles gardens at the end of this week. Most of this is already done, but you will both work the event and keep track of social media mentions and engagements. I will handle press."

A pop-up at the Versailles gardens? Holy hell.

"Next week we have an influencer event." Yvette winces a bit as she says this, I think, but then she collects herself. "We will host in the Tuileries garden, and this will be focused on handbags. We will unveil two of the bags from the resort show during this event. Again, you two will serve as hosts and keep track of the mentions."

I'm sensing a pattern, now that I think about it.

"Apart from the resort show, our final big event will be our gala at the Louvre."

The Fête à Minuit. I wondered if I would be allowed to work on the event—maybe I'd get to help plan or carry out some small tasks to assist with setup—but at least it sounds like I'll actually be there.

Renard Florin began the tradition of the Maison Dauphine Fête à Minuit—or the "party at midnight"—in the sixties. Back then, it was a marketing ploy, I'm sure, to have a party begin so late. It has transformed over the years, and is now a traditional gala, with Fête à Minuit as more of a title and an opportunity for some theming references.

It's one of the biggest nights in fashion. In the various entertainment industries, really, with a star-studded guest list and a ledger of famous moments over the years.

"You will be tasked with running the Instagram and TikTok during this event. Pascal will unveil one gown from the resort collection at the end of the evening."

Rhodes nods. "This all sounds brilliant."

"And each event is a clue," I say.

Yvette raises her brows.

"Right? Because Maison Dauphine has only referenced L'or des Fous at three shows in the last eighty-eight years—one at Versailles, one at the Tuileries gardens, and one at the Louvre."

Nodding, Yvette locks her iPad. "Very good, Milo. I must say I am impressed."

I don't look to Rhodes, concentrating on Yvette's tiny hint of a smile instead, but I bet he is probably foaming at the mouth right now.

"We also have a reshoot for the resort campaign after the gala, which we will likely ask you to assist with. Just logistics, but we will discuss that closer to the shoot." Yvette nods. "If any questions arise, please let me know. I expect the two of you to use your best judgment and represent the house well at all times, through emails, on social media, and at all events."

I do glance at Rhodes now, and I think—based on the way his eyes are a bit wider than normal, and his bottom lip seems to poke out ever so slightly—he's *nervous*.

"Milo, I'll have you lead for the Versailles pop-up," Yvette says.

My heart races. *Oh my god. I did something right.*

Then, as I am apt to do when I am given an inch, I test the possibility of getting a mile. "Of course. And if you need any ideas for some subtle references—just for the brand's most loyal audience members—I'm well versed on the history of L'or des Fous."

Yvette purses her lips.

Did I just push it too far?

She looks me up and down, and then she gives one very slight nod. "Send me any thoughts by end of day. Rhodes, until I have those ideas, please handle all messenger requests today."

Yvette leaves, and by the look on Rhodes's face, I know one thing for sure.

The game has just begun.

Chapitre Sept

Among my less brilliant ideas? Offering up brilliant ideas to Yvette without actually having any.

Rhodes has been gone all morning on messenger errands. Before rushing samples to French *Vogue*, he had to grab a watch from a boutique that wasn't open yet, ringing the manager, who was fast asleep. Then he had to pick up samples from a studio where some assistant had left them overnight, which is apparently a major, huge no-no. Such a huge no-no that I think Yvette's forehead vein almost burst when she came in and told us about it and how the assistant had been fired.

I'm not sure where Rhodes is now, but it's lunchtime and I have no freaking clue what brilliant ideas I'm going to deliver to Yvette by end of day. I know plenty about the history of Maison Dauphine. I know so many extraneous details, studying for this apprenticeship harder than I ever studied for the SATs, but they're not connecting to a creative way to package an Easter egg for a pop-up event at Versailles.

Note to self: Don't say "Easter egg" around Yvette. I think she'd hate that.

Yvette and I have been getting along really well today, though. She said, "Thank you" when I sent her an email with a delivery confirmation of an international carnet containing some resort samples.

My email notification dings, and it's Sophie.

> Milo, do you happen to know if you have FW25 Look 34 available to send overnight to NY? We loaned it for a shoot in Arizona, and we really need it if possible—*Vanity Fair* is requesting and we're thinking it might make cover.
>
> LMK!
>
> xx Sophie

I really like emailing with Sophie. It's nice how warm she is. It helps me feel like I'm not entirely alone, even if I am.

Scrolling through our inventory, I see that the look she's asking about is available.

> Hi! Yes, we have all items. Do you want the accessories too? Or just suit?

I don't think Sophie sleeps, since it's only six a.m. in New York. She replies instantly.

> The belt would be great! TYSM! Can send to my ATTN. I'll take it to the shoot.

I confirm, inputting all the shipping information and printing the label. I scan out the suit and the belt, and then I make up one of the cardboard boxes from the supply closet, lining it with tissue paper and carefully folding the look. Once it's all packed and the label is affixed, I go to drop the box off at the mailroom on my way out to lunch.

"Merci," I say, setting it on the outgoing table.

The mail lady gives me a sweet smile. "It's good. Try like . . . *merci.*"

Got it . . . less *mare*-see, more *mehr*-see.

I sigh. "I'm sorry. I don't know why I am so bad."

"No, it's good. You know, it's nice that you try. Go ahead. *Merci.*"

Mehr-see.

Clearing my throat, unable to fight my slightly embarrassed giggles, I nod. *"Merci."*

"Merci," she says. "Bit quicker. More with the throat. Do you hear?"

"Merci." It sounds like I'm hacking up phlegm.

"Oui, voilà."

I thank her profusely in English before offering one more *merci*, which she seems to approve of.

Once I'm out on the street and on the prowl for a cafe, I notice my stomach is essentially numb. It's not growling, it's not empty, but it's also not full. This is the most annoying feeling ever, one I'm familiar with from big match days. Nobody ever seems to get the ways my anxiety affects my appetite, which is frustrating, especially because they assume that since I am an athlete, I must be starving all the time. Sometimes even when I am starving,

I can't stomach the idea of food. The dietitian at Citrus Harbor High got me on protein shakes, and they were a lifesaver, but I have no clue where I might find some in Paris.

Of course you don't have an appetite, Milo. You have, like, four hours to come up with a genius idea now that you've completely oversold yourself.

For a moment, I wonder where Rhodes is. I wonder if he's eating some delicious gourmet lunch. He's probably eating at Le Grand Colbert, and the chef probably made him something that's not even on the menu. I'm not sure, but I just imagine his celebrity status gets him all kinds of perks. He's probably enjoying seafood and posting stories about how amazing French food is.

I stop walking and it occurs to me I haven't even looked at his Instagram since we met, which is borderline off-the-grid behavior, so I navigate to his account.

Rhodes Hamilton's Instagram account is exactly what I expected. Two million followers, no bio, and a black-and-white profile photo from an editorial shoot where he's wet in a white button-up and black bow tie. Photos on a boat in a black swimsuit—annoyingly toned physique—holding a bottle of champagne with a girl who looks like a model. Photos in a pub with some guys in Armoury United kits and scarves. A photo of some flowers with a handwritten note, perched on a marble kitchen island. There is a photo of Rhodes and Ollie squished together on a big ivory sofa—Ollie has his feet up on the coffee table and is pinching Rhodes's cheeks, while Rhodes seems to fight laughter, arms folded and hoodie pulled over his head.

There aren't any photos of Paris yet, and he doesn't have any

Instagram stories either, so I haven't made any new discoveries, and as I look at the screen, I realize there is no purpose to this and I am only wasting time.

Okay, Milo. What kind of brilliant ideas do we have just waiting to be unlocked?

I look around, thinking there must be some inspiration in Paris.

I've come to a cobblestone roundabout at the end of Rue François 1er, with quintessential Parisian buildings that curve around the road and the fountain at its center. Each building seems to have a courtyard out front, with wrought-iron fencing and gold-gilded accenting. Greenery grows over much of the fence, with flowers blooming behind the gates, and trees line the fountain.

As motorcycles and cars drive past, tourists take photos. It's gorgeous—an absolutely beautiful French vignette, with a blue sky and emerald foliage—but I can't seem to fully appreciate it because I'm desperately searching for the tiniest seedling of an idea.

The ticking clock in my mind only gets louder.

This is an opportunity, *Milo. Think of it as a positive opportunity.*

And it is, but I'm blanking.

I wish I had someone to talk to about this. Celeste is probably in-flight, and even if she were back home by now, I don't want to bother her about something like this when she's dealing with so much. My family is asleep, and honestly I don't know how helpful they'd be for this. The only person who could truly understand without needing a full debrief is Rhodes, and that is obviously never going to happen.

I can practically hear Celeste now: *Couldn't hurt to brainstorm together!*

My phone buzzes.

> Hi, Milo! Long time no chat. Do you happen to have the updated guest list for the Versailles pop-up handy? Seems mine is not the most recent.
>
> xx Sophie

I forward her the latest, and then, as soon as the idea strikes, I figure it's worth a shot.

> Also, do you by any chance have time for a quick call? It's totally cool if not, I know it's early. If you do, here is my cell.

And within a minute, a 917 number is calling me.

"Hi, Milo!" Sophie's voice is cheerful. Frantic, and a bit shaky, but cheerful. I can hear her smiling somehow.

"Hi, Sophie. Thank you for taking the time to chat. And I know we haven't had a full, formal introduction. I'm in Paris for the summer to—"

"Oh, I know. We all were very impressed by your entry for the apprenticeship. You should have seen the Teams messages about it. We've all got our eyes on you. I mean, no pressure." She chuckles. "It was great, though. A timely and innovative idea for the house."

I laugh. "Oh, wow. That's really nice of you. Thank you."

"Of course," she says. "And just for your reference, I'm the main PR assistant here in the New York office. I report to our PR manager, who reports to our US director. But you'll be working with me on everything."

"Awesome," I say. I cringe a bit, because it feels so unabashedly American of me. Then, of course, I remember I'm speaking to another American. "I was wondering if you might want to help me out, and if you don't have time, I get it. But Yvette is allowing me to send her some ideas for the Versailles pop-up—ways to subtly hint at the resort theme."

I glance around, as if someone might hear me, or I might be bugged.

"Nice," Sophie says. "Very nice. So, what do you have so far?"

"That's the thing." I sigh. "I don't have anything. And I really, really need to come up with something good. I need something that's quiet but makes a point. Something the house hasn't ever done before, if I can push the envelope that far. I really want to make a good impression, especially since this is sort of my first project."

Sophie hums on the other line. "I totally get it. It's hard to think of something the house hasn't done before."

"I know."

"It's also a bit hard to think of something subtle that wouldn't give away the L'or des Fous theme. We want some theories and speculation, but we don't want to indirectly confirm yet."

"Very true."

"I'm sure there is something. . . ."

Even though we've made no progress, it's nice to have someone to talk to who doesn't seem to be at odds with me in any way.

"How long have you been with Maison Dauphine?" I ask. It sort of just comes out, but I want to learn more about Sophie and her career.

"Two years," she says. "I interned with a PR agency during my last semester in college and met my current boss through that. She let me know about this job before it was formally posted. It was a blessing."

I nod. "That's amazing. Damn, that's such great luck. Well, of course you worked really hard and earned it, I didn't mean—"

"No, it's true. Luck and timing. I will say, the majority of jobs in fashion come down to who you know."

Rhodes's face pops into my mind, and it takes everything in me not to groan.

Trust me, Sophie, I know.

"But you got here on your own," she says. "Which is pretty cool."

"Thanks."

"Of course." Then, after a beat: "I'm about to get on the train, but I'll continue to think, and if you need anything at all, this is my cell. Feel free to text."

Somehow, this small gesture means more than I can even express.

"Okay, will do. Thank you again for taking the time. Or rather, *merci*."

I do my best to make the throaty phlegm sound.

"De rien," Sophie chirps, and then the call ends.

I'm still here, standing in the same spot, and I am crushed to not have a single new idea, but at least I have an ally.

Totally detached from the world around me, I begin to wander.

I'm not even sure entirely for how long or in which direction. My thoughts are incomplete and erratic, zipping around my head, trying to join and fully form like dogs chasing their tails before disappearing. The frenzy in my mind distracts me from the beauty of Paris—everything blurs together as I walk and walk and walk and think and think and think.

Some ideas come to me, but they're not right. Gold macarons are too obvious. Gold flowers or edible plants seem way too gimmicky.

Maybe it isn't about gold at all, but I don't know how else to reference L'or des Fous. We're already referencing the locations, and like Sophie said, this needs to be subtle. It needs to be something people piece together in hindsight and can't believe how genius of a clue it was.

The pressure is overwhelming, but the good news is, with all the walking, I finally feel hungry just as I stumble upon a cafe.

I'm seated outside immediately, and I absent-mindedly look over the menu, body in search of food, and brain in search of brilliance that is evading me with everything it has.

"*Bonjour*, how are you today?"

Oh. I guess I don't even seem like I am going to speak French.

"*Bonjour*, I'm great." Reflex. As American as it gets, probably. *I'm actually floundering, my fear of failure is threatening to expand until it's larger than the Arc de Triomphe, and then crush my bones and squish my organs into the cement.* "How are you?"

"Wonderful. Would you like something to drink?"

"Water, please."

"*Oui, bien sûr.*"

I sit with the menu.

The only thing that even sounds remotely good is a cheeseburger, which I know is hardly embracing the new culture I'm supposed to be immersing myself in. It wouldn't be so bad to just have a comfort meal and try to relax.

Maybe, if I can relax, an idea will come to me.

Besides, it's not entirely off-brand. I remember reading that Renard Florin fell head over heels with a cheeseburger in America, and it became one of his signature conversation topics. They called it *malbouffe*, or junk food, and Renard even—

Oh my god, that is it. So brilliant.

Malbouffe.

Renard Florin's love for *malbouffe* was controversial.

In 1957, one of the most famous articles associated with Maison Dauphine was published with the title "Guilty Pleasures." Let's just say while Renard found it comical, the rest of the company did not.

Then there was an entire campaign against *malbouffe*, because the stakeholders all thought it was distasteful. The house expanded its flagship location, purchasing another attached space, and opened its gourmet Restaurant Dauphine—all an attempt to prove it was a luxury brand with no real association with the *malbouffe* that Renard was becoming notorious for, which later became something fans of Maison Dauphine found endearing.

The campaign that resulted from Renard's guilty pleasures was all about opulence and indulgence and luxury—though also a subtle "fuck you" to all naysayers, if they only thought twice about the meaning.

After all, it was fool's gold.

L'or des Fous.

When the waiter comes back, I order a burger and fries, and I even ask for a Coke. I haven't had a soda in a while, but it sounds comforting, and it sounds like what I'd imagine Renard would want me to do.

I email Yvette my idea once it's more fully formed, and once I've finished my food, I use my maps app to navigate back to the office, where I sit and wait.

Chapitre Huit

Waiting for Yvette to get back to me on my idea is excruciating. Maybe even more excruciating than not having one at all—if I've gone out on a limb and suggested something too far in the wrong direction, that could be terrible. This is a situation where I can't afford to take one step forward and three steps back.

Rhodes is working through errands all day, so I don't see him for the rest of the afternoon.

Finally, right before I think I'm not getting a response, which could be a response in itself, Yvette walks in and nods, even going so far as to lift her chin. "Good idea, Milo."

I'm on cloud nine. I could ride this high all the way to Versailles. My idea—a pop-up café inspired by Renard's *malbouffe* motif, called Café 57—is going to be actualized. *My* idea is going to be all over Instagram and probably on *WWD* and *Vogue*, and it will become part of the Maison Dauphine lore forever.

It helps me to move past all the terrible emotions I'm feeling as I head back to the apartment, knowing Celeste won't be there. She hasn't texted me yet, and so I fire off a quick check-in message just to make sure she has made it home safe.

Celeste: I'm home! Sorry, I'm exhausted after traveling. Gran is doing fine at the moment. Hoping she will improve. But I want to hear all about your day. Distract me!

I make a wish—also hoping Gran improves. And then, with nothing else to do, sitting on the sofa, I fire off several long texts, regaling her with the events she's missed to distract her. I don't go into details about the theme or my idea, because Yvette has instilled the fear of God in me, but it's clear there might just be a chance for me yet.

Celeste: I think it sounds like things are going to work out after all.

Celeste: Try to have some fun while you're there.

I eat some fruit, scroll through social media, and mentally prepare myself for the rest of the week with Rhodes.

But Rhodes doesn't come in on Wednesday, and he doesn't come in on Thursday.

He's responding to emails, but this means I'm left with all the random grunt work for this event. Running around Paris picking up linens, calling to confirm bookings, sending things to print (which sounds, and is, very official and very stressful), and anything else the PR department needs me to do. It is at this point that I am relegated to cappuccino maker as well.

On Friday, when we arrive at the office an hour early, I've got every detail of the event memorized, and it seems like Rhodes just has his signature charm. I haven't seen him doing much for the event—all his errands have been related to magazine requests—so I'm not sure he's at all prepared.

I am stuck in the back of a black town car with him to Versailles, which is unfortunate because this is going to be at least a forty-minute ride, if the GPS is accurate. Forty long minutes with this guy who unknowingly demands all the available oxygen circulate to him, leaving me to suffocate.

He's staring out the window, phone in his hands on his lap. His jaw is particularly pronounced at the moment, clenched and bulging when he narrows his eyes on something as we drive past.

My emails are going off, plenty of things being confirmed, whether directly to me or to Yvette, with my email address just copied for awareness. Rhodes isn't on all of them, and while part of me believes this is a good thing—that I'm involved and trusted—part of me resents the fact that he's had it so easy the last couple of days.

Everybody just loves Rhodes.

Okay, Milo. Relax. Deep breath.

Everything has to go right.

I scroll up to an email Sophie sent me at five a.m., when it was 11 p.m. in New York.

Hi Milo,

Attaching a couple of sample requests. If we can accommodate, would be great. Some of these editors are making big asks, but we'll be shooting September issues soon, so should try to send as much as we are able to. . . . I've sorted them by priority.

(Also, LOVEEEEE the Café 57 idea. Another win for Milo in the Teams chat. You didn't need my help after all! Best of luck at Versailles tomorrow. Or today, for you, I guess!)

xx Sophie

I'm not sure how to tell Sophie I don't think it's entirely true that I didn't need her help, and that her kindness on Tuesday made a huge difference.

It's silent as we drive toward the Arc de Triomphe, and I want to ask Rhodes where he was the past two days, but I also don't want to be the first to speak or to express any interest in his whereabouts or agenda.

We're both in light blue button-downs and khaki linen pants, provided to us as uniforms for today.

Of course, since it's Rhodes, he's wearing a navy leather belt bag across his chest, and he's also wearing a gold chain. His shirt brings out the striking cerulean in his eyes, and it's physically frustrating how good-looking he is.

And I mean physically frustrating. I'm only human, and my pants might be a bit tighter momentarily when I catch myself taking in the way his pants stretch across his muscular thighs, or how the cotton of his shirt shows off his pecs and biceps.

I catch myself, though, and take several breaths, looking out the window to find things that I don't find arousing, though my mind keeps getting caught up in what Rhodes might look like in one of those tight little Armoury United kits like his brother.

"Café 57 is clever," Rhodes says, turning to face me.

"Thanks," I say.

"The year of the *malbouffe* disaster." He laughs and then wiggles his brow. "First your Waitlist campaign, and now *malbouffe*. Does somebody like controversy?"

"I don't," I say. "The best campaigns push the boundaries a little. People like it when you surprise them. Even the most extreme brand loyalists."

Rhodes holds up his palms. "I was only messing around. Though, to be fair, the idea *is* centered around a controversy."

It's no secret I don't respond very well to anything less than praise, and I don't know if he even means for this to be a criticism, but it feels like a cheese grater being dragged across my brain.

"Café 57 is an elevated experience that pays homage in a clever way." The buzzwords feel a bit overdone as they tumble out of my mouth, but it's true. "If it weren't for *malbouffe*, we wouldn't have L'or des Fous. Anyway, people like this kind of stuff. In the eighties, when Philippa Granger was creative director, she did an entire cheeseburger campaign."

He scrunches up his nose. "Well . . ."

"Well, what?"

Rhodes frowns. "That campaign was horrendous."

"Nobody had ever seen anything like it at the time."

"Philippa Granger's campaign caused one of the most controversial periods Maison Dauphine has ever gone through,"

Rhodes says. "None of the shareholders wanted to see the models eating giant cheeseburgers—getting grease and ketchup all over their faces and the clothes. Do you not remember that the head of the beauty division quit over that campaign?"

I shrug. "I do know from research that it generated the most sales of any campaign, historically and until the early 2000s. It was such a huge hit in America. That campaign is in, like, every eighties advertisement coffee table book."

"A huge hit in America," Rhodes echoes.

I grit my teeth. "Do you have thoughts?"

"I only think that campaign was a marked departure from the sophisticated image Maison Dauphine had worked hard to earn. *L'ors des Fous* was the first step in reestablishing the house as a serious luxury brand, so bringing up the whole *malbouffe* thing again . . ."

"Well, I'm sure Philippa Granger would love to hear from you. In fact, I'm sure all of the stylists, photographers, set decorators, models . . . I bet they all would like to hear what Rhodes Hampton thinks about their landscape-changing campaign."

Rhodes stares at me. "Have I struck a nerve? And are you trying to tell me that shock value equals success? Or sales, even if the DNA of the brand is compromised?"

"You're acting like this campaign was pornographic or discriminatory or something. It was models eating cheeseburgers. Grow up."

"Grow up?"

"Yes, you're so offended by . . . what? Women eating?"

Rhodes barks a laugh. "Oh, now I'm misogynistic. Is that right?"

"I can't seem to understand why else you're so annoyed by the campaign," I say. "The photo of Amalia Astor? The one where she's in the limo with the evening gown and satin gloves, eating a cheeseburger and fries with her Oscars beside her?"

There isn't a single model or actress who's associated with Maison Dauphine the way Amalia Astor is. People have aspired, but there has only ever been the organic, natural chemistry that Philippa and Amalia brought to the house.

Amalia's film career was taking off in the eighties. She was in iconic cult-classic dark comedies, brooding romances, cutting-edge coming-of-age films, and avant-garde psychological thrillers. Her portrayal of the bride of Frankenstein won her an Oscar, and so did her role in an early nineties adaptation of *Wuthering Heights*.

Her first campaign with Maison Dauphine was in 1983, after she wore one of their feathered gowns to an award show and made every best-dressed list there was.

The eighties *malbouffe* campaign—the one that featured her after-Oscars limo photo—cemented her spot as the unofficial face of the house. She would exclusively wear Maison Dauphine for the Oscars every year, which was unheard-of, and led to new pressure for the house to innovate in ways that provided new surprises even when everybody knew they'd be dressing her.

That photo changed the game in so many ways.

"I'm familiar."

"That's one of the most famous editorial photographs of all time. How many girls have that framed? Black-and-white, matted. Hung next to their framed photo of Audrey at Tiffany. It's elegant, even with the juxtaposition of the *malbouffe*."

"I'm so happy I have you here to explain this to me. I suppose now that you've enlightened me, once I'm done looking down on women, I might decide to change my opinion."

"You're the one who brought this up," I point out. "I would have been fine just sitting in silence."

Shifting in his seat a bit, he shrugs. "I didn't know you'd get so worked up over one comment."

"You said it to get back at me."

Rhodes laughs. "To get back at you? Why would I want to get back at you?"

"I don't know. Maybe because Yvette stuck you on messenger service to hear my idea, and then she liked it. She liked my idea so much they allocated a pretty decent chunk of the event budget to it. And fairly last-minute, as well."

"Yvette didn't stick me on messenger service."

"She literally did."

Rhodes unzips his crossbody and pulls out a pair of sunglasses, sliding them over his face. "Milo, please."

"Rhodes, please." I scoff. "I had a good idea, and you can't stand that now I might be ahead, so you're trying to knock Café 57."

"Ahead? All right, whatever you say."

It's *infuriating*. He's so sure he's going to win.

My jaw is clenched, my palms are sweaty, and my forehead is hot and clammy.

"I'm not just some moron, you know. They chose me." And, without even thinking through the implications: "*I* earned this."

Rhodes removes his sunglasses again, and those eyes—less gorgeous ocean, and now jagged, burning ice—bore right into mine.

"What did you just say?"

"I'm not going to let you treat me like I'm an idiot. I deserve to be here. My ideas are good."

His lips part, and he goes to speak before he chuckles, glancing over and then back at me.

"Where in the world is all this coming from? And are you actually implying I didn't earn my way here? Are you implying I don't deserve to be here?"

"Maybe I am," I snap. The tension between us feels impossibly constricting, like the car is closing in on us, and with each nanosecond of suffocation I just want to explode. "No, you know what? I'm not implying anything; I'm saying it outright. This is ridiculous, and you and I both know it. You didn't earn your way here."

"You're impossible. And you have no idea what you're talking about." He looks out the window. "Here I was feeling bad about us competing against each other. And the funniest bit? I bet you think you've got my number—you think I'm entitled and that I fancy myself a genius and everyone around me a bumbling idiot. You think all I care about is myself and winning. Isn't that right? But it's rich, since that sounds a bit more like you."

Before I can argue, Yvette is calling me.

After I walk her through some things for a magazine request, I hang up and Rhodes has his AirPods in, so we sit in the silence for the rest of the drive.

I use the quiet to calm down and improve my mood before we get to the event—after all, this is going to be my big moment. Whether he likes it or not.

Chapitre Neuf

The Palace of Versailles is breathtaking.

I get a sweeping view of the chateau when we arrive. It's extravagant and dramatic, with so much to see it's difficult to take it all in. I can almost make out the front gate, ornate and gold and bordered by stone statues. The gilding has a sort of magical effect on the palace: the grand gate, the detailing atop one of the buildings. The sun dances across it, a brighter gold than I've ever seen.

Since Maison Dauphine has only booked a portion of the gardens, the palace is still swarming with visitors. It's hard to conceptualize the history—that this used to be something so different, not overrun by tourists or part of a city with a McDonalds and KFC around the block. Where there are now soccer moms in Reeboks and sunburned dads in visors with cameras crossing the streets, there used to be horse-drawn carriages. It seems strange there was ever a quiet stillness here, separate from Paris, because now it all seems so busy and loud.

Rhodes doesn't pay any attention. He might glance up a couple of times from behind his sunglasses, but I gather he is too cool to be concerned with Versailles. His parents probably took them all to Paris all the time, especially given the fact that they have a flat, so I wonder if for him, this is more like Disney World or something. I can't imagine that, but then again, there is a lot about Rhodes's life I can't imagine.

He is much more preoccupied with his phone, either way, and that's for the best, because there is an awkward, seething tension between us now after this drive.

When we pull up to a side road and are let out, I want to sprint away from him. I don't, of course, if only because I have to figure out where we're going.

Haydée and Zoe rush out of a side gate, looking around as if to determine if we've been spotted. By whom, I'm not sure, but they usher Rhodes and me back through the gate, and they walk alarmingly fast, even for me. We make our way through what seems like a back alley, though a touch more glamorous for the architecture alone. I don't have much time to take anything in because we're zipping through, and then we arrive at the main gallery of the Orangerie.

The gallery is long and grand, with vaulted ceilings and light flooding in incrementally throughout the corridor from the arched windows. A large statue stands tall at the end of the hallway; I know it's the king on his horse because of the extensive research packet Haydée provided me.

A lot of the pop-up has been constructed: mannequins line the gallery like sculptures in a museum, and they're all dressed in ivory and beige. There's a soft, almost pop-y jazz track playing throughout. Some of the orange trees, which are typically placed out in the garden during the summer, have been brought back in to add a sense of season, sprouting up from green wooden planters. Woven baskets and rattan chairs are peppered along the perimeter of the hall. Some of the most popular wicker purses are displayed on stone pedestals. Clothing racks are set up, though they're far and few between, with limited offerings.

There's no need to have extensive inventory, because Maison Dauphine will sell out of every single one of these pieces today, and quickly. Anyway, as Haydée and Zoe have made very clear, the goal of this pop-up isn't sales, but awareness. Most of the guests will get gift bags anyway. Sure, they'll buy out the clothing and accessories, but more importantly, they'll generate a wild amount of buzz about what the house will do next.

Thankfully, Haydée takes me, and Zoe takes Rhodes, so we're finally separated, and I can take a deep breath.

I follow Haydée down toward the end of the hall, where Café 57 is being set up.

"Don't forget, our focus item today is the wicker Darling Dauphine," Haydée says, heels loud and echoing throughout the gallery, even with the quiet music to combat their volume. "Any time you have a chance to talk with a guest and there is a chance to weave it into conversation, be sure to."

"I see what you did there," I say, offering a grin.

Haydée stops and gives me a strange look. "What do you mean?"

"Oh," I stutter a bit, suddenly feeling incredibly stupid. "I thought you were doing, like, a play on words. '*Weave* it into conversation.' The wicker bag." She doesn't find this amusing, so I shake my head. "Never mind. You were saying?"

We continue walking. "If anyone on the standard guest list asks to purchase, we will have to refer them to the waitlist."

There are two guest lists. Both are laborious, especially for me since I am still struggling with my French, but one is shorter, and full of the names we must treat like royalty, while the other is longer, listing those who are still valued but will receive no special treatment.

"Right."

"And you're comfortable with these lists?"

I nod. "Yes, absolutely."

"Okay. And now, the *pièce de résistance*."

We stop walking, and I am floored by how large of a space they've given Café 57. Past a small entrance blocked off by waist-high shrubs, there are bistro tables and chairs set up for the guests under decorative striped umbrellas, just as if they were dining on the Riviera. Palm trees have also been added down this way, seemingly to separate the café from the rest of the hall visually.

A long marble-and-gold counter has been built in front of the equestrian sculpture of Louis XVI, which is also now flanked by short palms, and gold script on the front of the marble reads:

Café 57. Maison Dauphine. Paris.

There is a large black-and-white menu on an iron stand, and it's all the *malbouffe* one could want, though positioned elegantly with names like *Hamburger Florin* and *Gâteau du Dauphine*. I see Yvette even took my suggestion about the neutral-colored Pierre Hermé macaron tower.

To really tie everything together, they've framed that black-and-white photo of Amalia Astor with her burger after the Oscars.

"Good work," Haydée says, keeping her eyes straight ahead on the café.

That makes me feel warm and even distracts from all the shit with Rhodes on the car ride here. I'm doing a good job, and all those things he said don't matter.

After Haydée runs me through some of the itinerary one more time, as if I have not studied this over and over and played it all back in my limited sleep, she sends me on a wild goose chase to capture content for Instagram and TikTok. She wants establishing shots of Versailles—not only the gardens, but interiors to set the stage quickly as the beats of the music open the video.

I have an hour and a half to get as much B-roll as possible, and I have to make sure there aren't any of the general visitors in the clips.

At first I attempt to consult a map I find online, but then I realize I'm only wasting time, so I just start to power walk through the halls, taking videos wherever it seems appropriate. I capture close-up shots of glittering chandeliers, slow zooms of sculptures against floral wallpapers, and somewhat moody shots behind the paneled windows overlooking the gardens, which I think could be the perfect transition to the pop-up clips.

I find myself enraptured by the glamour of it all. I've seen the Sofia Coppola movie with Kirsten Dunst, of course, and I'm vaguely familiar with the *Versailles* Broadway show since Benji Keaton starred in it, and everyone knows about that, but the grandeur of it all is overwhelming in person.

I capture a bunch of details in the Queen's Apartments. The bedchambers are dripping in gold—the carved baluster that acts as a divider for the room, the border of the floral headboard, the ornate detailing on the canopy. The lustrous carvings that cover the ceilings and line the walls, and the giant chandeliers with crystal teardrops.

After zooming in and getting the perfect angles, I wander around a bit more.

I find myself in a stone gallery without any other visitors, and I bask in the quiet for a moment. Daylight brightens the pale pastel doors at the end of the hall, makes the brass lanterns shine, and illuminates the checkered marble tile and antique statues.

I look out at the gardens and wonder where the hell Rhodes is. Though this is a peaceful moment, and one I am trying to savor, I imagine he is getting a VIP tour of the parts of the palace that are roped off to guests. He's probably having a grand old time, not stressing about the lists of guests, because he can get by on his charm alone.

Damn it.

Eventually I give up on the peaceful moment when it becomes clear my mind is not going to shut the hell up, and I capture a few more snippets for Haydée.

Once I've navigated back to the Orangerie and found her, I AirDrop the files to her and she seems pleased, though she doesn't say as much.

"Where is Rhodes?" I ask. It sounds natural, I'm sure, and not at all like I'm worried or competitive or want to lock him in one of the storage closets until the event is over so he can't screw anything up for me.

Haydée looks around. "I'm not sure, actually." She shakes her head. "Guests will begin arriving soon. We're going to turn up the music and start to circulate cocktails out in the gardens. You can go wait by the rope, and once someone is inside, get a feel and escort them to the appropriate area."

"Get a feel for what?"

"What they're here for."

I nod slowly. "Right. What they're here for . . ."

Very obviously masking a newfound sense of annoyance, Haydée flicks her hair over her shoulder and straightens up. "Some of the guests are here to shop. If they are wearing a lot of Dauphine, they might be collectors. Some are here to socialize with friends in these circles. Some want to try and sweet-talk their way onto a waitlist, and some are very introverted—they will just want the most photographable moments and to be left alone. Are you following?"

"Yes, absolutely. Of course. I will go and do that."

And while I'm not entirely sure how I'm supposed to read people without knowing anything about them, as people arrive, it is much simpler than I thought.

A gaggle of British girls in their early twenties are some of the first to arrive. They're all wearing dresses—a green toile, a white toile, a couple of solid-cream variations, a light beige stripe—and accessories from last year's Dauphine resort line. The sandals and totes and scarves are one thing, but two of the girls have the exclusive blue resort Darling Dauphine bags that were only available at the pop-up at Chateau Marmont. That bag is instantly identifiable after all my studying, and it immediately tells a story: these girls have an affinity to the brand, and they are going to buy something.

I lead them to the shopping, subtly implying how limited the stock is today, and they take off like hunters in search of geese. Well, geese wearing designer sweaters, I guess.

Once I return, the crowd in the garden is larger. People are mingling, clinking champagne glasses and taking photos. It's a proper garden party, which is perhaps a stupid observation, because if there's ever going to be a proper garden party, it's going to be hosted by Maison Dauphine at Versailles. Still, I can't help but be in awe of the luxury and sophistication. It's certainly grander than anything I'd ever been to in Citrus Harbor, and I only feel a pang in my chest that I couldn't have snuck Celeste into this.

I snap a photo and send it to her, and then go on to greet more guests.

I greet executives and bring them to Yvette and board members who are huddled around speaking French and laughing, big beards wearing suits and big watches and signet rings. Yvette stands out in her slim cream dress, but she seems to command their attention as if they all answer to her and not the other way around.

I greet models and athletes who clearly want to feel like they're getting the VIP treatment—keeping their sunglasses on and heads ducked as I guide them past the crowd of influencers and into the gallery. They seem intrigued by the *malbouffe*, though the way they laugh, I'm not sure if they're excited to partake or just find it cute.

I continue to greet and work the event. There is no sign of Rhodes anywhere, but it's fine by me because Yvette keeps an eye on me and seems to be pleased. I'm learning her subtleties—when she's around other people, it seems her brow will only raise ever so slightly, and her lip will only offer the most minimal twitch of approval. It's enough to keep me on cloud nine, though.

I am not only doing well, but compared to Rhodes, I'm fucking winning.

This is going better than I could have even imagined. Honestly, I shouldn't even be shocked. He's probably taking photos in Marie Antoinette's hamlet, pretending he's the mayor of his own little town, better than everyone else.

Sure, it's a bit surprising he'd just admit defeat, especially given how defensive he was in the car, but I guess when it's obvious I've won, what is there to do other than go have fun and avoid facing the music?

I'll be sure to bring up what a success it was to Yvette as soon as the three of us are together.

I log into our creator platform, where we are tracking mentions and tags from the influencers and celebrities we've invited, and they're almost all posting Café 57. The burgers look incredible, and so do the fries, the small slices of pizza, and the onion rings. The desserts are magnificent—rich chocolates and buttery creams on wedges of fluffy ivory sponge cake, perfect scoops of pastel ice cream, and delectable milkshakes topped with cherries.

I'm bracing myself for even the slightest dig at the menu, since this is a bit out there, and if anyone hasn't heard of Renard Florin's love of junk food, it might seem like a total miss. Luckily, though, it's all love. One of the TikTokers even went so far as to say this was the best pop-up shop she'd ever attended.

Rhodes, you are so out of your league.

This is a great feeling after the initial trepidation I faced about doing this apprenticeship with him. If things go on like this,

Yvette will give me the resort show in no time, and then the job is mine.

But just as it seems like nothing could possibly get in the way of me and a win, there's Rhodes. He's grinning in a way that's entirely concerning, but before I can even theorize what he might be up to, he steps to the side—and everyone in the garden gasps.

Rhodes Hamilton has brought Amalia Astor to Versailles.

Chapitre Dix

It's not like I want Rhodes to find me sulking in the gardens of Versailles.

Seriously—dramatic, much?

When he does, indeed, find me sulking, I pretend to be on a very important business call. It's then, of course, that Celeste texts me and it's clear I'm not talking to anyone.

I pocket my phone. "The signal sucks."

Rhodes holds his palm out to reveal a few orange, green, and yellow macarons on a Ladurée napkin. He grabs a lemon and takes a bite, glancing down and gesturing for me to do the same.

"We had Pierre Hermé macarons for the event."

"There's a Ladurée in the palace," Rhodes says.

I raise a brow. "Why would you go out of your way?"

"Because you prefer Ladurée."

A lump forms in my throat.

He remembered? And not only that—he went and got these for me?

But of course I remind myself this is a tactic. Obviously.

À bon chat, bon rat. These are the macarons the cat leaves out for the rat in lieu of *fromage*.

Except I don't want to be the fucking rat!

"I'm okay." I shake my head, though my eyes might linger on them a moment too long.

"Come on. You want a macaron."

Obviously I want a delicious sugary almond confection, and obviously I'm not a rat and he's not a cat, so I take one of the pistachio macarons and begrudgingly take a bite. It's perfect. Sweet, light, with the most subtle crunch.

"Thanks."

Rhodes nods. "Course. So . . ."

"So?"

"Are you upset with me now?" He winces and draws in a breath. "I know things were tense with us in the car, and I really didn't mean to offend you. That got a bit out of hand. I shouldn't have said those things. And now I've brought Amalia. . . ."

I shrug. "You didn't do anything wrong."

"I did make sure to play by the rules," he offers with a sympathetic lift of his brows and tilt of his head. "Still, I'm sorry if you're upset. I just—well, we're competing, aren't we? So we both had to bring our A game. I thought Café 57 was brilliant. I mean, I *do*. I think it's brilliant. Present tense. It is genuinely so clever."

He's infuriating. He just rolls up to Versailles with a famous reclusive actress and upstages me, and then he has the nerve to stand here, looking irresistibly handsome and offering me macarons while complimenting my brilliance.

"But I really did feel bad after that car ride," Rhodes says, surveying the grounds. "I was thinking we should do something fun now that the event is over."

I blink. "Something fun?"

"Yeah, something fun." He places an entire macaron in his mouth and nearly coughs, laughing. "Lighten up, Milo. We're done for the day."

Easy for him to suggest I lighten up. He's the one who has just won.

Rhodes hands me the last macaron, crumpling the napkin. "Go on. Lighten up."

I glance down at it. "I am not going to put this whole thing in my mouth."

"You can do it."

"I can, but why would I?"

"Because."

"Why?"

Rhodes furrows his brow. "It's what Marie Antoinette would want, don't you think?"

I roll my eyes and stuff the macaron into my mouth. Immediately, I can barely chew, and I place my hand over my lips, bursting into giggles.

"There!" Rhodes snaps his fingers. "You laughed. *That's* why."

I chew and swallow. "I laughed because that was ridiculous."

"And now that you've laughed, don't you feel a bit lighter?" He wiggles his arms and shakes out his legs, looking absolutely absurd. "Don't you feel like now you're in the mood to do something fun and let the stress of the day slip away?"

"Are you high?"

"I'm not," he says. "Okay, come on. We'll go to the Petit Trianon. It'll be nice. I've never seen it."

Rhodes doesn't give me a chance to protest. He begins walking and, without stopping or slowing his pace, simply turns back to see if I'm going to follow him. I'm not sure if it's the way the sun causes his hair to glow like god-spun gold or if it's how his eyes are like glistening blue waters, but something compels me to follow him.

We ride the tram to the Petit Trianon, a smaller château on the grounds of Versailles. Marie Antoinette used the Petit Trianon as her little private escape, and I am at least curious to see what it's all about.

When in Paris.

There's a line at the entrance, and it shouldn't be surprising that the Petit Trianon is still fairly massive and impressive, with its own gilded gate and several buildings and sprawling gardens just visible from here. I imagine it's incredible inside if it's anything like the château.

"So," I say. I stare down at my feet as we wait. "Do I even ask how you managed to get Amalia Astor to this event? Or is it just a famous-person thing?"

Rhodes laughs. "A famous-person thing?"

I shrug, glancing over at him. "I don't know. I wouldn't know where to even begin with something like that. I mean, she's not only a celebrity, she's so . . . mysterious. Nobody's really seen or heard much of her in so long."

"She's a friend of my mum's," Rhodes says. "So I know her quite well."

I process this and decide to wait to follow up until we're past a small courtyard garden and inside the ground floor of the Petit Trianon. The floor is all white-and-green checkered marble tiles, and there is a giant ornate staircase with gold detailing, including the queen's monogram along the banister.

Once we're up the staircase, making our way into one of the elaborately decorated rooms, I finally break.

"Okay, wait. You *know* Amalia Astor? Quite well?" I gawk. "Sorry, I just am wrapping my head around what your life must be like."

Rhodes clicks his tongue against his top teeth. "My life feels too big sometimes."

"Too big?"

Like this place? I want to ask. Everything is so grand and luxurious—flourishes and touches of opulence in every detail, from the bronze gilding to the polished stones to the intricate crown molding.

"Yeah, too big." He interlocks his fingers, staring at them as he spreads his palms out away from him. "Not in some 'poor Rhodes' way. It's kind of hard to describe, but having famous parents and a famous brother, it makes everything feel really . . . big. And when you ask about Amalia Astor, who's just, like, Mum's friend, it's a reminder of how lost I might be in this big thing. Dunno. I'm not making any sense, am I?"

I nod. "I sort of understand. Maybe. Probably not."

We laugh when our eyes catch in one of the mirrors.

"Though," I add. "One thing about all that—you're famous too, you know."

"Tangentially," Rhodes says. "Fame by association is honestly so much different. Ollie has fans, and Mum and Dad have fans. I've got people who want an autograph because of my family members. Or because they think I'm fit, I guess. But that's not actually anything." He shoots me a look. "I know that sounds more 'poor Rhodes,' but I'm just stating the facts. It isn't something I expect to change. Unless . . ."

He pauses, shaking his head and stifling another laugh.

"What? Unless what?"

"Unless I make a name for myself," he says. "Bit silly out loud."

"I don't think it's silly."

"Reckon you're being nice," Rhodes says. "Which I'll take, considering just a few minutes ago you were furious with me."

I scoff. "I was not furious with you."

"Admit it, you were so annoyed with me. Absolutely fuming."

"I was *not*."

"Your tone is convincing," he says with a smirk. "That's okay, though. Look at us now."

"Why do you think it's silly?" I ask.

Rhodes purses his lips. "All right. So, this is going to sound like the most 'poor Rhodes' of everything I've said, but honestly, I don't mean for it to be. People don't exactly want to see me succeed. They'd like to write off my efforts as half-assed or, better for the press, a total failure. They'd like me to live in Ollie's shadow, I think because it helps for them to feel like he's the golden boy they all want him to be. Nothing makes somebody look good like somebody worse to directly compare them to."

I frown. "I'm sure people would be happy to see you succeed, Rhodes."

"People love to watch other people fail," he says. "I don't know why. Don't get it at all. But have you seen a tabloid recently? Seen the kind of news that makes its way all over social media about celebrities? Embarrassing stories. Things they've done wrong.

And I'm not saying it's not deserved sometimes, because if someone really does something bad, that's obviously different. But why should a wardrobe malfunction or a bad hair day be so entertaining? Why should a private drunk karaoke session go *viral*?"

"Oh my god."

His face flashes red. "So you've seen it."

I wince. "I mean . . ."

"To be fair, it was *everywhere*. It isn't even that interesting. People embarrass themselves all the time."

"I thought it was an inspired rendition," I offer.

He shrugs. "Everybody knows 'You Belong With Me.'"

"Was it Taylor's Version?"

"I'm not sure."

I fake a gasp. "Blasphemous. Though if I remember correctly, the meme was that it was *Rhodes's Version*. . . ."

He hangs his head. "It was bad. I wonder if she saw it."

I don't mean to laugh, but it is a funny mix-up. I apologize immediately, covering my mouth. I try to focus on one of the marble busts atop a fireplace, hoping not to rub any salt into the wound.

"No, it's all right, laugh. I can admit it's funny. The point isn't really that anyway . . . it's just the way people absolutely love to see someone embarrass themselves or fail. They can't get enough of that, really."

"Sure," I say. "I don't have the same level of experience with this, obviously, but one time I did post a really, really hideous accidental selfie on my Instagram stories. I didn't realize it was up for, like, three hours. I couldn't seem to live it down, either, which is so silly considering it's just a dumb photo."

Rhodes nods. "Any chance you have this selfie on hand?"

I roll my eyes. "I guess what I'm saying is I can only imagine how that felt for you. On that large of a scale."

"Absolutely phenomenal," he says, beaming. "How did we even get to talking about this?"

"We were talking about you succeeding and making a name for yourself," I remind him. "There are definitely people who will root for you. People who *are* rooting for you."

Rhodes groans. "I don't know, Milo. Sometimes it feels like my mum is the only one rooting for me. How pathetic is that?"

"Well, it's not true, and even if it were, it isn't pathetic."

"If I'm being honest, Milo, she practically spoon-fed me the idea of Amalia." He puts his hands in his pockets. "It was my idea in the end, but she did seem to sort of guide me there."

I'm not sure how to feel about that, but I guess he still hasn't done anything outside of "playing by the rules."

As we walk through one of the reception rooms, I consider how much I don't know about Rhodes. There's so much about his life here in Paris that's a mystery, and as for his life in London, I have next to no details at all.

"So you and your mom are close?"

He smiles. "Yeah, we are. She's the best."

"That's so nice," I say.

"Yeah. She's the reason I've come to love Maison Dauphine so much, obviously. After watching her wear their designs my whole life, and seeing how she's got this relationship with the brand and everything. She's taught me a lot about the history and the craftsmanship. Actually, one year, Mum said if I got a seven on my maths GCSE, I'd be able to go as her plus-one to a show."

"Oh? Did you get a seven?"

"Got a bloody nine, didn't I?"

"And a nine is better, right? You half lost me at GCSE, but I'm using context clues."

He grins. "Nine is the best, actually. My only nine ever."

I perk up. "That's a good motivator, I'd say."

"Oh, yeah. While Ollie's smashing it in the academy with Armoury—Dad bought him a car for being top scorer one season—I'm cramming for an exam so I can go to a fashion show."

"I think it's kind of cute."

Rhodes squints. "Cute?"

"W-w-well." I stammer. "Cute, like. Just that you wanted to go with your mom to a fashion show."

He turns his attention to a window, looking out at the gardens. "Right. Cute."

"I didn't mean it in any kind of—"

"It's okay, I'm only messing with you about it." He shrugs. "Guess it's kind of cute."

Looking out at the gardens beside him, I smile.

"You know—again, smaller scale—but it's kind of similar with my mom and me. She has a boutique back home, and she's opening a new store in the Hamptons. She's taken me to some trade shows and things like that. A lot of them are in New York, which is always really fun. I learned it all from her. She had this

Maison Dauphine coffee-table book, and as a kid I was obsessed. She always picks a few pieces from each collection to sell in the store too. Mostly accessories, but some ready-to-wear every now and then."

"Wow, that's really cool." Rhodes's gaze drifts. "Must be a really nice shop."

"Yeah, it's her whole world, basically." I catch myself. "*Our* whole world."

"Mums. Where would we even be without them?"

"No idea," I say.

"Honestly, I reckon I'd be much worse off." He pulls a face.

"Same, probably," I agree.

We spend the rest of the afternoon wandering around the Petit Trianon and the grounds, mostly just sightseeing like two pals who aren't competing. I didn't believe it could be done, but I was wrong, even if I do have to shove down the random thoughts that pop up about Amalia or Café 57. We wander until our feet are sore and it's about dinnertime. We take the train from Versailles, and Rhodes nods off for a moment but quickly jerks awake, complaining about how much it'd hurt his neck to sleep like this. We spend the rest of the ride going through some of our emails until we reach the Pont de l'Alma stop.

While we might have spent the afternoon like we're just two pals, there's still this distinct understanding between us that once we've emerged from the station, we are going our separate ways.

So once we've said good night, I ground myself, and then I text Celeste as I walk back to the apartment.

Me: How are things? How is Gran?

Celeste: Things are okay. She seems to be doing okay? Stable. Just not eating a lot.

Me: I'm glad she's stable. Hopefully her appetite will pick up

Celeste: Hope so!

Celeste: Distract me. How was the event?

Me: Well, I'm sort of confused . . . Me and Rhodes had this argument in the car, and then he totally outdid Café 57 by bringing Amalia Astor, but afterward he just brought me macarons and insisted we "do something fun."

Me: Even typing that, I can see it is clearly a tactic

Me: And to think it almost worked.

Celeste: Hmmm . . . maybe he just wanted to hang out

Celeste: Or if he brought you macarons, maybe he still wants to do a lil more 😉

I blink at the phone in my hand as there is a frenzy of butterflies in my stomach at the idea. I need to mow them down at any cost necessary, because if Rhodes—with all of his charm and good looks—did want to take me on a date still, that would only be a distraction, and one I made clear is not an option.

Focus, Milo. Stay focused.

Me: He brought Amalia fucking Astor! How do I even compete with that

Celeste: I guess if you really think he can't be trusted, you have to just keep an eye on things

Celeste: But try not to jump to any conclusions?

Me: I would never

Chapitre Onze

I spend my weekend trying to maintain a sense of normalcy, though nothing is normal, and I can't seem to pin down how I feel about Rhodes.

On one hand, I want to believe he's genuine. On the other, I should protect myself.

He definitely won this round by bringing Amalia Astor. She's rarely been sighted for the last twenty years, which meant Rhodes not only made the event a huge success, but he also made international headlines.

So, throughout the weekend, I avoid those, even though it seems everyone from back home wants to send them to me like I might not have heard about it.

Celeste checks in on me, but I tell her everything is great. I don't feel like there's much to say about it all, and it's the last thing I should be complaining to her about right now. I let her know she can reach me anytime, and I say a prayer to whoever is listening for Celeste and her family.

I decide to go to the Musée d'Orsay first thing in the morning on Sunday, desperate to get out and do something. After going with Celeste that first time, it's become one of my favorite spots—and it's quite peaceful by myself—but I can't seem to pay attention to anything. I walk through the exhibits in silence at first, mind racing, but then I pop in my AirPods and put on old film scores and classical music. Still, nothing seems to keep my thoughts from swirling around, and the more they swirl, the more I feel like it might be a hundred degrees.

I take photos as I wander the streets of the 9th Arrondissement, the Palais Garnier Opera House literally taking my breath away when I first stumble upon it. I debate going in, but I just spent the money going to the Musée d'Orsay only to get dangerously close to my first panic attack in Paris, so it seems fresh air is the move for the rest of the day.

Eventually, I pass a McDonald's and, having not eaten all day, I decide it's as good a time as any to try something new off the French menu. I feel completely alone, but the salty fries provide a small amount of comfort, which makes me think maybe Renard Florin really was on to something with all that *malbouffe*.

I send Celeste a photo of the Parisian McDonald's spread, and she sends back a sticker of Kirsten Dunst as Marie Antoinette.

Celeste: Ooh la la!!

Celeste: J'adore malbouffe

Thinking about the *malbouffe* and the pop-up is such a gut punch. I thought I had it all in the bag. Yvette was so impressed and things were going so well—until a giant Rhodes-sized shadow eclipsed everything.

I don't sleep well, and when I wake up around four a.m., staring at the ceiling like I tend to do, I consider the fact that this next event at the Tuileries is actually the perfect opportunity to make a comeback.

To truly one-up Rhodes, I'm going to have to utilize the element of surprise. He can't see it coming, so I'll have to let him think he's defeated me. I can't ham it up too much, or else he'll see through it, but a subtle hint here and there that I am intimidated by him? That should do the trick.

On and off the tennis court, one thing is consistent: Nothing holds an opponent back like complacency.

Sophie texts me to let me know she is now coming to Paris for the Tuileries event and the Louvre gala. I know she and I aren't exactly BFFs, but she's the closest thing I am going to have to a friend over here, so this feels celebratory.

I scroll through some emails that came in over the weekend. Yvette doesn't want us answering them unless she's specifically stated it's a high-priority item, so I have had to just let them pile up. British *Vogue* is requesting a bunch of accessories, a stylist in New York has emailed and gotten intercepted by Sophie, and a few questions have rolled in from the beauty division about upcoming events and photo shoots.

While I get ready to go into the office, I do everything I can to hype myself up.

Eyes on the prize.

I'm greeted by a grinning Rhodes, who is standing at one of the closets and sorting through looks.

"*Bonjour,* Milo. I had a workout this morning and didn't have anything to do, so I came in a bit early."

Another way he's a more model employee than me now, I'm sure.

"I've just gone through some of the media hits for the event," he says. "It was a success all around."

All around? It sounds like he means "Even your little café was well received!"

Am I overly sensitive? Or is there truly a condescension with a painfully cacophonous texture—like blades against my skin? He's riding this high of a win, getting in a workout, and showing up early to stay ahead?

Setting my coffee on the desk, I remind myself I have a plan. And breathing fire again isn't going to accomplish what I want.

So, I do my best to sulk.

"I know it was all about Amalia," I mumble, pulling out my chair and turning my attention to the computer.

Out of the corner of my eye, I think Rhodes makes a strange face before returning to the accessories he's pulling.

"No, no. Café 57 was a total hit. Scroll through the campaign! There were so many hits. Especially considering Amalia—I think it did as well as it possibly could have."

Ha! Isn't that generous?

I'm not a violent person at all. I've never gotten into a physical fight. Once, at a districts match, this kid Leroy thought I had a thing for his boyfriend. It was completely untrue—he was taken, but he was also the furthest thing from my type. Leroy had all these ideas, though, convinced he saw me making eyes at him. I guess at one point I accidentally watched the boyfriend's Instagram Story, though I still don't think that's even true, and this meant war.

Leroy absolutely pegged me with the ball every chance he got. He was incredibly accurate and had a powerful swing. I was getting bruised, and for the briefest moment, I wanted to lay him out on the court. It was probably a nanosecond that I had that thought, but my dad and brother—also athletes—always taught me that violence isn't the answer. Instead, we just win.

So I won, and when I saw Leroy at a party a couple months later, he apologized and admitted he was insecure and shouldn't have taken it out on me.

It was such a great feeling. I hadn't resorted to pegging balls back at him or beating him up, I just played my best and won, and in the end, I was validated.

This doesn't feel like the fucking Leroy situation at all. I am not sure what is happening right now, but it doesn't feel like winning is going to be enough. I want to take away Rhodes's win and any of his smugness.

"As well as it possibly could have!"

I calm myself down with the 4–4–4 breathing exercise my coach taught me while Rhodes stuffs a pair of strappy sandals into a linen dust bag.

Rhodes has to believe I've lost my fire, so he won't try as hard for the next event, I remind myself.

"It was just a silly café," I mutter.

Yvette walks in, looking incredibly cool in striped tracksuit bottoms and a T-shirt with Maison Dauphine sneakers. I've never seen her so casual, but it also still possesses her unique and powerful *je ne sais quoi.* I think Yvette could command the house in her bathrobe and nobody would question her authority.

Weird visual.

"Oh, good. You're both here."

She eyes me like I'm late because Rhodes decided to get in early.

"The pop-up was a total success," she says. "Rhodes, thank you for sending over that recap. I've shared it with leadership."

You're not going to throw anything at him. You're not going to throw anything at him.

"Milo, we can discuss how to pull the data and prepare the report after our next event."

I nod. I would have done it if I'd known it was a thing we were even supposed to do. Never mind any of my amazing networking or how I memorized those lists; it's just all overshadowed, and now that I didn't take the initiative to create a recap, I'm back at square one with Yvette.

"Now, we have the Tuileries garden event in two days. Everything is mostly set; we just need you to show up and work your magic. While the pop-up guest list included some influencers, that was a bit more elevated and exclusive. The Tuileries event is more curated for content, is solely focused on influencers, and we have a wider range of creators attending. Some have very, very large followings and some are a bit more micro. You should review the list in the creator portal as you have time."

Rhodes clears his throat. "I actually was wondering if I could run an idea by you."

Yvette looks beyond pleased, giving him a smile that's all *fromage*. "Of course, Rhodes. What do you have?"

"Okay, so I was looking at the renderings for the event and noticed there are some areas where we might be able to maximize content opportunities while also giving another very subtle clue for the L'or des Fous theme."

Great, what is he up to now?

"I know we have two of the gardens around the Grand Bassin Rond reserved," Rhodes says. "I thought we might be able to showcase some of the gold accessories from the Enchanted Garden line Pierre Allard did in 2003. Placing them among the flowers like art installations. Since those were a nod to L'or des Fous themselves. I mean, they are truly iconic pieces of Maison Dauphine history. That was the first time the latest Dauphine Monogram was introduced. It set a precedent for the house."

Yvette considers this, intrigued. "I love this idea."

Fucking hell, Rhodes.

"But I am not certain where those samples are." Yvette looks off. "They might be in our American archives, if I recall correctly. We won't have time to get them."

I immediately want to jump out of my seat and gloat like a child.

Rhodes picks up one of the dust bags on his desk. "So, I did some research on it this weekend, just in case. They are actually in a museum in New York."

He's so smug I almost groan. Where is he going with this?

"But my mother has five of the pieces—her own personal collection, you know—and she was happy to send them over. Just got here this morning." He pulls open the bag and reveals a couple of small boxes, and three more dust bags, which he goes on to show us are protecting two small gold handbags and a pair of heels. The famous Maison Dauphine monogram is all over the bags, and it is a bit wild to think that this was where that all started.

Yvette purses her lips. "Oh, Rhodes, I am not sure. I would hate if anything were to happen to them."

Rhodes waves this off. "I think it'd be a brilliant addition to the event. These pieces are famous, and they're so of the era that these influencers are capturing with their looks right now."

"But your mother—"

"Mum has already said she's happy to *donate* them if need be." It almost seems like he's exaggerating there, but I'm not sure. "She's actually very excited to see them get some use. They're just sitting in her closet, after all."

"They're incredibly valuable collectors' items," Yvette says. "We'll get display cases for them, at the very least. And we'll make up plaques to showcase the details and attribute them to your mother's collection."

When Yvette leaves, Rhodes is absolutely thrilled with himself. He packs up the stuff for the Tuilieries event in a few ivory Maison Dauphine boxes, labeling them for Haydée, who is going to take them to be put in display cases. He then says he's going to make some calls, and when he leaves, I cannot believe I am going to lose to him again. And it's just so easy for him.

I work through some requests and send some emails. It does excite me a little that I am going to meet Sophie in a couple of days, but I'm still beyond annoyed with Rhodes.

I take inventory of some shirts and pants from a request, carefully putting them into garment bags. Then I make up labels for a French magazine and I place them on the designated piece of plastic on each bag.

Haydée sends a message saying she will grab any boxes we have ready at the moment. I tell her we have a big British *Vogue* request to go along with the boxes for the Tuileries event.

And then it's like a switch flips.

There are boxes addressed to British *Vogue* in Rhodes's handwriting, and they're just sitting right there in a neat little stack. Since these aren't local, they won't be hand-delivered, which means the shipping company is going to deliver whatever boxes have those labels on them—nobody is going to double-check the contents.

Nobody would notice if the gold accessories from Rosie Hamilton accidentally got swapped. Nobody would have any idea, realistically, until it was much too late.

Anyway, it's not like these pieces are going to be lost. The assistants at British *Vogue* will open the packages, realize they are the wrong ones, and send them back.

Maybe it isn't worth it if I have to win this way.

But there's so much to lose if I don't.

At the end of the day, I don't have the luxury of playing fair with Rhodes. So, before I can talk myself out of it, I peel off the labels and switch the boxes.

Chapitre Douze

Movie and TV characters make ruthless ambition look so easy. Some of them make it look so sexy—alluring, even, is the ability to effortlessly get ahead and win using some intellectual prowess and cunning.

Though, come to think of it, how often does that end well for them?

This might be a new world record for how quickly someone learned a major life lesson the hard way. After all, I have always known I am competitive and driven, but it turns out I might not even last as a season regular on *Succession* or *Game of Thrones*. Hell, I probably wouldn't last one episode if this is what scheming feels like.

Once I'd left for lunch, I immediately had a sick feeling in my gut and turned around before I made it two blocks. When I got back, however, I was met with the unfortunate realization that Haydée had already taken the boxes. The mailroom would find it far too suspicious if I asked for them back, though I did consider if the risk might be worth clearing my conscience and trying to make amends with karma.

I spend lunch overthinking and going in circles. I want to text Celeste for her advice, but I am beyond ashamed of this shortsighted misstep. It seems like admitting it to someone else will only feel worse in this moment.

There's also the fact that I am torn about Rhodes in general.

I realize I am experiencing some silly emotional—and physical—response to him after our stroll through the Petit Trianon, but it's not like I can just abandon everything I have come to Paris for because of a crush. I was wrong to resort to such drastic measures, but was I wrong to take a step back and realize he is still very much a threat? Regardless of how cute he is?

All I know for sure is that it would be impossible to face him, so I spend the rest of the day claiming tasks that send me on errands around Paris. Errands that are far, far away from Rhodes.

While I'm in the back of a car toward the end of the day, practically drowning in boxes of Maison Dauphine scarves, I send Sophie a meme on Instagram and find comfort in scrolling through posts of some friends from back home. My mom's boutique is posting about a fundraiser they're hosting at the Hamptons store in a couple of weeks. My mom would be so disappointed in me—she's doing something so good, while I just did something so bad.

Sophie reacts to the meme with a skull emoji, and moments later a text from her pops up.

Sophie: Are you on a sightseeing kick?

Me: Lol no, what do you mean?

Sophie: You're just voluntarily trekking all across Paris today

Sophie: Haydée is convinced you're up to something

Me: Great

Me: I'm not. I just wanted to get out of the office!

Sophie: Fair

Sophie: Omg, we meet IRL in two days

Me: I literally can't wait

Sophie: Same, I just wish we were gonna have more time to hang out!

Sophie: Maybe you should come back to New York with me

Sophie: The office would be so much more fun

Me: Haha I do love New York

Me: But alas my apprenticeship is en français

Me: Did that even make sense?

Sophie: I'm not sure but I knew what you meant lol

As I near Maison Dauphine, I search the inbox for another task so I can make sure to avoid Rhodes for the rest of the day. If I'm lucky, he'll even be packed up by the time I finish my last to-do.

I try to volunteer to take Yvette's dry cleaning back to her flat once I'm back in the office, but Haydée insists I'm done for the day.

So, I swallow and tell myself that interacting with Rhodes for five seconds won't be bad. I can keep my composure, and there's no way he'll be able to tell I am riddled with guilt over my little indiscretion.

He spins around in his chair when I enter the fashion closet, taking off a pair of over-the-ear headphones and setting them on his desk.

"Well, *regarde qui c'est*!" Rhodes holds his arms out wide. "I thought you'd come back with a souvenir beret, at least."

"Why is everyone acting like it's so weird for me to want some fresh air?"

Chuckling, Rhodes cocks his head. "For a moment there I thought maybe you were avoiding me or something."

"Avoiding you?" My voice cracks and I stand up straighter. "No way. Why would I be avoiding you?"

He's still smiling, but his brows turn down. "Of course you weren't. Only joking. It was quiet around here, but kind of good, actually. I got to spend some time learning more about the archiving system for a lot of the rare and delicate old dresses. I've always found it so fascinating how they preserve the fabrics. They're sensitive to all kinds of things—the tiniest droplet of moisture or the wrong lighting."

"I didn't realize you were so passionate about textiles."

He laughs, which is probably for the best, because it came out with a bit of a threatened bite. I mean, I know he likes Maison Dauphine, and it's increasingly evident he does have some proclivity toward fashion, but he's constantly outdoing me. And I could have learned some of this if I'd been here, which all goes back to me avoiding him after what I've done.

I am such an idiot.

"It's interesting stuff," he says. "Honestly!"

"Sure," I say.

"Anyway, I'm wrapping up for the day. How about you?"

Oh no. That tone sounds eerily like he is going to ask if I want to hang out after we leave.

But there's no way out of the fact that I don't have any work left.

"I'm wrapping up too."

I try to think of something else to add. Some possible plans, maybe, to get ahead of him extending any sort of invite, but nothing comes to me.

Rhodes nods. "Want to grab something to eat?"

"Well . . ." Interlocking my fingers and walking over to my desk, I shrug. "I had such a huge lunch, I'm honestly not hungry yet."

"Fair," he says. "I'm not quite starved, either. Maybe we could just go for a drink or something? Fancy a glass of wine?"

I open my mouth, but with no poised response or excuse, I stand there silent.

Rhodes catches it immediately. "Ah, okay. No worries, then."

"It's not that I don't want to—"

"I get it," he says. There is such a vulnerability in the way his eyes widen. He glances down. "I know we sort of had this established, didn't we? I just misread . . . I kind of thought we had a nice time together at Versailles."

"We did have a nice time together."

The words come out quickly, almost all running together.

Damn those big, sweet eyes. I don't mean to give in, but I can practically physically feel his disappointment tugging at my heartstrings.

"I mean, if you wanted to keep it work related, I could tell you more about the textile preservation," Rhodes says. "Or we could spend some time coming up with ideas for content? For the gala? I also found some really cool decks on the server about the work Pascal is doing to modernize Maison Dauphine—there's a whole ten-year plan. He's pretty incredible."

Get it together, Milo. There is too much at stake to get caught up in a crush. Not to mention you screwed him over six ways from Sunday this afternoon.

I stay quiet.

"Right. Okay, okay. I understand." He locks his computer and grabs his wallet from his desk, standing before he pockets it. He gives me a weak smile before staring down at the floor.

Damn it.

It's like I finally understand why people lose their minds in love. I mean, obviously this is the furthest thing from *love*; it's just that right now my sensible side—the one that knows Rhodes is still the opposition—is absolutely being squashed by whatever the other side is—the side that just wants to admire his slightly Herculean features.

"I'll see you tomorrow, Milo."

He walks toward the door, and I curse my weak, human emotions and instincts.

"Wait!" I say. "Maybe we could go over some of the Pascal stuff. We could walk back to the 7th together?"

Rhodes laughs. "You need more fresh air?"

"Walking outside has a number of benefits, Rhodes—"

"I know, I'm only messing with you." He holds out his hand, gesturing for me to lead the way. "I'm good with walking back together."

And I am too. It was my idea, after all.

Except for the fact that as we walk, I have this sort of gooey feeling of guilt that just gets heavier, like Rhodes wouldn't be so eager to walk me through this Pascal strategy document if he had any idea what I've done.

"I think some of the new marketing verticals are really brilliant," he says. "Maison Dauphine has always really toed the line between classic, exclusive couture and innovation. They're somehow preserving the past but paving the way forward."

We stop at the middle of the bridge overlooking the Seine, and Rhodes looks out at the water. Across the way, the Eiffel Tower is tall and stark against the bright blue sky—since I got to Paris it has served as the landmark that tells me which way back to the apartment.

Maybe I should just tell him.

I'm not even sure how such a silly thought could pop into my mind right now, so I ignore it and focus on what Rhodes is talking about.

"Pascal is a genius," I say.

Eyes still fixed on the river, Rhodes smiles. "He is. My mom and I went to his exhibit when it was in LA. All those archival pieces. It was incredible."

I place my hands on the railing and sigh. "I wish my mom had the time to do something like that."

"Oh? I thought you said you would go to New York together."

"True," I say. "And I love those trips. It's just, you know. Those are for her stores. Work trips."

Rhodes turns to face me. "What do you guys do apart from that? Like, outside of work trips?"

"She's busy," I offer. "First the Citrus Harbor boutique, and now this Hamptons thing . . . and my parents divorced two years ago, so she's been doing it all alone. I guess she was always doing it alone, looking back."

"Are you saying you guys don't spend any time together?"

I shake my head. "No, we have dinner together. A few nights a week! And I see her on weekends, though she's either usually busy or tired, which is understandable. I have a ten-year-old sister, too, and there's just a lot to do all the time. But I mean it's mostly work stuff. I help out at the boutique sometimes. She doesn't need my help as much now that she has a bigger team, but I still like to give my ideas."

Lifting one shoulder, Rhodes purses his lips. "Well, maybe you should try to set up some kind of tradition outside of work trips or dinners. You know? Something fun."

Though I don't think he's trying to sound condescending, it irks me slightly the way he says this. As if I've never thought of it or it would just be so easy.

I do my best to avoid sounding irritated. "Maybe."

"It'd be good for you both. And your sister. And your brother could join too. If he's not busy watching Clyde Circus lose a match, of course."

"We used to have family game night. Sometimes we'd go bowling or to mini golf. And it'd just be the four of us, since my dad was always way too busy. He makes her calendar look like a dream—but it was fine because we had a lot more fun without him, to be honest."

Rhodes snorts. "So you're not close with your dad?"

"No," I say. "I guess things with us are fine, but we've barely even spoken since I've been in Paris."

"Oh," he says, eyes going duller as his smile falls. "I'm sorry."

"It's okay." I hold up my hands. "Really, I promise. No need to be sorry."

Rhodes bites his lip. "If you say so. I do think game nights sound really nice."

"They were. Obviously, this was all before she opened the store. I don't think we've done a game night for at least the past four years." I dig my fingernails into my palm. "I don't know, it seems silly to act like it's . . . her business is a big deal, and it's important. She supports us with it. You know? It's not like she's just choosing not to hang out with me."

Rhodes's eyes narrow. "I'm not sure. It sounds like she's making a choice to me."

Who is he to say that?

"It isn't that simple," I snap.

"It sounds like she's only going to get busier," Rhodes says. "And opening another boutique in the Hamptons? That's far, and it's going to require a lot of travel, isn't it? Away from you and your siblings?"

I shrug. "She'll take us with her when she can. Mostly she tries to only go up when we're with our dad, so it doesn't affect us as much."

"How did that even come about?"

"She and her friends have always gone up there for as long as I can remember," I say. "And she recently found a location, and then worked with a firm to do all this planning and research. She's been sourcing inventory and overseeing the remodel of the unit. . . ."

"Sounds like it's just another really big thing on her plate," Rhodes says.

"It's a huge opportunity," I tell him.

Frowning, Rhodes takes a tiny step toward me. "You know, it's all right if you're not happy about your mom's priorities."

"It's ungrateful," I counter.

"But if you—"

"Look, life has been fine without game nights." I can hear a bit of that irritation I was trying to avoid. It burns in my chest. "It doesn't matter anyway, because I'm going to be busy too. I have big goals and plans, and I won't have time for that kind of stuff myself."

Rhodes's forehead creases for a moment, but then his expression softens, and he just nods. "I didn't mean to strike a nerve."

"You didn't," I say. "There is no nerve there. I should have never said anything."

"All right." He points over his shoulder toward the Eiffel Tower. "Should we keep going?"

I'm beyond grateful that Rhodes is back to admiring Pascal's strategic vision for the rest of the walk home. We seem to both pretend there wasn't a slightly awkward, tense moment at the end of our conversation on the bridge, and I am also grateful for that.

Once I'm back at the flat, I kick off my shoes and text Celeste.

Then I navigate to my texts with my mom.

She hasn't replied in three days.

It's fine, though. I'm sure I'm only feeling sensitive about it because of Rhodes. She's busy, and I'm busy too.

Besides, soon enough I will have amazing news about my future with Maison Dauphine, and she'll absolutely respond to that.

Chapitre Treize

I'm not as superstitious as a lot of the athletes I know, but ever since the sixth grade, I always had this deep fear instilled in me that if I ever cheated to get ahead, I would not only lose, but I would get seriously hurt, one way or another.

I can't remember exactly when it started, but I think it might have been something my mom said or maybe a pro tennis player, even, since I went through a phase of researching them as obsessively as I researched Maison Dauphine to prepare for this.

In the heat of the moment on Monday, I went against years of superstitious caution to best Rhodes, and now I am sweating bullets in the back seat of a town car on the way to the Tuileries.

Rhodes is beside me, perfectly calm as always.

He had to take a call the moment we got in the car, and now politely apologizes as he hangs up. I'm not ready for us to launch into conversation after how quickly yesterday became a therapy session about my family life, so I tell him I need to focus on some emails.

For this event, we're both in thick white T-shirts that have the tiniest Maison Dauphine monogram on the sleeve. We've tucked them into cropped blue pants just as we were instructed. All the PR assistants and, well, everyone else seem to wear whatever they want to these things, but I'm guessing the reason we get strict uniforms must be because we're the only apprentices. That, or because we're both guys and Yvette doesn't want to risk us misrepresenting the brand, which is only women's wear.

I'm struggling to catch my breath back here, wanting to roll down the window, and Rhodes is nonchalantly scrolling through Instagram, excited for his perfect plan to pan out.

What have I done . . . ?

Specific superstitions aside, I've always been a fan of the more general idea of karma.

Do unto others . . . what goes around . . . those kinds of things.

But now I'm terrified of karma. What if I threw away all this hard work just to pull one over on Rhodes and lose it all anyway?

The fresh air is much needed after the awkwardly quiet car ride, no matter how short it was, and it's beyond cool to see the event come to life just like in the renderings. There are signs along the dirt path that will direct our guests to the garden, which has been transformed into an extravagant floral wonderland. The perimeter is secured by gold velvet rope, and there are tall installations of greenery decorated with perennial blooms.

Rhodes is off, hopping on the phone like always, and I look around for Yvette or Haydée, though neither of them is anywhere to be found.

"Milo!"

Sophie's voice is like music to my ears, especially right now, when I am so nervous I want to hide among the rows of trees farther down the path. I turn to find her hurrying toward me, wearing a midi skirt, button-up, and white tennis shoes. She looks exactly like her photo, actually, with dark brown skin and curly black hair, her eyes and smile both wide with delight.

She pulls me in for a hug, which is so welcomed, and then she takes a tiny step back.

"It's nice to meet you in person. I feel like we practically know each other, anyway."

I nod. "I know. You have no idea how nice it is."

"French offices a nightmare?" she whispers.

I shake my head. "Not a total nightmare." An image of Rhodes flashes across my mind. "Maybe some slightly nightmarish aspects. But I'm sure the New York offices have nightmarish aspects, too."

Sophie's eyes bug. "You have no idea. Luckily, in PR, we don't deal with as much of it in New York. Honestly, the magazines can be a bit wild. And there are some stylists in the city who are a lot. Overall, though, I bet you'd love it." She studies me. "Are you okay?"

I try to stand up a bit taller. "Yeah, totally. Just a little nervous."

"Don't be nervous," Sophie says. "This event will go off without a hitch."

"I hope so."

"It will. Influencer events like these are some of the easier ones. It's all about making sure they feel like they're getting a luxurious, hosted experience, and from there it's all a piece of cake. Which, by the way, Café 57 was incredible."

I shrug. "Not as incredible as Amalia Astor."

"That was absolutely nuts," she agrees. Then, sensing she said the wrong thing, she shrugs. "But a lot of people were trying to figure out the Café 57 thing. Like, why was there all the *malbouffe* or whatever. There are some luxury YouTubers who have made entire videos speculating. Have you seen?"

"I watched a couple."

I play it cool, but I totally watched them all. My idea was not only selected and implemented, but it was well received *and* achieved its goal: to create some additional mystery and intrigue. It's surreal seeing people share their photos and videos and theories, all stemming from my pop-up.

Sophie nods. "It was a hit. Really. And this will be a hit too. Should we do a quick walk-through?"

I follow her to the gold rope, where a bouncer in a black suit lets us in. It's still early, so there aren't any guests, and security is doing their best to stop people from taking photos as they pass by. I'm sure things are being posted early, but that's fine since the main event will be the bag unveiling toward the end.

At the far end of the garden, there are tall shrubs with MD monograms placed strategically in gold, and five stone pedestals are lined up among the shrubs, just like in the newest renderings in the event-planning deck. The glass enclosures are empty, though, missing the items from Rosie Hamilton's collection. The sight makes my stomach drop.

This is so ridiculous. All this anxiety, and it's my own freaking doing. If I had just let Rhodes have this, I could have maybe enjoyed this event. Now I'm just waiting for someone to realize the items aren't here and for all hell to break loose.

"So, just a quick refresher—though I'm sure you're super on top of everything—we have a *citron pressé* bar," Sophie says, gesturing to her left. "It's basically an elevated lemonade stand. Super refreshing. And then next to that, there is a little cart where people can grab finger sandwiches, small pastries, that sort of thing. There will be waiters walking around with other hors d'oeuvres, which I'm sure you remember from the brief."

We walk around, and I do my best to admire the way all of this has come to life—the *citron pressé* bar and the photo booth and the harpist. At every turn, however, the pedestals seem to taunt me, whisper how terrible a person I am.

Rhodes is over with Yvette, and the boxes that should contain the vintage pieces are on a table beside them.

He flashes a smile, and for a moment, that grin is all that exists, I think.

Jesus, Milo, come on.

Only, there's no way anyone wouldn't think he looks handsome right now, with the Louvre off in the distance behind him, surrounded by flowers, and practically some sort of Greek god—tall, sculpted, drenched in the golden sunlight.

"We really just want the creators to enjoy themselves," Sophie says, bringing me back to reality. "They'll get some content, and then, of course, the main event will be the unveiling of the resort bag. It's gorgeous. Have you seen it yet? I know everyone is going to be obsessed."

I shake my head. "I haven't."

"Oh, you have to."

I nod thoughtlessly before glancing back over to Rhodes. When Yvette walks away and he's left typing on his phone, my heartbeat quickens.

"You know what? I just remembered something super important. I need to remind Rhodes. I'll be right back."

Sophie grins. "Sure. When you get back, we can try the *citron pressé*. It's to die for."

I don't really know what a confession is going to do now, especially since the damage is done, but I can't take this anymore. I'm too superstitious and too guilt ridden to stand by and watch my terrible scheme unfold.

I hurry over to Rhodes and tap him on the shoulder. He glances down, looking over the rims of his gold Ray-Bans and quirking a brow.

"Milo, you're all fidgety."

"I'm not fidgety."

He cocks his head. "You're scowling and your breathing is a bit off. What are you stressed about?"

Shaking my head, I swallow. "No, look, I need to tell you something."

"Okay, just *one* second." He holds up his phone. "I've got to send a very important email, and it really must go now."

I take a deep breath. "No, I need to—"

He holds up his finger, repeating: "Just one second, okay?"

Watching him type, his jaw flexes a bit, and his bright pink lips are pursed in a way that makes them look way too kissable.

God, I wish things were different. I wish we didn't have to compete with each other, and we could have just gone to dinner, and I could have found out what it was like to feel those lips on mine.

Of course, that thought is fleeting. These are the cards we've been dealt.

The longer I wait, the more I realize a confession isn't going to help much. He's going to freak out, rightfully so, and then we're not going to have any solution. The items are in London now, and there is no way we're going to get them here in time.

"All right," Rhodes says, pocketing his phone. "What is it?"

I take a deep breath.

"You've got something in your hair." He reaches forward, palm warm as it brushes against my forehead, and his fingers twist something out of my curls. My breath catches, and I'm not sure if his does, but he holds out a small little yellow petal between us before flicking it away. "Little bit of flower, it seems. Odd."

"Really odd."

He sniffles, which seems to be more of a response to being uncomfortable. "Sorry. I shouldn't have—I don't know why I did that."

"It's okay, I appreciate it."

"Right. So, what did you need to say?"

The harpist begins to play, and Sophie rushes over to us, tugging at my sleeve. "We need some help setting up a few of the high-tops, do you mind?"

I shake my head. "Of course not, I'll be right there."

She hurries off, waving for Haydée to help her too.

Rhodes pulls off his sunglasses and stares at me. "Milo, you look like you're about to be sick."

I nod. "I feel like I'm about to be sick."

Now he nods, a small smile forming. "Does this have anything to do with the fact that you completely fucked me over today?"

As I blink, everything goes silent, and my mouth hangs open.

Rhodes looks amused, but he doesn't look angry. He gestures

toward the boxes stacked beside him, and I do think this is the closest I've come to actually being sick.

"Look, I'm really sorry. I shouldn't have done it. I was upset, and it was really impulsive and irrational."

He nods. "Maybe I was wrong about you, after all."

I shut my eyes. "I get it if you want to rat me out to Yvette. It's what I deserve. I'm not a cheater, really, and I think it's one of the most terrible things I've done."

When I open my eyes, Rhodes looks puzzled. "This is one of the most terrible things you've done?"

Frowning, and afraid my eyes might be going hot with tears, I bob my head up and down. "I don't know what came over me. I mean, I've always been competitive, but this was something else."

Rhodes squints. "You mean it? This is *actually* one of the most terrible things you've ever done?"

"We have a rule in my family against cheating or lying, and I have always followed it. Even when I had to play against the worst guys—just total assholes . . ." I wince. "Not that . . ."

"I was a bit of an asshole," he says. "I know it's not an entirely level playing field between us. But to be fair, I didn't cheat to win."

I nod. "I know. That's why I'm apologizing and taking responsibility."

"The pieces are collectors' items that belong to my mother, do you realize that?"

"Yes. And that makes it even worse. It's just that I know they'll be sent back immediately, and they won't be—"

"How do you know? They could get damaged in transit or

stolen. There's no record of them in our logistics spreadsheet since we didn't log them to be shipped."

I swallow. "You're right."

Rhodes reaches over for one of the boxes and hands it to me.

The box is heavy, and I don't know if that's metaphorical or physical, since I am currently going a bit numb all over from the embarrassment and shame I'm experiencing.

He lifts his brows, gesturing for me to open it.

When I do, I find his mother's monogrammed bag in a glass display case.

"Oh."

Rhodes nods.

"Wait . . . you knew I'd switch them?"

He shrugs. "I had a pretty good feeling."

"But you let me do it?"

"I did."

My head is spinning. I'm overwhelmed with relief—the items are here, the event is going to go smoothly, and everything is fine—but then I have so many questions. There's also a new-found sense of disappointment in myself: Rhodes thought this poorly of me, and I proved him right.

"Why?" I ask. "Is it somehow satisfying to see me freaking out over this?"

He shakes his head. "It was more of a test than anything. And when you got back from all your errands around Paris, I almost told you, but you were a bit . . . cold. And then we actually started to have some nice conversations, and I didn't want to ruin that."

"So you just let me stew in it."

"To be honest, I'd *hoped* you were stewing in it—that you're the guy I think you are—but I wasn't sure. Truthfully, I'm glad you feel bad about it." Then he frowns. "But I don't love watching you squirm, obviously. I feel a bit bad about it now."

"This one is on me." It's annoying, but it's true. "Are you going to say anything to Yvette?"

Rhodes shakes his head. "No, I'm not."

"Thank you. I really am sorry."

"How about from now on, we just play fair?"

"Sure," I say. "Right, we play fair."

Because we're still competing. This changes nothing.

Rhodes smirks. "Good. No more tricks, no more scheming. I won't use my connections anymore—keep it fair."

He holds out his hand, and when I shake it, I get that conflicting notion again. Part of me wants to win at any cost still, but part of me wants to hold his hand and find out what more there is to him.

With a glimmer in his eyes I can't read, he smirks. *"Que le meilleur gagne."*

I slowly piece it together in my mind, then nod. "May the best man win."

Thankfully, the event goes perfectly. Sophie and I are attached at the hip, which makes it feel more like fun than work at some points.

The influencers all love the garden and the art installations, and the collection pieces are a huge hit. On our creator platform, I check in on some of the mentions, and they're *mostly* about Rosie Hamilton's iconic pieces. Until, of course, Pascal Dumas appears and gives a short speech before unveiling the new resort bag. People *ooh* and *aah*, and they snap photos and videos. It's like a new iPhone being revealed or something.

Pascal is gone in a flash, as quickly as he appeared, and I don't get an introduction, though I was waiting with bated breath, just hoping Yvette might wave me over. He does say something quick to Rhodes, of course, and while I am relieved of my superstitious guilt because this event has gone off without a hitch, there is still a sharp sense of panic surging through me. When Rhodes is fawned over and congratulated for his brilliant idea, I am reminded that the resort show is slipping further and further away. The urgency bubbles and boils inside me, but there isn't anything I can do.

I'm so ready to cocoon at the apartment now after the roller coaster of guilt and anxiety and overthinking. Nothing sounds better than a bath and then becoming one with the couch.

I say goodbye to Sophie, and I am about to slip away when Rhodes waves me down, running over.

Is this becoming a pattern? Is he about to ask me to do something fun now that the event is over?

"Do you have plans after this?"

I just lift a brow. His tone and expression seem much different than they did at Versailles—warmer and more familiar somehow.

"Yvette wants us to verify all of the gala invitations from the calligrapher," he says. "To get them out first thing in the morning."

"I thought you already did that. Also, I don't understand why we're sending them so late."

Rhodes shrugs. "It's really just a formality. Everyone's already confirmed. Tradition. I did pick up the invitations the other day, and I meant to start double-checking them, but then Zoe sent me on a wild goose chase for a necklace."

"So we'd have to do them all tonight?"

"Yeah. But the invitations are back at my flat—we're both in the 7th, maybe makes more sense to just do them there than to take them back to the office?"

I sigh. "I guess I owe you, don't I?'

Rhodes flashes a devilish grin. "You said it, not me."

Chapitre Quatorze

The Hamilton flat is otherworldly. It's actually more of a private mansion, which makes sense given everything I know about Rhodes's parents. Three stories of French windows overlook a cobbled courtyard complete with potted palms and shrubs at the entrance, and once we've walked into what appears to be an obscenely large sitting room, I can see that there is a private garden in the back.

Rhodes has kicked off his shoes at the front door, haphazardly, like we aren't in a miniature French palace. One of them even knocks against a tall chinoiserie umbrella vase, and he doesn't seem to notice. I'm careful when I take mine off, placing them neatly and making sure the toes don't touch the wall.

Apart from the door closing and our footsteps, there's an almost eerie stillness here. It's so big and so empty. Sunlight bathes the sitting room, intensified by the large, ornate gold mirrors, but all the high-end furniture looks untouched and unlived in.

"Chez moi," Rhodes says, spreading his arms out and taking a slight bow before laughing. "Sorta."

I follow Rhodes through the sitting room into the kitchen,

which is massive and obviously renovated while still somehow fitting the style of the house. It has one of those really big, fancy stoves that look like they are just meant to make your kitchen more Instagram worthy. The crown molding details on the absurdly tall ceilings are carried throughout the apartment, from the living space into the kitchen and into the breakfast nook that sits beneath more windows.

"All right, Milo, what are you in the mood for?" He pulls open the fridge, and I take a seat on one of the wicker bistro stools at the pearly island.

"Shouldn't we—"

"I've got it all. Plenty of things to cook. Could do a pasta dish? Also have leftover pizza—you should've seen the waiter's face."

I cock my head. "What do you mean?"

Rhodes furrows his brow. "The waiters hate it when you don't finish your food. Haven't you noticed?"

"I haven't noticed that," I say.

What I do notice, however, is that Rhodes has made this kitchen feel a bit more like . . . his. There are some matchbooks on the other side of the island—the fancy kind, like you get from a nice restaurant or hotel. There are also some museum pamphlets and magazines and his passport, plus an Armoury United cap that looks stiff, like it's never been worn.

"Leftovers aren't really a thing here," Rhodes says. "Except pizza, I guess. But I believe it's a cultural thing? I reckon they find it disrespectful if you don't finish your food." He frowns, turning to the pizza box on the top shelf. "It's an honest mistake, really. Eyes were a bit bigger than my stomach."

I stifle a laugh. "You don't have to feed me."

Really, I'm a bit uncomfortable with this whole situation. Why has Rhodes invited me over? I just tried to fuck up his apprenticeship. Like, majorly.

Then, as if he reads my mind, he chuckles. "I'm not going to poison you."

"I'm not entirely sure I'd blame you," I offer.

Rhodes closes the refrigerator and leans over, propping his elbows up on the island across from me. "You're not hungry?"

"We just have a lot of invitations to get through, don't we?"

"Sure." He shrugs, standing up and heading over to one of the cabinets and pulling out two wineglasses. "You didn't answer my question, though."

My stomach answers for me, annoyingly, with a growl that's just loud enough for Rhodes to hear across the kitchen. He offers a smug smile, sets the glasses down on the island, and walks toward the arched doorway on the opposite side of the kitchen from where we entered.

"Right, come on. Let's go pick a wine, and then we can decide on dinner based on that."

I don't have a chance to interject with any follow-up questions or comments, because he's gone. Following him into another hallway, we turn and head down a curling wooden staircase with an iron railing. It looks like an ancient castle down here—uneven stone floors and walls, vaulted ceilings and columns. It sort of smells like an ancient castle down here too, though there are huge Diptyque candle jars on nearly every console table, as if they've had the same thought.

"Before you judge my family for being pretentious, this wine cellar has always been here." Rhodes says, guiding me up one small step at the end of *another* hallway and tugging on the handle of an aged wooden door.

"This place having a wine cellar isn't exactly surprising," I say. He shoots me a look, but then his lip curls up in amusement. I wince. "I didn't mean that to sound like an insult. It's incredible. I've just honestly never seen anything like this."

"It's okay, Milo."

The cellar is more modest than the rest of the property, all stone with another arched entrance to a wall of shelved bottles that become backlit as we get closer.

"Do you have any preference?" he asks.

"No," I say. "I don't really know a ton about wine."

He nods. "That's right, the drinking age is twenty-one in America."

"I mean, we drank at parties, but not wine. Plus, Europeans have such a different culture when it comes to wine, I think."

"This is true," Rhodes says. "Though, in England, it's not like we're having wine with meals in secondary school the way they are in France. At least we weren't, and my mates certainly weren't. Ollie always wanted to have wine if my parents did. They let him, in fact, and now he's a proper wine snob. You can't take him anywhere; he'll ask obnoxious questions just to prove he knows what he's talking about."

I laugh. "Is that right?"

"Honestly. Okay, this is one of my favorites." He picks up a bottle—they all look the same to me—and holds it up, grinning like a proud dad with a newborn. "I think we should have this, and I'll make some salmon."

"Are you sure?"

Rhodes is already ushering me out of the cellar, shutting the door, and heading up the stairs.

"You honestly do not have to cook," I say. "If I'm being honest, I'm confused why you are cooking for me when I . . . well, if anything, I should be cooking for you. To apologize."

He shrugs, stopping a few steps above me and turning around. "We've got to eat, Milo. It's not a big deal. I'd be cooking for myself anyway. I don't mind. Besides, you can get a head start on the invitations while I make dinner."

I roll my eyes as he starts back up the stairs. "That's why you want to cook. So I do most of the work."

"You're much more cynical than one might initially assume," Rhodes says with a laugh.

Once we're back in the kitchen, I sit on my stool, and he places the wine bottle and the glasses in front of me.

"Let me grab the card stock," he says, holding up a finger before rushing off again.

I sit there in the silence as his quick footsteps get farther and quieter.

On the counter beside the refrigerator, there is a photo of the Hamilton family in a thick silver frame, between some cookbooks and a floral ceramic jar. It's cozy, with them all gathered around this kitchen island making gingerbread houses. Rhodes and Ollie are pulling faces in sweaters and Christmas pajama bottoms, while their mom poses with a huge grin and Liam Hamilton offers an award-winning smile while stretching his arm out for the selfie.

"Right, here you are."

A mint-green box thuds against the countertop, and my

attention is yanked away from the photo. Rhodes removes the lid and studies the contents of the box, crossing his arms and pursing his lips. He then lifts his chin and huffs before grabbing the wine and fishing through one of the drawers for a corkscrew.

"Why were you looking at the invitations like that?" I ask.

"Like what?" Rhodes grabs the neck of the bottle and then glances over at the box. "Oh. I'm just wondering if that's all of them."

My jaw falls open. "What do you mean?"

"I could have sworn there were more." He waves me off, uncorking. "I'm sure I'm only imagining it."

While Rhodes pours us wine, I pull the box closer and find a printed spreadsheet with all the names and addresses for the invitees.

"It's sort of sadistic they make us double-check these," I say.

Rhodes nods, bringing over a black gel pen and setting it down in front of me. "Feels like a power move."

"But why? We're already at the bottom of the totem pole."

He shrugs. "Sometimes things like this serve as a reminder of that."

"Consider me reminded." I shake my head. "It's fine. We'll get through them."

"That's the spirit," Rhodes says. "Right, we'll have it all done in a pinch."

"In a pinch," I say, putting on an English accent.

He quirks a brow. "What was that?"

"That was me being British."

"I'm impressed."

"I was just joking around." I roll my eyes.

Fighting a grin, he nods. "No, no. Don't stop there. Go on, then. Give us some more."

"No, that was all you're getting."

"What if I do an American accent?" Rhodes asks. He holds up a finger, and with great Midwestern articulation says, "I'd love to visit a Five Guys in America."

Uh-mayr-icuh. It's so boldly pronounced.

I bark a laugh. "A Five Guys?"

"Yes," he says, continuing with an accent that has his mouth making the oddest shapes. "America is the birthplace of Five Guys. We have them in London, and they're delicious, but *the guys*—there are five of them—they're American."

I pinch the bridge of my nose, determined not to snort at his impression.

"Rhodes, I don't know what you think that is, but it's not quite an American accent."

He guffaws, deflating a bit as he turns back to pull something from a drawer. "It was an American accent. I'm not sure you've spent enough time in America if you don't know that."

"You're probably right." I sigh.

"Maybe you could show me around."

"Around America?"

He lifts his shoulders. "Sure."

"What? Like some Great American Road Trip?"

His eyes light up. "Is that a thing? Do you all just go driving around America?"

I shake my head. "Not exactly."

"Well, I've been to New York and LA. That's it. Oh, actually, I've been to Orlando. Obviously."

"Obviously? Why do you say it like that?"

Rhodes pulls a face, walking around to lean against the island beside me. "British people love Mickey Mouse, Milo."

"Is that so?"

"I'm fairly confident in saying this."

"Well, I don't know what else there is to show you. You've seen America."

He throws his head back as he laughs. "Well, I haven't seen the White House."

"That's true. I haven't either, to be fair."

Rhodes's lips part and he blinks. "You haven't been to the White House?"

"No. Rhodes, America is really big—"

"I know, mate," Rhodes says, reaching over and placing his hand on my shoulder. "I'm only messing with you."

His touch is alchemizing—like he's Midas and the only thing I want is to turn golden to match everything about Rhodes. Butterflies dance around in my stomach, and I'm not sure if they've been here the entire time, but they're uncontrollable now.

There's something brilliant about the color of his eyes—like a sparkling sea—that I've never seen in my entire life.

"What is it?" Rhodes asks.

"Hmm?"

"Why are you looking at me like that?" He pulls his hand back, lips forming a tight smile.

"I'm not looking at you like anything. Or any specific way, I mean."

He nods. "Okay, Milo."

"Okay, Rhodes."

Rhodes opens the refrigerator and pulls out a huge blue Ladurée box with silver etching along the sides that I instantly recognize.

"I don't know if these go well with wine," he says. "But help yourself if you'd like."

I open the box and take a lemon macaron. "You just have boxes of macarons in your fridge?"

"When in Paris," he says.

Studying the box, I lift a brow. "You haven't eaten any of these."

"Je prévoyais de les manger."

I know he said something like he intended to or meant to eat them, and as quickly as my brain will allow, I respond to ask when: *"Quand?"*

"Je ne sais pas."

"Quand les as-tu . . ." I glance off. How do I ask when he bought them? *"Achetés?"*

He grins. *"Je les ai fait livrer hier."*

Something about yesterday. I nod.

"They wouldn't last two days in my fridge," I say.

Rhodes furrows his brow. *"En français?"*

"I can't." I frown. "I don't know enough."

"Je savais que tu les mangerais. C'est pourquoi je les ai achetés pour toi."

I catch that last part, though.

That's why I bought them for you.

"For me?"

"Pour toi." He nods. "I mean, for us, I guess. After how they cheered you up after the Versailles event, I thought it'd be a nice gesture before the gala. But since you're already here."

My chest swells. Blood rushes to my face.

Rhodes was thinking of me and bought a box of macarons.

I swallow. "Rhodes. Why are you being *so* nice?"

Brandishing a knife and splaying out a salmon onto a cutting board, he chews on his bottom lip. "Dunno. Is it bad?"

"You got these macarons even thinking I'd switch those boxes and screw you over?"

Rhodes shrugs. "Look, I come from a very competitive family, Milo. I grew up in a very competitive world. If there's one thing I've learned, it's that you can't judge a person by one low moment."

"I guess that's . . . very mature." I say. "This is just not how things are supposed to go."

"They're just macarons," Rhodes says. "It's not a ring."

The very idea nearly makes me choke on the bite of pistachio I'm chewing.

"Look," Rhodes says, slicing the fish. "I'm not going to stop being nice to you just because we're competing for a job. I want it, and so do you, and I know that means . . ." He sucks his teeth. "I know at the end of all of this, one of us is going to be disappointed, but I still like spending time with you."

This brazen display of sensibility makes my eyes sting with warmth.

Why am I conditioned, though, to not take it at face value? Even when my entire being is practically swaying to the symphony of these nice words, and when I'm consumed with butterflies, I can't help but wonder if it's all some ploy so that he wins at the end.

"We had an agreement, though. We have to keep things professional."

"Getting my coworker some macarons isn't an HR violation. Or is that just something you expect from *guys like me*?"

I wince. "No, but . . . you're making us a salmon dinner and opening a nice bottle of wine."

"We have to eat," he says, shrugging. "And when in France, you should enjoy some nice wine."

This isn't in my head, though; I know it. I know there's *clearly* more to these nice gestures. Is he simply trying to change my mind? Or are my instincts right, and is he just a much more cunning competitor than me?

I work through the invitations and eat a few more macarons while he cooks.

When he's done, we eat salmon and asparagus and potatoes. He lights ivory candles on the table, insisting it gives a French ambiance, and we drink wine while we eat.

He tells me about his family traditions in this apartment—how they've done Christmas here twice, and how then this entire kitchen is draped in fresh garland and berries, and how they always come here during the summer for at least a week. He tells me about a time he shattered a cookie jar and tried to glue it together, which was unsurprisingly a failure. He tells me about Ollie's ex-girlfriend making out with an Irish rugby player in the very seat where I'm enjoying my salmon.

With each story and each sip of wine, as we laugh harder and catch each other stealing more glimpses, I know this is *not* professional at all.

After dinner is done, I scrub the plates and we get back to the invitations.

My phone buzzes, and I realize I've missed several notifications, but most recently a text from Sophie.

Sophie: Want to grab dinner?

Me: I just ate 😭

Sophie: No worries! I'm just hanging alone tn. You're welcome to come chill if you don't have plans

Me: Rhodes and I are actually working on some invitations right now

Sophie: Omg? It's getting kind of late

Sophie: Are you at the office? I can help if you want

Me: We're at his apartment

Me: He had the card stock here

Sophie: Oh, I see, I see

Sophie: So you and Rhodes are at his apartment

Sophie: After nine p.m.

It's already after nine? I swallow and focus on our thread.

Me: It just made more sense to finish them here than bring them back to the office

Sophie: Of course, of course

Sophie: 😉

Me: No, no, no

Me: Truly just working

I send her a photo of the invitations spread out on the counter.

Sophie: Avec du vin!

With wine.

I wince. This is not something I need spreading around the office. Sophie and I are friends, but I don't know if she'd tell anyone.

Me: We're only friends

Me: And we're actually almost finished with the invites, where are you staying? I'll come chill

"Let's knock the rest of these out," I say, pushing my glass of wine away on the counter. "I have to go, I totally forgot."

Rhodes blinks, shifting on his counter stool. "Oh. Okay, yeah. I mean, if you have to go, I can finish the rest."

"No, I'll help you."

"It's all right," Rhodes offers. "It was my task to begin with."

"You made me dinner," I say. "And got me macarons. I can help."

Rhodes shakes his head. "It's nothing. If you have plans . . ." Then he scratches the back of his neck. "What, um—if you don't mind me asking—where are you off to at half past nine?"

Oh.

I clear my throat. "I'm just going to hang out with Sophie."

"Oh," he says, exhaling as if relieved.

Did he think it was a date or something?

"Not that it's my business anyway," he adds.

I shrug awkwardly. "It's a fine question."

"Would she want to join us here?"

"I don't think . . ." Damn, I don't have a good response. "Well, we had this whole plan, that's all. I just totally blanked and lost track of time."

His Adam's apple bobs, and he blinks quickly, cheeks flashing a bit rosy before he turns his attention back to the invitations. "Totally understand. We'll finish these quickly, then."

Once we're done with the invitations, I thank him for everything, hurrying out with impressive speed. I'll do damage control with Sophie, ensuring she knows Rhodes and I are only coworkers and making sure she doesn't tell anyone else we were working late at his apartment—there's no way I want that spreading around the office and having some absurd story added to it.

Because it would be absurd. It'd be absurd for us to be anything but realistic about the fact that we're competing against each other.

No amount of macarons, unoaked wine, or lingering eye contact over a candlelit dinner changes that.

No quickening of my heartbeat, no tug in my stomach when he laughs.

Rhodes is the competition. He's the opposition.

So it would be absurd if my feet met the sidewalk and I found myself missing his company and wanting to turn around.

Chapitre Quinze

After nibbling on some leftover room service and watching a French reality dating show in Sophie's glamorous hotel room for a few hours, I head back to the apartment.

I kick off my shoes and take a long, hot shower.

I'd love to revel in what a fun night I had with my new friend Sophie, but my mind is stuck on Rhodes.

While I'm sitting in the couch on the dark, Celeste FaceTimes me, and I flick on a lamp and do my best to stay chipper, because I know she's going through something way harder than I am.

"Hi," she says.

"Hi. How are things? How is Gran?" I ask, lying on the sofa and holding the phone above my face.

Celeste shakes her head on the other end; she's wearing a light pink hoodie, her hair in a bun. Tears begin to spill down her face. "She passed away this morning. I just found out about an hour ago, and everything has been really intense."

I bolt up. "Oh my god, Celeste. I am so sorry."

She frowns, wiping at her face. "I don't know what to do. It feels like nothing is ever going to be the same. I just feel terrible."

"I can't believe this," I say. "I'm just so sorry."

Considering this isn't even my grandmother and I feel hollow and stunned, I can't imagine what Celeste is feeling right now.

"It happened so quickly," she says. "I mean, at Christmas everything was fine. I just don't understand."

I'm not sure what to say.

We sit there in silence for a bit as Celeste cries, and then she sniffs, wiping her nose on her sleeve. "My mom and Aunt Angela want me to go back to Paris."

I blink. "What?"

"Well, to visit you. They think it'll be good for me. But I just got back, and I don't know. It's a long flight both ways, and you're going to be really busy. I don't want to mess up the rest of your summer or anything, I'm sure now you're in a new routine and . . ." She sighs. "You're going to be really busy," she repeats.

"No way, I will make time for you. Are you kidding? Or if you want, I can come back to be with you. If that would help. I really would."

Celeste shakes her head. "You can't. Gran made me promise her that we'd all keep living our lives, and that we'd make her proud. She even specifically said to tell you that—I've been really worried about you over there all by yourself."

"You don't have to worry about me," I say. My chest was already tight this evening, but now it's almost unbearable. I let out a long, deep exhale. "I'm just so sorry, Celeste."

"Thank you," Celeste says. "We're having a service on Sunday. I don't think they want to put it off or drag it out, you know? Which I guess I understand. But my mom is really serious about sending me to Paris after that. I wonder if it's because she doesn't want me to see her mourn, but she swears she just wants me to go off and enjoy my summer. Like Gran would have wanted."

I nod. "I will do my best to be, like, the fun committee. Help you to take your mind off it a bit. I know this is so hard."

"It's crazy because I knew it was going to happen, but I kept getting my hopes up that it wouldn't or something," she says. "Which was stupid, I know."

"No, it wasn't stupid. I think that sounds really normal."

"Well then, I'll keep you updated on when they ship me back to Paris," Celeste says. "Sorry to put a damper on your night like this."

I wave her off. "You didn't. Don't worry about that. You need to take care of yourself."

She peers into the phone. "You're going to be the fun committee and you're spending your night alone in the apartment? Milo."

"I'm not!" I insist. "I just left from hanging out with Sophie—the girl from the New York office I mentioned."

"Good! And how is Maison Dauphine?"

It doesn't feel like the time to get into any of it.

"It's good."

"Oh no!" Celeste cries. "It's that bad?"

"No, it's good!"

"I know you, Milo. What's going on? Your Instagram stories seem like everything is going great."

I throw my head back. "Celeste, this is so not important right now."

"Distract me just a little," she presses. "Tell me what's going on."

"We don't have to talk about any of this now."

"I want to hear. You said you'd help me get my mind off things. You're living this grand Paris adventure and I know we talk, but I want to know every detail."

"I just don't want to bother you with all of this. I mean, we're talking about, like, fashion events. When you compare what you're dealing with . . ."

Celeste tilts her head. "Just tell me about the apprenticeship. Please."

So I tell her some of the details. About the Versailles gardens pop-up, the Tuileries event today, and a bit more about Sophie. She seems eager to hear it all, even though I think she must be in physical pain. I don't want to burden her with any of the details, but she keeps asking.

"I can't believe you cheated," she says. And then she's laughing. Actually belly laughing on the other end of the FaceTime call. I force laughter along with her, but I feel pretty empty inside, recounting all of this while I'm still shocked about Gran. "Wow, Milo. This guy has really gotten you worked up."

I only nod. "But we're just going to play fair from now on."

"Do you think he likes you?"

I stare at her. "What?"

"Well, he bought you macarons. And he's not getting you in trouble when you tried to majorly screw him over. I mean, he did ask you out when you first met. Maybe he has a real crush on you."

"Who's to say everything he's doing isn't part of some longer game? If he's Machiavellian, I'm falling for it all."

Celeste shrugs. "I want to meet him. When I'm back over there."

I chuckle. "All right. I'm sure that can happen."

We sit in silence again.

"Celeste, I love you. I know this is impossible right now, but you are going to be okay. I'm always here for you if you need anything."

She smiles. "I know that. And likewise. I know you think you can't talk to me about this stuff, but I'd rather you do. You're literally by yourself in another country."

"Sounds like that'll change soon."

"Yeah, maybe it really will be good for me. Right now, I don't even fully know how I'm feeling. I kind of just don't want to think about it, which sounds silly, but it's like it isn't *fully* real yet."

"I don't think it sounds silly."

"Thank you." Then: "And Milo? Can you promise me one thing?"

I nod. "Sure, whatever you want."

"Promise me you're not going to give up. You inspire me every single day, and I believe in you. So, play fair, but kick some ass. You're there for a reason."

"Thanks, Celeste."

"Promise?"

"I promise."

We say we love each other, and when we hang up, I set my phone on my chest and cry.

I cry because I'll miss Gran, and I cry because Celeste and her family are going through this terrible thing. I cry because there isn't really anything I can do to help. And then I cry because I'm just feeling everything all at once—loneliness, disappointment, embarrassment. And then there is an odd sense of shame for crying at all, because I shouldn't make any of this about me.

I consider calling my mom, but I know she'll be busy, so I get all the tears out until I fall asleep on the sofa, and for the first time, I don't wake up until my alarm goes off.

Chapitre Seize

When I wake up, the first thing I think about is Celeste. I think about how she must be feeling, and after I arrange for flowers to be delivered to her house, I think about the promise I made to her.

So, once again, I muster up all the motivation I have, and I get ready for another day at Maison Dauphine. This isn't going to be easy, but we're preparing for the gala at the Louvre on Friday, and it might be my last chance to stand out next to Rhodes. Currently, I am fresh out of ideas—I feel like a battery that has been completely zapped—but I'm hoping something will come to me.

I do my best to stay positive on my walk into the office, and I replay my promise to Celeste over and over.

I'm not going to give up.

When I get to Maison Dauphine, it's a happy surprise to find Sophie working in an office at the end of the hall by the fashion closet. I stop in the doorway, and she looks up from her computer before smiling.

"*Bonjour*, Milo."

"*Bonjour*," I say. I don't think it sounds half bad. "So, this gala. It's a big one."

She nods. "It is. Honestly, I think the Fête à Minuit might even be more important for the house than the shows in some ways. Maybe they can't actually be compared, but the historical significance of the Fête à Minuit is so major."

I take a deep breath. "Do you have any tips?"

"Tips?" She smiles. "What do you mean?"

"I don't know . . ." I rock back on my heels. "I want to make a good impression on Yvette. If there's anything extra I can do to make the gala even more perfect or something? I'm not sure."

Sophie nods. "Milo, you do know you've made an *amazing* impression on everyone?"

"Thank you," I say. Then, deciding to just lay it out there, I shrug. "I haven't made as good of an impression as Rhodes has. I know that."

"Oh, I see." She furrows her brow. "Well, I'm not sure if I'd worry about that. Rhodes is . . . Rhodes. You know? You're doing so, so great. It's not like it's a competition, anyway."

I shake my head. "But only one of us gets to work the resort show, and I really thought it'd be me. Because originally there was only one apprentice. But somehow Rhodes became one too, and now I think he's going to get to work the show. I mean, I know—it's not my place to act like he isn't earning it, but . . ."

Sophie is quiet for a moment, biting her lip and glancing around. "Milo, I'm not sure Rhodes has exactly earned anything."

"I thought the same thing," I offer. "But he's been doing a good job. And he does really care about Maison Dauphine. He wants this way more than I thought."

"I don't know if you should compare yourself to him, though.

I mean, everyone knows he got this apprenticeship because his mother made a call."

I feel a jolt of irritation, but I do my best to quickly cast it away. He only said his *father* didn't make a call, after all. I should have put two and two together. Anyway, all things considered, this isn't exactly surprising.

"And I'm not so sure he cares about Maison Dauphine," Sophie continues. "He took this apprenticeship because his mom made him. Apparently for some reason she was adamant about this over Louis Vuitton."

That doesn't sound like the same version of the story Rhodes told me. Though, thinking back, I don't know if he ever went into much detail.

"I don't know," I say, wanting to give him the benefit of the doubt. "He knows this means a lot to me, and I don't think he'd compete unless it meant a lot to him too. I think he really does care."

"He might care about what his mom thinks, but I don't know that he actually cares about Maison Dauphine or the resort show one way or another." Sophie frowns. "Look, just don't be too hard on yourself over this, that's all I'm saying."

"I just don't understand. He made it sound like he chose Maison Dauphine specifically."

Sophie bites her lip and lowers her voice to a whisper. "One of the PR girls over at Louis Vuitton said Rosie Hamilton was negotiating to void Rhodes's contract for a couple of weeks and Rhodes had no idea. Apparently, the day they were finalizing everything, Rhodes even sent an email asking why he had a new meeting invitation. He definitely didn't choose Maison Dauphine."

Then he lied? Why?

"I'm not trying to start something," Sophie insists. "I only want you to—"

I take a step back. "Thanks, Sophie."

"Milo—"

"It's okay! Don't worry. It's good for me to have some perspective."

And when I walk into the fashion closet, I am overcome with perspective.

Rhodes may like Maison Dauphine and fashion. He might be doing all this research and he might be putting in the hours, but does he actually even care about this at all? How can he act like he cares about me when he's just mercilessly competing for something he doesn't even really want?

And of course, now Rhodes wants to play fair and promises not to use his connections, but does that even matter? Is the damage not already done? Can we ever play fair when the playing field has truly never been level? His mother made this happen. It sounds like he didn't have to apply or even interview. Did he have any qualifications?

And anyway, how do you grow up in a competitive world from a competitive family and just lack the gene that vilifies the competition? Is that even humanly possible? In theory, he is conditioned to want to win against me at all costs, and what Sophie just told me only reinforces that. While I know Celeste means well, I think she might be wrong about him.

I've seen friendships end in betrayal as quick as a ball crosses a net—who's to say it's not possible he's just manipulating me?

I stop beside Rhodes's desk. "Why did you want this apprenticeship?"

Rhodes is scrolling on Instagram, and he looks up, dumbfounded by my question. "What?"

"I'm just curious."

"What is going on now?"

"You said you chose this over Louis Vuitton," I say. "And I've heard that isn't true. So, I'm just trying to piece this together. Why you're here."

"Oh, here we go again." He hangs his head. "I thought we were past all this."

I lift my shoulders. "I'm just curious what the truth is. Are you just doing this because your mom is making you? Because it's confusing to me why you say you need this so badly, yet it seems like it just fell into your lap."

"Like it didn't fall into yours?" Rhodes looks up at me. "You made an entry in response to a social media post, Milo. You didn't exactly cure a disease or solve one of the world's problems to get here."

"But I did earn it," I say. "I put in thought. And time. And effort. My submission won out of thousands. This is an actual, real, big thing to me, Rhodes."

"Which explains why you cheated?"

"Yes," I say, a tinge of desperation in my voice, pulling my chair out and taking a seat. "Yes, that *is* why. I've never done anything like that before, and I regret it so much, but I got carried away by how much this means to me."

Rhodes inhales sharply, setting his phone down in front of him. "What are you getting at here, Milo? Are you asking me to just give you the resort show? Because you want it more? Because *you're* not trying to prove a point at all—is that right?"

I prop my elbows up on my desk and bury my face in my hands.

The door swings open, and Yvette bursts in with garment bags draped over her arms. "Oh, boys, we have much to do before the Fête à Minuit. Here are your tuxedos."

She drops them onto our desks, and I stand up, grabbing the bag labeled for me and unzipping it. Inside, there is a gorgeous black tuxedo jacket with satin lapels, along with matching pants, a white button-down, and a bow tie the color of obsidian.

"Whoa."

Rhodes peers over at my tux and lifts a brow.

"They're custom to the measurements you gave Haydée, so hopefully they fit." Yvette taps her chin. "Now, listen, it is more important than ever that you boys really work together at this gala. Stick together. I know typically you each do your own thing, but this cannot happen, because we have to make sure the content across our platforms is cohesive and elevated. I would suggest one of you on Instagram and one of you on TikTok, but you can decide how you'd like to divide this. Do you have any questions about the gala? I'm sure you have gone over the binders many times by now."

I tilt my head. "Just a thought—you said we should stick together at the gala. Might it be better if we get different angles and content? For variety?"

Yvette gives me an odd look, like I've just said something inconceivable. "I don't believe so. We are looking for an especially unified approach across platforms for this event. We want it to feel as polished and intentional as possible. I want you two at each other's side the entire night. Attached at the hip, as you say." She says this to me, and it makes me question if this is actually just an American saying.

"We could just share content," I offer. "If that would be even more unified? Using the same video for Instagram that we post on TikTok?"

Yvette sometimes does this thing where her patience is depleted, and she brings her hands together in front of her stomach and then sighs a big, long sigh. She does this a lot with Haydée, I've noticed, but she's doing it right now to me.

"Is it too much to ask you boys to collaborate on creative, innovative ways to share this content? This is all you are required to do at the gala. If it's too difficult . . ."

"No, it isn't too difficult," I say. "We'll make sure the content is all creative and fresh, but polished and unified."

Rhodes nods. *"Absolument."*

Yvette narrows her eyes and leaves the fashion closet.

"I would like us to have one event without any drama, and to be done with all the arguing and animosity. My family will be there," Rhodes says.

"That's right," I say, remembering how he breezed past them when we verified the invitations. "Ollie will be there."

Rhodes turns back to his computer. He ignores the garment bag with his tux—probably not impressed, having worn custom designer tuxedos his entire life—and just starts typing into our sample loan spreadsheet.

"So? Can we just get along for one night?"

My face goes warm, and I feel like a child being reprimanded. "Yes."

"Okay, good. I really am making an effort here. I honestly don't know what else I can say." Rhodes sighs. "I thought we'd sorted everything out between us. Remember? May the best man win?"

I can tell my expression is less than polite by the way his eyes tighten. "I'm just wondering if the best man actually will win."

"You have to let this go," Rhodes says, exasperated. "I mean honestly, don't you find it all a bit exhausting?"

And there is the condescension. There is the "I'm actually much too important and self-assured to be nearly as impacted by this as you are."

"Rhodes, I am in Paris. I am here for one thing, and one thing only. To start my career."

"Well, to be fair, I have wondered myself—why did *you* want this apprenticeship? Why aren't you going for Wimbledon?"

I blink. "What?"

"Why didn't you pursue tennis?"

"I was never going to pursue tennis," I say. With what I've learned, I think he of all people should understand that loving a sport doesn't mean you want to make it your entire life.

"You just played for fun?"

I stare at him.

"Because you don't seem like somebody who'd spend all that time on something just for fun, that's all. I don't even mean that in a bad way."

Something about his constantly friendly tone is so grating in these moments.

"Well, you hardly know me, to be fair," I say.

"That isn't entirely true. Has something changed since last night?" Rhodes huffs. "Have I done or said something I'm not aware of? I don't get what's happening here."

I sigh. "I just don't know what to think about you, Rhodes. And if I'm being honest, it kind of makes me feel like I'm losing my mind. I want to believe all the things you say, but I feel like the moment I do, it won't end well for me."

"And I fully understand that, but I'm trying to tell you, I'm not some big bad enemy." He frowns. "In any other circumstances, I'd actually be on your team, believe it or not."

Against my more competitive instinct, I exhale.

"Okay. No drama."

"Who knows, we might even have *fun*." Rhodes smiles.

As I'm getting ready for bed, I get a text from Celeste.

Celeste: Okay, we're getting there next Friday since you have the gala this week

Me: Yay! I submitted a request to have that day off at MD

Who is "we"?

Me: Is Aunt Angela coming?

Celeste: Nope, just me and your mom

Me: My mom?

Me: Wait what?

She types and then stops. Types and then stops. Finally:

Celeste: Shit. I think it was supposed to be a surprise. It's all making more sense now

Me: My mom is coming to Paris?

Celeste: You have to pretend to be surprised!

I can't believe this. No wonder my mom hasn't been reaching out very much—she's probably worried she'll spoil the surprise.

I'm so excited I can hardly stand it. I'm *humming* as I get ready for bed.

My mom is coming to visit me in Paris, I feel pretty good about how things are with Rhodes at the moment, and I get to experience the Fête à Minuit gala.

Everything is finally looking up.

Chapitre Dix-Sept

I once told Celeste I was worried that in all my obsessive research and social media scrolling related to Paris, I might have spoiled too much of the Louvre. I might have seen it all, I'd said.

I was an idiot.

The Louvre is *massive*. It's unlike any museum I've ever been to.

My mom loves *The Da Vinci Code*, so I've always thought that the huge metal-and-glass pyramid outside was beyond cool. Especially when it was lit up at night. But the scale of it was something I somehow didn't expect. It's major, and it honestly looks even cooler when taken in the full context of the grand palace that wraps around it. I already sent the family group chat a selfie of me in my tuxedo with the pyramid behind me.

Paris is amazing, and it just keeps getting better.

Everything about the museum is incredible, and though the sun is only beginning to set, the Louvre has closed two hours early. I am fairly certain the only reason they were able to shut it down like this is because of some of the more high-profile guests. Seeing it empty feels like an immense gift, and one I try to savor as much as I can.

The guest list is expansive. Diplomats, rock stars, painters, magazine editors, actors and actresses, the most famous athletes, and at least three *Time* people of the year. French *Vogue* is involved somehow, though I'm not entirely sure if it's just that they promote or sponsor or how it all works. Either way, it will be wild to just walk around getting content and experiencing such a huge event.

This is going to be a dream come true.

Of course, there is the fact that I'm standing next to Rhodes, who is zooming in on his phone and squinting like an old man.

"Right, so we need to get a few establishing shots. Those are just clips we can use to—"

"I know what establishing shots are," I say. "It's sort of self-explanatory."

He chuckles. "Of course. All right, I think we should just get some shots of iconic painting halls. The main portion of the gala is here in the Cour Marly." He pinches the interactive map on his screen and points it toward me. "We could quickly run up here, to the Grande Galerie, and get some of those shots and maybe you can get some IG stories that tease the night ahead as we make our way back to the courtyard."

His plan is fine, it's just slightly annoying that he's running the show. I realize, of course, that this is incredibly petty.

No drama.

"There's one thing I want to see," I say. "Especially with nobody around." Then: "I can use it for content too."

He doesn't say anything, just lifts his chin slightly as if considering this, before giving the smallest nod and starting to walk.

Quick footsteps echo loudly in the empty lobby, and Rhodes's twin brother, Ollie, is rushing toward us in a tuxedo, with a brunette girl in a chartreuse silk slip dress.

Ollie Hamilton, holy shit. I mean, I know Rhodes already, and so his famous footballer twin brother shouldn't make me feel starstruck in any way, but I'm caught by surprise and find myself nervous like I'm queued up for a meet-and-greet and I might say the wrong thing.

Bizarre.

"Ole buddy boy!"

"Ollie?" Rhodes cries. There's a bit of a crack in his voice, and I can tell he's not wholly thrilled by this surprise. When Ollie pulls him in for a bear hug—one that's a bit aggressive in my opinion, considering how expensive and well fitted these jackets are—Rhodes laughs. "How did you get in?"

Pulling away and making a face, Ollie clicks his teeth against his tongue. "You're not part of the welcoming committee for this gala, I hope."

"It's just that you're two hours early."

"Right, why isn't the Fête à Minuit at midnight?" He waves off the question before I can answer him, sliding his arm around his date's waist, pulling her closer. "Mum and Dad are back at the hotel, but I thought I'd like to show Phoebe a private tour of the Louvre."

"Did you?" Rhodes holds his hand out. "Pleased to meet you, Phoebe."

Pleased to meet you?

It sounds awfully formal, and for some reason just not what I'd expect from Rhodes when meeting his twin brother's girlfriend. Or date.

"Wait, Mum and Dad are at a hotel?" Rhodes asks. "I thought they'd be staying at the flat. I just had it cleaned."

Ollie shakes his head. "They're in and out. Didn't they tell you?"

Rhodes pokes his tongue in his cheek. "No, they didn't."

My chest burns. I recognize that look anywhere. I can feel that look in my bones. It's the feeling of looking out at a crowd of parents at a match and realizing your mom is nowhere to be found.

I study Rhodes and Ollie as they stand beside each other. Where Rhodes has wavy blond hair with a middle part, Ollie has a shaved head. They've got the exact same aquamarine eyes, the same full lips, and the same square jaw with a defined chin. Both tall, both have an athletic build with muscular thighs, large hands and feet. It's a miracle for one person to be blessed with such good looks, but it's mind-boggling for two.

"And is this your . . . ?" Ollie gestures toward me.

Rhodes and I exchange quick glances.

"No!"

"God, no!"

"Right," Ollie laughs, now offering his hand to shake. "I'm Ollie Hamilton."

"Milo," I say. "Milo Hawthorne."

Ollie grins. "Ooh, that's got a nice ring. Very well, Milo. And all of us have got surnames that begin with H."

"Mine is Hack," Phoebe says with big eyes and a wide smile.

"Fancy that?" Rhodes says. "Well, it's good to—"

"Do you work for Maison Dauphine, Milo?" Ollie asks. Phoebe seems intrigued by this, her emerald-green eyes boring into my soul.

I nod. "Well, I'm an apprentice. Same as Rhodes."

"That's fantastic," Ollie says. "I hope you've been looking after my baby brother. He sometimes needs extra supervision."

Rhodes shakes his head and, not to me, but to Phoebe, says: "He always acts like he's so much older. We're talking *minutes*."

"And all the wiser for it, I reckon." Ollie laughs. He turns his attention back to me. "I remember you now, I think. You're the American with the social media campaign. Brilliant. How do you like France? Is it a culture shock? I love America, but I bet it's tough to adapt."

I shrug. "It's a little tough. Mostly just because I'm here all by myself."

Phoebe's eyes bug and she frowns a big, dramatic frown. "How sad."

"Sad indeed." Ollie seems personally affronted. "Has my baby brother not been keeping you company outside of Maison Dauphine as well, then?"

"I wish you'd quit with the baby-brother thing," Rhodes says, going red.

Ollie ignores him. "Because he's all by himself, as well. He just sulks around the flat, as I understand it. Isn't that right?"

I turn to Rhodes. I didn't quite form a full picture in my mind of Rhodes's life in Paris, but I did expect it to be glamorous and social and exciting. I imagined he had parties in that giant apartment, and now imagining him there alone all the time kind of makes my heart sink.

He shakes his head though, forcing a laugh. "Ollie, have you been drinking?"

"Not yet." Ollie echoes his brother's laughter. "You two ought to come up to London sometime if you're both bored. Come see a match!"

Something he's said has struck a nerve with Rhodes. He immediately stiffens and his jaw clenches.

"They're a lot of fun," Phoebe says to me coolly. "They have Dom in the box."

Rhodes remains quiet and Ollie looks perplexed. "You really ought to, I think it'd be nice. You haven't been in ages." He looks to me. "Rhodes came to my academy matches a bit, but he's been too busy lately. Now that he's going to have a career in fashion, I suppose football is less intriguing. Though don't let him fool you, he loved it as much as I did once."

"Ollie."

"What? It's the truth." He waves him off. "Just because you—"

"Ollie." Rhodes is sterner now, and Phoebe seems shocked at the shift in tone. "Milo and I have got to get some work done. We'll see you round the gala, yeah?"

Taken aback, Ollie nods. "Right. Yeah, we'll see you round the gala. I'm sure Mum and Dad will text you once they're here. You know Dad'll want a family photo. Even if you're a waiter or whatever." When Rhodes doesn't laugh, Ollie rolls his eyes and shoves him in the shoulder. "I'm only joking, mate. Relax. Mum and Dad are proud you've got a job now."

"Sure thing," Rhodes says. He looks to Phoebe. "Lovely meeting you, enjoy your private tour."

Phoebe smiles. "I will. Lovely meeting you. And you as well, Milo Hawthorne."

"You too, Phoebe Hack."

She seems to love this, bursting into giggles as she and Ollie rush away.

Rhodes and I stand there in silence for a brief moment, and I instinctively look down at the ground, kicking together the toes of the patent leather shoes. He takes a deep breath and pulls his phone out of his jacket pocket, recalibrating the map and mumbling to himself about the route we're going to take to get our content quickly.

I consider if I should say anything at all, but I can tell he's upset. I opt for levity, thinking it may not be my place to get too specific:

"That was . . ." I say with a chuckle that might sound too forced.

"That was . . . ?" Rhodes snips.

"Oh, I don't know. It seemed like you were tense with Ollie."

Rhodes shoots me a look. "What are you on about, Milo?"

"Sorry?" I bite my lip. "I thought maybe Ollie was picking on you a bit."

"I don't know what you're talking about," he says. "We just mess around. We're brothers. You've got that Circus clown of a brother, you should know."

"Don't talk about him like that, you don't know him."

"Fine. Okay, whatever. To the Grande Galerie we go."

Chapitre Dix-Huit

It doesn't take us long to get some impressive shots—the Louvre, it seems, is impressive by nature, and even more breathtaking when there aren't crowds in the frame. It gives full command to the art and the architecture, each detail coming alive. We get photos and videos of halls with arched ceilings and maroon marble columns, and corridors with gilded detailing. Many of the paintings are so massive they take up their own wall.

I'm working on an event teaser, so I get close-up black-and-white shots of ornate flourishes and unique aspects of the buildings' designs.

Rhodes and I aren't really speaking, which makes this a bit more tense than it needs to be, but I know he's still defensive over whatever that was with Ollie. I'm not sure if it's just that he has a complex about his brother being a famous footballer, or if their personalities are just those of teasing boys who never grew out of it. The problem I have with that theory is how one-sided it seemed back there.

The longer we spend in silence—though I am annoyed about his Clyde Circus comment—the more I feel a bit sorry for him.

This is the Rhodes effect, I'm sure of it. How am I here, in the tranquility of the Musée du Louvre in absolute quiet stillness, feeling sorry for Rhodes Hamilton? At every turn, he's insisted I don't know him, and I don't understand, but the facts are still the facts. He's still mega wealthy and famous, even if less than Ollie, and he still got this apprenticeship because his *mum* called and took care of it for him. By any standard, I think he should be doing just fine.

Which makes me feel more like shit. I guess, deep down, I know all those things aren't going to amount to happiness. I'd imagine they make life easier, definitely, but I wonder what it's like to actually *be* Rhodes.

I didn't, for instance, realize Rhodes was spending his evenings alone as well. I wonder, if we had gotten off to a better start at Maison Dauphine and become friends, what that could have looked like. Maybe we would have each had a bit more fun in Paris this entire time.

It's pointless to imagine, but we're not speaking, so my mind wanders until he claps his hands together and the sound is so sharp, the echo so loud, I nearly jump out of my skin.

"That's a wrap," Rhodes says. "Well, until we get to the Cour Marly, anyway. What was it you wanted to see?"

"Oh, let me see."

I pull up the map and find what I'm looking for quickly. I think it might be one of the more famous pieces of art at the Louvre, but that could just be my interpretation.

Pointing to our right, I start walking, and Rhodes follows.

"You're not going to tell me?"

"You'll see."

We walk back through the halls and head down a level when we get to the massive grand stone staircase with the *Winged Victory of Samothrace* statue on its landing. We pass a few more exhibits, and Rhodes asks a couple more times where we're going, before we end up in a large room of red marble at the end of the Galerie des Antiques.

Alone, in the center of the room to pronounce its distinction, the *Venus de Milo*'s stark ivory contrasts against the dark stone she stands on and the rustic carnelian blend of marble surrounding her.

"The *Venus de Milo*." Rhodes chuckles. "Of course."

"I just wanted to see it," I say, getting as close as I can. "To see her."

She is magnificent, and I can see why she is so famous. It's amazing to imagine this was once only a block of stone. It's amazing to conceptualize Alexandros of Antioch chipping away, no blueprint or DIY tutorial, the figure emerging from the marble born purely from his imagination.

I remember reading that because the statue's arms had broken off, and typically the Greek goddesses could be identified by the items they held, there were difficulties with identifying her. In fact, some might argue she is Amphitrite, the sea goddess of Melos, while some will insist she is Aphrodite, the goddess of beauty.

"What do you think?"

"She's stunning," I say.

Rhodes stands next to me and knocks his shoulder into mine, glancing down. "Did you want to see her because she's got *Milo* in her name?"

I nod. "Ever since I was a little kid, I thought it was the coolest thing. I don't know. Milo isn't *that* common of a name. It's not as unusual as Rhodes, but."

He barks a laugh that bounces off the marble throughout the empty room. "Touché."

"Rhodes Barley Hamilton."

"Done some googling?"

"Like, what does *Barley* have to do with anything?"

He fakes offense, putting his hand on his heart. "It was a family name. I suppose it means my great-grandparents were farmers or something. Something to do with barley."

"Probably older than your great-grandparents," I offer.

"You're just going to make fun of my name? Just like that? What's *your* middle name, then?"

"I'm not telling," I say. "And you're right, sorry. I was only kidding around, but—"

He laughs again. "It's okay. It's a stupid-sounding name. Rhodes Barley Hamilton. How absurd. As usual, Ollie got the better end of the stick." Our eyes meet and he quickly glances away, like he's said too much. "Anyway, do you want a photo with her?"

There are these moments where Rhodes temporarily wipes my memory of our ups and downs, and when he holds his hand out to take my phone and proceeds to art direct me so that I get a good photo, that's one of those moments. He makes me laugh, and it's like we're old pals.

"I think you're going to need some peace signs," Rhodes says.

I lift a brow. "I don't think she would want me to throw up a peace sign."

"She would too. She's probably bored of the same old thing all the time."

Rolling my eyes, I take a few sillier photos as he calls out ideas, and then when he hands me my phone, we both seem to recognize that we're getting along again. I'm struck by the electric blue of his eyes like lightning. It's brand-new every time, like that day on the sidewalk all over.

It's so quiet, I can hear him swallow.

"We should get over to the Cour Marly," Rhodes says, voice a bit gravelly. He runs his hand through his hair and looks around. "I'm . . . I think it's that way."

I nod and follow him through the museum, winding through exhibits I wish we could stop and marvel at, until we get to the giant courtyard where the gala is being held.

The Cour Marly is incredible. I imagine, when filled with daylight from the glass ceilings, that all the ficus trees and white stone architecture create a sense of calm unlike any other. Large equestrian statues are stately without feeling too extravagant. Sculptures of gods and goddesses are the main focal points—I instantly recognize Daphne being chased by Apollo, and Neptune with his trident.

Round white-linen-dressed tables have been added between the sculptures, with centerpieces made of tall branches and stems of green. The wooden chairs surrounding each table look antique, though they are actually brand-new and very expensive, per the presentation we went through with Haydée and Zoe. Dim uplighting casts a warm ambient glow over the room, along with the pillar candles surrounding the foliage on each table.

People wearing all black are scurrying around like chickens with their heads cut off. Some carry iPads, some are talking into headsets or walkies, and some are transporting brown cardboard boxes. The energy and stress are palpable. We're about an hour out from when people start showing up on the midnight carpet outside, so it's go time.

Haydée rushes over to us, wearing a sparkling black off-the-shoulder cocktail gown. "Have you got everything you need? I must attend to the guests soon, so I will not be available to you."

"Where are the tripods?" Rhodes asks.

Her marked annoyance hits me like a brick wall, and I shake my head quickly. "I'm sure we can find them."

"They are in one of the closets," she says. "Please, you do not have the tripods yet? Do you boys both understand the importance of the Fête à Minuit? This is not a garden party or *malbouffe* stand, we need to be . . . how would you say . . . steps ahead. Do you understand?"

Rhodes glances over at me and sighs. "We'll find the tripods."

"Quickly. *Allons-y!*"

We wander around but we don't find any unlocked closets.

"Maybe we could ask someone else," I offer. "I think Haydée is just stressed."

"Or maybe we don't need tripods," Rhodes says. "I mean, these iPhones have stabilization built in."

We've wandered pretty far from the Cour Marly now, but it's quiet and I can think, so focusing on the time, I start posting some of the teasers to the Maison Dauphine Instagram Story. We normally have to use a third-party scheduler—since it's clearly not the most secure option to just give the password to two apprentices—but tonight Haydée has logged into the accounts on our phones.

The official Maison Dauphine account has over fifty million

followers, and I do think Haydée should probably be approving our content regardless of the rush, but tonight she's told us to just use our better judgment because she doesn't have time. She also provided the not-at-all-terrifying warning that there will be consequences for any mistakes, so to say I'm nervous posting is an understatement.

The first of the teaser stories is a super zoomed-in shot of a clock with arms set to midnight, in black-and-white and with a slight grain that gives it an older, cinematic feeling. The rest follow suit—just small, clever details from the Louvre.

I double- and triple-check everything. It's all fine. It's elegant, on-brand, and it's just what fans of the house or followers of the Fête à Minuit will be glued to their phones hoping to see until the red carpet looks start rolling out all over social media.

I go to post the last one as Rhodes yanks me by the arm, pulling me down a hallway with him.

"What the—"

He shushes me, and as footsteps approach, Ollie, Phoebe, and a docent walk past us.

"Rhodes."

"Milo. Don't."

There's some issue with the Instagram Story upload, but it prompts me to retry, so I tap it and watch as it finishes posting before pocketing my phone.

"Why are you hiding from your brother?"

"I'm not."

I throw my arms up, gesturing around the dimly lit hall. "We are literally hiding."

Rhodes sighs. "It's just complicated. I don't want to get into all of it."

He takes a few steps away before leaning his back against the stone wall, hanging his head and shoving his hands into his pockets. I can tell he's genuinely overwhelmed, so I am slow to move closer, but I do.

"I don't mind."

When he looks up at me, he looks more pained than I've ever seen him.

"It's a bit of a cliché, I'm afraid," Rhodes says, gaze falling again.

"Well, that doesn't matter." I kick my toe into the stone next to him. "Look, maybe I was wrong. I don't know . . . we're kind of in the same boat here in some ways. All alone here in Paris. On our own. After the way I've treated you, you probably hate me, but—"

Rhodes's head jerks up, and he furrows his brow. "I don't hate you."

The sincerity in his voice gives me goose bumps. "Well, I just haven't exactly given you the benefit of the doubt, so I'd understand. Honestly, most people in our situation probably *would* hate each other."

"Do you hate me?"

"Well, no. I don't *hate* you."

"That's quite convincing."

I throw my hands up. "Things have felt complicated, to say the least. You can't act surprised that I don't exactly think of us as friends."

He shrugs. "I suppose you're right. I dunno, I just would like us to be. I've tried to make that clear. Tried to prove I'm not here to screw you over, Milo. It's honestly got nothing to do with you."

I believe him, though I'm not sure why.

"But then . . . what *is* it about? I mean . . . why is this so important to you?"

Rhodes points down the hall. "You saw Ollie. You heard him. Can't you piece it all together by now? I'm only Ollie Hamilton's brother. And I suppose, out loud, that doesn't sound so terrible. I can see that. But you don't know what it's like, especially when my father only ever wanted us to be footballers like him. Ollie has gone and done it, and I've failed at everything I've ever tried."

"Surely that isn't true."

"You want to know the truth?" Rhodes asks. "I didn't even make it into the academy with Ollie. Not even with my father's influence. He even offered to buy my way into the club. How pathetic is that? I know my problems aren't the worst to have, but I feel it every day. . . ." He makes a fist. "I feel like nothing. All the time. I just feel like nothing."

My heart aches at this.

How can this boy—this boy threaded gold and blue, so bright and charismatic—feel like nothing?

"You're not nothing."

"I appreciate that," he says. "But I've disappointed my father my entire life. Maison Dauphine just . . . It's my last chance to actually do something for myself. Make a name. Ollie's career is about to absolutely blow up, and by the time it does, if I don't have something to show . . . I don't know. It's complicated, I guess. Family dynamics and all that."

I know a thing or two about family dynamics, but this sounds next level. On a scale I can't even imagine.

When I don't say anything, he frowns. "I know you've got your reasons. But I've got mine as well. It's like every time I see an Instagram post or get a Premier League app notification about Ollie, I just get this reminder—this feeling like I've got to win. Otherwise, I'm stuck being Ollie Hamilton's brother."

That need-to-win feeling is one I know very well.

"I don't *want* to compete with you," he says. "I wish we could just both win."

Desperation rises within me. "Maybe there's some way we can?"

He shakes his head. "I've already asked Yvette. I tried twice now. She said there's one position. That's it. And it sounds like whoever works the resort show will have the advantage when all is said and done. Since Pascal and the whole team will be there. One of us will be at the show, and the other will have to man the desk and watch press hits all night. Haydée and Zoe will be staffed, and if I'm honest, I think I did more harm than good. It seems like my asking only irritated her—like maybe now she'd keep it that way to spite us. It makes no sense. You'd think they'd want the extra help."

My breathing slows as the gravity of this dawns on me.

"You asked Yvette?"

He winces. "I know. I'm sorry."

"No, I didn't mean it like that." I don't even know how to express the sense of appreciation I feel in this moment. "It's just . . . I didn't realize you'd asked her."

"I really do want us both to win," he says.

"That's really nice of you to ask Yvette," I say. "I mean, I'm with you. I don't get why it's so impossible. It's almost like they want us to compete. Like they think we'll give them better ideas if we're both vying for something."

Rhodes shrugs. "You could be on to something for all I know."

"À bon chat, bon rat."

With a quizzical expression: "*Pardon*?"

"It's better for them if we compete, I think. The rat challenges the cat and vice versa."

He snorts. "And who's who?"

"I fear I might be the rat."

"No way."

I roll my eyes and shrug. "I might be. But seriously. You shouldn't feel like you're nothing, Rhodes. You're really clever, you know."

He smirks. "That's true, isn't it?"

"And you're funny. Sometimes."

Rhodes scratches his chin. "There's no way you ever find me funny."

"Why would you say that?"

"Have we ever actually had a laugh together?"

I think we may have had a laugh together at his family flat. Anything else would be having a chuckle together—and even that could be a stretch.

"We did both laugh in that staff meeting—the one where Haydée made you pronounce French words in front of everyone."

I roll my eyes, stifling a smile. "You laughed *at* me, that's different."

"You laughed as well! From where I was sat, I was laughing with you."

"Of course I had to laugh it off, I sounded like the world's biggest doofus."

Rhodes' eyes go wide. "Whoa, *doofus.*"

"Yeah, doofus. Me, trying to speak French. You'd think I'd have improved by now."

"I think you're improving," Rhodes offers. "You know, Milo, nobody can ever say you don't put effort into things. Even if something seems impossible, I reckon you're going to try."

Full-on smiling like an idiot now, I can't pretend I'm not enchanted by the way his eyes twinkle when they meet mine.

"I can't believe you thought I hated you."

"I thought it was entirely possible. I wasn't the best."

"I feel like it was pretty clear. I did ask you to dinner the first time we met. That isn't exactly what you do with people you hate."

"Well, sure. But we didn't follow through on that. Things change."

Rhodes considers this. "Things certainly change."

Maybe Celeste was right all along. He did try to hang out with me several times. And he did get me macarons.

"Did you want to follow through on that?" I ask.

There's a moment of shared quiet. I study him—his posture, the way he turns toward me, and his gaze that falls to my mouth—and I wonder what he's thinking right now. I wonder if I've spent all this time misreading him.

I guess now I'm going to find out.

My phone will not stop buzzing in my pocket, so I fish it out. I'll silence whatever this is quickly.

Celeste: LMAO at you on the Maison Dauphine IG story

Celeste: who approved this

Celeste: I'm crying!

What is she talking about?

My stomach immediately drops as I navigate to Instagram. There are way more notifications than usual, even for Maison Dauphine. Our latest story seems to be getting a ton of reactions and replies and—

Oh my god.

It's a photo of me in my tuxedo, holding up a peace sign in front of the *Venus de Milo*.

On Maison Dauphine's Instagram Story.

Chapitre Dix-Neuf

This is like that nightmare where you show up to school naked, but a million times worse. My stomach plummets so fast I could literally be sick all over the floor of the Louvre right now, though I quickly become aware that would make this entire situation that much more humiliating, so I fight a gag.

How did I make such a stupid mistake? Now thousands of people have seen this photo of an intern making a peace sign in front of the *Venus de Milo*—there is no way anyone would think it's anything other than a mistake, given how off-brand and unprofessional it is.

"That's . . . that can't be."

"What is it?" Rhodes asks.

I'm deleting the story as he looks over at the screen.

He exhales. "Shit . . ."

"Shit is right, Rhodes." My voice cracks and I shake my head. "This is terrible. Yvette might kill me. Or even worse, they might fire me. I'm going to be sent back to Florida on the first flight they can book."

Gaze unfocused and wandering, Rhodes reaches for the back of his neck. "How did this—"

"I don't know, there was this error screen on the last story I posted, and I just pushed it through, I didn't triple-check that one."

My heart is beating a thousand miles per minute. I simultaneously feel like my skin is on fire, scorching hot, and like I am submerged in ice, prickly frostbite turning me blue. I feel clammy and like I can't inhale enough—if my lungs are balloons, they're leaking, deflated, with no chance of holding any air. My usual breathing exercise doesn't work.

"I can't breathe."

Rhodes grabs my shoulder. "Hey, it'll be fine."

I shake my head, panic setting in. I'm consumed by a fear that if I can't catch my breath soon I'll suffocate. "No, I really mean it—I can't breathe."

"Okay, it's okay." Rhodes takes my other shoulder and looks around. His eyes finally land on mine. "Milo, you're okay. You're all right."

Tears well in my eyes. I can't swallow, can't focus. Everything is going hazy.

"Hey, hey." Rhodes says, his face blanching. "Has this ever happened before?"

I nod, tears spilling down my face. It feels like I'm drowning. Like the room is becoming exponentially smaller each time I desperately attempt to inhale and still draw in no breath.

"When?"

"Semifinal," I wheeze.

Rhodes's eyes bug, as if he's beginning to understand, but I can't read much more of his expression as everything becomes blurrier and blurrier.

"How did you come out of it?" He squeezes my shoulders.

I only give a weak shrug.

I'm convinced there's no way my chest can withstand this much longer. I'm more than just lightheaded, I'm beginning to feel tingling in my lips and cheeks.

He draws in a deep breath. "I know you must have figured it out before the match, because there's no way you'd let this stop you, Milo."

I nod quickly.

"You did, huh? You figured it out before your match?"

I nod. "I had to play."

"That's right. And you got through this back then. Because you . . ."

"Because I had to *play*," I repeat. "I don't have that now. I just—"

"You have the gala," Rhodes offers.

I sob.

"Shit, okay. Not helpful. Right, okay . . . so then look. Here's the thing, Milo. My father was actually a bit of a head case, did you know?" Rhodes smiles. "He'd absolutely crush practices or matches that were a given, but if they weren't favored, he'd clam up. Fuck the whole thing up, really. All in his head."

I try to swallow, though my mouth is too dry. "Is this supposed to be helpful?"

"Well, I haven't gotten to the helpful bit yet, I was just trying to help you relate a bit."

"By calling me a head case and implying this whole thing is in my head?"

Rhodes grins. "Exactly. Well, no, not the head case part. Sorry. I just meant he would get really anxious. You're not a head case. Fuck."

"Great. So far, off to a great start."

"The point is, he'd just go absolutely mad. Honestly, he even threw up on the sidelines once. Was in the paper."

I nod. "I would love if we could get to the motivational part."

"One of his coaches taught him how to cope at Armoury, during his academy days. Basically, he had this technique, which is called Everything's Shit."

I groan. "Rhodes, I literally can't breathe and this—"

"No, really. Listen. You can approach fear of failure any number of ways, but this one always seemed to work for him. I mean, look at his career; worked well enough, didn't it?" He places his palms together. "You just have to ask yourself, 'What is the worst thing that's going to happen?' and you work your way down that spiral until you get to the very end, and then you realize everything's shit, but it's actually not as bad as you think."

I blink.

"Are you fucking with me?"

He shakes his head quickly, holding up his palms. "No, I swear. This will help you get to a place of believing everything is going to be fine. Because at the end of the day, it always is."

I imagine how this might be appealing for one of the most famous living athletes and his family, but it sounds like a way to spiral down a rabbit hole of worst-case scenarios until this panic attack finally does me in for good.

"I don't think Everything's Shit is for me."

"Everything's Shit is for everyone." He squeezes my wrists. "So, go on. Do it. Everything's shit. What's your worst-case scenario?"

My whole face feels numb at this point and I'm struggling to even focus on what he's saying, but I do my best.

"I'd have to go back to Citrus Harbor and tell everyone I failed and be humiliated."

Rhodes nods. "Right. Would your life be over?"

"Yes."

"Would it actually?"

"No. I guess it wouldn't."

"What could you do?"

"I could find something else," I say. "Go to college and figure something else out."

"Right, because you're eighteen. And you're already doing so well for yourself. You *would* be okay. Better than okay, I bet."

Somehow, as if by some miraculous breakthrough, I believe him. It truly must be magic. I don't know if any one person has ever made me feel so instantly calm, as if a wave washed over me and brought back feeling to my nerves and cleared my vision. This belief Rhodes has in me is enough to make me believe in myself again.

I draw in the biggest breath I possibly can, holding it for a moment before exhaling. I repeat this a few times, and it feels like I'm emerging from ice. It feels like I'm being brought back to life.

"Look," Rhodes says. "Even if everything's shit, you're going to figure it out, Milo. You made it here in the first place."

"Thank you, Rhodes." I wipe the tears from my face.

He goes to speak, but his eyes widen at something behind me. When I turn around, I see it's Yvette. She's storming over, black ball gown twisting with each step.

"What are you two doing down here?"

Rhodes steps forward. "We were taking photos and—"

She holds up her phone, and I have to blink several times, because it's not adding up—I deleted the story.

"Milo, what is this?"

"It was a mistake, but I deleted it."

"This is a screenshot, Haydée has already taken it down. I can only assume this was a very careless mistake, but it is one that is going to cost you nonetheless. Do you have any idea how many people have already seen this? We are trying to think of how we can possibly address this should we start receiving inquiries. If stakeholders and shareholders find out our apprentices are abusing access to our marketing channels this way—"

Rhodes takes a step forward. "That wasn't Milo's fault. It was mine."

Yvette and I both look to him.

"What?" she asks.

He nods. "I took that photo, and I should have paid attention to what I was uploading, but I was going too quickly."

Yvette narrows her eyes. "You posted it?"

"I wasn't being careful. It was so stupid. I'm so sorry."

We both know the consequences for Rhodes will be minimal, but I can't believe he's doing this.

"Well."

Yvette's eyes wander the empty hall. "We will discuss this on Monday. For now, I suggest you both get back to creating content. And from now on, Haydée and Zoe will approve every post before it goes out."

"It won't happen again," I offer.

Rhodes nods. "Really. My apologies."

Yvette walks away, and my stomach is in knots.

When the coast is clear, I want to sink into the ground.

"Rhodes, thank you. But why did you do that?"

He just shrugs. "Honestly, I'm not too worried about it."

"But that's kind of a huge mistake," I say. "I made a mockery of—"

"You didn't make a mockery of anything," Rhodes says. "You were in an expensive tuxedo at the Louvre, this wasn't a scandalous photo or something."

My stomach lurches at that. "I just can't believe you took the blame. You didn't have to do that."

He takes a step forward. "I know. But nothing will happen to me." He lifts his shoulders and smirks. "Nepo baby perks."

"I should have never said that."

"Perhaps not, but perhaps you're right after all. We both know Yvette will just tell me to be more careful."

I exhale. It's a long, deep breath. In fact, it isn't enough. So, I take a deep breath in through my nose for four seconds, hold it for four seconds, and then exhale through my mouth for four seconds.

"Dad taught us that one too," Rhodes says. He cocks his head. "You're always so tense."

"I know." I inhale and hold it. After I've let the breath out, I shrug. "I think it's a personality trait, at this point. I'm never calm. And it's, like, the most annoying thing. Sometimes I just—"

Rhodes blinks. "Sometimes you what?"

"I don't know. A lot of things. But, anyway, thank you. I can't ever tell you how much I appreciate you doing that. I think my time at Maison Dauphine might have been up, even."

He clicks his tongue against his teeth. "Nah. Doubt they'd sack you like that. But now we don't have to worry about it. I'm glad to help. I'd like to keep you around, after all."

"You would?"

Rhodes takes a step closer. "Milo, you are one funny guy."

"Why do you say that?"

Before I get an answer, he lifts his hand to my chin and leans down, his mouth finding mine. My eyes fall shut, my body goes still, and then our lips melt into each other with ease. His other hand finds the small of my back and he pulls me in close as I take his face in one palm and rest my other on his chest. The kiss is slow and tender and so perfect like it's just been waiting for us to discover it.

This kiss belongs here, in the Louvre.

We break apart and he rests his forehead against mine, those blue eyes magic.

My heart swells and there is a delicate tension, like a golden string between us I don't want to test. I stand still, his heartbeat steady against my palm, and he nuzzles his face into the other, kissing my skin and then raising his brows.

"Was that okay?" he asks, though he knows the answer, which is oftentimes Rhodes's way.

"More than okay." Then I blush. "I mean, it was really good."

He grins, licks his lips, and leans in again.

As we kiss, I know this changes everything, but I'm swept up in the romance of this city.

Chapitre Vingt

I've been absolutely giddy since Rhodes and I kissed.

The rest of the gala was honestly uneventful compared to the kiss. I almost met Rhodes's parents, but they were in and out quickly, I think really just to get their photo taken. He didn't seem too upset by it, but Ollie and Phoebe ditched pretty early as well.

I suppose it's a good thing nothing of note happened—everything went according to plan, and we made great content that got approved and posted. Nobody at the gala seemed to recognize me from the photo, which gave me peace of mind that maybe it didn't blow up to be some large-scale issue.

After the gala, Rhodes had to dash away to go meet his family, and he kissed me again outside the Louvre. It felt like a fairy tale.

Rhodes Hamilton was kissing me. I was kissing Rhodes Hamilton. Under the stars in Paris.

He's had a busier Saturday than me already, having a brunch with the Hamiltons before they are off to London—a brunch that was heavily photographed, which I know since Celeste has already forwarded me an Instagram post from two different American tabloids.

Rhodes: You free by chance?

I glance down at my ratty plaid pajama bottoms, and then around me at the takeout containers and the various cords I have connected to charge my phone and laptop and AirPods. It looks like I am practically plugged into this couch, with *Gilmore Girls* playing on the screen. Lorelai's absurdly fast talking has been a nice reminder of home somehow. It's season three, and I've seen it a million times, but somehow I've spent hours here already, gripped like this is my first viewing, and drowning in coffee.

Me: I am free!

I've sent the text, but I retroactively study what I've written.

Exclamation point? A bit eager, Milo.

Groaning, I lock my phone. I don't want to sit here and wait for the little gray bubble with the three dots. I don't want to acknowledge the fact that texting with Rhodes gives me a delightful if not nearly nauseating stirring in my stomach.

Rhodes: Brilliant

I stare at the preview of the text on my lock screen. I stare, and I wait. Because surely he's going to say something else, right? What kind of line of questioning is this? How is it only brilliant that I'm free? Why isn't he saying anything else?! He must have a reason for—

Rhodes: Let's hang out

Rhodes: We had brunch in the 6th, would you want to come meet me around here? I have a couple of hours to myself before we've got some fitting for Ollie

Rhodes: Have you explored much over this way?

It's silly, but there's something oddly comforting about him so unabashedly texting me like this. In my previous experience, texting guys can be like pulling teeth. A simple, short response to a message can feel like a rare gem sometimes, even when they *are* interested.

Me: I haven't been over there too much, so I think that would be fun!

Jesus Christ with the exclamation points, Milo.

Rhodes doesn't respond for about ten minutes, but it's fine because I'm up and cleaning my mess before jumping into the shower.

I throw clothes around the room in search of the perfect "casual stroll through the 6th Arrondissement with a guy I just kissed" outfit. It should be put together but effortless. Flattering but casual. Parisian but still me. Whatever that means.

Rhodes drops me a pin, and after consulting two maps apps, I figure the best course of action is to walk back to the Pont de l'Alma station and take the train to Saint-Michel Notre-Dame. I've gotten pretty good at the New York subway after trips with my mom for apparel-buying conferences and other boutique-related trips, and it turns out the Paris Metro isn't that much different once you figure out the start and end points and the colors of the lines.

As I ascend the steps, I realize I've been sweating profusely on the entire train ride, which is mortifying, but luckily I decided on a green button-down that's so green it's almost black in certain lighting. I shouldn't even be nervous. Maybe, in fact, I'm not?

Maybe this is . . . excitement?

Rhodes is standing on the sidewalk, scrolling on his phone. When I reach street level, it's like he senses I've arrived, and I think his face might light up as he spots me.

"There he is!" He rushes over and pulls me in for a quick hug, which is new for us. He's stepping back just as quickly, studying my face as if trying to judge how touchy he should be at this point. "My brave metropolitan traveler. I'm impressed you're so savvy, Milo."

His brave metropolitan traveler. I hope I'm not blushing, and my face is already probably flushed from working myself up over this exact moment.

"It's honestly not that hard. My mom and I learned the subway, and it's kind of similar." I say, gesturing over my shoulder toward the station. Then, like a little kid, beaming, I can hardly contain my excitement. "Oh my god, I didn't tell you. You'll get to meet my mom!"

Rhodes grins. "Oh?"

"Yeah, she's coming to visit. It's a surprise, so I'm not supposed to know. But she'll be here. In Paris!"

"That's awesome, Milo. I'm glad you guys will get some quality time together. And not work related!"

"I know," I say. My cheeks are actually sore from smiling so much. "I'm so excited."

Rhodes nods. "I'm looking forward to meeting her."

"It'll be great. So how was brunch?"

"It was nice," Rhodes says. Then he rolls his eyes and shrugs. "What am I saying? It was annoying." He nods. "It was really annoying."

Rhodes starts to walk away, and I follow.

"What? That's it? No additional details?"

"Well, if you were a fly on the wall, you'd have no idea they were all here in Paris for the Maison Dauphine gala."

"I'm sure they were mostly here to see you."

With his brows pressed together, Rhodes's lips form a tight line. "You'd think they were here to tell me all about Ollie's footie career. As if my being away for a few weeks has rendered me completely unaware and out of the loop. As if I don't know literally everything he's doing at all times."

I sigh. "I'm sorry."

"That's okay." He shakes out his shoulders. "Let's not talk about that. Let's talk about . . . anything else." Then he points across the street. "Have you been to Shakespeare and Company?"

I shake my head, eyeing the small green shopfront. "I haven't."

"I really like it," Rhodes offers.

"Oh yeah?"

Then he chuckles. "Sure. When I fancy a stroll through the stacks, I'll pretend I know how to read for a bit. It's nice."

Laughing, I stand beside him as we wait to cross. "You might even enjoy the shop if you actually learn how to read."

"Why would I do that? Who needs to know how to read?"

"That's a good point," I agree. "It's probably much more fun to just guess what the books are about based on the vibes."

Rhodes nods. "Some of them have pictures inside."

"You're ridiculous."

"Come on, we'll go have a look. It really is a nice little bookstore. It's a tourist trap, to be sure, but I think you'll like it. You do strike me as the type to love the smell of old books."

I roll my eyes.

"No?"

"I may or may not have an old-book-scented candle."

"Whoa, I'm good."

When we get to the store, there are a few people queued up outside. It seems they're limiting the number of guests in the shop at a time. I half expect Rhodes to seek or get some kind of special treatment—do famous people stand in line?—but he doesn't. We go to the back of the line and wait until it's our turn to go in. As we wait, I admire how everything is vintage and riddled with character—the painting of Shakespeare above the door, the writing in chalk on panes, the mismatched wooden benches, and the sign that reads ANTIQUARIAN BOOKS, which seems like an objet d'art itself.

Once we're inside, the shop is as charming as I'd expect, with old wood everywhere and hanging ivy. Mosaic tiles and signs with antique lettering—one seems to lead to a room called the Blue Oyster Tearoom, and some others are in French, which I should probably be able to understand by now. As far as the smell of old books goes, it blows any candle out of the water; it's as if the magic of the pages wafts through the air.

Rhodes leads me through the crowded rooms, past tufted seating and whimsically uneven stacks of books on every possible surface. His finger trails along some of the spines.

"I do love the *idea* of reading," he says with a smile that gets a few odd looks from customers around us.

Then he starts up some crimson stairs that creak a bit, with an ascending inspirational quote hand-painted on the risers. He wanders away, and I find myself at the top of the stairs looking at myself in a big mirror surrounded by wood detailing, almost like it's part of something, like a bench or stall that has been repurposed.

I snap a quick mirror selfie—I am still a tourist in Paris, after all—and I try to make it quick and unnoticeable, but Rhodes rushes over, slinging his arm around my shoulders and offering a big, cheesy grin.

We get a few together, and then he gestures toward my phone. "Send me those, yeah?"

"I'm sure they're—"

"I'm sure they're cute." He lifts his brows and then leads me into another room, beneath another hand-painted quote. This one is about not being inhospitable to strangers in case they're angels in disguise, and it's the absolute cheesiest thought I've had, but as I watch Rhodes turn around—with his gorgeous blue eyes and flowy blond hair—to make sure I'm following, I think I might get that quote the most of any in this store.

It's a cheesy enough thought that I both cringe at my own brain and blush, shaking it off and hurrying to join him in the next room of books.

This room is the first we've had to ourselves, and he gestures around.

"Do you like it?"

There are a few verdant plants in the corners of the room, which also has exposed rafters, a built-in bench lined with pillows beneath one of the walls of bookshelves, and a desk with a typewriter in front of a window. The colors are all inviting, and a mirror on the wall seems to bounce the light and warmth all around.

"It's . . . charming."

His smile widens. "Yeah? I agree. Ollie hates it. And so does Freddie." Then: "He's my best mate."

I'm very vaguely familiar with the existence of Freddie from social media, but this is the first time Rhodes has ever mentioned him to me. It seems like a big step for some reason, which may be silly, but we haven't discussed much about him outside of his family now that I think about it, even in all the stories he shared when he made me dinner.

"Is he back in London?"

Rhodes furrows his brow, turning to one of the bookshelves. "Mmm, no. What's it, now? June . . . he's on holiday, that's for sure. Mykonos, maybe."

"Oh, of course."

He laughs. "What does that mean?"

I shake my head. "No, nothing."

"Tell me!"

"It's just that we come from different worlds, that's all. I don't have friends who go on holiday to Mykonos. I'm still getting used to these kinds of things being casual phrases."

Rhodes nods. "Well, to be fair, going on holiday within Europe is a bit easier than from the States. But I see what you mean overall. Freddie's big into travel, actually. He just doesn't quite like hanging around old bookstores."

"Well, it's a nice chance for some alone time, then."

He shifts to face me, lowering his gaze and bringing his hand to my chin. "Or time with a cute boy."

Then he kisses me, and when our lips meet, it's got to be a better feeling than any kisses written within any of these pages. I'm lost in all of it—his palm on my cheek, our noses brushing, his teeth tugging gently at my bottom lip. With his other hand on my waist, he pulls me in, until we hear the stairs creaking behind us and break apart.

We fight laughter, pretending to look through the books, and I hold my hands down around waist level to hide anything potentially embarrassing.

"So." I clear my throat. "How did you and Freddie become friends?"

Rhodes pulls a face. "Thinking about Freddie during that kiss?"

"No!" I knock him lightly in the chest. "I just like getting to know you."

"Sure," he says. "Freddie and I met at an Armoury match, big surprise. The beginning and end of life itself seems to be Armoury United."

Grabbing a dusty brown leather book off the shelf, he flicks through the pages.

"We were in the box—I think Ollie was playing with Under-14s at the time, and whenever his schedule allowed for it, we were going to basically all of the professional Armoury matches. Freddie's dad is a financial something-or-other in London . . . to this day I actually still couldn't tell you."

He closes the book and hands it to me, but when I pay it no attention, he smirks and continues.

"Right, they were in the box with us, and Freddie was just playing bloody *GTA* on the telly. Dad's box has all the amenities, really."

"*GTA* is . . ."

"*Grand Theft Auto.*"

"Right, that's what I thought."

Rhodes holds his palm out to take the book back, and then he shelves it. "We haven't played it since we were fifteen or so, to be fair, but I can assure you it is good fun. Yeah, I guess that's the story, really. I sat with Freddie and we took turns playing."

I nod. "Did Ollie play with you as well?"

Shaking his head, Rhodes eyes another book. "No."

Before I can ask anything else, he's off to another shelf, lifting his finger to the wood.

"Should we buy a book?" Rhodes scrunches up his face. "Maybe not. I have this terrible habit of buying books and not reading them."

"Oh yeah?"

He hangs his head. "I love the prospect of it—a new book, a new experience or world or educational opportunity. I'll find a book, and I'll have this sort of grand idea of how it'll be so nice to escape into it. Set the scene, something cozy like those reading TikToks. But I never do it. Literally just never do. My attention span is too short."

I fold my arms. "I'm sure your attention span is long enough to read a book."

"Afraid not, Milo."

"When was the last time you read a book?"

He grimaces. "I did almost finish a book about the fashion industry before starting the apprenticeship. It's a fictionalized account of Renard Florin and his contemporaries—like Chanel, Dior, and Givenchy. It was interesting to fact-check and see what was really happening in Paris and in fashion during the time period, though the fictionalized drama was a bit over-the-top for me. Bit indulgent, and the language was way too flowery."

"I haven't even heard of a book like that."

I'm impressed by Rhodes yet again. For his dedication and also for his critical analysis. I don't think I've ever had such a strong opinion on writing. Maybe if it was something I got graded on, but even then, I haven't found myself to be particularly sensitive to the style of prose.

He's surprising, yet again.

"I might have finished it if it were a bit better."

"Fair enough."

"I have actually read Pascal's book front to back," he offers. "Before I found out about this apprenticeship or anything. When it first came out. I know it's a coffee table book, but, like I've said before, he's a real talent."

My eyes widen. "I've read it front to back too."

"Have you?"

I nod. "My best friend, Celeste, said she'd never heard of someone actually reading a coffee table book."

"People are missing out," he says. "They're as utilitarian as they are decorative."

We laugh.

"You really do love Maison Dauphine," I say. "I'm sorry I ever questioned you. Wasn't really fair of me."

He waves me off. "No worries. I think, in context, your assumptions were all sort of fair. But I'm glad it sounds like I'm proving them wrong."

"Definitely."

Rhodes kisses me again. He sneaks a kiss every chance he gets, in each room of this little whimsical bookstore. With every kiss, I find myself wanting more. No amount of him seems to be enough. He locks his fingers into mine for little moments when nobody is around, and the last time, when they break apart, he looks down at me, very seriously.

"I'm not hiding you or keeping you a secret," he says. "It's just that these things tend to blow up pretty quickly once someone snaps a photo or something. And since we are still working together . . ."

I bob my head up and down quickly. "Of course, you don't have to explain."

As if on cue, someone asks Rhodes for a photo.

Once we're back outside, someone else asks him for one. They hand me their phone and I snap the perfect shot with a gorgeous Parisian backdrop.

It's nice to be in his orbit, really.

When we're alone again, Rhodes brushes some hair from his forehead and then catches me smiling at him like a lovesick puppy. "What is it?"

"Nothing." I blush.

"Right." He puts one hand in his pocket as we walk across the street into a park. Then he points across the way, past a fountain and people sitting on stone steps and benches, toward a tree with a massive leaning trunk, beside what appears to be a church. "You know, that's the oldest tree in Paris."

"Wow. You seem to know so many interesting things."

"You sound surprised," he says, clutching his chest. We approach the tree, and it's sweet the way he seems to revere it, softened eyes set on the greenery. "I reckon I just love this city. I wish I knew everything about it, really."

Studying the grooves and edges of the tree, I tilt my head. "Do you love Paris more than London?"

Rhodes blows a raspberry. "Oh, definitely. I don't know. It's my escape. Having a twin is the best thing in the world, but sometimes it's nice to have something that just feels like it belongs to me, I guess. Ollie's never cared for Paris the same way, and it's always felt like mine." Then he kicks his toe into the dirt. "Does that even make any sense? Probably sounds really silly, doesn't it?"

I knock my shoulder into his. "Not at all."

"I'm so glad to be here this summer," he says, shutting his eyes and taking a deep breath. Then he turns to me. "I'm glad you're here too. And, look, I know this new *thing* between us . . . I know it doesn't change the circumstances. We both want the job. But I'm hoping we can separate it. I'm really hoping we can."

"One of us is going to win and one of us is going to lose."

Rhodes lifts his shoulders. "We can figure it out together."

"Sure. I hope that's true." I shake off the dread that comes along with those thoughts, desperate to get back to the way I felt kissing him in the bookstore. "Come on, I want at least five more interesting facts about Paris before you have to go."

He tosses his head back laughing. "Okay, Milo, now be careful what you wish for."

Celeste: WELL??

Celeste: HOW DID IT GO

Me: the apartment speakers might currently be playing Today Was A Fairytale

Me: (Taylor's Version)

Celeste: FUCK YES

Chapitre Vingt-et-Un

Rhodes: Did you see Sophie's gala post?

Rhodes: She is living her best life

Rhodes: #SophieInParis

Me: Be nice!

Rhodes: Ain't hating

Rhodes: I love it

Rhodes: What are you doing?

Me: Cleaning a little

Rhodes: Oh yeah?

Me: Yeah, my friend is coming back to Paris on Friday

Rhodes: That's exciting

Rhodes: Celeste, right?

Me: Yeah. She's the blonde on my wallpaper collage

Rhodes: Ah right. Nice. Hope to meet her.

Rhodes: Fancy dinner tonight?

Me: You will. She'll love that

Me: And yeah, that'd be nice

Rhodes: Brilliant

Rhodes: Do you want to go to a restaurant? Or I could have them make something for us at mine? While it is hard to beat my cooking, it's still good lmao

Me: You have a personal chef?

Rhodes: Well, not exactly.

Rhodes: Kind of, yes. Lol

Me: Let's go somewhere

Rhodes: You're right, it is our first date

Me: Exactement

Rhodes: Tu es si doué pour parler français.

Me: Oui.

Rhodes: Haha I'll text you in a bit, have fun cleaning

Me: It'll be the most fun I've had in Paris, I think

Celeste keeps insisting I don't need to do anything to clean, but I seem to have had a minor slip into some not-so-great mental health territory over the past couple of weeks. All alone, and mostly petrified by anxiety, the dishes have begun to stack in the sink, the laundry is a blur of chaos, and all my products in the bathroom or bedroom have lost any sense of organization.

I tell myself this is okay, but it does happen somewhat regularly. It's like I become so transfixed with anxious thoughts or spirals, I either forget to take care of smaller, routine things, or I just outright choose to neglect them.

This spell has been made particularly worse by loneliness and sleepless nights.

After the gala, however, I was able to really, truly rest. It took a while for me to actually fall asleep, going over the night—every word Rhodes said, the way his mouth looked redder after we'd been kissing for a while, and the way his eyes were both wild and sweet—but once I did, I was out like a light with no restlessness or waking in the middle of the night.

I clean the apartment while listening to music, and it doesn't take as long as I'd expected at all.

Like a schoolboy with a crush, I check my phone every five seconds to see if Rhodes has texted me. We've been talking pretty much nonstop since we each left the gala, and we were going to see each other yesterday, but he was busy with his parents and Ollie. Now they're all gone, and I'm practically buzzing because I am so excited to see him and kiss him again.

This is absurd.

This is an emotional response.

But this is Paris.

And this is Rhodes.

He texts in the early afternoon with some dinner ideas, and we pick a restaurant in the 2nd Arrondissement. He says we can probably go on a nice walk after if I'm up for it, which I definitely am.

While I'm getting ready, my mom calls. This must be *the* call. She's finally going to let me in on her little surprise.

"Milo?"

"Bonjour, Mère!"

"Sounds like you're in a good mood."

I smile. "It's the magic of Paris."

Soon you'll be here too!

"So you're completely fine?"

"I'm fine. Why wouldn't I be?"

She's quiet for a moment. "Well, I know you sometimes get a bit anxious, and I don't know what exactly happened, but I do know there was some debacle with a photo of you on the Maison Dauphine Instagram?"

I swallow the newly formed knot in my throat. "No, it's all fine. It wasn't a big deal."

Cue criticism.

"You've got to be more careful, Milo. You're just starting your career. Once something is on the internet, it's there forever."

I nod, even though she can't see me. "I know."

"And I saw a photo of you and Rhodes on *WWD*. If I didn't know better, I'd say you two looked *very* friendly."

"We're friendly," I say. "We're going to dinner."

"Just take it slow," she says. Ever the pragmatist. "It can get messy to mix business and pleasure."

I'm so happy you're happy, Milo. And I know you can make good decisions. Would that be so hard?

I want to groan, but I don't. "I'm being smart, Mom."

"Good."

Mom hums. "Did you meet Liam Hamilton at the gala? Was he handsome? Tall? Does he look the same in photos as in real life?"

I laugh. "I didn't meet him. I did see him, very briefly, and I'd say he looks the same. Definitely tall."

"Amazing. Well, I've got to run."

Oh, come on. I want her to let the cat out of the bag already. It would be nice to start coming up with a little itinerary together.

"Big week?" I ask.

"Of course," she says. "We're partnering with Kate Kensington for a huge local launch event next weekend."

Next weekend? As in the weekend she's supposed to be here?

"Oh. Next weekend? You're going to be there for it?"

"I will be. You know I need to make sure it all goes perfectly."

"My boss at Maison Dauphine says she hires good people, so she lets them do their jobs." I say it like it's a joke, and we both laugh. But I wish she'd consider the possibility that she could miss the event. "No, of course, I understand."

A familiar feeling of disappointment washes over me.

I swallow, and my eyes begin to sting.

This is way worse than her missing a match or a parent teacher conference. I'm across the ocean, all alone, and I guess it was stupid of me, but I thought maybe that'd be enough. Maybe she'd prioritize me. At the very least, maybe she'd prioritize a trip to Paris.

She sighs. "Celeste told you, didn't she?"

I wipe away my tears and try to sound like I'm not upset. "She did, but it's okay. It's a big event."

"If I could be there, I would be. I wanted to. And this is why I didn't say anything—I didn't want to get your hopes up."

"My hopes weren't up, it's okay." I even force a laugh. "It's a Kate Kensington launch, I get it. Huge."

"Thank you for understanding," she says. I almost roll my eyes. "And I will just say, there is still a surprise arriving in Paris with Celeste."

My mouth falls open. "A surprise? What kind of a surprise?"

"You'll just have to wait and see. Now I really have to run. I love you."

"I love you too."

When we hang up, I realize she mentioned the surprise to distract me from the disappointment. It's sort of working, because what kind of surprise could Celeste be bringing me?

There isn't any time to think it over now, but I'm sure I will start to obsessively go over all the possibilities as soon as I get home tonight.

I feel like an idiot for thinking my mother was going to come visit me in Paris, and I feel like even more of an idiot for still feeling so sad even after all the other times this has happened.

At least I've got tonight with Rhodes.

After I've showered and gotten dressed—in a nice button-down with slim green trousers and brown shoes—I get a text from Rhodes that he's almost here.

We've already kissed, and we already know each other, but this still feels so monumental and special. This is our first date. For all I know, I'll be getting to know an entirely new side of Rhodes. Even our texts since Friday night have been so warm and different and exciting. We didn't stop speaking Saturday from the moment we woke up until I fell asleep.

Rhodes: Je suis arrivé!

I head down to the street, where he's leaning against a cherry-red vintage Porsche convertible, arms folded with a big grin beneath his mirrored sunglasses. He's wearing a similar outfit to me, only his shirt is ivory and striped, and his pants are a blue-gray. He looks so cool with his windswept hair and confident smile.

My jaw drops, and he pushes himself off the car, gesturing toward it. "What do you think?"

"This is probably the coolest car I've ever seen," I say. "It looks like it's from a movie."

He nods. "It's my dad's. A 1960 Porsche 356."

"Are you allowed to—"

"Of course." He laughs.

Rhodes takes a few steps onto the sidewalk and takes me in his arms. He smells fresh and woodsy, a scent that isn't too strong, but still pronounced. I'm not sure what it is, or how this happened so incredibly quickly, but I feel a sense of safety when he's holding me like this—his arms around me, hands on my back, my cheek against his chest, and his chin on the top of my head. I could stay like this forever, which seems silly because I'm not someone who cares for hugs in general. But this doesn't feel like it's just a hug; it feels like a silent promise.

Rhodes moves back just a little, pulling one hand around to graze my jaw, lifting my mouth to meet his. His tongue parts my lips, and I instinctively follow his lead. When we've kissed for a moment, he opens his eyes, glancing down at me. "What?"

Rhodes laughs when I lift my shoulders. "You're smiling *so* big."

"I am."

"Just a massive smile." He kisses me again, and then he walks back to the car and opens the passenger door. *"Monsieur."*

I get in, and he closes the door before he gets in on the driver side and cranks the engine.

"Allons-y, Milo."

It's like a dream, Rhodes's profile against the blurry streets of Paris in this car that's too cool to even be real. How is this my life right now?

When we roll to a stop, he turns to me. "Did you get everything ready for Celeste?"

I nod. "Yeah. I talked to my mom a bit ago. It turns out she can't make it after all, but she did say Celeste is bringing me a surprise."

"She can't make it?" Rhodes frowns. "I'm sorry, Milo."

Shrugging, I watch his hand grip the wheel. He presses on the gas. "It's fine. I should have known better than to get excited."

"Still, that's shitty," he says. "Do you want to talk about it?"

I shake my head. "It's fine. Par for the course."

"All right. Well, at least you've got Celeste. And a surprise on the way?"

"True. I'm not huge on surprises. As a general rule. But I guess I'll do my best to focus on that."

"You? Not big on surprises?" He sticks his tongue out, laughing. "Could have guessed that, mate."

I knock him lightly on the arm. "It's kind of the anxiety, I guess. It doesn't exactly lend to appreciating the element of surprise. I think it's the unknown."

Rhodes nods. "I completely understand."

"Do you?"

"Yeah, I don't get anxious the way you do, but I definitely have had moments." He raps his fingers against the top of the wheel, as if thinking whether he should go further. "Sometimes, when I used to play football, I'd make myself crazy. Work myself up so bad, I'd nearly be sick. I suppose that's what you go through? Maybe?"

I nod. "Yeah. It's a nightmare, because it's sort of all the time. And I have 'coping mechanisms' "—I use air quotes—"but they're all much harder in practice."

"I think you're doing well," Rhodes offers. "From my perspective, anyhow. You are in another country—on another continent, even—all by yourself, which I reckon is really difficult. But you're doing just fine, Milo. Doing just fine."

"Thanks," I say. "So that's partly why you're so into the Everything's Shit exercise, then? From football?'

Rhodes sticks out his bottom lip. "Hmm. Yeah, I think that's probably how I became most keen on it. It actually does help me a lot, though. In general."

We valet the car, and I follow Rhodes into a restaurant that also feels like it must be out of a movie. Brass-paneled mirrors line the walls, and there are palms and sculptures and giant oil paintings. The whole place basks under the warm glow of lanterns and candlelight, and a pianist in the middle of the restaurant sets the tone—a low, hushed whisper respects the music, doesn't compete with it.

We're guided back to a little booth with some extra privacy, and I can't ignore the way heads turn as we walk. I'm with Rhodes Hamilton, after all, and I wonder how he feels about being seen with *me* like this. Not that I'm worried about my looks or appearance, exactly, but I'm not *someone*. I'm not a model or an actor or an athlete.

I slide into the U-shaped black-leather-tufted booth, and he sits diagonal from me. The square table is covered in a thick, buttery white tablecloth. Small candles are placed in the middle, and they make Rhodes's eyes flicker.

"How do you feel about splitting a bottle of wine?" he asks.

"That sounds nice," I say.

Even with more privacy, I can feel people slowly turning to look at us. I might be imagining it, but I think there are whispers and nods.

Rhodes must catch on. "What is it? Do you want to sit somewhere else? I could see if they've got anyone in one of the private rooms if you'd prefer. I know it can be a bit much. I'm sorry, I didn't really consider that it might be a lot for you."

I shake my head. "No, it's totally okay. Just new."

"If it's any consolation, you do get used to it." He draws in a breath and takes his napkin off the table, unfolding it and then smoothing it over his lap. "And they'll all get tired of looking at us. I'm not sure why people find it so terribly interesting to just look at other people."

"Well, you're Rhodes Hamilton."

He furrows his brow and gives me a very serious look. "And you're Milo Hawthorne."

"Yeah, they don't know who I am."

"They will," he says.

"Can't wait to see what they'll say."

"What's that supposed to mean?"

Searching for the right way to phrase this so that my insecurities around this don't come off as too unattractive, I study the melted wax pooling in the ivory candles. "I'm just not what anyone would expect. I'm not a model or famous or—"

"Don't be silly, Milo." He takes my hand. "Who cares about fame? You're incredibly smart. You're loyal. You're so driven—you rival Ollie for the most driven person I know, which is really saying something. And . . ."

"And?"

He squeezes my hand. "I think you bring out the best in me."

My chest warms.

"And anyway, you're fit enough to be a model."

I laugh.

"Right, so I think we should do a nice white wine. It's summer. But we could easily do a red if you prefer."

I shrug. "I'm pretty new to the wine game, remember?"

"Course," he says. "I think this is quite a lot of responsibility, then. Picking out the wine. But it's a responsibility I will eagerly take on."

Rhodes orders us a bottle of Ladoucette Pouilly-Fumé, which doesn't exactly mean a whole lot to me when I watch him drag his finger across it on the wine list and effortlessly pronounce it to our waiter.

"It's from the Loire Valley," he tells me. "Pouilly-Fumé is one of the regions."

"Impressive."

"Learned some things from Ollie," Rhodes says. "I think I mentioned he's a wine snob. At his flat in London, he has this entire wine cellar . . . er, well, I'm not sure if that's what it's called—it's not like the one at our flat here, it's all modern and it's like a big glass closet. It's a whole thing. Don't ever ask him about wine, Milo. Not unless you're really interested in getting a lesson."

Their relationship as siblings, particularly as twins, is so interesting to me.

"Do you and Ollie get along? I know there are some things that make it complicated, but in general?"

The waiter brings over the bottle, uncorks it, and pours a small amount into Rhodes's glass. Rhodes swirls it, brings it to his nose, and then takes a tiny sip. He offers an expression of general approval, then the waiter pours some into both glasses.

"Merci."

We clink our glasses together and I take a sip. It's drier than any wine I've had so far, but I like that, I think. It's light, and it tastes a bit like grapefruit and maybe some other citrus.

Rhodes sets his glass down. "Okay, what were you asking? Right. Do Ollie and I get along? Of course. We're twins. We spent our whole lives as best mates. I think with Ollie, things are just a bit complicated. He's got a chip on his shoulder for some reason, and I know what you're thinking—I do too. But Ollie's is different. I mean, I'll put in effort, and I'll give something my all. Really. I'm driven enough."

He stares off, eyes narrowing a bit. "Ollie is . . . relentless."

"How so?"

"He'll do anything if it means he won't fail. For instance, when we were lads, I'd say we had the same level of talent when it came to football. Or rather, the same lack of talent."

We both laugh at that.

"Honestly, though, it's true. Except where I did my best—did all the trainings and drills and everything Dad wanted—Ollie became absolutely obsessed. Ollie figured if he didn't have the same talent as Dad, he'd train until it seemed like he did. It was his whole life, 24/7. Lived and breathed football. And I obviously can't say it didn't work for him. I mean, he's going to crush his career as a footballer."

"And you don't think there's still a chance for you? You're still young."

"Mate, there are players who are seventeen years old." He barks a laugh. "I haven't been on a pitch in ages. My chance has come and gone. I've come to peace with it, honestly, but I just need to find my way now. Anyway, it's a bit exhausting having all the media paint me as some bumbling idiot compared to my dad and brother. Not that they matter much, don't get me wrong. But it would be nice to shut them up."

I nod. "I can imagine."

"And what about you? You really just played tennis for fun?"

"Oh, this again." I force a chuckle, sipping my wine.

He nods. "Yeah. I just don't know if I buy it."

"And why not?"

"Well, it's like I said. You don't strike me as somebody who's going to play tennis just for fun. It's a competitive sport. You're competitive. Bit like Ollie in the way you are so determined. So I guess that doesn't add up for me. Obviously, I could be completely wrong, but I'm curious."

I shrug. "You don't even know if I'm any good."

"Again, I don't imagine you'd play if you weren't."

How has he got my number so precisely? Am I *that* predictable, or does he pay that much attention?

Taking a deep breath, I fidget with the corner of the tablecloth.

I hate talking about this, and normally I wouldn't, but it seems Rhodes might be one of the few people to understand.

"My mom used to come to my tennis matches," I say. "In the beginning, it was great, but eventually she was too busy, so she only came to the big ones. Championships, pretty much. And it worked well that way, in retrospect, because it motivated me—if I didn't make it to the championships, she wouldn't see me play. So I really pushed myself. Worked as hard as I possibly could."

Rhodes frowns.

"But along the way, I did fall in love with it for myself. I wanted to be a professional tennis player pretty badly, actually," I say. "But it just wasn't in the cards for me."

Rhodes runs his finger along the stem of his glass. "Why not?"

"Never was the best," I say. "Maybe sometimes, but overall, I didn't have what it took to make it something bigger. I just didn't have *it*. Never stood out enough, no matter how well I did. No matter how hard I tried. Just always felt like I was second best."

"Damn. I'm sorry," he says. "If it's any consolation, I completely know what that feels like."

Our eyes meet and I can't believe it, but it does make me feel a bit better.

My phone goes off a couple of times in my pocket. I apologize and check it, just in case it's Celeste or something about her travel.

"Everything okay?"

"Sophie is texting me," I say. "She has something important to talk to me about before she leaves."

The tone seems different from our other texts. This feels less like we're friends and more like coworkers—she's using periods and perfect capitalization, and she begins with a jarringly formal "Hi, Milo."

He furrows his brow. "Huh. Wonder what it's about."

I pocket my phone. "Sorry about that. No work talk."

But there's a slight tangible shift now that Maison Dauphine has come up.

We're here, about to have a romantic candlelit dinner with wine and live piano, but this might just be a bubble that bursts on Monday morning.

Chapitre Vingt-Deux

It's a beautiful, sunny Monday morning, and Sophie has asked me to meet her for breakfast before we get to Maison Dauphine.

I typically hate breakfast, and I absolutely *despise* any type of meeting for breakfast. What tiny appetite I might have is dashed by the worrying or anticipating that comes along with a serious discussion.

Like, if our coach wanted us all to meet for breakfast when we were on the road for a tournament, I'd purposely schedule training early so I could work off some of my anxiety and drum up a need for more fuel. Otherwise the guys would all be like, "Milo, you never eat."

Which is about as helpful as you might think.

I'm walking over the Seine now, listening to music and trying to be totally zen. Because I'm sure this isn't about anything bad. Maybe Sophie just wants to chat through our strategy for some of the quicker-turnaround international loans. They can get pretty stressful, and with the resort show coming up, I bet it's only going to get worse.

It is of note that ever since this thing with Rhodes, I feel a bit more . . . capable. It's weird, because while everything is essentially the same, I also am highly aware of the fact that Rhodes thinks so highly of me and wants me for me, not despite what I think are some of my worst traits, but because he seems to understand them. This could either be amazing or awful, I know, and it's just the beginning of getting to know each other, but there's a confidence that comes along with a guy like Rhodes Hamilton wanting to kiss you. There just is.

After our dinner, we walked through dimly lit streets until we passed the Louvre and went down to the cobblestones beside the river. We watched boats and spent time talking. Off in the distance, as we walked, the Eiffel Tower glittered. Rhodes held my hand, and I didn't think anything could be better.

I wished I could just spend the entire night with Rhodes. I wanted to talk about everything with him. Memorize everything about him. It's a strange feeling to find so much time with somebody can still not be enough. I know we've got plenty ahead of us, but for the first time since Celeste left, really, I don't feel like I'm alone.

When I get to the little cafe Sophie suggested, I see her standing outside, eyes glued to her phone. She's wearing a black dress and slouchy brown boots with a massive Maison Dauphine hobo bag on her shoulder—it's hard to decide if she looks more Paris or New York, but she certainly looks the part for working in fashion.

"*Bonjour,*" Sophie chirps. "I love your outfit."

I glance down. Same Dunks I wear all the time. Same wide-legged cropped pants with a slightly boxy Uniqlo T-shirt. "Really?"

"Really. You look very effortlessly cool, which I fully mean as a compliment."

We sit at one of the little blue-and-white woven bistro tables outside; we each order a cappuccino. I've learned, fairly quickly, that Paris is not at all like America when it comes to coffee. The first time I ordered a latte, I ended up with a café au lait, which I attribute to them thinking I was speaking French poorly, which, to be fair, wouldn't have been far off base if I had tried. I'm sure there are places that do the sugary coffee drinks we have back home, but I want to embrace the culture, so I've only been getting cappuccinos.

"The gala was a huge success," Sophie says. "I heard about Rhodes's little incident with the Instagram Story, but I also heard people thought it was a fun photo and that it seemed like it was on purpose, even. A way to resonate with the Gen Z audience, I think."

Rhodes's little incident.

I shut my eyes and sigh. "So embarrassing."

"Honestly, I saw a screenshot and I thought it was cute. Anyway, that's a social media trend, I think. You see it all the time—meet the interns, that kind of thing."

"Right. Well, I'm not looking forward to hearing about it in the office."

"I doubt anybody will even talk about it," Sophie says. "They'll all be on to the next thing. It's not like Rhodes will be in trouble. I'd say it's all in the past." She browses the menu. "What are you getting?"

"Honestly, I think just the cappuccino."

"You're not a breakfast person?"

"Not really. I'm just a bit—well, I just don't usually have too big of an appetite in the mornings."

Sophie nods. "Well, as long as you eat lunch and dinner, I guess."

I shrug. "Most of the time. I'm sure you get it, like, if we're working or really stressed, it's harder to keep up."

"I definitely get it," she says. "It's important to take care of yourself, though. Are you doing okay? With everything? I'm sure this is a big adjustment."

I sip my cappuccino. "Yeah, for sure. I just tend to get a bit anxious in general, so sometimes it spikes a bit worse. It's not like I don't eat on purpose or anything like that, really. It just is more so my body doesn't . . . I know, it sounds horrible."

"No, I *really* get it. Do you take anything for your anxiety?"

Now I shake my head. "I've tried some before, but the side effects weren't great. I actually lost *more* weight. And I was playing tennis then, so it was dangerous to not eat and then go practice or play. Especially in Florida, and in the sun." But the way she says she *really* gets it and asks about medication, I wonder what her experience is. "Do you take anything for it?"

Sophie nods. "I do. But I know it's not for everyone. It might just be worth looking into. You don't have to commit to anything, but maybe you could find one to take only as needed. Or maybe you don't need medication at all. I'm not sure, I just know it helps me. And there's nothing wrong with you if you do need some help to manage your anxiety."

"Thanks," I say, hands around the warm cup in front of me. "Though I have no idea how I'd even go about that while I'm here. I'm not sure how insurance and health care works when you're an American in Paris."

Humming and rocking back in her chair a bit, Sophie drums

her fingers on the edge of the table. "Well . . . what if you were back in the US?"

"I'm sure back home it'll be a lot easier."

"Right," she says. "So that's actually why I wanted to talk to you today, Milo."

"I don't follow?"

"We want to bring the apprenticeship to our New York office," Sophie says. "It'd be a paid opportunity, and it's very important we get someone amazing, because it's a pilot program. If it doesn't do well, it'll reflect on my team. We want someone innovative, who works hard, and who knows Maison Dauphine."

I understand what she's saying, but I wait for her to bring it home.

"We want you."

Drawing in a shallow breath, I blink and swallow and look around, again expecting some sort of *Candid Camera* situation here.

"Sorry, did you just say . . . You're trying to tell me . . ."

"I'd love to hire you," she says. "It'll be thirty hours a week, so almost full-time. And we can work together to figure out housing options."

"Wow."

"Is that a good wow or a bad one?" Sophie smiles, indicating she's not even entertaining the idea of the latter. "I actually have a girlfriend who lives in the East Village, and she's looking for a roommate. I'm sure she could cut you a great deal if you wanted to sublet the room. There are other options too."

I stare at the foam of my cappuccino that is stuck on the sides of the cup. This is a lot, and it's amazing, but it's also so unexpected.

"I'm not sure what to say."

"Do you want to do it?"

I shrug. "I mean, New York is so cool. I never really . . . I don't know. My plan was to try and stay in Paris."

Sophie bites her lip. "Really?"

"Well, yeah."

"It's just . . . you don't speak French. Plus, there's the whole visa thing. . . . And I'm as optimistic as anybody, truly. But—don't take this the wrong way—there's only one job in Paris at the end of the apprenticeship."

Of course it's what she doesn't say here. *Rhodes is going to get it.*

"I honestly am not sure. I just . . . I wanted to stay in Paris and I guess I figured if I really did a great job, maybe it could be me."

Sophie orders a ham omelet from the Le Petit-Déjeuner menu, and the idea of that makes my stomach turn, but I don't say anything.

"I get it," Sophie agrees. "But it's not guaranteed. And this opportunity in New York is guaranteed. We wouldn't even make you interview or anything. You'd just transfer over. Keep your email and everything. Maybe a few extra forms, but it'd be seamless. We have an assistant position opening up, and the apprentice will transition into that role. You'd be all set in New York, Milo."

"Okay," I say. "Right, okay. I guess you're right. I don't see why I couldn't . . ."

This is what I wanted. Even if it's being presented in a different way, this is ultimately what I came here to do. The plan was to kick ass at Maison Dauphine and find a way to stay on with the house. So I'm on track. Plus, Sophie is right, I don't speak French and I don't even know what that visa process would be like.

"Perfect," Sophie says. "I leave tomorrow morning, but we could give you a couple of weeks if you need to get everything in order."

I blink. "Wait, a couple of weeks?"

She nods. "Is that okay?"

"Oh, I thought this would be for the fall or something. . . ."

"Well, it'd be great to have you in New York before the resort show. That way you can take the lead on a lot of American requests when the line is live. Leadership feels there is enough staffing for the show, but stateside there will be a lot of press attention we'll need help with. Only one of you is going to be working the show here, anyway."

And there it is. There's the gut-wrenching twist.

I'm only just now starting to get used to being in Paris. I'm only just now starting to fall for this ridiculously cute guy who is like a dream come true. I'm only just starting this story, and now . . . how can I turn down an offer for an apprenticeship in New York? And one that could lead to a job?

"Is there any way I could stay a bit longer?" I ask. "I want to come to New York, I really do. But I just got here. . . ."

She frowns. "I get it. I wish things were different, but if we don't have someone in place before the resort show, we'll have to open up applications, and from there, I can't guarantee it'd be you, unfortunately. It's not that I wouldn't still want to pick you, but HR will need to treat every applicant fairly, of course, and that means if someone with more experience comes along . . . it's a gamble."

I nearly spill my cappuccino because I sit up so quickly. "No, I get it. I completely understand."

There are a million thoughts swirling around in my head, and I can't seem to wrangle even one of them, so I just figure the best and only option is to buy time.

"I'll need to talk to my parents," I offer. "And figure out some of the logistics. When would you need to know?"

Sophie sucks her teeth and looks off, eyes darting around as if she's calculating. "I'd say by next Wednesday at the latest. That's when we have our departmental meeting, and they'll want an update. There won't be much I can do once it gets beyond our team, so if you're not signed on, things just get really complicated."

I nod. "Sure, okay. By next Wednesday."

"At the latest," Sophie says. She makes a strange humming noise, leaning a bit closer. "Milo, I'm a bit surprised here, I can't lie. You seem so determined, and I know you want to stay with Maison Dauphine. This is really a once-in-a-lifetime opportunity we're talking about here. This isn't something many eighteen-year-olds would get offered."

"I know. Trust me, I am so grateful for the opportunity."

"Is there anything that's holding you back here? I just sort of thought you'd be thrilled and jump at this. Maybe that was presumptuous of me, but—"

I can hear her tone shifting, and I suddenly feel desperate to shift it back.

"No, you're so right. I am just really surprised, that's all. I'm in shock. This doesn't happen to random guys from Citrus Harbor, Florida. At least not that I know of." She laughs at that, and I can tell she's feeling less offended by my initial lack of enthusiasm.

"But this is amazing. I'm going to talk to my parents, and I'll figure it all out."

She smiles as the waiter sets the ham omelet down in front of her. "Okay, good."

"I really am grateful," I say. "Thank you for putting me up for this."

How is it I've gotten this amazing opportunity but won't even let myself feel excited?

I can practically hear Celeste now.

Milo Hawthorne, a boy with a choice.

Risk it all for Paris?

Or start fresh in New York?

Chapitre Vingt-Trois

When Sophie and I get to Maison Dauphine, I expect a reception from hell after the Instagram Story debacle at the gala. Even if they think Rhodes posted it, the embarrassing photo is of me. But nobody pays me any attention at all.

It's just a normal day.

Rhodes isn't in the fashion closet, and Yvette is nowhere to be found either. I slide down in my chair, brain going a million miles per minute, unable to focus on the inbox of requests waiting for me. I pull out my phone.

Me: where are you?

Rhodes: Ah sorry! Didn't want to bug when you were with Sophie. I've been sent on a wild goose chase. La Défense. Yvette seems to have quite the list of tasks for me today. I reckon it's my punishment.

Me: Oh, okay. Let me know if you need any help!

Rhodes: How did it go with Sophie? What did she want to talk about?

This is kind of a major thing, so I figure it's best to have this conversation in person, not over text.

Me: It was good! I'll update you in person - a lot to text

Rhodes: Glad it was good. That sounds like a plan

Rhodes: I hoped we could have dinner tonight, but I might have to meet with one of Mum's pals who doesn't know her way round Paris . . . not sure why I've been assigned to be her tour guide tbh

I groan. Not because he's got plans, but because this means our conversation will be delayed even more.

Me: lol sounds like quite an evening

Rhodes: You could always join if you want. But I don't foresee it being fun. And you probably want to get ready for Celeste's arrival, right?

Me: Yeah, I probably should. I wanted to get her some flowers and things to make it a bit nicer. I imagine she'll be sad about her grandma and I want to try and help how I can

Rhodes: That's very considerate. I have your address, but not the apartment number? I want to send some flowers as well

Me: You don't have to!

Rhodes: Ofc. But I'd like to

I blow a raspberry. Why would the universe do this to me?

First we're competing, and then we're going to be separated by the Atlantic Ocean. I can't imagine what could possibly be next.

I send him the full address, and then I turn my attention to some of the emails I have to answer. I'm always very on top of our editorial requests and returns, so there's nothing out of the ordinary, and the ease with which I am able to clear the inbox helps me to breathe more like a normal person and less like a chronically anxious one.

And then, of course, the doors swing open and Yvette is standing there with her thick-framed black sunglasses and black cape over a black dress with black shoes. She looks annoyed, and she holds her palms out.

"Well?"

I blink. *"Bonjour?"*

She sighs, and I can imagine she's rolling her eyes behind those glasses. "Are you ready?"

"Am I ready . . . ?"

"Mon dieu, Milo. Avez-vous des nouvelles d'Haydée? Épuisant. Nous devons être quelque part et nous ne pouvons pas être en retard." She lifts her brows. *"Dépêche-toi!"*

I can put together that she's annoyed, I should have heard something from Haydée, we are going to be late, and that I need to hurry up. My computer is locked and I'm out of my chair in record time.

"I'm so sorry." We're sprinting down the hallway and Yvette seems disinterested, if she's even listening at all, but I ramble on for whatever reason. "I had no idea we were going anywhere. I would have prepared if I'd known. Is this a meeting? If there's anything I can—"

"No, you do not need to prepare anything," Yvette says.

We walk out a back exit to a black car, and when the driver opens the door and Yvette slides in, I follow suit. This is all very mysterious and very stressful, but part of me is excited—this could be an adventure.

Or Yvette could know Rhodes took the blame for me, and she's taking me to an undisclosed location where they will dispose of my body.

We're driving for six very long, silent minutes before Yvette removes her sunglasses and looks over at me.

"We're going to a closed set, so you will need to give me your phone when we arrive."

I nod. It's not something I'm thrilled about, but there isn't even the slightest suggestion that this would be optional.

The Palais Garnier comes into view, and I marvel at the majesty of the Beaux Arts facade that the boulevards seem to culminate in—an abundance of arches and windows and balconies and columns. There are sculptures on seemingly every level, with golden busts looking out over the streets of Paris. Atop the building, on either end, famous symmetrical statues of Harmony and Poetry stand tall, like gilded guardians of the opera house.

"Are we going to the Palais Garnier?"

Yvette nods. "We are shooting some of the creative to accompany the resort show. Billboards, bus wraps, some digital advertisements. We'll use some of it organically, as well. The opera house is the perfect place to exhibit L'or des Fous resort."

"So I'm going to see some of the resort looks?"

Everyone on the PR team has seen the line . . . except for me and Rhodes.

"Yes, you will see all of the resort looks," she says, taking out her phone. "Some will be on the models, but I will have Haydée send them to you now so you can review. When we get these photos, we will need help tagging them in the database. You'll mark them with highest security restrictions until the embargo lifts."

"Wow."

I cringe, not sure where "wow" even came from, but it's too late.

Yvette locks her phone. "You should get a pdf shortly. Milo, it is of the utmost importance that you do not share this with anyone. Do you understand? Not a single person."

There's something specific she's saying. *Don't share this with Rhodes.*

"Of course. I understand." My fingernail digs into my thumb. "Though . . . I guess I was under the impression—rather, I had assumed . . ." It's no wonder I can't speak French when I can barely speak English. "I thought the resort assets were off-limits for the apprentices."

"They are. But if you are going to be working the resort show, you will need to be acquainted with the ins and outs of the line and all the moving parts of the event and campaign." Yvette puts her sunglasses back on.

Before I can respond or even really comprehend what she's just said, the car comes to a stop.

We walk along the sidewalk to the entrance, but Yvette just sort of announces herself and says *"Pardon"* quite assertively so that everyone moves out of her way. Once we're inside, while other visitors wait in line, a man in a navy T-shirt and jeans unclips the rope for the queue and lets us pass through before quickly ensuring that no other guests follow us.

He leads the way until we are huddled between two marble staircases, beside a sculpture of a woman with such incredible detail it actually appears she is frozen in motion.

"Bonjour, Yvette."

They exchange kisses on the cheek, and when she introduces me, he does the same. I do my best to not be visibly startled, but I think he senses my discomfort, which only makes him laugh and lightly touch my shoulder.

"This is Jean Paul," Yvette says. "He is a brilliant art director."

"I do my best," he says with a thick French accent. "Come along.

You are going to be astounded. Everything has come together so perfectly. It is as if some little fairies plucked the vision from my brain and brought it to life."

Yvette *snorts*. I've never heard her make such a noise, but as we follow this man up the staircase, I am distracted by how overwhelming the opera house is. Everything is so ornate and massive, with a sense of timeless luxury emanating from the baroque detailing that adorns the entire building. Among the arches, with their intricate ornament-like carvings, there are more sculptures and candelabras, more domed ceilings with colorful embellishments and paintings.

We end up at a door where two security guards talk to Jean Paul in French before letting us in.

For how impressive the grand stairwell was, the auditorium we've just walked into is a fever dream. It's all deep shades of red and gold, with the bright famous fresco painting on the ceiling, anchored by a truly massive chandelier.

The auditorium is closed to guests for the time being, and sultry, synthy music is pumping through the room. The stage has been transformed into a lavish beach resort. Like a classic stage play, there are layered wooden ocean waves in the background, while a facade of gold makes up the foreground—palm trees, sand, surfboards, a cabana. There are Maison Dauphine logos placed strategically throughout, and there are also added stage lights that seem to give a behind-the-scenes feel to the image.

"The concept has come to life wonderfully," Yvette says. "And you were right, it's not *too much* gold."

"Just enough." Jean Paul nods. He looks to me. "She thinks sometimes I will go overboard, but I never do."

"It kind of reminds me of home." I say it without thinking, and Yvette and Jean Paul both look to me with quizzical brows. "The palm trees and the surfboards. All the beach stuff . . . it's like a much more luxurious version of Citrus Harbor."

Yvette offers a pinched smile.

Some models are sitting in the front row of the theater, and they are called up, one by one, until five or six of them are situated throughout the scene like Barbie dolls. One leans against the cabana as if ordering a drink, while one sunbathes and, beside her, one pretends to prop up the Maison Dauphine surfboard.

It's incredible, seeing these pieces that are going to soon become famous and sweep the editorials. Gold is present throughout: threaded through an ivory tweed suit and bucket hat in a subtle way that makes it sparkle when it catches the light; painted on one model as a one-piece beneath a billowing sheer white kaftan; hammered onto metal in the form of hardware on rattan bags.

Jean Paul hurries up the aisle and starts to shout something in French, which causes the photographer and a few set assistants to go wide-eyed and rush over to him.

Yvette is surveying the auditorium. "We will be debuting a new line of the Dauphine's Jewels along with this resort show, which is unprecedented. The house hasn't had a new addition since the fifties. We anticipate this will eclipse the new Darling Dauphine bag and the finale gown. If you work the resort show, I want you to create content around them. Something fresh that the house hasn't done. Something other houses aren't doing either."

I stand up straighter and focus on the models, who look so

glamorous. It's in these moments that I realize what a gift this entire experience is. Even a few months ago, I never would have thought I'd be standing in the Palais Garnier watching the Maison Dauphine resort campaign photoshoot. I never thought I'd have access to confidential documents or information about the Dauphine's Jewels, one of the most famous collections of rare, fine jewelry in the entire world.

"I'm sorry if this is a dumb question." I scratch at my palm. "It sort of sounded like . . . you've decided I'm working the Resort show?"

Yvette purses her lips and clasps her palms together. "Not officially. I know the New York office wants you to transfer, but we will need someone here we can trust. Someone who won't make mistakes. I might be more inclined to let New York have Rhodes."

My heart nearly stops.

Oh, god. This would be a great time to be a good, honest person, Milo. This is your chance to come clean.

But Rhodes was the one who took the blame.

And now you're going to take this opportunity from him without him even realizing the full implications of what he's done.

Except he must have known there would be consequences? He wouldn't have done it if not?

It's not like he'd have done it if he knew it would mean the resort show. Or that he might get transferred to New York!

"Rhodes doesn't—"

"I know you two have formed a friendship," Yvette says, seemingly very proud of herself for being so astute. "While I appreciate whatever it is you're about to say, as it is, I'm sure, very chivalrous or loyal or *good*, it won't make a difference in whatever decision I make."

I nod, a bit relieved by that wording. "So you haven't made the decision yet."

Yvette shakes her head. "I haven't made a final decision."

Okay, this is good. So from now on, we play fair and square, and things will be fine.

"But . . ." she says. "One of you is here, with access to the resort lookbook, and one of you is decidedly not."

Fuck.

Chapitre Vingt-Quatre

It's Thursday night, and I haven't seen Rhodes all week.

Yvette has kept him busier than ever, on errands all over the city. Some run into the evenings, and when he's been free, his mother's friend has guilted him into entertaining her and her family.

I've kept our text thread pretty light, and we've FaceTimed a couple of times before bed, but luckily he's forgotten about my meeting with Sophie and I've avoided telling him what happened with Yvette and the resort shoot.

Now, back to the sleepless nights, I head over to the window, past the kitchen island with the bouquet for Celeste from Rhodes, and I look out over Paris.

I think Sophie was on to something with the whole anxiety medication thing.

I could make this right. There seems to be one option that would be painless: accept the New York position and leave before the resort show, which automatically gives that to Rhodes. Then Yvette doesn't ever have to know the truth.

But it pains me to go down that path for some reason. It feels like I've barely made my mark here, like Paris would just forget me if I left now. And maybe it'd forget me anyway, and maybe I'm more worried, deep down, that I'd forget it. That I'd forget Rhodes. That he'd forget me.

I hate to imagine Rhodes staying behind without me. I'm sure we'd have every intention of finding each other again, but the reality is so different. Given enough space and time, he'd realize he doesn't need me—there's a whole wide world of guys better suited for him anyway. What could it be about me that's worth crossing the ocean for?

That's a depressing thought, and I crawl into bed, getting smaller and smaller until I'm certain I'm going to disappear.

Rhodes could do better, I know that. He could find someone more successful, more attractive, more *everything*. Someone with affluence and influence, who brings more to the table than I could even dream of, I'm sure.

I may be ambitious, but we're not from the same world.

These thoughts are like the devil, but in the dark they're winning.

Eventually, going over different scenarios a million times, I fall asleep.

I wake when I hear the key in the front door, along with the sound of luggage wheels rolling over the wooden floors. Sunlight is filtering through the curtains and the city is awake beyond the windows.

"Miloooo!" Celeste calls.

Blinking myself to consciousness, I tap my phone screen. How did I sleep until nine?

Yawning, I pull it together and slide out of bed. The sight of my reflection in the mirror is a jump scare—my curls going in every direction and my Citrus Harbor Boys' Tennis T-shirt twisted around from restless sleep I hardly remember—but I pad out into the living room anyway, my pajama bottoms catching the heels of my feet.

I hold my hand up to wave at Celeste, a bit too groggy to be proud of my greeting. She's wearing one of her beige Lululemon headbands, an oversized hoodie, biker shorts, and a grin that is refreshing if not a bit confusing.

And there's someone walking through the front door behind Celeste.

It's only for a nanosecond, but I wonder if I'm hallucinating or still asleep until it hits me that I recognize that person.

"Noel!"

Celeste looks pleased with herself, and I'm instantly jolted awake by the sight of my brother, who is wheeling in his suitcase. The corners of his mouth turn up a bit, which is about as much as you can hope for from the guy who was likely born scowling. His black hair is a bit longer than normal, though it still is better kept than mine ever is, and he has the tiniest bit of a five o'clock shadow. Noel is taller than me or Celeste, and he's wearing black soccer pants with a white Clyde Circus training kit.

I rush over and pull him in for a hug. He wraps his arms around me and grunts.

"You look like you just woke up," he says when I take a step back. The door closes behind him and he looks around the apartment. Noel is a year older, and he plays soccer at Stanford. I think he wanted to go somewhere else, but he followed his best friend out there like a puppy, which is one of the easiest jokes I can make to get under his skin super quickly.

Celeste hugs me next. "It's so good to see you."

"You too," I say. "I'm really sorry about Gran."

She hugs a bit tighter. "Thank you." Then she pulls away. "But now we're in Paris. And we're going to have an amazing eight days."

I nod, and she heads over to the kitchen island, plucking the card from Rhodes's bouquet.

"This *is* a surprise," I say. "But this is amazing. I'm so glad you're here."

"Me too," he says. "It's weird not having you around to bug me."

"Laura isn't filling that void?" I ask, knowing very well that he has some bizarre otherworldly patience for our little sister.

"She's doing her best."

"Is she upset she couldn't come?"

Noel shrugs. "She said she wants to wait to visit Paris until she's getting married. Little kids, you know."

That certainly sounds like Laura.

"I cannot believe I got flowers from Rhodes Hamilton," Celeste squeals.

Noel narrows his eyes on me. "You had to pick a Hamilton."

"Is that why you're wearing this?" I take the sleeve of his shirt between my fingers.

Lifting his chin proudly, Noel smirks. "I thought maybe he'd be here."

"They're not at sleepovers yet," Celeste says. Then she tilts her head. "Are you?"

"No," I say.

Noel frowns. "Is he a prick?"

"Why would I like him if he was a prick?"

Celeste plops down onto the couch and then immediately gets up and walks back toward the kitchen. "I have way too much energy. What are we going to do today?"

"Yeah, Milo, what are we going to do today? Are you going to take us to Maison Dauphine?"

I shake my head. "I took today off. I figured we could find some fun things to do."

Celeste leans up against the island, gesturing toward her flowers. "When do we meet Rhodes?"

Noel makes a growling noise. "Yeah, when do we meet Mr. Armoury?"

"Dinner, probably," I say. Then I turn to Celeste. "He said he really wants to meet you." I glance over at Noel. "I'm sure he'd love to meet you, but I'm going to have to request you wear something a bit more neutral."

"Fine," Noel says. "I'm actually really interested in meeting him, honestly. I bet he's got a lot of great stories. Imagine having Ollie Hamilton as your twin brother."

"Well, he has a lot more to offer than just being Ollie's twin brother."

Noel pinches his brows together. "Easy. I get it, I get it."

Celeste shows Noel to his room, which is smaller than ours, but he doesn't make any fuss over it. In fact, he practically *bellows* "Ho-ly fucking shit!" when he sees the view from his window.

Noel is sort of another best friend in a lot of ways. Nobody else around us really gets the pressure of being in a councilman's family, and when our mom opened her boutique and things started to change, we realized that was another storm we could weather together. We both like sports, and we both are pretty driven and competitive. We played tennis together all the time, and he taught me to play FIFA against my will, which is where I learned most of my Premier League knowledge.

I've cried to him, laughed with and at him, wanted to punch him in the face, and also never wanted him to leave when he first went to Stanford.

Celeste and Noel both have a lot of energy for having just landed after a long flight, but that's fine with me, since it'll make for a more fun day, and I really need that right now with all the racing thoughts surrounding Rhodes and Maison Dauphine.

They shower and change. Celeste looks cool and stylish, like always, in baggy jeans and a ribbed tank with a black leather bag. Noel also looks stylish, which is a bit out of character for him, but he's wearing an oversized graphic tee with carpenter pants and Adidas. They honestly both look more Parisian than I have this whole trip, I think.

Now that I'm an expert on the Tuileries and the Louvre, we spend most of the day wandering the gardens and the halls of the museum. Celeste *ooh*s and *aah*s over the sculptures and romantic paintings, while Noel marvels and mutters expletives at the scale of the larger art pieces. We eat at a little cafe inside the Louvre, and the food is surprisingly delicious—even Noel's practically grinning by the end of the meal.

Rhodes is preoccupied with errands, but we text on and off all day. Initially, my entire being is split into two—one half of me wants to talk to him and be with him all the time, eager for this crush to develop into more, while the other half of me wants to avoid him like the plague to try and assuage the feelings of guilt, like I'm betraying him after the conversation I had with Yvette.

Still, I keep it together. I focus on the fact that this is what we signed up for, and that *he* took the blame on his own accord. I repeat this to myself over and over until the guilt truly does seem to smooth over.

For now, anything could happen, so there's no use in blowing everything up.

We like each other, and this is exciting and new and fun.

Celeste is here, and she's brought Noel, and this also is exciting and new and fun.

Everything is fucking exciting and new and fun!

We decide on a restaurant in the 8th Arrondissement for dinner. It's casual, since none of us will have time to go change, and I think the more laid-back vibe will help this all go as smoothly as possible.

I'm not sure what I'm more worked up over: Rhodes meeting Celeste and Noel, or the opposite.

The more I try to dive into the thoughts, which I do somewhat obsessively as we make our way to the restaurant, the more I realize it might be the opposite. After all, Celeste and Noel know me, and they're important figures in my life. It's not so much that I want them to approve of him, I don't think, but there's a distinct desire for them to be happy for me. And I know Rhodes is charming and likable, but I just want this to feel *right*.

Noel has only ever met one guy—one ex-boyfriend, and while that went well enough, I think Noel had a sixth sense that allowed him to say nice things while never being truly ecstatic for me.

Said sixth sense was prescient, and that relationship did not last long, so maybe that's why I'm particularly concerned with how Noel perceives Rhodes.

One thing about me? I'm going to find a reason to worry.

"This is going to be so fun," Celeste says.

Noel, with his hands in his pockets, nods.

It isn't until we're standing outside the restaurant that I realize I have a string of texts that make my heart sink.

Rhodes: I am so, so sorry but I'm stuck at this magazine shoot forty-five minutes away and I don't think I'll be out of here for an hour at least

Rhodes: I've got to drop the samples back off at MD after as well

Rhodes: You should eat without me. Please tell Celeste and Noel I'm very, very sorry. I'll make it up to you all somehow

"What is it?" Celeste asks. "You look like you've seen a ghost. Is it some Miranda Priestly shit?"

I shake my head. "No, no. Well, I guess kind of. It's Rhodes. He can't make it. He's stuck at a photo shoot."

Noel harumphs. "I'm sure he is."

"He is," I say.

Now, of course, it's like a tiny seed has been planted in my brain.

Would he back out like that because he didn't want to meet them yet? Is it too soon for him to meet my best friend and brother? Was it a dumb idea to try to make this happen?

Celeste waves her hand. "No big deal. I mean, we have plenty of time to meet him."

"Right," I say. The disappointment stings like acid on an open sore and I'm anxious about the potential for this to be something bigger, but I point to the restaurant. "Are you guys hungry?"

"*Oui, j'ai une faim de loup,*" Noel deadpans.

Celeste and I stare at him.

"It means I'm as hungry as a wolf," he says. "What?"

"Since when do you know French?" I ask.

He pats me on the shoulder. "You know, Milo, when one plans to go to France, one should learn some French."

Dinner is delicious, and it's nice to hear about how things are going back home. My dad is about to run for reelection, which he will definitely win. Laura's making a lot of new friends at her dance camp this summer, and Noel is coaching some youth soccer programs in his free time with Zack, the friend he went to Stanford with. Zack's return also explains why Chip has also been in an especially good mood in the group chat, since they've been dating for nearly a year.

I'm surprised how jealous I get when they tell me about how the Fourth of July festival is going to be the biggest ever this year—apparently one of the local surfers, Foster, is going to compete in the US Open of Surfing, which is the first time someone from Citrus Harbor has qualified. Because of this, the whole town is celebrating, which is amazing and gives me some FOMO, even though I'm in Paris and should just be excited about that.

Noel and Celeste are still not tired after we leave the restaurant, so they decide to go out on the town. I am exhausted and can't possibly hang with them at this point, so I head home to try and get some rest.

Sophie and I are following each other on Instagram now, and she sends me a fair amount of DMs—funny memes, looks she likes, things to do around New York. When she sends me something about the city, I almost forget that I've decided to stay in Paris. It's like I have to convince myself all over again every single time.

I pass out around nine thirty, and at around three a.m., Noel and Celeste get home. They're obviously drunk, laughing as quietly as they can and rummaging through the pantry. I almost get up and go out to the kitchen to have fun with them instead of trying to force myself to sleep, but then all the lights go off and it goes quiet when they head to their rooms.

In the morning I wake to a text that makes me sit up, smiling like an idiot.

Rhodes: Are you guys free this afternoon?
I found a way to make it up to you

Chapitre Vingt-Cinq

Typically, when someone says they'll make it up to you, they might buy you a cup of coffee or offer to let your dog out. They might do something small but generous and call it a day. And if we're being a bit more cynical, most people might say they're going to make it up to you, and then do nothing at all.

When Rhodes Hamilton says he'll make it up to you, apparently, he means he'll use his connections to pull off something seemingly impossible and so major it makes you want to pass out.

I had some suspicions about what we'd be doing when Rhodes advised us to wear athletic clothing, but something this cool never even crossed my mind.

My feet are firmly planted on the red clay court of the Stade Roland Garros, where the French Open was played less than a month ago. It's absolutely massive and feels like a dream come true to be here, under the bright blue cloudless sky among the sea of empty green seats that tower over the court. It's a bit chilly for me, since Paris doesn't get nearly as hot as Florida in the summer months. Still, the day is gorgeous, and I know I'll be warm as ever once we get to playing.

We've been picked up in a car and then escorted into the stadium by some PR person Rhodes knows. Also, we've been given shoes to wear during our session, and Celeste and Noel are both taking photos and videos on their phones. Noel forces me to take a photo, and I act like I'm cringed out to pose like some dorky fanboy, but really I'm excited to have this memory documented. Me, standing beside the net with the magnificence of this famous stadium roaring behind me.

I might immediately send it to the Deuce Bags.

I've watched so many huge matches played at Roland Garros. I wasn't even two years old yet, but I've rewatched the 2008 match between Rafael Nadal and Roger Federer several times. I've rewatched plenty of Nadal matches here, actually, but apart from that, Alcaraz versus Ramos-Viñolas was wild in 2022. All that time spent watching matches and it never occurred to me I'd be here, not even a glimmer of a daydream when I'd found out I was going to be spending the summer in Paris. Why would I ever end up here? How could I ever?

Leave it to Rhodes.

Celeste smacks me on the arm so hard I think she might be swatting a bug, but her eyes are big and when I follow her gaze, I realize she's watching Rhodes as he makes his way onto the court. He looks like he could be a tennis player, of course, in white shorts that hug his thighs and a white polo that hugs his chest and biceps. He's got a sweatband around his forehead and sunglasses with blue-and-purple lenses.

When I see him, all those doubts from before are washed away. He has more than made up for missing dinner, and I think this goes to show it was as innocent as I'd have assumed without Noel's little remark.

When I see him, in fact, I almost forget where I am. I almost want to run up to him and throw my arms around him, kissing him like I haven't seen him in ages. It's only been less than a week, but there must be a reason they say absence makes the heart grow fonder. All these days spent without the feeling of his hand in mine or his lips pressed to mine—I'm surprised how much my heart absolutely swells at the sight of him.

"Good morning!" Rhodes has his signature charm on full display, with a huge grin and his arms open wide, racket extended from his palm. "So glad you guys were able to make it."

When he meets us at the net, I expect he'll treat me like a friend or an acquaintance. It's all so new, and there are some staff members at the entrances of the court, plus Noel and Celeste are here. I imagine he'll go for something quite conservative.

Instead, he pulls me in by my waist and kisses my cheek. "Hi, you."

"Hi," I say, wrapping my arm around him. He's bringing out this bashful side of me that I wouldn't have anticipated, but all the day's sunshine isn't as bright as the feeling I get because he's so happy to see me.

After our little greeting, which has left my cheeks hot and my heart racing, he takes a few steps forward before he stops and pulls off his sunglasses. His grin extends when his eyes land on Celeste. "A gorgeous blonde—you must be Celeste."

She's blushing like a schoolgirl, and she glances down at her feet before pulling some hair behind her ears. "Thank you for having us. This is beyond amazing."

"*Absolument*," Rhodes chirps. He places the racket under his arm and claps his hands together, gesturing toward Noel now. "And you must be Noel." He offers a cheekier smile. "I hear we've got a bit of a difference in opinion when it comes to football."

"Luckily today we're focusing on tennis," Noel says, a bit less gruff than usual, with a put-on smile that almost makes me break into laughter.

Rhodes doesn't know the difference, though, and just nods. "Of course."

"Thanks for having us." Noel echoes Celeste and shakes Rhodes's hand when he approaches him with his palm extended. "This is a very kind gesture."

"I'm happy to meet two of the most important people in Milo's life," he says. It's a bit cheesy and a bit cringe, except for the fact that I really believe it's sincere. "I figured a little private session here would make up for how I so rudely missed our dinner. And I do apologize for that. It was unavoidable."

"We understand," Celeste says. She's practically flirting, but it's a bit entertaining. Innocent, really, like a little girl meeting one of the princes at Disney World. "You and Milo are both so busy with Maison Dauphine."

Noel nods. "Saving the world one dress at a time."

"Shut up," I say, punching him in the arm.

Rhodes barks a laugh. "One dress at a time."

"It really is cool," Noel says. "I was only kidding."

"Hilarious," I say. I decide to shift the focus. "I can't believe we're here. At Roland Garros. I think this is probably one of the most famous stadiums in the whole world, wouldn't you say?"

"Yeah, I'd say so."

Celeste wiggles her foot on the ground. "The clay is interesting."

"In the 1800s, they used terracotta to cover grass courts," I say.

Celeste smiles. "Did you know Milo likes to research?"

"A lot," Noel adds.

"It's good for joints." I ignore them. "The clay is easier on the knees than other surfaces."

Rhodes smiles. "The more you know."

"But I hardly play on clay," I say. "Or *played*, I guess. Mostly hard courts."

Turning over the tennis racket in her palm, Celeste pinches her brows together. "Is that bad?"

"It just means I won't be as good," I say.

"I'm sure you'll be brilliant." Gripping his racket and scoping out the court, Rhodes draws in a breath. "All right. So we'll play doubles. How would you all like to split up?"

"Milo, you have to play on my side," Celeste says. She grabs my arm and pulls me over to her, my foot dragging along the clay. "I have literally no skill."

Noel frowns. "Well then."

"Sorry." Celeste laughs. "But I stand by my decision. Now if it were soccer . . ."

Rhodes pats Noel on the shoulder. "Then it's me and you, mate." He points to me. "Don't worry, I'll go easy on you."

I laugh. "Thank you."

We set up on the court, and a sense of confidence washes over me. There's something reflexive about it. I'm in my domain, in a way, even if it's on a particularly intimidating court. The stands are empty, so the pressure is lower. In fact, I'm feeling excited about the audience I do have. Noel and Celeste might not be too surprised by my game, but I expect Rhodes will be really impressed once he sees how I play.

I certainly don't expect to play with topspin like Rafa, but I might be able to experiment a bit with the clay court once I get a handle on it. Maybe I'll have some flourish in my slide or pull off a killer slice.

We're playing with a standard doubles formation, with Rhodes and me at the baselines, and Noel and Celeste diagonal from each other at the nets. I know I've got a mean serve, so I figure this is a good way to start, and if it gets to be too much for Rhodes and Noel, we can just switch up the formation. I want it to be fun, after all, so I don't want to completely dominate and not have any volley action.

When we start, I'm first to serve, and Noel is set to return.

With my feet firmly on the ground, I toss the ball up with my left hand. My right foot drags up a bit, and then I'm on my tiptoes before bounding into the air and slamming the racket down onto the ball. The blur of neon green speeds past Noel, and I realize I've put way too much power behind my initial serve as Rhodes's eyes dart toward it.

For the next point, I try to hold back a bit on the power, but it's still got a solid backing to it. Noel doesn't even attempt to return the ball, and it seems Rhodes is resigned as well.

But it doesn't get by him. Rhodes leaps over and hits it back.

His racket meets the ball with an impressive precision, like it is truly an extension of his arm, and it flies right at Celeste, who jumps out of the way.

I'm so shocked he got it back to us that I'm a nanosecond too late to return it, and they gain the point.

Noel and Celeste exchange glances and a single shallow breath passes through my lips in a quiet exhale.

"Fifteen-fifteen," Rhodes says, beaming.

"That was great!" I shout.

I guess it's not outside the realm of possibilities, since he comes from a super-athletic family, that Rhodes will have some sort of genetic predisposition to excelling at whatever sport he tries. That's a good thing, though. It'll keep things interesting.

This time when I serve, I catch myself feeling a bit rattled. It's a slight change in perception that affects my timing in the slightest way, but not *knowing* I'm about to dominate makes me second-guess where I'll place the ball on their side and just how much power I should utilize. It's the tiniest, externally imperceptible shift, but it's just enough to screw with me. The ball is practically gifted to Noel.

He and Celeste volley it back and forth over the net, and they erupt into laughter when Noel narrowly gains the point.

I'm glad they're having fun, but I'm a bit frustrated with my gameplay, and we're only starting.

This should be a well-choreographed dance—my serve should leave them panting, and we should take the first game. We should easily take a set, really. I'm one of the best tennis players in Citrus Harbor, and I'm serving, so there's no way I can blame this on not being brought up on clay courts.

I know it's friendly and this is only meant to be fun, but Rhodes sends my next serve back with ease and I practically feel an overly competitive demon curling up the back of my neck and whispering in my ear: *Shout, get upset, show that you're bothered because you're doing so fucking poorly when you should be the best by a mile.*

Remaining composed, I prepare to serve again.

I do my breathing exercise quickly, and I am ready to go.

This time, I'm all in.

Maximum power. Maximum precision.

Left foot extended, I toss the ball. It's like slow motion. I'm off the ground and I slam the ball so hard my right foot nearly kicks my glute from the unbridled momentum, and it's like a bubble pops as time resumes normally in an almost cartoonlike manner, with the ball flashing by like lightning.

It's a brutal serve, with all the intensity I have to offer.

And Rhodes sends it back.

I slide to my left, barely making a backhand and getting the ball over the net. Noel saves it, and then so does Celeste. Rhodes sends it back, but without much power, so I have a moment to breathe and calculate my next move as it flies toward me.

With the next few possibilities playing out in my mind, I get ready to send the ball back toward Noel, but my foot slips a bit more than I anticipate in the clay, and when I swing, it's short.

They take the point.

When Rhodes and Noel win the first game and we break for water, I know I need to do some breathing exercises and calm down, because my aggravation is wildly disproportionate to the situation.

I take a squeeze bottle of water and walk away, taking deep

breaths in, my chest rising and falling rapidly. I wipe sweat from my forehead and try to relax.

This is meant to be fun. You don't need to win.

But this is tennis. I should be winning. This shouldn't be happening.

It's like instead of some amusing game of enjoyment and levity, I'm right back at every match when I felt this way—when I felt like I should be better, and I just couldn't quite crack it. When I could play a greater game, but my muscles would only operate at ninety percent despite what my mind knew to be true. When I wanted to rip off my own flesh because my body betrayed me, and I knew it could perform better.

I guess Rhodes was right in that sense—I'm not great at just having fun, after all.

"You all right?"

He's reaching for me, and I instinctively jerk away as if he's only an opponent on the court, though I quickly remedy by pretending to be startled by him.

"Sorry," I say.

"Bit jumpy?" Rhodes chuckles nervously. "Must say, for someone who hasn't played much on clay, you're doing rather well."

With the squeeze bottle at chest level, I pivot to face him. "And what about you? Never mentioned you're so good at tennis."

"I'm not that . . ." He kicks his toe into the clay, biting his lip. "Right. I've played my fair share. Mum and Dad are quite into tennis."

"You learned all that from playing with your parents?"

"I've taken a few lessons," he says. "But really, that was mostly luck. Have I done something wrong?"

Grinding my molars and trying to stay rational, I shake my head. "No. Of course not."

"It's just that you seem a bit off. Something's annoyed you, hasn't it?"

"I'm not annoyed," I say. "I'm just cooling down from the game."

Rhodes takes the tiniest step closer to me. "Are you upset that we won the game? Milo, I don't want to—"

"I'm not upset you won the game."

"But if you are, and you want me to—"

I hold up my hand. "I don't want you to do anything differently, Rhodes. We're playing tennis. So keep playing."

There's a terseness and a bite to my words that he absolutely recognizes, and I wish I could take it back, but I know there's also a sourness to my expression that I can't seem to shake. It's more than a bit irritating that he's all but offering to throw in the towel so I can take the win. Like there's any pride in claiming a victory that was handed to me out of pity.

"Sorry if I've said something wrong," Rhodes offers.

"You haven't," I say. "Let's play our next game."

So we do, and when Rhodes serves and they take each point like Celeste and I are just stationary decoration on the court, my temper is unmanageable.

This internal tug-of-war is raging on, and it's happening in record time.

One hand, I want to appreciate that Rhodes has brought us here. It's a gorgeous day, and I've got basically all my favorite people together. This is one of the coolest things to ever happen to me.

On the other hand, my competitive compulsions and sensitive

ego are being stoked like coals in the belly of a dragon, with no recourse but to cough despite the fiery consequences.

I don't want to let this part of me win over the part of me that has come to really trust and care for Rhodes, but I'm agitated, and unfortunately this is difficult to mask, since I tend to wear my emotions on my face.

I've never had romantic feelings for an opponent before, and I've never had an opponent change from potential date to competition to *friend*? To competition et al. Just trying to recount the sequence of events that got us here is making my head spin more.

When Rhodes and Noel celebrate winning the game, I kind of get how some players submit to blind rage and throw their rackets.

Of course I don't submit to blind rage, I just head over to the squeeze bottles and try to breathe until we play our next game.

We lose the set, and then we lose the match.

I know I'm supposed to be having fun. I know I should enjoy it when Rhodes sneaks a few kisses in, but I find it hard to even look at him without feeling that same sense of fervent animosity I felt the first time we sat together in the back of the car on the way to Versailles.

Maybe it's my nature.

There's one question circling my mind that is haunting, really.

Even on the days when we're supposed to be the happiest, is it always just going to be a competition?

Chapitre Vingt-Six

It's late Sunday morning and Celeste is sleeping in, so Noel and I go for a stroll along the Champs-Élysées. It's a touristy spot, I know, but I haven't really explored it much—apart from mad dashes out of the Maison Dauphine boutique or cursory glances from the back of a car during an errand—and Noel has never been to Paris, so it seems like a somewhat natural time to see what it's all about.

Anyway, it's not like I'm *not* a tourist. I guess I've gotten to know the arrondissements where I'm staying and working more than most tourists, but for a lot of the neighborhoods, I don't know my *droite* from my *gauche*.

As it turns out, the Champs-Élysées is sort of like Times Square, but Parisian. Less flashy and chaotic in general, but still very crowded and commercialized. The classic Parisian architecture, along with all of the trees and the view of the Arc de Triomphe, differentiates it pretty distinctly from Times Square.

Noel is wearing a familiar vintage cream Clyde Circus T-shirt with camouflage carpenter pants and white Adidas Sambas, and

I'm in a retro-inspired Grand Slam T-shirt from Abercrombie with jeans and Nikes. Based on our graphic tees alone, we look like a very athletic pair of siblings. Not the *most* athletic pair of siblings I know, obviously, but still.

We wander around for a bit, marveling at the grandeur of some of the windows—displays of luxury goods in intricate, if not over-the-top, sets. The artistry is incredible. One window looks like an under-the-sea landscape with pearl jewelry floating among glittering fishes. There's such an art to window design, which I know since Maison Dauphine has an entire team dedicated to visual merchandising.

"I want to run something by you," Noel says, the words spilling out quickly.

"Sure."

He clears his throat. "I want to take Celeste to Champagne."

I raise my chin. "You want to *what*?"

"I have some money saved and I know she wants to go, so I thought while you're working this week, I could take her." His mouth forms a tight line. "Tomorrow."

"Tomorrow? You want to take Celeste on a trip? To Champagne?"

Noel, ever the emotive one in the family, nods once.

"You and Celeste? On a . . . are you actually asking what I think you're asking?"

He gives one more bob of his head.

I consider this. I wonder why I'm so surprised, since they have always gotten along really well. There were times when I thought she might be eyeing him more than normal at the pool or in his soccer uniform. I certainly noticed Noel would laugh a bit more with her than anyone else, but none of this struck me as anything worth paying any mind to.

There was once, now that I think about it, when they took care of me after my wisdom tooth surgery. They were both so giggly, but I thought it was just a mixture of delirium from my pain medications and their shared amusement about my chipmunk cheeks and nonsensical musings about *Break Point* on Netflix. They did seem to have a bit of a banter going, if I'm remembering correctly.

"Does she like you?"

Noel furrows his brow. "What?"

"I mean . . . I don't know what I mean. I'm a little shocked. Are you guys together?"

"No," he says, voice squeaking a bit. "I wouldn't do that. Not without making sure it was okay with you first. But I do think she likes me. I think . . . I think she wanted to kiss me when we went out in Bastille that night."

I blink. "Whoa."

"Look, if it's too weird—"

"No." It's a gut reaction, not one I really think much about, but one that comes instinctively. "Just try not to screw it up. You're both going to be in my life either way, so if you could just . . ."

"Right, the goal is to not screw it up." Noel says. "So. You're actually cool with it?"

"I'm cool with it."

"Not just saying you're cool with it but actually stewing over it?"

I shake my head. "I really am cool with it."

"Okay," he says. "Nice."

"Nice," I agree. "Champagne will be fun. Bring me back something?"

"I imagine we'll bring you back some champagne."

"Right."

There's silence between us as we keep walking, but I'm actually sort of excited about this. They wouldn't be the worst couple, the more I think about it. Noel seems to be off in his own thoughts as well, but I swear I see his lip twitching into a smile every few steps before he catches himself.

We decide to stop at Ladurée. The bakery and tearoom has a massive storefront with a big mint-green outdoor dining extension enclosed by glass. Everything inside feels ornate and decidedly French—more marble, more columns, lots of gold and chandeliers. The cases are filled with brightly colored tartlets and eclairs, and Noel orders us a large box of sixteen macarons, which seems a bit excessive. They are packed into a little green box, assorted flavors with a small card atop the tissue paper that tells us which colors are which.

I order a pistachio latte—it seems lattes do exist in Paris, just in the more touristy areas—and Noel gets caramel, and then we continue down the sidewalk away from the arc and the more crowded areas.

My mind is preoccupied, of course, as it always is. I'm bouncing around from Maison Dauphine New York to Maison Dauphine Paris, to Rhodes.

"All right, which are you having first?" Noel asks. He's taken the lid off and set the box inside it, stuffed the little card along the side, and now he's holding the macarons out for me to choose.

"I'll do a chocolate one."

So I do. The bite is perfect—the shell is airy with the slightest crunch, and then it turns a bit chewy in the middle with the ganache. The chocolate is rich and elegant, not sickeningly sweet, but not too sharp or bitter.

"Well?"

"So good, as usual."

Noel nods. "We're in Paris, after all." He pops an entire one into his mouth and bobs his head from side to side. "Yeah, that's good. It tastes just like the ones at Sucré back home."

"I'm sure they'd take that as quite the compliment," I say.

We walk for a while, making a dent in the macarons and our lattes, until we pass a roundabout and find ourselves wandering through a little park. I take a lemon macaron from the box, nursing small bites.

"You're being unusually quiet. What's wrong with you?" Noel huffs.

"A lot of things." I say it without meaning to. But it's Noel, so there isn't really anything I can't say, and maybe that's all the comfort I need right now. "Things are really complicated."

He's got macaron crumbs in his stubble, which he must catch me staring at, because he wipes them away before knocking back more of his latte. "What's complicated?"

"Everything," I admit. "At least everything feels complicated."

"Assuming this isn't just some bout of existential dread . . . is this about Rhodes?"

"Sort of," I say. "Yeah, I guess."

Noel looks off. "What did he do?"

"Nothing. This is pretty much all me." There is one thing I

wonder if he'd understand: "I did something I never do. And it still makes me feel terrible even thinking about it now. Because I knew it was wrong, and I know it is wrong now, but I felt like I had to do whatever I could to get ahead in the moment, and I sabotaged Rhodes the second I got the chance."

"How so?"

And the floodgates open. I tell Noel everything. From the first moment I met Rhodes on that sidewalk, through each of our events and all the little random details in between—the errands and the emails and the meetings and the tiny ways he had a leg up and the sliding competitive scale I operated on that was so small it was almost invisible, because I never *truly* even got close to competing with him before the Louvre.

Once I've spilled my guts, Noel shoots his empty coffee cup into a trash can a few yards away.

I think he must be exceptionally disappointed, because he hasn't stopped me a single time to clarify or ask for more details. I've painted the picture, it seems, and judging by the way his brows are pinched and his mouth is turned into a frown, I have let him down.

When he finally opens his mouth to speak, he shuts his eyes for a moment, and I swear he does his little growl thing. "So is Rhodes a prick or not?"

"What? That's what you have to ask after all of that? I mean, I'm the one who—"

"Milo, you are competing with Rhodes Hamilton," he says. "This isn't like 'Be on your best moral behavior' at a little Citrus Harbor tennis match. No offense. I'm trying to figure out Rhodes's part in all this."

I shake my head.

"What you did with the boxes was wrong, yeah, but it was remedied, and in fact he set you up." Noel grabs a purple macaron and chomps down on it. As he chews, he glances away. "Sounds like he was a dick."

"I don't know," I say. "Maybe in that instance. But not really outside of that. And to be fair, I was a dick to him."

"I'm failing to see what the actual issue is here now," he says. "If you're both being pricks but you still like each other, then maybe you just have a weird dynamic. I'm sure there are weirder ones out there."

"Well, there's more."

I tell him about the consequences of the Instagram Story at the Louvre, and going to the resort shoot, and that it's basically mine but Rhodes has no idea, and then I launch into the whole thing about the New York apprenticeship.

"Plus, there's the fact that he just *happens* to be better than me at tennis and annihilated us the way he did. When he was supposed to be making it up to us!"

Noel takes a breath. "I think that part is a bit of a stretch."

"He practically offered to throw the match. Like I needed the charity."

"All right." Noel forces a smile. "Let's rewind to this whole New York thing. I can't believe this is the first I'm hearing of this. Milo, that's huge. Do you have any idea? I mean, this sounds like a legitimate opportunity."

"But the resort show," I say. "It's like I finally really have Yvette in my corner. And I think something could come from that."

He offers me another macaron, but I decline.

"It sounds like you've got something to prove. I can't see why you'd stick around to work one fashion show, with no guarantee of what happens next, when you could just go to New York and work your way up and then, likely, work more fashion shows in the future."

This is a succinct way to knock me on my ass. A firm shift in perspective.

"So I should go to New York. . . ."

"I think so," Noel says. "Look, can I give you a little tough love?"

Bracing for impact, I draw in a breath. "Sounds like you're going to."

"You are going to lose yourself in this competition with Rhodes," Noel says. "You haven't even done anything wrong, really, but you've already compromised your values. And you're sitting here, feeling guilty about having a leg up on him with this fashion show, when I know for a fact he wouldn't give it a second thought if the roles were reversed."

"No, that's not him. You don't know it for a fact."

"Don't I? He's told you he intends to win, Milo. And I'm sorry to be harsh about it—I don't want to hurt your feelings and I know you two have something that feels exciting and romantic, but those sparks are very likely not enough to change things. You said it yourself, and while it is a bit blown out of proportion, he's the kind of guy who will annihilate you during tennis when he's supposed to be making it up to you."

The sadness in my mind washes over my face involuntarily.

"I'm sorry," Noel says, squeezing my shoulder. "But this is bigger than what you're used to, Milo. The scale of this . . ."

I know what he means, of course. The biggest, most dramatic thing I've ever faced before was probably the state championship. And even then, we knew we weren't going to win, so it was really more of an exercise in controlling my perfectionism and temper. Two of my teammates, Chip and Miguel, were more at peace with losing and pretty much acted as my therapists. Much like Noel is now.

"I do have feelings for him, though." I hate to pout, but this feels like one of those conversations with my parents where I already knew the answer wasn't what I wanted to hear. "When we're not focusing on Maison Dauphine, things are different."

"Then *maybe* there's a chance for you if you're not competing," he offers. "Maybe if you go to New York and he stays in Paris, you could work out something long distance until you figure out the specifics. But I know guys like this. He's going to choose to win every time."

"It's tough for him. With his father. With Ollie. Think about how hard things can be with our dad. Can you imagine the shadows *they* cast?"

Noel swallows hard, shuffling his feet a bit. "I can't. But I think that only means it's going to be harder for him."

"Harder for him.?"

"To choose you. If it came down to it."

I don't know what to think, really.

"If I choose New York, I could lose him."

"You could lose him either way, Milo. Honestly, how well do you even know him? Really? You know what he wants you to know at this point. That's it. And I'll try to stop the tough love here, but you're eighteen. You can't make these big life choices around him."

"I'm not—"

"You are. A bit. And I think that's normal to some extent, but you have to level yourself out. You have to remember how hard you've worked and what you want to accomplish. You have to have some discipline here, even if it's going to be tough."

I groan. "You sound like Dad."

"I hate when that happens." He sighs. "But I need you to be realistic here. I know you want to show our parents you can make it in fashion and all that. Do you think choosing to stay in Paris is really the right idea? You don't even speak a lick of French."

"Je parle un peu français."

"S'il te plaît, sois sérieux, Milo."

I sigh. "Why is it so hard for me to just commit to New York?"

"This is classic you, really," Noel says. "You've set your mind to this, and it's not easy for you to change course. I also think deep down you want to win, and maybe you won't admit it to me, but I do believe that. And I don't think there's anything inherently bad about that, but maybe it will help you recognize the truth. Because you and Rhodes are going to fail if you both have to succeed."

"Jesus Christ, you sound like an old wizard delivering a prophecy."

"Fuck off." Noel laughs. "I'm sorry. I know tough love isn't fun."

I roll my eyes. "There's a reason it's called tough love. And I know you are just looking out for me."

"Somebody has to, because you're easily one of the most stubborn people I've ever met." Then his face softens. "And I know you're disappointed Mom isn't here. I think part of this internal battle you're having is related to that. Maybe you feel like if you don't make Paris work, you're failing. But surely you can see that getting a job at Maison Dauphine in New York is a huge accomplishment? Hardly a failure."

My breath hitches. "You're right. I guess Mom would still be really proud."

Noel shakes his head. "That's the thing, Milo. It's not about her. I know it's hard—but we can't ever be happy if we're trying to do things for our parents. Once I figured that out, I swear, everything changed."

I sigh.

"They may never get their priorities straight," Noel says. "I hope they do, but we can't spend our lives trying to make them. You are a great kid—or *man* now, I guess." We both laugh. "You have to know that. For your own sake. If someone doesn't show up to your tennis matches, or if they don't surprise you in Paris, that doesn't mean you're worth any less."

But now I smile. "Only someone did show up to my tennis matches. And surprise me in Paris."

He blinks and inhales sharply. "Are you going to get emotional?"

"I won't." I chuckle. "But you're right. Our parents are who they are. And as usual, I am really glad I have you as a brother."

Noel nods. "I'm glad to have you as a brother too."

After a beat: "So New York?"

"Obviously only you can decide what to do," Noel says. "I'm

just trying to give reasonable brotherly advice. I want you to be happy. But I want you to be happy in the long run. Not just for a few dates in Paris." He winces. "I'm really not great with anything but tough love."

"It's okay, I know this about you."

"Honestly, I think New York could suit you."

I take a long, deep breath and grab one more macaron. It's one I read about in Ladurée—the Marie-Antoinette, light blue with a special black tea filling. It has notes of rose and honey and a very subtle tangy citrus. It's delicious, and it reminds me of Versailles and the Orangerie and everything in Paris. It reminds me of the blooms of the Tuileries and the citrus candles in the Maison Dauphine beauty boutique. It reminds me of the loose-leaf tea I smelled with Noel and Celeste in the Louvre gift shop. I'm suddenly aware of the magic in every cobblestone in this city now that it might be a bit too late.

I never even really had Paris, and I'm about to lose it already.

I never had Rhodes, either, and it seems I have to gamble that too.

Chapitre Vingt-Sept

This is maybe the worst I've experienced *le syndrome du lundi matin*.

In America, we'd probably call this the Monday blues or something similar, but since I am me and tend to skew a bit dramatic, this is *far* worse.

I've been texting with Rhodes like normal since we last saw each other at Roland Garros, but I am just waiting for the moment I tell him about New York. Everything is going to be different.

Celeste and Noel seem to believe he'll take it well. Noel's more cynical view of Rhodes foresees him happy to be rid of competition, while Celeste's romantic ideal sees him seizing the opportunity to make a transatlantic romance work despite any potential challenges.

I don't know what to expect or what to hope for, even.

There's also the fact that I need to tell Sophie and Yvette. I'm excited and nervous and not sure how that will work, exactly. Do I tell Sophie and then Yvette? Or the other way around? Will Yvette be unhappy now that it seems she wants me to stay?

Mon dieu.

Starting the week off with a bang, we're doing an accessories shoot. I got to the set way too early, with no real sense of what the fuck I am going to be doing today apart from trying to keep my composure.

The studio is minimalistic and simple: two white cyclorama walls, curved in the same way a skate ramp would be, though that's a very odd way to interpret what I'm sure is a thoughtful design choice. There are soft box lights and LED panels, thick black wires run along the floors like snakes, and bright neon-colored tape is strategically placed as markers. Clothing racks are empty and pushed to the side, since this is all about bags, shoes, hats, and jewelry.

The general chaos of the shoot is overwhelming at best, as the photographer and his assistant are tinkering with the equipment while the creative team are working on the set and the PR assistant from the accessories department is barking something in French into her phone with such furor I fear for the person on the other end of the line.

I'm assigned to untangling all the jewelry and laying it out on a table. Once that's done, I'm to cut out small squares of paper and write numbers on them, placing one next to each asset before photographing it for our records. Once I'm done with this, I am to neatly stack all the boxes and baggies, place them under the table, and then move on to the hats, and then the shoes.

This isn't a particularly daunting task, but it's a bit too rote for me at the moment. I am desperate for a stimulating intellectual distraction to stop me from glancing up at the door every three seconds in case Rhodes has strolled in.

I manage the pieces with the utmost care, lining up the fine metals and jewels as symmetrically as possible. There's a silver necklace with curving wreaths of diamond leaves, and there are big, square sapphire earrings. A topaz heart on a thick gold chain choker is next to delicate gilded dewdrop earrings. There are vintage rings mixed in with the new, and rectangular watches with diamonds glittering beneath the glass.

"Got started without me?"

Rhodes is here, and he's not being handsy or doing anything overt, but he is sidling up pretty close, his shoulder brushing mine, so I glance around and try to take the tiniest step to my right to make it clear he can't do that here.

"I'm on jewelry duty," I say, uncapping the marker and working on the numbered squares.

"Oh yeah?" Rhodes rests his knuckles on the table. He's in trousers today, with trainers and a gray T-shirt that's a bit snug so his triceps bulge when he leans forward a bit. "How long do you think this will run? I was thinking maybe we could go for lunch."

I shrug. "I'm sure we'll be done by lunchtime. No models."

Rhodes catches on to my shortness immediately. "What's wrong?"

"Nothing," I say. Then I shake my head, realizing that my inability to mask emotions is going to be the end of me. "I didn't sleep well, and I'm stressed. But I'll be fine."

Not convinced, Rhodes pushes off the table and runs his hand through his hair. "All right. What's going on? Have I done or said something?"

I shake my head, starting to take the photos of the jewelry.

My heart is thudding in my chest and trying to make its way up to my throat as I'm consumed with thoughts of how all of this could go wrong. Not only am I still unsure of how to broach the subject of New York, I am now seemingly responsible for the well-being of thousands and thousands of dollars' worth of precious jewelry.

A boy can only take so much pressure.

It's amazing, honestly, how anxiety can heighten the most ridiculous of thoughts and turn them into full-fledged fears. Ever since tennis with Rhodes, I've been going back and forth about the metaphor of it all—what other secrets could he be harboring? This is peak anxiety versus rational thoughts, but honestly, Rhodes could be, like, a werewolf, and I'd have no idea. He could be a murderer or in the mob or a murderer in the mob. He could be a spy or a body snatcher. Not that I even know what a body snatcher is, but the point is he could be one.

And then, of course, more realistically, he could be pretending to like me to eliminate the competition.

But that would be nuts, right?

It seems like that would be nuts, and I don't feel that from him, but I don't trust my thoughts, and it's making me have trouble trusting him.

"You're acting like I've said or done something wrong," he insists. Then he grins. "You're not already breaking up with me?"

Disarmed, I laugh, finishing the photos and pocketing my phone. "Rhodes, I—"

"I mean, that'd be a new record."

"Well, we can't break up since we're not together," I offer.

There's a bit of an unnecessary harshness in the delivery that is stemming purely from all these stories I'm telling myself about Rhodes.

His smile falters. "I was only joking."

"So was I."

Rhodes tilts his head. "I'm really confused here."

I walk over to the table with the hats, and Rhodes follows.

"Okay, you're right. I'm being weird. I'm sorry. I have this thing where I can't *not* act weird if I feel weird."

He nods. "I have learned this about you."

"But it's a whole thing. And I can't get into it all right now, because . . ." I unpack a sky-blue tweed newsboy cap and hold it up for him. "I have to finish unpacking and labeling and recording everything."

Rhodes grabs one of the boxes. "I'll help, then. We'll be done faster."

"I appreciate the offer, but this is my task, so I should be the one to do it."

"Do you not trust me?" he says with a smirk, unveiling a bucket hat wrapped in tissue. He places it on his head.

Do you not trust me?

The question circles around in my mind way too loudly and for way too long.

It's not like this guy is a villain from a Batman movie or something, after all. But damn it if Noel hasn't gotten me overthinking every tiny detail about Rhodes.

Honestly, how well do you even know him?

This summer is giving me whiplash.

"I just don't want us to get in trouble." I say it convincingly as I set down another newsboy hat, this time in a bubble-gum pink. "You know how it is, they probably want you doing something specific, too."

Rhodes stares at me. "I am very interested to hear whatever it is you have to tell me after this shoot."

"What's that supposed to mean?"

"I'm so confused with what's happening," he says. "I mean, I thought we were . . . just a few days ago we were . . ."

"We were what?"

He grimaces. "Don't do that."

"Rhodes, I told you I'm stressed, and I can't talk about this right now, and this is just making it worse, honestly."

"Okay, fine. I mean, I guess I should have seen this coming, since thus far, this whole summer has been some variation of this Jekyll and Hyde schtick, but—"

"What's *that* supposed to mean?" I repeat, this time even more annoyed.

He rolls his eyes. "One minute you're up and the next you're . . . I *literally* don't even know! But I thought by now we'd moved past it. I thought we were putting all the weird shit behind us since we were really getting to know and like each other."

"We were," I say. He raises his brow at that. "We *are*. I don't know. It's not like I'm trying to do a Jekyll and Hyde schtick on purpose. You just confuse me. I have all these mixed signals and I don't know what to believe or trust, because one minute—"

Rhodes throws his hands up. "No, Milo, that's what I'm saying. Didn't we move past all that? When we started going out? Or not . . . You know what I mean. We've hung out. We went on a date. We've clearly moved into a new territory."

"We have, but we're still here." I gesture around. "I don't know how to navigate this, if I'm honest. I don't know how to let myself just trust you when we're still competing."

"That's where you're wrong. *You're* still competing. I told Yvette this morning I wanted you to work the resort show. That ought to help you trust me, though I honestly didn't realize I was that untrustworthy in your eyes. Sure, we've been competing, but we agreed to play fair, anyway."

I blink. "What?"

"I know, it's not quite a mixed signal, but it's something to go off, I'd say. I let her know you should have it. And I also . . ." He shakes his head. "I can't believe this."

"Rhodes." I'm not sure why, but this is only making me more irritated. His constant chivalry makes me feel worse about myself, probably. "I was going to give you the resort show."

"Well, to be fair, it might not have been yours to give."

"Well, it sort of . . . was."

His face hardens. "What are you talking about?"

"Yvette told me it was as good as mine," I say. "When she took me to the resort shoot last week."

Rhodes scoffs. "Yvette took you to the resort shoot?" He brings his fingers to his temples. "Milo, let me get this straight, then. You went to this shoot with Yvette, and she said you'd be working the resort show, and you just didn't tell me? Didn't think I'd want to know?"

"Because she thinks you posted that Instagram Story at the Louvre."

Now he's silent.

The tension between us becomes so thick I can't swallow.

"You've got some nerve, Milo."

"Well, look, you must have known there would be consequences when you took the blame. What did you think was gonna happen?"

"I'm not sure! I guess I was just thinking we had something more to us than the competition, and that we'd figure it all out together. Now I'm just thinking I'm a fucking dolt. I should have known better."

It stings, of course. The implication that I've betrayed him. It's more than an implication, I guess, because I didn't tell Yvette when I had the chance.

"This is all we will ever be," Rhodes says. He echoes Noel's sentiments, and it causes a dull ache in my chest. "This could never have worked."

Suddenly, when faced with the realization of how quickly this is all devolving, I shake my head.

"Okay, look. I fucked up by not telling you about the resort show. I would have," I say. I think I would have. I hope I would have. "But there's another option, and—"

"I don't care about another option," Rhodes spits. "You're unbelievable."

"But this way we could—"

He raises his hands. "Why are you saying 'we'? There is no 'we' here. Honestly, we got on for five seconds in the grand scheme of things."

It's like the wind is knocked out of me, the way he minimizes this thing between us. That can't really be how he feels. I know he must feel something deeper than that. I know there is more to this.

"Don't say that," I try.

He shakes his head. "It is what it is. We're only fooling ourselves otherwise."

You don't believe that.

"But I really think we can get past this," I say. "You can work the resort show and have Paris, and I'll be in New York. I'm not sure about the long-distance thing, but I'm sure we could figure it out."

Rhodes's eyes bug. "New York? What are you on about now?"

"Sophie offered me a position in New York," I say. "An apprenticeship. And I wasn't going to take it at first, but I think it could be good. And it could be good for us."

"Something else you've kept from me," Rhodes says. "Wow. No, I don't see how that'd be any better for us. I really did like you, Milo, but this is clearly just not going to work. Everything else aside, it isn't realistic to have some long-distance relationship based on text messaging and FaceTimes."

He *did* like me. As in past tense.

I want to sink into the floor, slide away like a puddle.

My eyes are welling up, which is beyond embarrassing, and he looks incredibly pained as he stares at me. Seeing the hurt in those gorgeous eyes—the ones I admired so many times—feels like a twisting knife.

Rhodes is right. I am Jekyll and Hyde. One minute I'm hot and one minute I'm cold and even I can't predict it. All I know right now is that I don't want to lose him—don't want to lose this before it even has a chance to get off the ground.

"Can we just have a real conversation about all this?" My voice is breaking. The feeling of weakness adds insult to injury. This vulnerability of being openly shattered is new to me, and it's only making everything more confusing. "This is why I wanted to wait until after the shoot."

"There's not much left to say, is there? Or am I missing something?"

With a newfound desperation to save this, I begin to stutter. "There's plenty to say. We can figure all of this out. We like each other, and there's something here between us. It's something I've never felt before."

Rhodes doesn't look convinced. "Sometimes that isn't enough, Milo."

I'm not sure I realized the scope of my feelings for Rhodes, or the vast expanse they'd started to take up within me. Hearing him say that—say all of this—is devastating. I guess I didn't really expect to burn the whole thing down so quickly. We're standing on scorched earth now, razed to the ground at an impossible pace.

Rhodes drops his shoulders and rubs the back of his neck. "I forgot something at the office, I'm going to go back."

"Don't go. Not like this."

He frowns and leaves.

It's instinctive to follow him out into the hall of the studio. I run after him like a little kid running after his best friend, ready to beg him not to go.

But he doesn't stop just because I'm behind him. In fact, he takes the stairs down to the ground level, and when we're on the street, his eyes are misty as he looks up and down the road to figure out which way to walk.

"Rhodes, please. I get it, I fucked up. I fully own that. I wish I could take it back."

"It's not that simple," he says. "I should have known when you tried to switch those boxes—it's partially on me for not realizing it then."

"I shouldn't have. I know that. It was the heat of the moment, and I was desperate to—"

"To get ahead," Rhodes interjects. "Yeah, I know. You chose to get ahead, and you were going to do it again, even after we talked things out. It's who you are, Milo."

Tears mark my cheeks now. "That isn't true. I didn't do the right thing, in a moment of weakness. In *moments* of weakness. I see that. But it's not who I am. I've never been that person."

"The funniest thing is that you fancy yourself the rat because then you're a victim."

I swallow. "What?"

"Right? The rat has to run from the big bad cat. But you're not the victim here, Milo."

"I never said I was a victim—"

"Here's a better one for you, mate. *Chat échaudé craint l'eau froide.*" He scoffs. "A scalded cat fears cold water."

"But . . ."

"Proper shame."

He shakes his head again and buries his hands in his pockets, turning to walk up the sidewalk away from me.

There's nothing left for me to say or do right now. I know that. My mind is blank, without a single coherent thought. All I keep thinking is how I screwed this up and what it means I've lost. How I'm not going to see his bright blue eyes light up, because he'll never be that happy to see me again. How I'll never feel him hug me or kiss me.

I take solace in a park for a moment, trying to get all my tears out. I feel so stupid for having such a strong emotional reaction. I know we weren't even *together*, but the way I felt with him was different. The way I thought we'd grow into something—that was different.

There's this whole future Rhodes and I could have had, even as friends, that is just gone now, and somehow that has left me with a grief I didn't know I could even feel.

On top of this, I feel like a terrible person. All those things Noel said about Rhodes . . . were they actually true of me? Was Rhodes even wrong about me?

I can't stop crying like a blubbering fool, and I try my best to bury my knuckles in my eyes.

Paris has turned gray alongside me, and now I can't imagine spending more time in this city where I started to see Rhodes in everything so quickly. He's going to be everywhere—in every café and museum and on every avenue—and it's going to be unbearable.

The thought of escaping Paris for New York suddenly feels more appealing than ever.

I gather myself after a bit. I'm going to have to dust myself off, and then I'll email Sophie and let her know I want to start as soon as I possibly can. I don't want to spend any more time here, faced with my failures and all these new aches and pains. Once I do that, I'll talk to Yvette and figure out how we can get the transition started.

As if I summoned her, Yvette's name pops up on my phone.

I sniffle like a giant baby and pick up. "Hi."

"Milo, this is unacceptable. I have been told you were responsible for over thirty thousand euros' worth of accessories, which you left unattended. This is absolutely outrageous. This is not the first issue we've had, and you have shown such poor judgment here, I am left with no other option but to terminate your apprenticeship, effective immediately."

"Wait, Yvette, I'm so sorry." The melodrama of what actually transpired will mean nothing to her. If anything, it might make things worse. I'm scrambling for some excuse or something to get me out of this, but before I can say anything, she's clicking her tongue against her teeth.

"We will leave a box of your things with reception. Your time with Maison Dauphine has come to an end."

From: Sophie Rigby
To: Milo Hawthorne
Subject: Update re: New York Office Apprenticeship

Hi Milo,

I am so sorry to hear about your termination! Unfortunately, your employee profile has been marked Do Not Rehire due to the nature of the cause for termination. Regrettably, this means we are unable to move forward with the apprenticeship as discussed.

Wishing you all my best,

xx Sophie

Sophie: Hi, I'm sorry for the formality of the email. Had to blind copy some team members. I'm SO sad to hear. I hope you're doing okay. Please don't be a stranger and let me know if there's anything I can do. If you ever need a letter of reco or anything . . . I'm here. This is tough, and I know it isn't easy.

Me: Thank you, Sophie, I appreciate it

Sophie: I really did try to get around the Do Not Rehire status. Just so you know

Sophie: It's just a legal thing, I'm sorry

Me: No, I totally get it. Thank you again. It was really lovely working with you

Sophie: You too. If you're ever in New York, I better hear from you. xx

Chapitre Vingt-Huit

The recurring theme of me being sad and alone in Paris has become exhausting.

I guess it's good I'll be going home then, at the very least. I'll be sad back home in Citrus Harbor, with the most colossal failure ever under my belt. Worse than I could have even dreamed up or obsessed about in my worst anxious spirals.

Since Noel and Celeste are on their getaway to Champagne, I've got the apartment to myself. I eat a piece of croissant that's left over on the counter, definitely from Celeste since Noel would never be so messy, and then fall asleep on the couch.

When I wake up in the morning, it's bright and sunny and I realize I've fully slept through the night with no nightmares or anxiety at all. Didn't wake up once.

It's not exactly a good thing, of course, for lethargy to be setting in so immediately.

One thing I've learned is that along with an anxiety disorder, there are bouts of depression here and there. For me, it mostly presents situationally. A therapist told me I'm often mildly depressed, when we discussed my moods and symptoms, but I've learned that my competitive nature and setting goals are the best way to combat this. When I'm focused on a goal or achieving something, I'm much more prone to anxiety than depression. If I don't hit said goal or fail to achieve said thing . . .

All the brightness outside doesn't help the colorless torture in my chest. It's like yearning for *anything* to light me up, but finding that even yearning requires too much energy.

I've so spectacularly failed that I'm not even ashamed to indulge in some of this depression. I mean, I really managed to screw everything up in a royal way. This trip was a complete bust, it seems, and now there's no Maison Dauphine in Paris or New York. Now there's no Rhodes.

I open my text thread with Rhodes and send him a message.

Me: I'm sorry again. If you decide you want to talk, I'm here

Part of me wants to tell him about my apprenticeship getting terminated, but I think it might come off as attention or sympathy seeking, which is really not the angle I'm trying to go for.

Fuck, Milo. It's all so calculated with you. It's always about angles.

Again, I'm positive I am somewhat of a terrible person. Am I worse than an antihero, even? Am I just a villain? All the villains in the big stories are people who are blinded by ambition, driven to do terrible things. Justifying the means for the end is a villainous trait, and it's one I think I've acquired in Paris. Worse, what if I have had it all along and I'm really just incredibly unaware of my own character?

I wish this couch could swallow me whole and erase my existence.

That's how awful I feel about myself right now.

I've missed two calls from Haydée, and as I'm panicking over what she could want, she calls again. My finger hovers over the slider to answer it—do I even want to know? Do I want to face any further humiliation?

The anxiety of not knowing what she has to say wins, however, so I pick up.

"Hello?"

"Hi, Milo."

There's a long, drawn-out silence.

"What's . . . up?"

Haydée sighs. "Milo, you sound like hell. I'm sorry to hear about what happened. I thought I'd reach out to see if you're okay."

Another long, drawn-out silence.

"Really?"

She scoffs. "Yes. Really. Is that so shocking?"

Well, yes.

Haydée was nice enough mostly, but at times she could be really cold, so I'm a bit surprised she wants anything to do with me now that I've been fired from Maison Dauphine.

"I appreciate you calling," I say. "I guess I'm okay, yeah. As okay as I can be."

"We're all pretty upset," she says.

I keep pausing. This is a great example of how difficult it can be for me to find words in the English language, let alone French.

"People are upset? Like, about me?"

"Of course," Haydée says. "We all liked working with you."

I sit up straight so fast I almost faint. "You did?"

"Milo, are you quite all right? Are you drunk or something? Tell me you're not drowning your sorrows alone."

"No, I'm not drunk. I'm just surprised, that's all. I guess I didn't realize people liked working with me."

Haydée snorts now. "What do you *mean*? You were the best. You were on top of everything, and you were always so . . . what is the word for it? Peppy?"

"I was peppy?"

It's like I'm hearing her describe someone else entirely.

"You have a great work ethic, and you are very creative," Haydée says. "I know you must be disappointed. I understand. We will all miss you, and I know you are going to do wonderful things."

"That's really sweet of you," I say. I'm welling up, but I don't want to make it weird, so I do my best to swallow it. "I really needed to hear that, actually. I've been beating myself up about everything."

"It's not about you, even," she says. "There's just a lot of financial liability involved. Leaving the shoot like that . . . if any of us had done that, we'd have faced consequences, Milo. Try not to take it too personally."

Picking at the bouclé of the couch, I poke my tongue in my cheek. "I think I was too competitive. With Rhodes. I cared too much about getting that spot at the resort show. It's good he'll get to work it, but—"

"Rhodes isn't working the resort show." Haydée's voice goes

up. "He will be moving back to London, I think. His apprenticeship was terminated too."

I stand up now, as if doing so might make some difference in how surprising this is. "What?"

"He left the shoot too, Milo. Unacceptable. Like I said, it's not personal. You see now?"

I groan. "But Haydée, everything . . . all of this was my fault. Rhodes shouldn't be fired."

"This is not the way Yvette sees it," Haydée says.

"I can't believe it," I say. "Rhodes is Maison Dauphine's darling. . . . Rosie Hamilton doesn't know yet, does she?"

Haydée sounds confused. "Rosie?"

"We have to fix this before she finds out. I know how important it was to her that Rhodes worked with Maison Dauphine, and I know he—"

"Important to Rosie?" Haydée asks. "*Mais non.* Between us, she only called in this favor because Louis Vuitton decided they wanted Ollie instead. She did it for Rhodes, not for her."

What?

My heart sinks. I was wrong about the whole thing. Rhodes felt like second best to Ollie. Again. And me—a stubborn, headstrong know-it-all—I went on to presume I knew everything about him.

"I have to talk to Yvette," I say. "Do you know what her calendar looks like today? I don't think she's going to take my calls, and an email is going to take too long."

Haydée is hesitating, and I don't blame her, but then she exhales. "You want me to help you parent trap?"

"Um?"

"It's a classic setup, *non*?" She giggles. "I will do it. Let me look at her calendar."

She abruptly ends the call, and as I sit in silence waiting for her to get back to me, I feel even more terrible for how things went down.

All of my previous thinking about being a villain is reinforced. Not only was I totally wrong about why Rhodes was at Maison Dauphine, but he was taking himself out of the competition for the resort show, and now, because of me, he's lost the entire apprenticeship.

I have got to fix things quickly. I'm still hoping I can get to Yvette before Rhodes's family finds out. I'd imagine he is putting off telling them—at least, it wouldn't be the first thing he would want to do. So there's a chance this could all be contained. It might be a stretch, but I'm willing to do my best even if the odds are low.

Noel sends me a text with a screenshot of a *Daily Mirror* article. There's a photo of Ollie in his red Armoury United kit, holding up a fist and cheering. I click into the screen grab.

FOR HE'S AN OLLIE GOOD FELLOW!

Ollie Hamilton makes a dashing impression with his first philanthropic appearance as a member of Armoury United Football Club of North London.

Hamilton, 19, might be familiar to you as the son of Liam Hamilton—endearingly referred to as Left Boot Liam by football fans around the world. One of a talented pair, Ollie's twin brother, Rhodes, has been making headlines for his apprentice work in Paris with luxury fashion brand Maison Dauphine.

Yet to debut for Armoury, Ollie has captured the attention and hearts of millions across the globe on social media. Concurrent with the announcement of his signing with the club following an impressive run with the academy, Ollie took to Instagram with a moving photo of him with Liam and Rhodes when the twins were in primary school.

"Armoury United is my entire life," his caption read. "It's my being, really. It might be cliché to say it's not just a club, but it's the truth. Armoury means everything to me and to my family, and I'm glad to have a place where I belong."

And belong he does. Pundits have predicted Ollie will be a welcome and lively addition to the club. Preorders for the yet-to-be-revealed 2025 kit with his name on it have already sold out. Some social media users have pointed out that having a Hamilton back with Armoury United could have a number of overwhelmingly positive financial effects on the club, which has already seen record attendance and finished third in the league last season.

"Ollie Hamilton's going to change the game," wrote one user. "This'll be the best thing to happen to our boys in years."

Below that quote, Ollie's previously mentioned Instagram post is embedded. The photo shows two little blond boys in slightly oversized Armoury kits on either side of their father, whose face is instantly recognizable.

My heart sinks even further, wondering if Rhodes has seen this.

Armoury means everything to me and to my family.

Noel: Christ. That title. And this is just the beginning. It's about to be all Ollie, all the time, once he debuts

Haydée calls back before I'm able to respond to Noel. I rush to answer, nearly knocking over the vase of flowers Rhodes bought for Celeste.

"Yvette's calendar is private all day," she says wistfully.

I throw my head back. "Great."

"But," she sings, "I called her driver and I know where she will be."

"That's genius!" Haydée responds well to praise and affirmation, though it's much more effective coming from Yvette or the leadership team. I can practically imagine her beaming on the other end. "So? Where will she be?"

"She is having lunch with Pascal shortly, which is really your only chance. Otherwise, all private appointments that I don't think would work."

Lunch with Pascal?

"Are you sure there isn't another opening? Maybe I can try to stop her between meetings. I don't think ambushing her lunch with Pascal will go too well. . . ."

She clicks her tongue against her teeth. "*Non*. There is no other time. Perhaps you can pretend it is a coincidence?"

"I'm sure she'd believe I'm dining wherever she and Pascal are going." The sarcasm isn't intended for Haydée, so I apologize.

"Okay, if this is it, then I'll have to just make it work. Where are they going?"

"Le Relais Plaza," she says. "At the Plaza Athénée. It is only just down the street from the office."

I gape. "The Plaza Athénée? Is there a dress code? I don't know if I even have anything nice enough for that."

"Just wear something smart," she suggests. "Like trousers and a jacket." After a pause: "What exactly is your plan here?"

Now it seems like good news that Noel and Celeste are in Champagne. There's nobody around to tell me this is certifiably nuts. Nobody around to try and talk me out of it.

"I'm going to walk into Le Relais Plaza, and I'm going to talk to Yvette."

Haydée laughs. *"D'accord,* Milo. Welcome back."

Chapitre Vingt-Neuf

The Hôtel Plaza Athénée is, I think, one of the most famous and luxurious hotels in Paris. At least as depicted by a lot of American media. The five-star hotel is an elegant fixture of the Avenue Montaigne, with red awnings and ruby geraniums garnishing the iron-wrought windows and terraces.

So it doesn't feel like the ideal place to surprise Yvette when she's at lunch with the creative director of Maison Dauphine.

In all my overthinking on the way here, however, it's become clear there isn't an ideal place for this to happen. I've made my bed, and now these are the circumstances I am stuck with.

This is one of the more unhinged things I've done, without a doubt, but according to Haydée, this is the only chance I have, so I am taking it. I'd like to believe, after hearing how he wanted me to have the resort show, Rhodes would do the same for me.

I've wanted one-on-one time with Pascal since before I even got this apprenticeship, and now I am jeopardizing any chance of him ever having a favorable opinion of me. It's not, after all, considered very sophisticated or well-mannered to waylay people, much less in a restaurant operated by a Michelin-starred chef.

When I walk through the gold-adorned revolving door, I am overwhelmed with nerves. This is the type of thing that makes my vision go a bit blurry, my heartbeat get erratic, my pits start to sweat uncontrollably . . . thank god I'm wearing a sport coat. Sometimes before a big tennis match, I'd panic that the bottoms of my feet would sweat too much and I'd slide around in my shoes. This never happened, but it didn't stop me from worrying about it.

Standing in the lobby, I am surely out of my league here. Gorgeous, impossibly tall flower arrangements seem to grow beside the massive columns, and a grand chandelier anchors the room. Mirrored doors and rich paintings add a distinct feeling of luxury to the space.

Confidence, Milo. Confidence.

Je suis confiant.

I puff up my chest just a little, and I get into a mindset that doesn't belong to me.

In my head now, I'm someone more like Rhodes or Ollie. I'm someone who throws on a jacket and tie for lunch without even thinking anything of it—the tight, restricted range of movement for my arms doesn't feel limiting, but empowering. In my head, I'm someone who isn't going to look at the price when I order. I'll get one of the nicest bottles of wine without even asking anything about it, and when the waiter brings it over to taste, I'll *actually* taste it and consider whether it's worthy of my consumption. In my head, I fit in here.

I walk over to the front desk, resting an elbow on the marble. The woman at the computer is probably mid-forties, with black hair and red lips that match her dress.

"Bonjour, monsieur," she says with a wide smile. "Welcome to the Hôtel Plaza Athénée. Are you checking in?"

"Bonjour." Then, with all the confidence in the world, I shake my head. "No, I'm here to meet someone for lunch. Only I'm not sure how to find my way. Would you be so kind as to show me to Le Relais Plaza?"

The woman squints a bit, and I think she is evaluating me silently. Probably scanning me for details that would give away if I belong here or not. Stitching on my lapel or the structure of my shirting. How well-groomed I am, maybe?

It feels like forever that she examines me quietly, and I wonder if this was a terrible idea altogether. It would be humiliating to be asked more questions and get denied. Or, worse, what if they have some kind of blacklist for people who try to disturb hotel guests? Pascal Dumas is incredibly famous, after all, and I don't think they'd take this lightly.

The woman's face softens. "Of course."

And just like that, I'm being guided through the hotel to the restaurant. As I follow her, I silently exhale the stress from moments before. We come to the entrance, which is just as elegant as the rest of the hotel—an arched, lit doorway with gold lettering that reads LE RELAIS PLAZA in a fancy serif font.

She stops at the door, which I was crossing my fingers for, because if she wanted to show me to the table, things would have gotten awkward quickly. My backup plan was to thank her for guiding me but to let her know I wanted to use the restroom before joining my lunch date, which might have given me away.

"Here we are," she says. "Enjoy your lunch."

She's off, and when I walk in, I admire the restaurant. It's Art

Deco, which I'd read when I looked up the reviews and the dress code. Brass lighting, tall palms, and gorgeous gilded artwork that looks carved into stone, spanning the wall behind the bar.

I spot Yvette and Pascal quickly.

They're both smiling, which is a great sign.

It's somewhat surreal, seeing Pascal Dumas in the flesh. Obviously, he's a human, just like us. But I have his coffee table book and I follow him on Instagram and I've read and watched dozens of interviews. He's a revolutionary in many ways, but he brings a certain reverence to Renard Florin's legacy—shown through small acts like paying homage to L'or des Fous and its history. Pascal is revered in the fashion world for bringing Maison Dauphine into the contemporary space while maintaining its integrity and displaying a deep respect for the fashion house and its roots.

I cannot believe I am about to make a complete ass out of myself in front of this man.

One foot in front of the other. That's all I can manage to do or even think about as I make my way across the restaurant, over the blue-and-gold fan-patterned carpeting. I walk as if this isn't terrifying, because the only way I can do this is if I pretend I'm the type of person who might bump into Yvette at Le Relais Plaza.

She spots me as I'm approaching their table, and her smile falls immediately, which sends a shock of nervous chills down my neck and spine. I'm not sure what my first bodily response is—wanting to throw up, wanting to spin and run, or feeling faint enough to drop to the floor in cold unconsciousness.

"Milo." She says it in a whisper, hissing like a mother annoyed with her child. "What are you doing here?"

I glance around. "I'm meeting someone for lunch."

She narrows her eyes. "Who?"

"A friend," I say. "I just saw you and wanted to come say hello and apologize in person for what happened at the shoot."

Smoothing the napkin in her lap and pursing her lips, she sits up straight. "I assure you none of this is necessary."

But Pascal seems intrigued. He turns to me and studies me behind his thick tortoiseshell glasses. He's wearing a brown tweed suit, which seems like it'd be excruciatingly warm in the summer, but it fits him perfectly, like it was made just for him. Which I guess it probably was.

"To whom do we owe the pleasure?" Pascal asks, one corner of his lip quirking up.

"Milo Hawthorne, sir." I awkwardly nod, which is a million times better than the intrusive urge to *bow* that just occurred in my mind. *God*. "I was an apprentice for—"

"Ah." He places his forearms on the edge of the table. "I know who you are. Indeed."

Yvette looks displeased, eyes darting from Pascal to me. "It was nice seeing you, Milo."

Pascal, undeterred, gestures toward me. "Your entry into our apprenticeship program was my favorite. It displayed a deep understanding of Maison Dauphine. Renard's signature defiance and elegance wrapped into one."

"Thank you," I say. "Or, *merci*, sorry."

He barks a laugh that is so loud several people turn to look at us. My cheeks burn. "I like that." He says. "Very good. What is this you are apologizing for? At the shoot?"

I couldn't have asked for a better in, so I draw a deep breath.

"I had a lapse of judgment, unfortunately. I was meant to be responsible for the jewelry and some other items at an accessories shoot and I . . . well, I stepped away, and left the assets unattended. It was a terrible mistake," I say this to Yvette. "And it's one I am deeply sorry for. I wish I could go back and be more sensible."

Yvette nods curtly. "Rather awkward to discuss over lunch."

Pascal furrows his brow. "And were any pieces missing or stolen?"

"No," Yvette says. "But the financial liability was too great. We must uphold all employees and individuals affiliated with the maison to the appropriate standards of responsibility, which is why Milo and Rhodes were, sadly, unable to maintain their apprenticeships."

I'm watching the gears turn in Pascal's mind, the way his brow becomes more pinched and his mouth twitches ever so slightly. "Seems a bit rash, I suppose. From my perspective, anyway."

"I'm not here to appeal my termination," I offer. "Though, if I'm being honest, I don't think it's quite fair to Rhodes. He was, rightfully, a bit offended that day after he found out I was likely going to be working the resort show instead of him."

Yvette frowns. "And why would he be offended? Again, this is not a personal decision, but one based on merit and responsibility. His mistake—"

"Mistake?" Pascal asks.

"The Instagram Story."

"Oh yes." Pascal grins now. He points to me. "I quite liked that. Very . . . *enjoué*, I think. No harm was done."

Yvette lifts her shoulders, clearly at a loss for what to say next.

"Only the thing is, it wasn't his mistake. It was mine."

"Yours?" Yvette, unconvinced, leans back in her seat before gesturing to an iPad on the table. "Milo, I'm afraid we have important things we must discuss—"

"I will let you get to it," I say. "I'm sorry. I just wanted to tell you the truth. Rhodes didn't do anything wrong. Either time. I shouldn't have let him take the blame for my mistake at the gala, and I shouldn't have left the accessories unattended. Rhodes hadn't been assigned a job at the shoot yet, and it was my fault we got into an argument, and he was upset. It's quite understandable given how everything happened."

I swallow, because I know that what's going to come next will be bad for me. Painful, like when you're a little kid and you pocket a candy bar at the grocery store and your parents make you take it back and apologize for stealing.

"I also tried to sabotage him. Before the Tuileries event. I switched the labels on some boxes, so that his mother's pieces would go to British *Vogue*. Rhodes knew I'd do this, and he got ahead of it, so the event went smoothly."

Yvette's mouth is ajar, and her eyes are wide. "Milo . . ."

"Rhodes doesn't deserve to have his apprenticeship terminated," I say. "I do, I will admit that. But please don't make him go back to London. He has worked hard, and even when he did all those tasks after the gala that were clearly meant to punish him for a mistake that wasn't his, he didn't complain or give up. He should be working for Maison Dauphine, and he should get to work the resort show."

Yvette is rendered speechless, and she takes a sip of her water, glancing around the restaurant.

"Why would you sabotage him?" Pascal asks. "Why would you risk ruining the event?"

I visibly cringe. "I know, it was absolutely *awful* of me. I have never done something like that in my life, and I am so ashamed and embarrassed of it. Back home, I played tennis competitively for my high school, and one of our family values was to always have integrity and honor. Never cheat, never do anything to get ahead. It's not a reflection of my character, and I apologize for jeopardizing the event like that. It was thoughtless and selfish and immature."

Pascal chuckles. "Indeed, but I truly wonder *why*? What possessed you to do this?"

Yvette bats her lashes. "Yes, Milo. Feel free to expand on this."

It feels like I'm in the principal's office. Or something even worse. I'm beginning to get choked up by the circumstances and by the brutal reflection of myself I'm forced to face in this moment.

"I don't know," I say, voice shaking. "I guess I felt threatened by Rhodes. He's famous and wealthy and charming. I thought everything came easily to him. Before I got to know him, I assumed I knew all there was to know about him, and I viewed him as competition with an impossible edge. I viewed him as having an advantage over me I couldn't possibly hope to challenge."

Yvette's face softens just the tiniest amount, but she catches it and lifts her chin.

"Why adjust your own values, then?" Pascal asks.

"It was stupid," I admit. "Really stupid. But I wanted this so badly. I kept thinking . . . *You're here, Milo. You're in Paris, with this once-in-a-lifetime opportunity with Maison Dauphine.* I had the chance to experience and do things that people across the world would kill for. And I fully understood the gravity of it. I felt the weight of what it'd mean to lose, and I couldn't stand to accept that possibility, even if I never had a chance all along."

Pascal frowns. "That is a bit of a bleak outlook on yourself, Milo."

"Pardon?"

"Very often in life, we're faced with challenges and barriers. Particularly when we are going after big things. The bigger the dream, the bigger the obstacles." He adjusts a bit in his chair so he's facing me full-on. "In order to succeed, we have to fully believe in ourselves. We have to believe we are able to overcome any obstacle. That we can rise to any challenge. Otherwise, there is no point in moving forward at all. If we cannot believe in ourselves, after all, why should we expect someone else to?"

I try not to show too much emotion, though my bottom lip is beginning to tremble.

"I understand wanting to get ahead," Pascal says. He waves his hand. "I have done things I am not proud of, especially as a younger man wanting to make it in fashion. Many of us have seen ambition as a dagger, with which we stab ourselves or the back of another. But the truth is there is the option to sheath the dagger and not do any harm at all. We often seem to forget that."

Yvette seems bored of this conversation, letting out a near-silent sigh.

"Renard Florin himself had a slightly cunning side, I'm sure you know. He was a bit mischievous, a bit rebellious. Pushed the envelope. Wanted the best. Wanted to *be* the best. But sometimes that could present as being a bit too ruthless. A bit too cold and perhaps, at times, inconsiderate of the effect on others." He shrugs. "Renard was not a bad man, and most accounts of him are positive, but I know he had his moments.

"The point I am trying to make is that we have a choice, Milo. Those of us with a competitive nature—with ambitions and aspirations and a desire to be the best—we can act from a place of desperation and fear, or we can find confidence in ourselves and trust that what is meant to be, based on merit and hard work, will be."

I nod. "Right. Yes, of course. I'm sorry. I really am."

"I'm not asking you to apologize." Pascal laughs. "I'm asking you to do yourself a favor and learn from this. Grow from it. Don't make these mistakes again."

"Yes, sir."

"Very good."

Yvette claps her hands together. "Well, this was nice." With her eyes, as they shift toward the door, she tells me it's time for me to leave.

"I'm sorry again," I say. "For all of it. I hope maybe there is a chance you'll reconsider terminating Rhodes. I really believe he deserves a chance."

"Thank you," Yvette says. She looks at Pascal and nods slowly. "We will discuss."

"Bonne journée, Milo," Pascal says.

"Bonne journée."

It sounds like there might be a chance for Rhodes, so I leave. Though it's with a heavy heart I will leave Paris behind, at least I might have corrected some of my mistakes. No matter how humiliating it was to say all of that to Pascal and Yvette, it's freeing in a way. The truth is all out. I just hope they'll find it in their hearts not to punish Rhodes after everything I've said.

Standing outside the hotel, I open the maps app and look to see if there's anything in Paris I haven't done yet. I may be overwhelmingly depressed right now, but I may as well be overwhelmingly depressed at a Parisian landmark, since I won't have access to them soon.

I haven't visited the Sacré-Coeur, so that might be a start. There's also Notre-Dame and Place de la Concorde. I wonder if I should go back to ditch the jacket first or if I should—

"Milo."

I turn around to find Yvette emerging from the revolving door. Her heels are loud against the concrete as she comes to stand beside me.

Squinting under the sun, she looks pretty pissed, so I instinctively pocket my phone and face her. "Yvette, I'm really sorry about that, but I had to—"

"You haven't booked a flight home, I presume?"

"Not yet. I plan to tonight." Her face indicates this conversation might be going in an unexpected direction, and my chest is instantly lit on fire. "Why?"

Yvette rolls her eyes. "You made quite the impression on Pascal."

This can't mean what I think it means.

"I'll expect you both in the office tomorrow at eight thirty sharp. We've got a lot left to do for the resort show, which you both will be working."

"Wait, what?"

"Eight thirty sharp," Yvette says, turning on her heel and

walking back toward the hotel. She stops, glances back, and lowers her chin, eyes hooded. "No funny business, Milo. I expect you and Rhodes to both exceed all expectations, or I guarantee neither of you will ever get a job in fashion. In any city. Are we understood?"

I gulp. *"Oui."*

With a stony stare, she purses her lips. *"Bon courage, Milo."*

Chapitre Trente

Thanks to Google, I have learned what Yvette meant by her steely "*bon courage*," and I am not thinking it's a great omen for her faith in us. After all, while "*bonne chance*" might mean "good luck" when something is out of one's hands, "*bon courage*" indicates it's up to the recipient to make their own luck or outcome. The sarcastic tone of her voice tells me she's expecting me to fuck up the outcome.

It's a good possibility.

I texted Rhodes last night.

Me: You've probably heard from Maison Dauphine by now. Was kind of an awkward conversation with Yvette and Pascal, but I told them everything . . . I'm sorry again. Hope to see you at the office tomorrow.

No response, as expected.

One somewhat comical part of all this is that I haven't told Celeste or Noel anything, so they don't know about my termination, brazen waylay, or reinstatement. All in a day's work, I guess.

They also don't know that Rhodes and I aren't speaking, which is probably why they keep sending me things about the Ollie article and the corresponding social media attention he and Rhodes have been getting lately.

There are even photos of Rhodes and me circulating, taken from different Maison Dauphine events, with plenty of speculation attached.

People on social media seem to have a lot of opinions. I sort of expect a text, at least checking on me, since some people have had some less than polite things to say. Mostly they're nice, but some have questioned why Rhodes would go out with "some rando from Florida" or called me a downgrade from his last girlfriend, Imogen, who was a very gorgeous contestant on a popular British dating show.

I obviously didn't spend any length of time looking her up or finding photos of them together and comparing how he might look, aesthetically, at least, much better with her.

That would be silly.

There were the funny or slightly positive ones, of course, like the post asserting that next to Rhodes I'm a "short king," which feels like a bit of a stretch and is likely only because he's over six feet tall. Some people called us adorable, and a lot of people had nice things to say about my appearance, which helped soothe the sting from the others.

I should have started to think about this as soon as people were eyeing us together at the restaurant, but the speculation and the scrutiny of being linked with Rhodes are way more than I anticipated, and we aren't even officially together. Now, of course, we won't ever be.

Great, can't wait to see how that *all plays out online.*

Rhodes must not care about any of the stories swirling around, since he hasn't said anything to me or addressed the rumors, though he has posted a photo of a sunset on his story. I'm not sure why, honestly, but if I were to read into it with any sort of inflated ego, it might be to show me he is unfazed by everything going on and that he's very much ignoring my texts.

That could be absurd, though. It could have nothing to do with me at all.

Either way, I'm graced with another sleepless night. I have to physically fight the urge to see what people are saying about me online. I want to search our names together so badly, but I don't think it'll end in any positive way, so I don't allow myself to do it.

Once it's time to go into the office, I get dressed like always, and I look at myself in the mirror. Honestly, since getting here, my hair is more disheveled, my skin is drier, the bags under my eyes are darker and deeper, and I've got more of a pronounced frown.

It doesn't do me any good to dwell on any of these things, either, though, so I put in my AirPods and head to Maison Dauphine.

I finally open all the unanswered messages from the tennis group chat on my walk back. I've been ignoring it for a bit, mostly because I have been increasingly anxious and a lot of it is random stuff about TV shows or music or movies, but it makes me feel like a bad friend. I don't want to lose touch with my friends from the tennis team, and I feel extra removed from the group since I'm thousands of miles away and several hours ahead.

Of course, there are some things I'm okay with skimming as I catch up.

Deuce Bags

Isaac: Bro is literally dating Rhodes Hamilton and didn't tell us

Chip: We should have seen this coming

Isaac: Should we?

Miguel: hey don't act like Milo can't pull

Isaac: No, I mean obviously he can pull

Isaac: I am just in a state of shock

Chip: I'm waiting for Imogen to make a statement

After some more scrolling through enthralling segments with similar themes, I arrive at the most recent texts.

Isaac: Have we lost Milo?

Chip: He's a busy guy

Miguel: too busy for the deuce bags

Chip: One day we should change that

Isaac: No way, why would we ever change it

Chip: Idk, we're going to college and people around us will see our phones and not understand the context

Miguel: we cannot ever change deuce bags

Isaac: Yeah, if they don't get the context, it's an icebreaker

Chip: "Our rival tennis team used to call us deuce bags, so we thought it was funny"

Chip: Cue crickets

Chip: That your icebreaker, king?

Isaac: MILOOO, where are you when we need you!

Me: I'm here! Sorry sorry, I've been so busy and things have been a total shit show

Chip: How bad?

Me: Bad

Isaac: Oh no . . .

Miguel: catch us up

Me: I'm running into the office right now, but I will catch you guys up soon

Me: And Chip, I'm sorry, but we cannot change the name of the group chat

Chip: Fine, fine

Isaac: Sorry things are shit, Milo. But you got this! And don't forget, no matter how bad it all gets, you've always got your Deuce Bags

It's comforting, funnily enough. When we all graduated, I had mild moments of panic that we might lose touch—that Celeste would be my only friend and they'd all move on and forget about all of our fun times on the team—but we've been through so much together and become so close, it makes sense we'll continue on. Even if I'm the worst at texting back.

When I arrive, I'm surprised to find there is no awkwardness.

In fact, Haydée actually looks *happy* to see me. As I walk down the hall toward the fashion closet, she waves from behind the glass of the conference room where she's pinning printed-out photos to a foam board.

I stop before opening the doors to the closet. Even though I'm not sure what is going to happen when I see him, I'm hoping Rhodes is on the other side. I'm hoping he's sitting there in some stylish streetwear with one of his belt bags across his chest. Maybe he'll say something a bit snide, but maybe there'd be some chance for him to hear out an apology.

Drawing in a breath through my nose, I practice the 4–4–4 method. *Hold. Exhale out the mouth.*

I push open one of the doors, and there he is.

He's in a sky-blue hoodie, wearing silver over-the-ear Apple headphones and focused on one of the iPads they gave us to take photos of samples.

"Hi," I try, knowing he is wearing the headphones very purposely to deter me from speaking to him. I should have seen this coming.

I walk over to my desk and sit in the chair. It feels strange to be here, like I am on probation or something. I log in, and everything is the same. I'd expected to find my desktop reset or something, but I guess I hadn't been removed from the employee database yet, so it's all still there.

Rhodes won't look at me. He doesn't even seem remotely curious about my presence—which I'm sure of, because I have glanced over about a thousand times in the span of five minutes.

Sophie hasn't emailed me yet, and I wonder if she knows I'm back. I know she's normally awake at an ungodly hour, but it's only two thirty in the morning in New York, so I respond to a thread she's on and expect she'll pop up in my inbox in a few hours.

Obviously New York is off the table now. I'm hanging on by a thread, with everything resting on the resort show going smoothly. Specifically, I guess, it's about things with Rhodes and me going smoothly. No sabotage or bickering or silly mistakes. There's no risk of us getting off track because we've snuck off to make out, and while that is ultimately a good thing for our careers, it's a realization that makes my heart drop all the same.

He still won't look in my direction.

There's only one thing I can think of, so I tap him on the shoulder. He ignores me at first, even though he must feel it. I tap him again, this time a little harder, and he finally lifts the headphones off his right ear and offers me side-eye.

Seems like the best I'm going to get right now.

"Did you see this request from *Vogue* Italia?"

He nods once.

"Well . . ." I don't exactly know what to ask. I hadn't gotten this far in the plan. "I don't know if we have this belt either."

With a bit of a pout, he tilts his head toward one of the shelves, where the belt with the large gold MD is clearly rolled up and facing out.

"Right, but is that the—"

He puts his headphones back on and returns his attention to the iPad.

Great. This is going super well.

I figure it's best to give him a moment, because I'm only going to annoy him if I tap him again right now. I fulfill the *Vogue* Italia request, packing up the belt in a Maison Dauphine box that I place in a larger cardboard box. Then I make a shipping label and place the box in our outgoing mail pile.

Once I'm done, I let the PR assistant know we are sending the belt ASAP.

Rhodes hasn't looked at me once. A somber aching has replaced my heartbeat, and the room has grown chilly. I know we were really only ever strangers, but it felt like we'd made so much progress—we'd gotten closer so quickly, and now we're strangers all over again. There's a unique sadness here, because it's not like some breakup where we never see each other again. First, there's no true breakup at all, just like Rhodes had joked about. But second, he's reluctantly stuck with me, clearly with no desire to communicate at all.

I break, reaching over and tapping him on the shoulder. This time he takes his headphones off immediately, placing them on the desk and facing me.

"Yes?"

"Can we please talk? We're going to be working together, and I know you don't want to hear what I have to say, but I'd really like to try and get past this."

Rhodes is hardly moved by this, but he lazily lifts his shoulders, gesturing for me to go on.

"I made a bunch of mistakes," I say. "And I have learned a big lesson the hard way."

"And what lesson is that?"

"That I don't have to stab you or me," I say.

Rhodes's eyes widen. "*Stab*? Who said anything about—"

"No, I mean, that's abridged. It's something Pascal said." I shake my head and wave my hands around. "Pretend I never said that."

"What are you on about, Milo?"

"I am sorry I was so competitive and that I let my ambition get the best of me," I say. "I knew better, but I was insecure, and I didn't know how to . . . I felt so threatened I temporarily lost my mind."

"Several times," Rhodes points out.

"You're right. I lost my mind several times."

Rhodes crosses his arms. "Well. I suppose you're right. We're going to be stuck working together."

Stuck.

"I know things won't go back to the way they were. . . ."

"No, they won't." He swallows, sitting up a bit straighter and pulling his folded arms tighter together.

Our eyes lock, and I know he's saying it all right there. We're not going to have a conversation about it. Not a proper one, anyway. Whatever happened between us romantically is in the past. There's no more "us" at all. There's a sting of warmth behind my eyes, and a chill runs up my spine.

I clear my throat.

"But hopefully we can get along. I know this is important to you, and I am not going to do anything to screw it up. We just have to get through the resort show and show Yvette that everything is fine. In fact, anything you need, just let me know."

Unfolding his arms, Rhodes places his hands on his lap. "All right then. Sounds like a plan."

Sounds like a plan . . .

"And I don't know if you have any concerns about what's been going on . . ."

"What do you mean?"

A bit of an awkward topic to breach now. I shift in my seat. "Well. On social media, I mean."

"People on social media are blooming idiots," he says. "What's new?"

I don't show him how much it hurts that he doesn't seem to care how it affects me. I just shrug it off. "Yeah, that's true."

"They've always got something to say. You know what they say about opinions."

Right. Of course I know what they say about opinions. I guess I just don't exactly know what Rhodes's actual opinion is about all this.

"You just let people say whatever they want, then? I mean, some of the stuff they say is pretty out there."

He kicks the side of his Adidas into the desk. "Sure. But it's, like, they're literally always gonna do that. Just have to ignore it and ride it out. You'll see."

"It's just weird having all these random people speculate about my life."

"I don't know why anyone is so invested in who a stranger may or may not fancy." Rhodes blows a raspberry. "Quite lame, if you ask me. But oh well. *C'est la vie, Milo.*"

He's skirting around the fact that this affects me. I don't want to let it get to me, but I'm already feeling shaky—the sadness that accompanies our non-breakup is overwhelming to me on its own, so my emotions are particularly volatile, and I seem prone to a sharp annoyance at his flippant tone.

Still, this isn't the time for me to mouth off, and I am fully aware of that.

Lesson learned.

"I think the worst part of all those stories . . ." He sucks his teeth and looks to me. "Probably when the wrong person believes them. When they judge you before getting to know you."

I swallow, gaze dropping to the floor. "I'm sorry about that too. I know now . . . I know *you* now."

"And now you know how it feels," he says. "A bit, anyway. Though, believe it or not, I don't take any pleasure in that. For what it's worth, I'm sorry some of them are so vicious."

"Yeah, some of them have been tough to read. A lot of people who really love Imogen really hate me."

He groans, hand forming a fist. "Fuck. I'm sorry, Milo. All you can do is ignore those people. They're out of their minds. They have no lives. They're just spewing shit, really."

"It's not *all* shit, I mean . . . Imogen is . . ."

Rhodes looks at me very seriously. "Imogen and I were not good together. I don't know what that even was. Like, *at all*. And I don't mean to be disrespectful to her in saying that. But I need you to know there's no comparison there. Not even a small amount . . . the connection you and I have . . ." He clears his throat. "Had. Anyway, try not to let them get to you. It gets easier with time."

I want to cling to what he just said. I want to remind him we *do* still have that connection, but I don't want to screw this up any more than I already have, especially when we're so close to the show.

Instead, I nod silently and go back to work.

I make sure all my work is perfect and I don't irritate Rhodes, or anyone else at Maison Dauphine for that matter.

We get an email asking which of us will deliver the handwritten invitations to over twenty-five addresses around Paris. The invitations are a formality, just like the ones we verified for the gala. These people already know they're attending the show on Saturday, but it's something the house does for prestige and posterity. We can split them up, the email offers, or one of us can just spend the day doing this.

It sounds absolutely miserable, and I volunteer just so Rhodes won't have to do it.

I'm here, I remind myself. *I'm back, and I have to make the most of this.*

Because I got what I wanted. I got what I came to Paris for. Didn't I?

Chapitre Trente-et-Un

I sleep through the night now.

Mostly because Maison Dauphine has become its own waking nightmare for me for the last two days. There's an inescapable pain that goes along with seeing Rhodes every day, and there's a numbness in doing the requests and small tasks when I have already secured a spot working the resort show. Without a true goal or something to make progress toward, the fire is starting to dim.

On Thursday, when Noel and Celeste get back from Champagne, they are like two absolutely over-the-moon lovebirds. If I weren't lovesick myself, I'd probably find it to be the cutest thing I've ever seen. After all, they're basically two of my favorite people, and seeing them that happy is great.

But every time they do something cute, it's like this upset to my central nervous system. I don't know how my heart latched on to Rhodes so quickly, because it doesn't make logical sense, but I find myself practically mourning the way we won't do the little things they do. We won't look at each other the way they do. Won't burst into giggles when we say the same thing at the same time because we've just become *that* in-sync.

I don't tell them what's happened, of course. I can't bring myself to be a dark cloud over their perfect French holiday. Especially with Celeste looking so happy after everything with her grandmother. I'd feel horrible taking even a tiny bit of that away from her.

So, instead, I tell them I'm working the resort show, and Celeste is thrilled because they've got the perfect bottle of champagne from their trip. Noel doesn't bring up New York, thankfully, and puts on some Serge Gainsbourg as we pop the cork and pour it into fancy flutes from Celeste's aunt's kitchen, the golden bubbles fizzing and skirting up the glass with a light layer of foam at the top. We clink the glasses and celebrate my win, and we're probably also celebrating them being a thing, which I'm more than happy to do. In fact, I find that a bit more worthy of celebrating, given everything.

On Friday, I barely make it through the workday.

When I get there in the morning, I make sure all of my requests are out the door with record speed, but they keep coming in. Rhodes and I are tasked with a million things, and we are pulled into more meetings with Haydée and Zoe. They'll open up Zoom and talk through something with another Maison Dauphine team member, mostly in French so I don't actually know what's going on, and then we'll have another task at the end of the meeting that needs to be done in fifteen minutes.

We organize the resort look database and receive a document of approved first priorities and VIPs, since we know the floodgates for requests will open as soon as *Vogue Runway* posts all the looks after the show.

The energy has shifted from understated and poised to chaotic and fast-paced. Haydée and Zoe are working on gifts that I am going to drop off at hotels for some editors and celebrities this afternoon.

The good news is my sadness is only allowed to surface for very, very brief periods of time. I'm way too busy and overwhelmed to experience it otherwise, and the rush of chaos has been invigorating. I work well under pressure, and there is a lot of it.

The other good news is that Rhodes and I are forced to cohabitate, and we've *nearly* gotten friendly with each other. We've exchanged glances—shared disbelief at a timeline for a project, or a common feeling of being dumbfounded by the inanity of a task.

After I drop off the gifts, my last task is to do a pickup for Haydée, which I find out is her dress for the show. She thanks me profusely and apologizes for having me do it, but considering she looks like she hasn't slept or eaten in two weeks at this point, I mean it when I tell her I don't mind.

As the business day comes to a close, we finally shut the fashion closet door for the first time and sit in silence. There's absolute pandemonium on the other side of that door, but in here, it's quiet.

We sprawl out in our chairs, fully spent from the day. From the week, really.

"We did it," Rhodes says. "We made it to the finish line."

"Tomorrow is the real finish line," I say.

Rhodes cracks his knuckles. "Right. Tomorrow night I'll have the best sleep I've had in ages."

I nod. "My feet are killing me. I can't wait to just lie around all day on Sunday."

"I appreciate you taking on the invitations," he says.

He must realize how much I ended up walking around Paris, even with some of the transportation suggestions.

It's nice to hear him acknowledge that, and it's a big step forward for us.

"Of course. No big deal."

"I do find it a bit mad we have to hand-deliver invitations like that at all," Rhodes says, hushed like Yvette might hear. "These people have already reserved their spots. Or rather, their assistants have."

"Just the way things work," I say. "I guess it's a fine tradition overall. It is a nice gesture."

"Sure," Rhodes says. "Tell your feet that."

We both laugh, and it's like we're friends.

I'm exhausted, but Noel and Celeste are texting me that they're eager to do something fun for their last night in Paris, and they're just as eager to include me and Rhodes. I could easily use the excuse that I need to get a good night's rest before the show tomorrow, but I don't have a call time until five p.m., and they both know I'm not going to get much sleep regardless.

I'll make up an excuse for why Rhodes can't come. He's got a dinner to go to or something.

"What is it?"

"Hmm?"

Rhodes points to my phone. "What's got you making that face?"

I wasn't aware of any certain formation of my facial muscles. "I'm not making any face. Am I?"

"Bit of a face," he says.

I shrug. "It's stupid."

"Your face isn't *stupid*," Rhodes pokes.

I roll my eyes. "Good one."

"No, no. Okay, something stupid. My favorite." Rhodes chuckles. "Tell me, then."

"Noel and Celeste have been in Champagne this week, and now they're back and it's their last night in Paris, and they want us to hang out with them," I say. "But they've just been so happy, and after Celeste's grandma and everything, I didn't want to bring down the mood, so I haven't told them anything that's gone on."

"Between us, you mean."

I nod. "Or with Maison Dauphine, even."

Rhodes rubs his eye. "Whoa. So, what, they think this is all just sunshine and daisies?"

"They do," I say. "But it's fine. I'm just going to tell them you've got plans. Easy enough."

We sit in silence and Rhodes seems to study me, scratching the back of his neck.

As we sit here, essentially staring at each other, I wonder if he thinks this apprenticeship has affected my appearance as much as I have come to believe it has. It's not like Noel or Celeste have commented on the way my face seems more sunken in, and I wonder if I'm imagining things. Because when I look at Rhodes, his skin appears to be just as bright as the day we met. No bags beneath his eyes, no thin cheeks, just a perfect complexion that appears healthy and radiant.

Of course.

"I could go with you."

I blink. "What?"

"If you want, I could go with you tonight. I don't mind. I liked Celeste and Noel."

"Well, I'm sure you have something better to do," I offer. "I completely understand if you want to get more rest before tomorrow or . . ."

He folds his arms again. "Nah. I probably won't sleep too well, honestly. Bit anxious, between us. So it's fine. Unless you'd rather me not. Then your plan is good."

"No, I mean, I'd like you to come. If it won't be too weird for you."

"It's just one evening."

"But they're going to think we're . . ."

Rhodes cracks a smile. "I think I can manage one evening. If you can."

Chapitre Trente-Deux

Rhodes and I are a bit awkward together, and I wonder if Noel or Celeste will catch on. After all, at Roland Garros, he wasn't super shy about a little bit of affection. Now, even though there's only about an inch between us, he's much more distant.

We're wandering around the uneven cobblestoned streets of Montmartre, a charming little neighborhood in the 18th that I've seen in loads of movies and films and social media posts. Celeste and I took photos outside the famous little pink restaurant with its green shutters, La Maison Rose, before we went off for dinner. The quaint buildings still stand from the days when it was a small village, and there are vines sprawling across many of the facades.

Now that the stars are out and the lanterns light the streets, it's an entirely new kind of magical.

Noel and Celeste aren't holding hands or anything. It's been interesting to watch them navigate their new dynamic around me. They're sort of like two middle schoolers who aren't sure if they can brush hands around an adult, eyes darting around before they steal a little kiss or squeeze the other's arm, like they're sneaky and I don't see.

I want to tell them I don't care; I want them to enjoy every moment of this new, delicate stage of whatever this is.

"Okay, I know I have said this, like, a hundred times already, but I cannot believe you guys are working the Maison Dauphine fashion show tomorrow." Celeste gawks, stopping on the sidewalk to shake her head with wide eyes. "That's, like . . ."

"It's mad," Rhodes agrees.

Noel, with his hands in his pockets, pushes his toe into the stone wall we've stopped beside. "You've been to fashion shows, I'm sure?"

"I have," Rhodes says with a nod. "With my mum."

"Is she going?" Celeste asks. "I love her style."

He smiles. "She is. She gets a plus one. . . ."

Celeste's eyes bug, but Noel brings her back to earth. "You'll be in Florida."

"Milo, I bet your mom would love to go," Celeste says.

"She's got the fundraiser in the Hamptons this weekend," I say. Then I turn to Rhodes. "And anyway, I'm sure your mom has somebody she wants to bring."

He chews on the inside of his cheek.

"Right?"

Then he nods. "Right. Yeah, I'm sure she will."

"Will you guys get to watch it?" Celeste asks.

We both shrug.

"Maybe?"

"Either way, it's still pretty cool," Rhodes says. "I've never really seen it up close like this. The behind-the-scenes is intense. I'm sure Milo has told you all about it."

They look at me expectantly.

"He's been too busy," Celeste teases. "But that's okay. We understand he's got a few distractions right now."

Grunting, Noel eyes Rhodes. Heat flushes my cheeks.

"Well, what can I say?" Rhodes reaches out, puts his arm around me, and pulls me in tight.

Celeste grins. "I knew everything was going to work out." She points at me. "Didn't I say that? At the start of the summer, didn't I say it'd all work out?"

"I'm sure you did."

"I did," Celeste says. "And you were all like, 'This summer is not about love,' but . . ."

Noel laughs. "Leave them alone."

But I want her to be right. I want it all to work out. Because when I'm cozied up to Rhodes like this, it feels like the stars above Montmartre are shining just for us.

I've never had such an unexplainable feeling in my entire life. Before Paris, I was always able to map out a game plan and strategize. But ever since I met Rhodes, it's all gone out the window. Whatever strength my brain has is overpowered by this flurry of feelings, like butterflies covering a window so there's no light, leaving me to navigate through intuition and emotion.

The affection I feel for Rhodes is overwhelming. I want to right all my wrongs and undo all my mistakes so I can stay in his arms for all the starry nights to come. When I glance up at him and he looks down at me with those big blue eyes, I want to capture this and keep it forever.

Celeste holds up her finger and then takes a photo. She squeals that it's adorable, pinching her fingers on the screen before showing it to us.

The photo is indisputably adorable. I fit perfectly under Rhodes's arm, nuzzled into his side, and we've both got these happy, sort of lazy grins.

Rhodes chuckles, seemingly pleased.

At the sight of the photo, my eyes burn. My mind is flooded with thoughts, but foremost is that this photo will one day be a distant memory, and that whatever she's captured between us here isn't even real. It's just a brilliant act.

"Come on, let's keep walking."

I pull myself away from Rhodes and walk a few steps ahead, composing myself. There's no need to get emotional over this now. After all, I've got a night of staring at the ceiling in solitude ahead of me.

"Like I said . . ." Celeste hums. "Things always work out."

"You can't post that or anything," Noel says. "It'll be all over the tabloids."

Celeste scoffs. "I wasn't going to *post it*."

"Well, I'm just making sure."

With my back turned to them, I'm fairly certain I hear Rhodes pat Noel's shoulder.

"Appreciate that, but don't worry, it's all good. People make up whatever stories they want all the time. I don't care too much about all that anymore."

"Well, I hope you'll look out for Milo."

I turn on my heel. "Noel."

He holds his hands up. "I'm just saying. Sorry."

Rhodes's eyes twinkle, I think, as he looks to Noel. They actually fucking *twinkle*. "No, don't apologize. You're a good big brother."

Noel just raises his brows and looks at me like "See?"

But I know there's way more to this than that. Way more to the way Rhodes looks both enamored of my brother and so hauntingly disappointed in the relationship he has with his own.

"Not bad for a Circus fan?" Noel laughs.

"Class, mate."

They start talking about football—Clyde Circus and Armoury United stats and players and loans and transfers—and Celeste rushes up to walk with me as they fall behind.

"I don't want to leave in the morning," she says, locking her arm around mine. "It's like I just got here, and I'm being yanked away all over again."

I squeeze her hand and nod. "I don't want you to leave either."

"I'm glad this time I'm not leaving you here by yourself."

"Hmm?"

"Well, now you have Rhodes."

My heart skips a beat. "Right. Yeah, I'm glad too." Eager to change the subject. "So. You and Noel."

"Me and Noel."

We both burst into laughter, which causes both Rhodes and Noel to call out asking what is so funny, as if there's some sort of Spidey sense that goes off. We fend them off when they try to catch up and badger us about why we're laughing, and then they're settling back into their football discussion, which has evolved to something about the Champions League.

"I don't think I saw it coming," Celeste says.

"Somehow I both didn't see it coming at all and totally saw it coming."

With a gasp, she squeezes my arm. "Did you really? I think I've had a crush on him longer than I realized. And I think maybe he had one on me too."

"Definitely," I say. "Looking back, it's completely obvious."

"You really don't care?" she asks, a sincerity in her tone. "Because if you do, I want to know. You're my best friend."

"And you're mine," I assure her. "Which means I want you to be happy. And I want Noel to be happy too. So, from where I stand, this is a total win-win."

"Right." Celeste has the biggest smile as she glances down at the cobblestones. "A win-win."

We continue to walk, and Noel and Rhodes are laughing behind us like they're old friends.

"And look at you," Celeste says. "You accomplished what you set out to. I'm sure they're going to keep you on after the apprenticeship. You've been amazing."

"Yeah."

Celeste bats her eyes. "What is it? Why are you being weird?"

"No, sorry, I don't mean to be. Just a bit tired. And overwhelmed."

"Well, you've been busy and you're doing big things."

"What about you?" I ask. "We haven't *really* talked about everything. I've wanted to give you space and all that. But are you doing okay?"

She nods. "I'm good. Really, I am. I'm glad Gran isn't suffering anymore. And I'm happy I got to spend more time with her. And now . . ." She takes a deep breath. "I don't know. This is nice. It's a bit of an escape, sure, but being here is nice. In Paris with you and

Noel, and now Rhodes. It's probably the best possible way to get my mind off the sad parts of life at the moment, and it's reminded me of what's important."

"Yeah?"

"Yeah." She stares at me. "Milo, I know you want everything to be perfect, and I know when we got here you said this was all about business. And you did what you said you'd do, but what do you think you're going to remember the most when you look back on this summer?"

This summer is unreal—a sizzle reel of absurd moments, mostly featuring Rhodes. It's like no matter how I try to position this summer in my mind, there he is. The boy with the bluest eyes I've ever seen. A wild blond daydream. Rhodes is like the wind—he's always there and he's a breezy type of cool you want on a warm summer day. He made my blood boil at times, but he also made my heart beat.

"That's a good point."

Celeste smiles like she knows exactly what I'm thinking. "You're like the Billy Joel song. You know? 'Vienna'? You're rushing to the finish line, and I get it, but the finish line isn't the important thing, it's all the stuff along the way. All the people along the way."

She glances back at Rhodes and Noel, and once again, I'm actively fighting a stinging sensation behind my eyes.

"And what if things don't turn out the way we plan?" I ask. "I mean, it's all well and good to enjoy when things are going smoothly. But what if it doesn't work out?"

Celeste shakes her head. "I don't know. I guess I believe it always works out. Even when it seems like it's not working out, that just means there's something better. So things not working out are just things working out." She scrunches up her face. "You know what I'm trying to say."

I laugh and nod, leaning my head against hers. "Yeah, I guess I do."

I'm not sure how, but it's comforting.

Even if everything's shit, I guess it'll all be okay in the end.

Chapitre Trente-Trois

The big day is finally here.

It was mildly devastating watching Noel become pretty fond of Rhodes last night, knowing that friendship isn't going to go anywhere. It felt a bit unfair to Noel, and that left me with a sense of guilt that persisted long after we said good night to Rhodes.

Currently, I have the nerves to end all nerves. If I ever thought I had anxiety before a tennis match or a test, or even my first day at Maison Dauphine, this is a reality check. I am practically vibrating because I am so nervous about today.

Celeste and Noel left early, and it was all too familiar, hugging them goodbye as they wheeled their suitcases out, and then sitting in the silent apartment alone trying to calm myself down with breathing techniques.

The wildest thing is that I'm not even fully sure where all these nerves are coming from. In theory, this should be a piece of cake. We've talked through everything and gone over all the details a hundred times by now, and it's just keeping all the parts in place so this is a well-oiled machine. This isn't Maison Dauphine's first fashion show, after all, and it's not like Haydée and Zoe and Yvette aren't at the top of their game.

I think, in a very strange turn of events, I'm more anxious for Rhodes than myself.

Despite Celeste's vote of encouragement, I've come to accept the fact that this is my last hurrah. Yvette only brought me back because of Pascal, and I highly doubt there's going to be anything else to come from that one-time endorsement.

So today is more about Rhodes than anything. I want to make it up to him once and for all by ensuring that everything is perfect with no hiccups or funny business.

We're at the Jardin du Luxembourg. Specifically, we're at l'Orangerie.

Another day, another orangery.

The brick-and-stone facade is stunning, with large arched, multipaneled windows and white bust sculptures adorning symmetrically spaced enclaves. There are palms and orange trees in green wooden boxes, just like at the Versailles Orangerie.

And, similar to the pop-up, they have brought the greenery inside.

All the chaotic energy from the weeks leading up, all the frenzy and hysteria, it's all culminated here. There's a palpable feeling of urgency that emanates off everybody in the room—each crew member assembling or moving a set piece, each member of PR or marketing or global affairs, each security guard.

It'll look different at night, but the sunlight washes the stone runway that's been constructed down the middle of the space. Gold bamboo chairs are placed along the sides, with palm trees masterfully placed inside to add a sense of depth and dimension.

It's minimalistic, but there's a true sense of summer, along with an obvious nod to the L'or des Fous line.

The room will be ambient, with warm uplighting opposite the windows, where an artificial wall of falling water has been installed, and even softer lighting along the runway. The quiet luxury of it all is very aligned with Pascal's direction for Maison Dauphine.

I've read all about the lighting design in our prep deck. The purpose is to strategically accentuate the lines of the pieces and to illuminate the gold.

The room is already being pumped with the aromatics, which include a very light orange blossom, an even lighter sandalwood, and a hint of tonka. It's subtle, but it's suggestive of an upscale resort during the summer. Something else I learned from the prep deck.

All of us in PR are wearing black dresses or tuxedos. My feet are already sore from running around so much this week, and these new loafers they've given Rhodes and me aren't helping. They're a buttery black leather with cloth details of Maison Dauphine monogramming peeking out from the slot, but as soft as they may be, they're brand-new and they're killing me. I do really like this new satin bow tie we're wearing tonight, and we also got a really nice gold sans-serif MD pin to wear on our jackets. It is a bit heavy, but incredible quality, and something I'm looking forward to having as a keepsake.

Yvette is on the phone a few yards away, currently dressed in black pants and a white T-shirt, which is as casual as I have ever seen her. When she spots me, I notice her signature sigh of displeasure before she mutters something into the phone, locks it, and then walks over to me.

"Can always count on you to be punctual," she says.

It's one of those statements that actually has another statement hidden behind it. Like: *Can always count on you to be punctual, even if you're going to screw something major up.*

"I like to be on time."

Yvette gestures around the room. "Have you found Haydée yet? She'll have assignments for you and Rhodes. I'm off to find Pascal."

"I'll go find her."

"Bien." She starts to walk, but I clear my throat.

"Yvette?"

I'm a bit surprised as her name comes out of my mouth.

She turns around, and I think of how to phrase this. After all, this was not planned out or practiced or something I'd even considered. But, when faced with Yvette and the somewhat biting reality of this apprenticeship coming to an end, I feel just a bit emboldened.

"I know you didn't necessarily *want* to bring me back," I say. "I don't even think I blame you. But I am really grateful you did."

She turns up her nose, as if waiting for the other shoe to drop.

"It's just . . . I know Pascal is the reason I'm here at all, and I wondered if he might be available."

Yvette laughs. "Available? You want, what, a one-on-one with Pascal?"

Lifting my shoulders, I hesitate. "Not a one-on-one, actually. I was thinking Rhodes and I could both talk to him."

"Milo."

"I've looked up to him for so long," I say. "I don't think I really made quite the impression I wanted to—"

"Oh, you made quite the impression."

"But not my best," I offer. "Yvette, please. You must know that I regret all my missteps and errors in judgment. I am fully dedicated to this and have been since day one. Since before day one, even. I'd just really love a moment with Pascal if it's at all possible, and I know Rhodes would as well. I know the reality is that this might be my last chance."

What I haven't said is lingering between us. My fate at Maison Dauphine rests with Yvette, and we both know she's not going to keep me around any longer than she has to.

"Please?"

Yvette frowns. "I don't think so, Milo. If it becomes possible, I'll relay to Haydée. But I wouldn't get your hopes up."

She leaves without another word.

Rhodes arrives just as Yvette walks out the door, and I'm instantly breathless seeing him across the room, as handsome as ever in his perfectly fitted tuxedo, with his perfectly styled golden hair.

He crosses the room and it's like slow motion—all the absurd noise and busy energy disappear. The entirety of the Orangerie vanishes, and it's just Rhodes, and it's just me. As he makes his way toward me, I wish more than anything he'd close the gap between us once he finally greets me. I wish he'd take me in his arms, not to convince Celeste and Noel of anything, but because he never wants to let me go either.

And in this moment, as I wait with bated breath and watch every step, I know I'll forever regret losing him the way I did.

He stops about a foot away and smiles. *"Nous voilà."*

"Nous voilà."

"You look nice," he offers. "How are you feeling?"

"Thanks," I say, smoothing the fabric of my jacket. "What do you mean?"

Rhodes stifles a laugh. "Bit anxious or . . . ?"

"Oh," I say. I'd somehow forgotten that Rhodes had developed a sense for these things along the way. "A bit. I feel like I'm hiding it pretty well, though."

"Definitely. You can't tell at all."

Cheeks flushed, I roll my eyes. "Are you making fun of me?"

"No, really." He shakes his head. "You look very confident."

"I don't know if confident is how I'd describe myself in this particular moment," I say. "But thanks. You look really nice too."

Rhodes adjusts his hair. "You think so?"

"Yeah, of course. I mean, come on. Obviously."

"Obviously?" He quirks a brow.

I roll my eyes and do my best not to give in, but my smile stretches across my face immediately. "Whatever. Yes, obviously, you look nice."

"Thanks, I appreciate that. Noel and Celeste gone, then?"

"They're gone."

Rhodes almost looks . . . concerned? "Right. Well, hopefully they had a fun time. I'm glad to have met them."

There's a finality to the sentiment. They met, and that's all it will likely ever be.

"So what do we have to do first?"

"Find Haydée," I say. "She'll have tasks for us."

It doesn't take us long to find her, absolutely red in the face and barking orders at whoever is around to take them.

"Oh, good. There you two are. I thought you'd been fired again or something." When the joke falls flat, she pulls a face. "Sorry. Very stressed, bad joke."

"That's all right," Rhodes says. "I'm sure someone would find it funny."

Haydée gives him a death glare before turning to me and smiling.

"Dear Milo, do you think you could handle confirming our media credentials?"

I nod. "Of course."

"We'll want to make sure the credentials match the most recent confirmation list. If anyone has been removed, be sure to void their credential so they don't make it into the show."

"Sure," I say.

Rhodes rubs his hands together. "All right, what can I do?"

"Will you just do a quick check of our front row? Make sure it's all accurate—again, matching the most recent confirmation list? I think I've seen some changes and want to be totally sure it's all right."

We go about our tasks pretty quickly. Only one fashion reporter has been removed, and I am sure to invalidate and dispose of his pass. Rhodes has confirmed the front row is all up to standard.

Haydée finds more tasks for us—checking the batteries in the walkies we will use backstage, ensuring all gifting is placed on seats, walking beside the falling water to be sure it doesn't smell weird or spray anywhere it shouldn't. Once we are thirty minutes out from the show, Rhodes and I are officially placed on press duty.

We check people in, give them their credentials, and hold them in a small room they've constructed outside the Orangerie. I'm not entirely sure why they're not allowed to just go in and sit yet, but I'm guessing by the flashbulbs outside that it's because the celebrity attendees are arriving and being shown to their seats first. We're to keep these members of the media contained—they're here to cover the show, not join the paparazzi outside.

I do manage to sneak a peek at some famous editors and a few actresses, all wearing gorgeous Maison Dauphine gowns. Rhodes and I exchange satisfied glances, knowing we helped gift or loan those pieces to their stylists. My favorite is a ruby red dress from the 2022 fall/winter collection, and I also spot a champagne taffeta suit Rhodes secured for a British editor who is friends with his mom.

Eventually, Haydée gives us the clear to begin escorting press members to their seats.

"I know I recognize you. Are you the boy from the Instagram photo?"

"Are you *actually* dating Rhodes Hamilton?"

"What's the American teen perspective on Paris, then?"

Maybe I was born to be in PR after all, because I masterfully maneuver everyone's questions with grace and ease, even though I was not expecting them at all. Obviously I'm naive, but I figured there were unspoken rules in society about asking strangers questions about who they're dating.

I'm sure Rhodes is handling the questions all the same, with chatty older women clinging to his arm as he helps them find their seat.

Finally, when I go back to greet the final guest I'll escort for the evening and find her waiting for me, I wonder if I'm back in one of my stress dreams.

Because it can't be . . . right?

How can it possibly be . . . ?

"Mom?"

Chapitre Trente-Quatre

My mother is standing in the press room.

My mother is in Paris. At the Maison Dauphine resort show.

We've got the same earthy tones, the same nose, and the same resting bitch face, which she immediately corrects with a huge grin once we've locked eyes.

"Milo!"

She's wearing a stunning green cocktail dress, and her dark brown hair is done up to show off large diamond earrings and an emerald hanging from a silver clasp on her neck.

Instinctively, I rush over to hug her, though I have no idea what the fuck is happening right now. Still, it's nice to be wrapped in her arms and in her signature Tom Ford scent.

Once we've broken apart, I blink a few times. And then I wonder if someone can be so stressed they hallucinate.

"How are you here?" I ask, taking a step back.

"Well, a very determined young man with a very charming English accent called the store and was apparently endlessly persistent about speaking to me," she says.

Rhodes? Why would he do that? When did he do that?

"He invited me to the show, and said he wanted to buy every single item for the silent auction so that we could cancel the event."

My jaw falls open. "He bought everything?"

"Of course not. I wouldn't let him do that." She laughs, narrowing her eyes like I'm just as absurd as Rhodes. "They're holding the fundraiser without me."

"What? But you . . . are you sure? Who's going to make sure the hydrangeas aren't wilting? Who's going to check that the Sonos is on the perfect volume? What if someone tries to make chalk signs?"

"I hire good people; I should let them do their jobs."

I almost audibly gasp. *She did hear me.*

"Rhodes invited you."

It's overwhelming—my mother being here and finding out that Rhodes did this. I'm not sure when or how he could possibly have made this happen.

She nods, and her thumb traces the stitching of her clutch as presses her lips together tightly before exhaling. "As a mother, it's humbling for your son's boyfriend to make it sound like the only way to get your attention is to buy it."

"Well, he's not my boyfriend. And I'm sure he didn't mean to—"

"He didn't," she agrees, frowning. "But it still stands. I should have been here with Celeste like I first planned. I just . . ."

"Want to control everything," I say with a smile.

"You come by it honestly."

"I understand why you work so hard," I say. "I appreciate it, even. This summer I thought I could make Maison Dauphine work and I'd finally be successful. I'd finally win. I'd finally be like you."

Mom lifts her chin. "Oh, Milo. You're going to be so much better than me."

"There's no such thing."

She pulls me in for a hug, and for the first time in so, so long, I feel like I can take a deep breath. And then she looks around, lip quivering and grip tightening around her bag.

"I see you here. . . . You're a young man now. You really are. You've always been so independent and driven. You had a busy social life, signed yourself up for tennis camps, booked your own SAT tutors, and then one day you were packing your bags and going to France all on your own. And look at what you're a part of. Look what you've accomplished."

"I know this all seems so glamorous, but you know what they say—all that glitters." I blink back tears. "After everything, I still failed in the end. I'm not going to get a job after this."

"That's okay, dear. You haven't failed. You're eighteen."

"But then what was all this for?"

She smiles. "You have time to find out."

My shoulders drop. "I just wanted to make you proud, and I tried so hard, but . . ."

"Listen to me. I am so proud of you. No matter what you do. And the fact that you don't know that is my fault, not yours. I am going to do much better about making sure it's clear how proud I am of you, Milo."

"Thanks, Mom."

"And I should have known that just because you are

independent doesn't mean you don't need me. Doesn't mean I shouldn't be there."

She pauses and gives me a very serious look.

"And what do you mean he's not your boyfriend?"

I laugh, a kind of gross, snotty laugh, which I'm grateful nobody else seems to notice apart from her.

"It's a whole thing."

Across the room Haydée waves at me, pointing at an imaginary watch on her wrist.

"We'll catch up tonight," Mom says. "I'm sitting with Rosie Hamilton—can you believe that? I'm actually a little nervous."

"Don't be! You two will have plenty to talk about. Okay, *suis-moi.*"

"Ooh, *oui.*"

The room is buzzing. The guest list is incredibly prestigious, the traffic flow has been mastered with no hiccups, and the ambience and decor are flawless. Angèle's "Les Matins" is thumping as everything falls perfectly into place.

I walk my mother over to her seat and say hello to Rosie, who (in the twenty seconds I have with her) is as radiant and kind as every clip I've ever seen of her.

Once everyone is seated, I hurry back to Zoe, who is doing final checks on the models, impeccably lined up. They're all so tall, even the ones in flat Maison Dauphine resort sandals, and it's like a walking parade of shimmering gold with lush ivories and thick cream fabrics. None of the opulence or luxury is overstated—all refined and tasteful and true to Renard Florin's vision for the house, while also speaking to contemporary fashion.

I find Rhodes next, standing beside him backstage.

"You just love to make phone calls, don't you?"

He glances down at me. "She made it."

"She did." I nod. "Thank you, Rhodes. That was an incredibly thoughtful thing to do. Something I'm not sure I deserve."

Rhodes shrugs. "I think you might deserve more than you give yourself credit for sometimes." Then, without missing a beat, he smiles. *"Sometimes."*

"Right." I fight a laugh. "But really, it means a lot."

"You went to bat for me with Yvette and Pascal."

"That was me fixing my own mess," I remind him. "Just doing the right thing."

Rhodes nods. "I appreciate it, nonetheless. We might have had a bit of a bumpy road, but I do know you're a good person. And I can't say it hasn't been fun."

"Nearly time," Zoe says.

"Catch up after," Rhodes whispers.

Adrenaline rushes through my entire body.

The show opens to "Summer 3" from Vivaldi's *Four Seasons*, with a projection onto the falling water. Maison Dauphine hired a production company to do a short video: it's shot on film, and starts out black-and-white, with a woman in a flowing white gown and opulent gold jewelry running through an orangery. As she stops, hiding between the trees and believing she's in the clear, she takes a deep breath. Her lover catches up to her, though. We see a close-up of him nearly grabbing her hand before she pulls away, and we see the desperation in her face as she does.

He moves closer, but she urges him not to before she reaches out to touch one of the orange trees. As the tree slowly turns to gold, color gradually fades onto the projection. Her lover smiles, shaking his head—he already knew. He reaches out to a nearby orange tree, and when his fingers brush a branch, which also turns to gold, she realizes they suffer from the same affliction.

They're the same, after all.

Watching the lovers causes a deep, sinking feeling. My throat constricts, and I quickly glance over at Rhodes, who is watching intently.

They reach out and cautiously press their palms and fingers together. As they embrace and kiss, both become gilded, but neither heart stops beating. They smile into their kiss before they begin to turn the orangery to gold, making it clear they are creating their own paradise as the sun sets over the horizon.

The music then remixes to have synth and some bass as the first models start to walk out in their gold resort wear. We watch the livestream backstage on a large monitor, and everything looks truly perfect. As the models continue, the music transitions to a slow-tempo classical song with a bit of a beat and hints of the Vivaldi.

When the show ends, Rhodes and I watch from the wings as Pascal emerges in a tailored tuxedo, greeted by rampant applause.

Unexpectedly, I even get a bit emotional watching him take his bow. This is the culmination of all the hard work he's put into this. All the hard work so many people have put into this—I've watched it come to life over the span of my short time here at Maison Dauphine, and I know it has all been in motion for much, much longer.

There's an odd sense of graduation now as Pascal bows to close out the show.

For the first time since I've been here, I really and truly feel like I have accomplished what I wanted to. Maybe *this* is all I was meant to do after all. Maybe it's not about staying on at Maison Dauphine or in Paris, but about this once-in-a-lifetime opportunity. An odd sensation washes over me that is a bit like relief, but could also be described as a warmer version of grief—not quite full mourning, but something like a gratitude and appreciation for a wonderful thing that I don't think I'll ever experience again.

Rhodes is clapping too, and he pats me on the back. There's an immense sense of pride in his eyes . . . because we did it. The show went off without a hitch.

"Well done, Milo."

Beaming, I nod. "You too, Rhodes."

He will continue to shine, because that's what he does.

I've come to Paris, and I've had the most incredible, hectic, exhilarating summer. I worked amazing events and met beyond-talented people. I found romance and lost it.

But this . . . everything happening right now—the glamour and the fantasy of this Maison Dauphine fashion show . . . this isn't my life, and I think it's time for me to accept that I just can't force everything, no matter how much I want to.

Just like with tennis, I'm second best, but that's okay.

Mom is right: I have time to figure it out.

After everything, Rhodes will get the job with Maison Dauphine. Yvette will forget all about what happened this summer—especially with me out of the picture.

It's bittersweet, but this is it. It's time to go home.

Chapitre Trente-Cinq

After the show, my ears are literally ringing.

The falling water has been turned off now that the guests have been gone for a solid forty-five minutes. The models were out quickly—makeup removed and mostly reset, though it seemed like some of them were eager to leave, even with all the product still in their hair.

My mom is going to get a drink with Rosie Hamilton, and I've let her know I'll call her as soon as I'm able to leave.

There's no music, just lots of chatter and excitement. Bottles of champagne are popping all around us, and the PR team members are all sitting in the extra makeup chairs, excitedly shouting things in French as they track mentions on social media and across press outlets.

"Maison Dauphine prouve que tout ce qui brille est de l'or!" Zoe squeals.

Rhodes leans in to whisper. "Maison Dauphine proves all that glitters is gold."

I nod. "That's amazing."

"La maison de couture vaut son pesant d'or!"

"The fashion house is worth its weight in gold," Rhodes coos. "Very positive reviews, it seems."

They go on like this for a bit, drinking expensive bubbles from delicate coupe glasses. It's almost like what I imagine a sorority is like, the way these girls all have this bond and love for the house.

Rhodes and I end up helping Haydée and Zoe secure the samples so they can be transported back to the fashion closet. We cleared two racks for the assets yesterday, in anticipation. My email is already blowing up, and I just know Monday morning is going to be absolutely bonkers.

I've come up with a plan that I feel pretty good about. I'll do my best to get things started with the requests for the new looks and help ensure Rhodes is in a steady, comfortable rhythm with everything. And then, once things are as close to stable as we can hope for, I'll tell Yvette that I have to return to Citrus Harbor, as much as I want to stay. I'll come up with an excuse or something if I have to, but I'm hoping she won't ask too many questions. She will likely be happy to see me go, honestly.

After zipping up a garment bag, I go to answer some texts.

Sophie: Show was PERFECT

Sophie: Good job

Me: Well, it was hardly thanks to me

Sophie: Every member of the team made it happen

Sophie: You should be proud

Celeste: I bought the good plane wifi just to watch the stream

Celeste: AMAZING

Celeste: Noel is like so impressed

Me: Lol thank you both. I miss you already

Celeste: We miss you too

Celeste: Have fun celebrating tonight

Celeste: Ugh, I bet you and Rhodes are gonna have the most amazing, romantic night

Me: They've already busted out the champagne!

Deuce Bags

Chip: Congrats, Milo!

Isaac: That livestream went craaaaazy

Isaac: So good

Miguel: yeah bro if you ever get extra invites . . . 👀

Chip: I'm sure there are so many extra invites

Isaac: Hope you and Rhodes have a fun night celebrating

Isaac: 🥰

Me: Lol thanks guys, if I ever get to work another fashion show I'll be on the lookout for a group of seats just for the deuce bags

Haydée comes over, and I can't tell what she's feeling at all. She's very focused, that's for sure, but her expression gives absolutely no suggestion of what is going through her head.

"Milo."

She looks so serious; I'm honestly going to break a sweat. *What is going on?*

"Haydée?"

Drawing in a deep breath, she pulls me aside, a few feet from Rhodes, and then she lowers her voice to a whisper, leaning in close. "Yvette told me to tell you there is now an open seat at Pascal's table."

"I'm sorry, what?"

"At the reception. Someone got sick, I guess? So you're up."

"I'm up?"

"You're up. Pascal wants you. Yvette just called."

"But that doesn't make any sense."

Haydée groans. "Milo, are you trying to be funny?"

I shake my head with wide eyes. "No, sorry, I'm definitely not. I just don't know why they would possibly invite me to that."

"So you don't want to go?"

"I definitely want to go," I say.

Rhodes drops one of the shoes, and it makes a loud noise as it thuds against the floor. Red as a lobster when everyone looks at him, he immediately recovers it, holding the shoe up to show it is completely unscuffed. "All good!"

Haydée frowns.

And somehow that's all I needed to see.

That frown that says everything.

I remember when I thought I knew Rhodes. When I thought he didn't deserve to be here and that he didn't appreciate his lot in life. I remember when I judged him too quickly and didn't even give him a chance to speak or show me how different he was from what I imagined.

Most importantly, I remember when I thought he was ill-suited for this role. I had no idea how dedicated he is or how hard he works. I thought it was conniving or cheating to use his connections—Amalia Astor or his mother, even—but this is PR, and that's literally the job.

Rhodes Hamilton is amazing at this, and Haydée's frown is innocent enough, but it helps me remember he's still proving himself.

"Actually, I want to give the spot to Rhodes."

Her jaw drops. "You can't be serious, Milo. I say this without meaning to offend you, but you could use this opportunity more."

"Maybe," I say. "That could very well be true. But I think Rhodes will make better use of it."

She shrugs and goes to talk to him. He looks excited, like a little blond puppy, eyes lighting up and his grin huge, and when she walks away, he rushes over to tell me.

"That is going to be so fun," I say.

"I saw her talking to you." He presses his palms together and rocks on his heels. "He wanted you, didn't he?"

I pause. For a split second, I consider lying, but I figure there's no use. It could come out somehow, and this little white lie wouldn't be worth it. At this point, I think I owe Rhodes a little honesty.

"Earlier I asked if Yvette if we could get some time with Pascal," I offer. "I guess this is her answer."

"Then it's your seat, Milo."

There's a bit of disappointment brewing in those eyes as they turn to stormy glaciers rather than vibrant skies.

I slide the garment bag I've just zipped farther down the rack and grab one of the folded ones from a nearby chair, opening it up and stuffing in a camel-and-gold tweed suit.

"You go," I say. "I've met Pascal. He knows who I am."

Rhodes laughs. "I'm sure he knows who I am, too."

"Exactly," I say. "He should get to know the *real* you."

"Really?" Rhodes's face softens at the recognition.

"Yes, really."

"Thank you, Milo."

He's giddy as he squeezes my arm and then runs off with Haydée.

I feel like one of the little animals in Cinderella, though I guess I'm not exactly turning rags into a gown or a pumpkin into a carriage. Still, it feels nice to make it up to Rhodes and do what I know to be the right thing.

Continuing down the garment racks, I work on bagging the remaining pieces.

By the time I'm done, the party seems to have cleared out. There are a few empty champagne bottles, but the coupe glasses and laughter have disappeared. I hardly notice everyone leaving, lost in my own world as I admire the clothes, simultaneously reflecting on my decision to go back home and fighting the impending sadness that is going to hit at the end of this night like a tidal wave. The emotional hangover is going to be so real tomorrow.

"You do know you don't get overtime."

Yvette walks in wearing a stunning midi-length black dress with a golden snake necklace that seems to slither down her chest, along with charcoal-colored snakeskin boots. All Maison Dauphine from very different periods, paired so perfectly and in a way I haven't ever seen before. She seems to be a never-ending master class in style.

"Oh, I know, I'm just finishing up."

"Relax, I'm only joking." She gestures around. "Are you heading to any of the little soirées?"

I shake my head, counting the garment bags and then heading over to the labels and grabbing a Sharpie to start working on them.

"None?"

"No, I'm going to head home after this."

"I see. . . ."

"You're not at the dinner?" I ask. Then: "I'm sorry, I hope you didn't think I was being rude or disrespectful by not going. I just wanted to give Rhodes a chance to talk to Pascal. You know? Since there was only one seat."

"I am heading there after this."

Yvette pulls a bottle of champagne from a chiller and then uses one of the untouched, folded black towels from the makeup supply cart to pop the cork. There are a few clean coupe glasses, and she grabs two, pouring champagne into them and handing me one.

"I couldn't resist," she says, holding hers up. We clink glasses and she takes a sip, shutting her eyes to savor it. "Thank you for your work on the show. It was a beautiful success."

I take a sip too. The champagne is crisp, and the bubbles are lively and effervescent. "Thank you for having me back."

She nods. "And I didn't think it was rude or disrespectful. It was very noble, actually. You have really impressed me with the way you've so selflessly advocated for Rhodes lately. You have a strong work ethic, but also strong values."

"Thank you, Yvette. I really appreciate that."

God, I'm getting choked up again. Why am I always getting choked up these days?

"It's just unfortunate." Yvette frowns.

"What?"

She holds the champagne coupe up to her chin, pursing her lips and giving me a once-over. "I think I'm actually going to miss having you around when you transfer to the New York office."

Chapitre Trente-Six: Septembre

Though it's almost Paris Fashion Week, I am back on Eastern Standard Time.

And it is *glorious*.

The stress levels are high, but it's a much different atmosphere working in the Manhattan office. As a quintessential French fashion house, Maison Dauphine only shows during Paris Fashion Week. Some of the New York PR girls have been sent to France to work the show, but Sophie and I are here running things for all of the US magazines, stylists, and events.

"I think the messenger got lost on the way to *Vogue*." Sophie sighs dramatically, splaying out on the conference room table and resting her face on the pile of magazines we've been using to tab Maison Dauphine credits. "How have we not gotten a status update yet?"

I refresh my inbox, and while there is no status update about this delivery, there are immediately four more requests. The spring/summer show isn't happening for three more days, but people are chomping at the bit.

This line is going to be even bigger than what we worked

on for resort—the venue is turning into an immersive galactic experience to highlight the futurist themes with iridescent and metallic fabrics—so the volume of emails has been next-level. Some of the younger editors invite me to lunch or coffee, which Sophie has explained is a tactic to befriend me, in the hopes that I'll consider them first when the line drops and pieces get multiple requests.

It's hard to say no to a free lunch or coffee when I consider New York prices and my part-time salary, but it seems safer to avoid any kind of possible indebtedness when the motive is abundantly clear.

"I've handled all requests for the day," I say. "Are we ready for tonight?"

"So ready," Sophie says. "Can't believe we're already back to Fashion Week events. It feels like we were *just* talking about the resort show."

I nod. "Oh, I know. Somehow it's been two months."

How have I been here for that long already?

Everything has been going so well it feels like I'm in a dream. The only concern that is bound to come up is the cost. I spent two weeks living in a guest room that belonged to Sophie's friend, but then Celeste worked her magic. Her aunt easily decided she was ready to return to Paris and agreed to let us stay in her Brooklyn apartment until at least spring, so long as we keep the place clean and Celeste runs errands for her and her clients . . . the errands have mostly been showroom tours and measuring out spaces. She did have to meet with a contractor on her aunt's behalf, and that was a whole thing, considering she didn't even know what a contractor was.

(To be fair, I didn't fully know either.)

Our parents did both insist we pay rent since Celeste's aunt had already let us use her Paris flat, but Aunt Angela is a godsend and isn't charging us anywhere near what we'd pay if we'd found this place on StreetEasy.

It's horribly ironic that I ever judged Rhodes for privilege.

Celeste and I have been beyond lucky ourselves, and I've made sure to take stock of that as often as possible.

Before leaving Paris, I did break it to Noel and Celeste that Rhodes and I were no longer dating, and while I had hoped to leave it at that, there were loads of questions, which resulted in me spilling my guts about the whole situation. I expected a bit of backlash for keeping it from them, but I only got sympathy. They seemed to connect the dots with their reactions—it was like I told them I had lost the love of my life, and they were quite eager to assure me that I'd never find anyone like him, that this is very sad indeed, but that they're here for me and they're so sorry to hear.

Exactly the kind of response one hopes for.

Anyway, yes, it's been sad, but it's gotten better. Leaving Paris and saying goodbye to Rhodes was more brutal than I imagined it'd be, but it was for the best.

Rhodes and I are friends, and I am confident that's the best-case scenario here. We text a lot and we send each other memes on Teams all the time. I'm glad we've been able to maintain a friendship, even if I had at one point desperately wanted more.

It's not like either of us really has time to date, anyway.

So Celeste is sort of right after all. Things do always work out the way they were meant to.

I'm not sure how long we'll have this amazing deal with her aunt's apartment, but I've been making friends at work and I'm hoping to have a roommate lined up when the time arrives, especially because I know Celeste is likely scheming.

After all, Noel visited us before the fall semester started, and he's now back at Stanford. Though Celeste is having fun with me in New York for now, I just know she's plotting her escape to California. I'm not upset about it—I knew this was temporary as soon as she said she was packing her bags. I just want to make sure I'm ready and can make it in New York without her.

I also got to hang out with Chip, Miguel, and Isaac when they came up to watch some of the US Open. Overall, this has been a net positive.

"So you're going to meet me at the hotel, right?" Sophie is applying some lip gloss and logging out of her computer now that we've made our way back into the fashion closet.

I nod, firing off a quick email. "I just have to go home, turn in an assignment, change, and then I'm on my way."

I'm enrolled in Citrus Harbor Community College for now, doing three online classes until I transfer to a university here in the city. The plan is for me to do this apprenticeship until the assistant position opens, which should be in October.

My parents are absolutely thrilled that I am about a two-hour plane ride away and that I'm enrolled in classes with the prospect of a job already on the horizon.

Sophie and I leave and take trains in different directions from 57th Street. Celeste is out for dinner in Chelsea with a couple of girls she met at a kickboxing class, so I get home to a silent and pitch-black apartment. It's a bit wild how early it gets dark in New

York in September. I can't believe I thought the sun ever set too early in Citrus Harbor, honestly.

I bang out a discussion board post about academic writing—absolutely riveting, I assure you—and post it after reading it over three times. I'm trying to be better about the whole perfectionism thing, but old habits die hard. And some old habits aren't the worst, anyway, since my grades thus far have been really good.

After a quick rinse, I open my closet and find the silky black garment bag I've been avoiding since I moved here. Pulling the zipper down, I take a breath. Only one breath, since I've needed the 4–4–4 method a lot less lately.

The garment bag opens to reveal the tuxedo from Paris, with its gold MD pin. All the emotions come flooding back like I'm experiencing a sizzle reel on triple speed, but I don't have time to go on a trip down memory lane, so I swallow my feelings and get dressed.

Maison Dauphine pays for our transportation to and from events, so I take an Uber back up to 57th Street, where I am let out in front of the Plaza Hotel. It's a legendary institution of New York City, and one of the places I've been dying to see, so I take it all in as I stand on the sidewalk for a moment after the car has left. The cool air is refreshing, and the guests of this black-tie dinner all look so glamorous as they crawl out of town cars and make their way up to the hotel.

There are so many variations of quotes that basically tell us not to feel sad for losing something because we'll surely gain something else. As I stand here outside the Plaza, I wonder if it's silly to still think about things I feel I lost.

And then, when the wind picks up, I feel the oddest sensation, like the elbow of my jacket is being pulled.

I turn around, and all the lights of Fifth Avenue glow a little brighter . . . because there, sharply dressed as ever in his tuxedo, with that golden-blond hair and those bright blue eyes, Rhodes Hamilton is holding a light green box of macarons.

And he's smiling right at me.

Acknowledgments

I pinched myself so many times writing this book—what do you *mean* I get to play make-believe and spend a summer in Paris? I get to wander the Louvre and Versailles and daydream about macarons and delicious wine? I get to create a fashion house and write a runway show? I'm so thankful that I get to do this, and while I hope to someday revisit Citrus Harbor, this feels like the end of that chapter for the foreseeable future. It's been such a pleasure to write about these headstrong teenage boys as they find themselves and fall in love, and I am just over the moon that we're rounding out this Citrus Harbor quartet with Milo and Rhodes.

Mitchell. *Mon chou.* My favorite Arsenal supporter. Thank you endlessly. Your word count spreadsheet is the reason this manuscript was completed on time. Your ideas and your creativity made it better. Throughout the entire process of bringing this book to life, you amazed me by finding new ways to support me and inspire me. Your belief in me makes me feel like I can do anything. *Je t'aime.*

My family's support means everything to me—thank you Mom, Gabby, Reagan, Dad, and Erica. My late grandmother, Hola, encouraged me daily to meet my word count goals on this one, and I wish she could read it, but I am so grateful for her constant inspiration and love. My Geminis who kept me sane during the tight deadline—Kelly and Lizzy—*merci beaucoup*!!

Madame Griner: *Tu es la meilleure prof! Merci beaucoup pour tes encouragements. Les cours de français étaient amusants et mes préférés. Grâce à toi, je peux survivre à Paris! Tu as fait une grande différence dans ma vie. Je t'en suis reconnaissante.*

I have made so many wonderful author friends who always show up and support me and my titles—thank you Shawn, Adam, Jason June, Liselle, Adam Sass, Tobias, Robbie, and many more! As always, the biggest thank-you to the BookTokers, Booksta-grammers, BookTubers, and book reviewers!

We've arrived at Volume IV of *Why Kristy Hunter Is the Perfect Agent*—the multivolume leather-bound boxed set! Kristy, thank you for taking a chance on my little beach read romance five years ago. Thanks to you, the Citrus Harbor boys have had their stories told and, I believe, have made a positive impact on so many read-ers. I'm so proud of the work we've done to bring these queer joy stories to life together. Thank you for believing in me and advo-cating for me and for always being my rock throughout my pub-lishing journey.

Thank you to my editor, Tara Weikum, for helping to make this story shine. Thank you to Ricardo Bessa and David DeWitt for a cover I couldn't have even dreamed of!

And last, but certainly not least, thank you, reader. Thank you for you journeying to Paris with Milo and spending the summer with him. I hope you had the time of your life at Maison Dau-phine with him and Rhodes, and I hope this book leaves with you with a feeling that anything is possible. I hope, dear reader, your life may always be *la vie en rose*.